This edition of

CRESCENT CITY KILL

has been signed by the author

CRESCENT CITY KILL

BY JULIE SMITH

Rebecca Schwarz mysteries
Dead in the Water
Death Turns a Trick
Tourist Trap
The Sourdough Wars
Other People's Skeletons

Paul McDonald mysteries
True-Life Adventure
Huckleberry Fiend

Skip Langdon mysteries
New Orleans Mourning
The Axeman's Jazz
Jazz Funeral
New Orleans Beat
House of Blues
The Kindness of Strangers
Crescent City Kill

CRESCENT CITY KILL

A SKIP LANGDON NOVEL

JULIE SMITH

FAWCETT COLUMBINE • NEW YORK

A Fawcett Columbine Book
Published by Ballantine Books

Copyright © 1997 by Julie Smith

All rights reserved under International and Pan-American Copyright Conventions. Published in the
United States by Ballantine Books, a division of Random House, Inc., New York, and simultane-
ously in Canada by Random House of Canada Limited, Toronto.

http://www.randomhouse.com

Library of Congress Cataloging-in-Publication Data
Smith, Julie, 1994–
    Crescent city kill : a Skip Langdon novel / Julie Smith.—1st ed.
      p.   cm.
    ISBN 0-449-91000-8   (hardcover)
    I. Title.
PS3569.M537553C74   1997
813'.54—DC21   97–22099
                                                                            CIP

Manufactured in the United States of America

First Edition: August 1997

10   9   8   7   6   5   4   3   2   1

Dedication
For Lee Pryor, my adored husband

Acknowledgments

No one could be nicer than the ever-patient members of the New Orleans Police Department, particularly Captain Linda Buczek. This time I owe thanks not only to her, but also to Lieutenant Jeff Winn and Officer Bobby Norton. I hasten to mention that if I got anything wrong it was my own fault and none of theirs.

Thanks also to Betsy Petersen, Ken White, Kathy Perry, David Kaufman, and Lee Pryor. In addition, I owe a debt of gratitude to two people I've never met—Judith L. Rapoport, M.D., and Richard Sebastian. Their respective books were invaluable in determining The Monk's thought patterns.

A final note: Though there are many schools in New Orleans named after John McDonogh, there is no McDonogh 43.

1

• •

Theoretically, the point of Mardi Gras is that it precedes Lent, though it often seems no one remembers but the odd priest or nun. In New Orleans, no sooner do the Mardi Gras parades end than new revelry, in honor of Saints Joseph and Patrick, begins, with massive food altars and the throwing of cabbages from floats. Some people do go on diets during Lent, or at least give up sweets, though there is little talk of forswearing alcohol or cigarettes.

In general, if truth be told, Lent is a fitful time. Some days are balmy, some humid and sticky, some below freezing. It can seem as if the city is just marking time until JazzFest.

But officially, it's over at Easter and sure enough, the mood seems to change overnight. Good Friday is often gray and chilly, yet Easter Sunday generally dawns bright as a sequin.

It's a big holiday for most families, even those who aren't Catholic. To out-of-towners, used to nonobservance, it's a bit of a shock to see the young men still in their Saturday night eyeshadow rush home at mid-morning to wash their faces for Easter lunch with their mothers.

Since New Orleans is well known as the city where too much is not nearly enough, there are no fewer than three Easter parades, all in the French Quarter.

The first one consists of a caravan of horse-drawn carriages making their way from Arnaud's Restaurant to Jackson Square, where the occupants, ladies of fashion known as the Friends of Germaine Wells, alight to promenade before going to church at St. Louis Cathedral.

There is irony in the name they have chosen, as Ms. Wells, daughter of Count Arnaud and the late owner of the restaurant bearing his name, was no lady, it is said. Or at least her friends were no gentlemen. To be perfectly honest, rumor has it Ms. Wells's head was easily turned by a tattoo.

That head, however, nearly always sported outrageous hats, hence the Easter connection. The ladies of the Friends go all out. Some go vintage, some contemporary, some head-to-toe purple, some delicate peach. And these are only their frocks. Hat diameters have been known to reach a good thirty inches, and chiropractors to retire on the resulting sore-neck proceeds.

Before reaching the square, the ladies will have begun at Arnaud's for hat-judging and a Bloody, and after church, they'll return for brunch and more Bloodies.

About that time, Chris Owens's Easter parade begins. Ms. Owens is a Bourbon Street club owner and renowned dancer, though not a stripper. Be that as it may, she does bare quite a bit, and everyone agrees it's a splendid-looking body for anyone, much less a woman said to be somewhat Tina Turner's senior.

Besides herself, Ms. Owens's parade features a number of ladies, some in carriages, some in cars bedecked with pastel balloons, all wearing the requisite eye-popping hats. Many drip chiffon veiling, some sport bunny ears. These ladies, unlike Ms. Wells's friends, cover a range of ages, from eight or nine to well over eighty, judging by appearances. Those in between frequently display ivory fields of bosom and unsubtle makeup. They throw nice beads to the masses.

Around two o'clock, as the last of Ms. Owens's carriages disappears down Bourbon Street, the day's first drag queens begin to venture out. Theirs is the least formal parade of the day, consisting mostly of afternoon saunters between Good Friends Bar and the

Rawhide. Full drag frequently occurs, with all its high-heel teetering, but the point, as in the other parades, is hats. The gentlemen's hats can get outrageous (sometimes reaching three feet across), but for once, not that much more outrageous than those of their female counterparts. Easter's an all-out kind of day for everyone.

Biblically, it will be recalled, Easter signals renewal, resurrection, a rising of the spirit. For Skip Langdon, newly returned to work after a leave of absence, resuming her job as a homicide detective was more like Lent than Easter—more fitful than triumphant, more gray than sunny, more edgy foreboding than happy expectancy. In short, morale that spring in Homicide—indeed in the whole department— was so low she couldn't close herself off.

● ●

There were four detectives in the car—everyone in Sergeant Sylvia Cappello's platoon—on their way to a crime scene: A sixty-two-year-old woman had opened her door to a barrage of gunfire.

"D'y'all hear? Cooper's leaving." The speaker was young, cynical beyond his years and experience.

"Shit. That makes three this week."

"Fuck. What we doing here? Let's take a vote—anybody in this car wouldn't be out of here if they could?"

Another senseless shooting. Another resignation. Another hot, crowded ride because there was no money for more cars.

Skip tried to turn her mind off. If the job wasn't meaningful, what was? She wasn't waiting to collect a pension. She was too young for that, didn't have enough years in and didn't want to go anyway. She'd gone back to work after what amounted to an involuntary leave of absence (though technically it hadn't been) because she loved the work, because it was the only thing she'd found to do with her life that truly pleased her, that made her feel alive and healthy and useful.

But the mayor, when new blood was so sorely needed, had appointed a superintendent who was no more than a political pal. The City Council had decreed that officers who didn't live in the city had to move back to be considered for promotion. And every mugger in

3

town had heavy artillery; every other mugging, it seemed, turned into a murder. Two cops were currently on Death Row.

The best way to get through was not to think about it.

• •

The shooting was in the Seventh Ward. The victim's two sons and three daughters were on the sidewalk, one of them cradling a baby, some of them holding toddlers' hands, all of them crying.

The case wasn't Skip's—it belonged to Danny LaSalle, who assigned her the family. She walked over to the distraught little knot of humanity, and almost immediately one of the sons got in her face, or would have if he'd been tall enough—Skip was six feet tall and he was about five-six. "What y'all collectin' ya salary fo'? Who wanna kill my mama?"

"Who do *you* think would?"

Evidently defying him, one of the daughters stepped forward. "Somebody want Herbert."

Bingo, she thought. "Herbert?"

"Rudolph boy." The woman pointed to the short dude.

Skip said, "You Rudolph?"

"Tawanda don't know her pussy from her asshole. Nobody want Herbert."

It went like that for a while, but the story came out: Herbert ran with a bad crowd, Rudolph and his wife kicked him out, he sometimes stayed with his grandmother.

Herbert would probably know who wanted to kill him, and therefore who had mowed Granny down like some enemy soldier, but by now he was probably halfway to East Jesus, having no doubt killed a two-year-old who got in the way when he tried to retaliate on behalf of Granny.

Christ, she thought, *I'm thinking like O'Rourke*. Frank O'Rourke, the nastiest cop in Homicide.

Nonetheless, when they left the crime scene, Herbert was by far the best lead they had. They found him at his sister's in New Orleans East, bare-chested, wearing baggy pants and black running shoes, passed out on his nephew's bed. The little boy had answered the door promptly, trustingly, as his great-grandma must have done.

He'd apparently been watching television, lying on the floor in the living room. There was no one else in the apartment. The TV was so loud it had masked their entrance.

LaSalle said, "Herbert, wake up."

The sleeping man had a well-muscled torso. His body jerked, a hand reaching under the pillow.

"Police. Freeze."

He didn't—the hand came out with a gun in it.

Danny shot him. It was over in a millisecond.

Skip ran back to the living room and gathered up the nephew, soothing him, lying to him.

She wasn't that good with kids, or so she told herself. But she took this one on as a project, and it was harder than watching his uncle get shot.

Herbert died within the hour. After wading through the red tape surrounding the shooting, Skip was sent to interview his girlfriend, Renee.

Renee said she had no idea who'd want to kill a guy like Herbert.

By the end of the day, it looked pretty certain Herbert's granny was going to go unavenged.

"Damn shame, ain't it?" It was the same cop who'd reported Cooper's resignation, a three-year vet named DeFusco.

"Damned ironic. Herbert was home free—he just didn't know it."

"I'm thinkin' about the poor old lady. Bastard who killed her's out gettin' loaded right now."

Adam Abasolo chimed in from across the room. "Don't let it get to you, Joey boy. Seems like anybody we pop gets off, and if they don't they're back on the street in thirty seconds."

"Two minutes max," said Charlie Dilzell. "Least this way there's one less punk on the street. That's some kinda justice anyway."

"However twisted," said Skip, making a lame attempt to raise the level perhaps a millimeter.

"Shee-it. When was the last time you saw anything resembling fucking justice?" Frank O'Rourke was the speaker—not Skip's favorite person, but the words were spoken with such heartfelt outrage, they made her feel helpless rather than angry.

I've got to get out of here.

But Cappello caught her before she left. "You okay with what happened?"

"Hell, no, I'm not okay with it, but there wasn't any choice. Anyway, it's LaSalle's case; I can't worry about it."

"I didn't mean the case. I mean . . . what you saw."

She meant watching LaSalle shoot Herbert. Skip brushed unruly curls from her forehead. "No. I swear to God I'll never get used to watching someone die." She didn't mention it was all she could do not to wince. "But I take your meaning. Yeah. I'm okay."

"It didn't bring back . . ."

"It did. How could it not? But it was LaSalle, Sylvia. Not me. I watched him do it, and I knew he had to do it. It's a different deal. You know?"

"I needed to check."

"I appreciate that."

"I hear you were good with the kid."

"Sometimes you get a second chance."

Skip's leave of absence had involved a shooting as well; but the dead man had a daughter, who witnessed it.

Skip could work now; she no longer had nightmares, nor saw the girl in every child who crossed her path. Today she'd proven she no longer fell apart at shootings where there were children.

But she was glad Cappello hadn't asked if she was depressed. She was. She didn't think she'd be human if she wasn't.

And it wasn't only about Herbert. There was hardly a thing about the day that wasn't depressing. She couldn't wait to get home.

She frowned. Actually, there were certain things about home that depressed her as well. One thing, anyway. A big thing, about a hundred and fifty pounds' worth.

It barked as she approached. Barked and snarled.

"Napoleon, take it easy, boy. Come on, now, I'm your pal." *In a pig's eye.*

At least the dog didn't come any closer.

He belonged to Steve Steinman, her long-distance sweetheart, who was visiting from California. Steve yelled down from the balcony. "Napoleon! Take it easy, boy." The dog shut up and wagged his tail.

Skip said, "You're a dog magician."

"He likes people who like him."

"Don't be mean. I feel awful."

"Be right down. Napoleon—stay." But as soon as Steve stepped from Skip's slave quarters into the courtyard, Napoleon leaped up lovingly, spilling the beer he'd brought for Skip.

"Dammit. Maybe you're right about this creature." His T-shirt was soaked.

"Napoleon! Hey, boy! Hey, boy. Come on." Thirteen-year-old Kenny Ritter had dashed out of the Big House that also opened on the courtyard. "Want to go for a walk? Steve, can I take him for a walk?"

"Please do," said Skip. "Across I-10."

"Oh, Auntie."

"Now here's my *baby*." Angel, a black and white fluffball, frolicked at Kenny's heels. Napoleon sniffed at her rear end. Skip said, "You leave her alone or I'll kill you," and Kenny smiled, used to her. He left with the dogs.

Steve said, "Cappello just called. She said either call her back right away or just watch the news."

"That's weird." Skip plopped into a dark green patio chair. "I think I'll opt for the news."

"I was hoping you'd say that." He massaged her neck.

"That's better. I swear to God that's better."

"We're here to serve."

"How about you go be a cop for a while."

"Uh-uh. I'd rather watch you suffer." He was a filmmaker who'd become a film editor but never got over his first love. Right now he was back in New Orleans working on what was getting to be a long-term project: a documentary about kids who'd been shot—and, as Skip liked to say, the kids who shot them.

"You came to the right place. I've had a hell of a day."

"Can you tell me about it?"

Sometimes she couldn't, but this was different.

"Why not? It'll be on page one tomorrow."

When she had finished, he looked worried. "You . . . uh . . . dealing with this okay?"

"You sound like Cappello." There was a reason for it. She'd had a near breakdown after shooting the man who tried to kill her.

She patted Steve's knee, trying to reassure him. "Yeah, I'm dealing with it fine. Except, of course, for the part about the grandma. That gets to me."

"Do you ever think about Shavonne?" Shavonne was the little girl who'd watched Skip blow her daddy away.

"Oh, yeah. I don't even *want* to stop thinking about her—I don't think it'd be right to forget. I mean, I don't dream now—don't look so worried—but I try to keep tabs on her. I check up on her now and then, sometimes even . . ." she hesitated.

"What?"

"You're gonna think I'm crazy."

"Tell me."

"Oh, well. If you're here long enough you'll find out anyway. I take her little presents sometimes. Little surprises—anonymously, of course."

"You're right. I think you're crazy."

Skip felt her face get hot. She said nothing.

"But crazy good, of course. Crazy in a very sweet way."

"You really think it's nuts?"

"Of course not. No. You've got two really great projects—Shavonne and Jacomine. They balance out perfectly. Skip Langdon, Batwoman—flap one wing and nurture the innocent; flap the other, destroy all evil. You gotta love it."

Her cheeks warmed again. "It's not like that."

"Don't get huffy."

"Are you laughing about Jacomine? Do I actually hear you laughing about him? The kids could be in danger." She meant her friend Jimmy Dee's adopted children—Napoleon's pal Kenny and Kenny's sister, Sheila. Jacomine was someone with whom she had some history. He was crazy, he was evil, and he had reason to hate her. She could never shake the fear that he'd go after the children—or even Steve or Jimmy Dee if he couldn't get the kids. But there was no doubt in her mind, he'd try first for the children—it was meaner, it was nastier, and it was more likely to send her around the bend.

She said, "Let's go watch the news. Cappello's probably afraid they're going to crucify LaSalle."

But LaSalle's case rated only a sentence or two—there were a couple of giant stories pushing everything else to the back, one national, one local.

The local one was huge—a blockbuster, said the anchorman—so mind-boggling no one would believe it. But first, a bigger one.

It was the verdict in the Billy Ray Hutchison case, a murder trial the press was calling "O.J. Revisited." The thing was eerie, it was so similar to the O.J. Simpson trial: Billy Hutchison, an African American football player who did commercials, was accused of killing a wife who claimed a history of abuse.

But there were two major differences in the cases—the two were still married, and the wife was also black. To Skip, the evidence seemed overwhelming, and, to her mind, there wasn't a racial issue.

Open-and-shut, she would have said.

But because of the Simpson trial—and because of Hutchison's huge popularity—all eyes were on it.

The verdict was "not guilty."

"Shit. He did it."

Steve said, "FemiNazi."

Skip made her hands into claws, pretending to scratch his eyes out. "It's not funny. He bought himself a walk."

"Get used to it. It's the American way."

"Oh, hell. I wish I had a joint."

"Thought you stopped that shit."

"God, I'm in a mood."

"I don't see why you're so surprised. He's not the kind of guy who'd do a thing like that."

For the first time, she really looked at him, suddenly not sure what he was saying. "You're kidding, right?"

"I'm just a right-thinking American—the bitch had it coming. Probably gave him lip every time he brought home a bimbo."

Okay, he was kidding. "You're not helping my mood."

"Hey, who cares about evidence? I need justice—I work all day and when I come home I want a hot meal on the table. What do I get? Lip, lip, and lip. Billy's my man."

"I see what you're saying, but there were eight women on that jury."

"He's a good-looking dude. That goes a long way in this country—along with a few million green ones."

"I hate lawyers."

"Omigod. Listen."

The local story was on. Sometime between now and the time Skip left headquarters, the superintendent of police had resigned.

She said, "Holy shit! I should have called Cappello. Did I hear that right?"

"Even I don't believe that one."

"They said it though, right? Pinch me."

"They'll probably replace him with somebody worse."

"There isn't anyone worse. This dude's dumb as a rock and corrupt as hell. God, is he stupid! Every day he transfers somebody just for the hell of it—just to prove he can do it, I guess."

"Do you think he's resigning over this LaSalle thing?"

"Naah. I bet it's been in the works for weeks. Even the mayor can't stomach him—or more likely, can't stomach the increasing outcries of an angry populace. If he's smart, he'll bring in someone from outside."

"The problem is, he's not smart."

"Well, he may be desperate."

"I know I am."

"Well. Mr. Cynical finally comes clean."

He shrugged. "You gotta keep your sense of humor. Either that or go nuts."

"You know what? This is good news. We just heard good news on the boob tube. Mark down the date and time. Break out the champagne."

2

• •

Dorise was washing wineglasses in a great big old stainless steel double sink equipped with garbage disposal. She was in pig heaven.

"Dorise! That's lovely, but—"

Cammie Fontenelle had clicked into the kitchen on shoes so tiny, Dorise wondered if she had to special-order them. In fact, she was so petite she probably had to get her clothes somewhere in Asia. At the moment she was wearing a flamingo-pink spring suit that nipped in to show a waist about the size of a hummingbird's. Dorise liked her as well as it was possible to like someone from another planet.

Cammie's pretty little face was screwed up in distress, blue eyes all squinty. She didn't know how to ask for what she wanted.

What was Dorise doing wrong?

Singing. She hadn't even noticed.

"Oh, darlin'. I'm so sorry. I didn't even know I was doing it."

Cammie smiled, all better again. Her eyes were sparkly between their liner and their shadow. "It's beautiful. Really. Maybe you should come out and entertain."

Dorise waved a hand at her and smiled. She started humming again before she caught herself. All things considered, she'd rather be in the kitchen, washing Cammie's antique crystal, lovingly handling the gorgeous glasses, loading the china in the dishwasher, getting a gander at the silver as she put things back in the kitchen cabinets.

She liked serving, too, standing at the buffet table, ladling out the crawfish pasta and grilled vegetables, checking out the ladies' sleek bright suits. Cammie always requested her, and now so did lots of Cammie's friends, who also had occasion to give luncheons from time to time. She was careful, she was thorough, she was fast, and she was cheerful—those were some of the things that had consistently been mentioned in her evaluations ever since she went to work for Uptown Caterers. Her mama had taught her right.

It was easy to be nice in houses that were cool in the summer and warm in the winter, where you walked on Oriental carpets nearly as old as the houses themselves. Another lady, one the next generation up from Cammie, had explained to her that the more threadbare and tattered the rugs looked, the more likely they were to be valuable, thus the more careful she had to be.

In these houses, upholstery was always some soft stuff, like silk or velvet. The furniture was dark and shiny, crystal prisms rained from sconces, mirrors were framed with gold leaf, metallic-colored tassels tied the curtains. There was so much to look at, she could hardly work.

She didn't exactly fantasize about living in these places. That made no more sense to her than taking up residence in a museum—and anyway, she had an eight-year-old daughter. How did you keep a kid from breaking the Chinese vases? How did you get comfortable in a place like this? How did you keep it clean?

And then, of course, there was the problem of keeping the neighbors from shooting you. (Or more likely, shooting your brother or husband. Black men were viewed with suspicion in the Garden District. But she didn't think much about that—her own living room in the East hadn't been all that healthy for her late husband.) These places were just foreign—great huge rooms and high ceilings, more than a hundred years old. But she loved being in them, looking at everything, taking care of things. And the people who came to lunch! Judges' wives, legislators' wives, and for the night parties, the judges and doctors, too, some of them women. Some of them black. At Cammie's once, she had met Suzanne Nickerson, the most popular anchorperson in the city. A black woman.

"I felt like I was really hangin' out with the stars," she told her sister.

Her sister had said, "Dorise, don't you get it? You aren't hangin' out with anybody. You the help."

"You just jealous," she had said. "How else you gon' meet Suzanne Nickerson?" Her sister worked at a laundry, back in their old neighborhood.

Under questioning, even her sister would have said Dorise was doing good. Dorise knew she was. She'd gotten married young and had some piddly job at a video store until her husband insisted she quit working. He made plenty of money and she had a kid to take care of.

She didn't ask him how he got his money—he was a businessman with lots of investments. She didn't know he had his own apartment somewhere else and a life she knew nothing about, until the day he died. Leaving her with nothing. Leaving their daughter with nothing.

"Why didn't you know, Dorise?" her mother had asked. Her sister had asked. Everyone had asked.

But they hadn't known either. "Not for sure," they said. It wasn't polite to bring it up. Dorise came from a churchgoing family, and the day Delavon came into the video store with his fancy clothes and his fancy car and his silver tongue, he told Dorise he managed a band she'd heard of, everybody'd heard of. Later, when she asked why he never took her to concerts, he said he quit that job to "take care of some other bi'ness," and she believed him. He bought her a nice little house, or so she thought. After he died, it turned out they didn't really own it.

Dorise was strong, though. She picked up and moved to Gentilly, taking Shavonne with her. She kept applying for jobs until she got one, and because she was such a hard worker, she did well. "Just be nice," her mother said, "and people'll be nice to you."

Her sister said being nice to white people was bullshit, but Dorise enjoyed it. "Law, girl," her mother said. "You always had a good disposition. Miss Sunny Smile, yo' daddy used to call you."

She did have a pretty smile, to this day. She had a big butt and big hips, and she sort of floated when she walked. Her husband had picked on her, told her she'd gotten fat and he didn't want to "have nothin' to do with her no more," by which he meant sex (though what he did and what he said were two different things). But other people liked her. "You look like a nice person," the older lady had said, the one who told her about rugs.

"I try to be," she answered, and the woman smiled back. That was all there was to it—that and being careful, respecting other people's things. She was doing so good she almost didn't believe it sometimes.

She had a little apartment, and enough money to buy clothes for herself and her daughter, and her mother had given her her old Chevy. Half the women she knew—other single mothers—didn't even have cars.

She didn't need all those presents her husband used to bring her—stereo systems and bracelets and things. A good thing, too, because she'd had to sell them all.

She didn't at all miss that life. Shavonne was in second grade when he died—already, there was no one to be home for anymore. And Dorise liked working. She liked the people she worked with and she liked meeting the clients.

What she missed was having a man.

Sometimes she missed her husband, even though he had an evil mouth on him and knew how to hurt her feelings. But when they made love, there was nobody better, nothing sweeter.

"Mmmm-mmmm," she told her sister. "Chile, I *tell* you."

Lawrence came in to pick up the equipment. "Just about over?"

"Seem like it. Few people still drinkin' coffee."

"This some place, huh? How you like to live here?"

"Would you like to? Tell me the truth."

"You kiddin'? I got three kids and four rooms—now what you think?"

"But I mean *here*. With all this stuff in it—seem like home to you?"

He laughed. "Well, I sho' wish it did."

"I rather have a nice place out in the East."

14

"Well, I could see that, but in a pinch."

They both laughed. "Okay. In a pinch."

Cammie clicked back into the kitchen. "Hey, Lawrence. Y'all hungry?"

Dorise appreciated the way she always asked. She and Lawrence shook their heads. Dorise said, "I'm tryin' to lose a little weight."

Cammie looked at her watch. "Don't you have to pick up your little girl?"

She nodded. "Just soon's I finish here."

"Well, go ahead. I can do the rest of those."

Dorise thought Cammie one of the most considerate of the women she worked for, but Lawrence said, "She just don' want to pay for another hour."

She rattled off in her old Chevy, arriving five minutes before school let out. Once she had been twenty minutes late, and her daughter had stood alone in front of the school in the rain, hair soaked, clothes plastered to her body, tears streaming down her face.

But Shavonne had lied to make her feel better: "These ain' tears, Mama. They just raindrops."

That was worse than if she'd stamped her foot and sassed. Now they had a deal: If Dorise wasn't there as soon as school let out, Shavonne went home with her friend Chantelle.

Today she came running out in jeans and a turquoise T-shirt, hair neatly braided and held by clips. She was such a tiny thing!

Since Dorise had gained weight—shortly after Shavonne's birth—the idea of unpadded bones was inconceivable to her. Her own mama was heavy and so was her sister. Yet they had all been skinny little kids once.

She could barely remember her own thin body or her childhood. Even Delavon's memory was fading. Dorise prided herself on living in the present.

"How was school?"

"Good. You know about Passover?"

"Somethin' in the Bible."

"They still have it, Mama. Lady come in and tell us all about it."

"Well, ain't that nice."

"Some days be better than other days." Dorise didn't know if she meant school or her own state of mind. Shavonne had watched her father die, shot to death in their living room.

Dorise said, "Honey, you still dreamin'?"

Slowly, reluctantly, Shavonne nodded, but half-heartedly, only a couple of times.

"You don't call me no more." At first her daughter had screamed out in the night, terrified, desperate to be reassured.

"Ain't no point, Mama. I know it's a dream. Ain't nothing you can do." She was looking at her lap.

Dorise said nothing, wondering what all this meant. It could mean her daughter was growing up a little, getting over what had happened. But something about the way Shavonne spoke sounded so calm, so resigned, it worried her. She wasn't sure why, but it gave her the creeps.

She said, "Now don't you be like that. Mama be right there. Right in a minute. Promise me now."

"Okay." But she didn't raise her eyes. She was such a good girl. Some things just weren't fair.

"Tell you what. Maybe Chantelle like to come over. You like that, precious?"

The way Shavonne nodded was much like she had before, when Dorise asked her if she still dreamed—slow and not very convincing.

"What's the matter, baby?"

"Nothin', Mama."

Chantelle's mama said why didn't Shavonne come over there, spend the night even, give Dorise a night off? And Shavonne seemed to like that idea—but Dorise had a hard time reading her these days.

The upshot was, Dorise found herself home alone, something that hadn't occurred since before Shavonne was born, maybe. *Nobody* was there—not her sister, not anybody. She could take a nap if she wanted.

But Dorise wasn't the napping kind. *I could make gumbo,* she thought. *Then we'd have some for the weekend.*

I could call Troy.

Troy was a man she'd met at her sister's house, a neighbor, with whom she'd had a date or two. There was something about him she liked.

Yeah, said her sister. *Somethin' hang down between his legs.*

Dorise said, "How I know about that? I ain't even seen what he got down there."

She thought, *I might like to, though,* and the thought scared her a little bit. She hadn't been to bed with anyone but Delavon in ten years.

I need to get to know him better.

She called him at work. "Hey, Troy. I'm gon' be down at Jack's later on." A bar near her sister's.

"I was just thinkin' about you."

"You were?"

"Whatchew want to go to Jack's for? Why don't I pick you up, take you someplace nice?"

"I cain't be late, now."

He laughed. "Dorise, you worry too much."

They went out and had crawfish and beer. Before, they'd been to hear music, or to a party. They hadn't talked much yet. She knew what Troy did, he had a good job driving a bus, and he knew she was a widow with a little girl, but he didn't know about Delavon— or anything about her, really.

She was sitting there working on her crawfish, poking at the tail joints, delicately separating meat from shell, when he said, "You got pretty hands, Dorise. I been watchin' 'em."

She didn't know what to think. "That mean you don't like my face?"

He laughed. "You funny, you know that? I wouldn't be here if I didn't like your face. But you got pretty hands, too."

He reached out and grabbed one of them. "Know what I like? You don't put all that polish and shit on 'em."

Her sister did. Her nails were royal purple one day, pussy-pink the next, and half the time they had designs on them. Dorise giggled. "Little moons and stars—you don't like that? Gold-colored fleur-de-lis?"

"I like nice brown hands. Brown like God made 'em." He turned her hand over. "Nice soft pink palms."

He rubbed her palm with his finger and it gave her a funny feeling, the sort she'd almost forgotten. But she was embarrassed. She pulled her hand away.

"Dorise, what you do with those hands?"

17

"You don' know?"

"You never told me."

She could hardly believe it. "I work for Uptown Caterers." She said the name and everything because she was proud of it, like men were when they said they worked for Shell Oil or something.

Sure enough, Troy was so impressed he whistled. "Well, ain't that just—you know—uptown."

"They nice people. I'm real lucky."

"You cook and everything?"

"No, uh-uh, I'm a server."

"You serve the food?"

She nodded. "Yeah, uh-huh, I supervise the jobs, really. Make sure everything's there, then I serve—sometimes I tend bar if they want me to. And I wash dishes and pack up—do just about everything."

"You like it?"

"Yeah. You know, I really do. I love it."

"What you like about it?"

She had never had anyone ask her that. She told him, feeling as if she were giving him part of herself. Nobody else knew how she felt in those places, how comfortable and happy, as if she were Mistress of the Manor—but somehow, not at all grand. Simply as if she were in control for once.

● ●

In Skip's life, Errol Jacomine was the one who got away. He was a con man and a murderer, but so were lots of scumballs. Jacomine was something else, someone who treated human life like gardeners treat bug life. He had run not one but many a con, and murdered as often as he felt the need—or possibly the desire. She'd messed up a very good thing he had, and she knew it was only a matter of time until he came for her—or for someone she loved.

Every spare moment she had, she tried to reel him back in. The problem was, he'd come to prominence in a big way almost overnight. She'd been able to run down his early life in Savannah, Georgia, including a murder he'd once been accused of. Then he'd had a period as a minister with a minuscule denomination called the Christian Community, during which he made a big splash in Atlanta.

That one ended when one of the ladies of the church complained of sexual favors required as part of pastoral counseling sessions, and other ladies came forward in something resembling a stampede.

He was perfecting the art of healing in Atlanta—some said he could even raise the dead—and he continued that when the church took away his congregation and sent him to southwest Louisiana. Eventually, he started his own church, the Blood of the Lamb Evangelical Following, which was about the time Skip encountered him. As a minister with growing influence, he began to dabble in politics.

The Christian Community had kept poor records. All Skip had was this: In Atlanta, he had a family—in Louisiana, none.

After things blew up in her face, his wife, Tourmaline, had quite literally gotten out of Dodge. The Community had three missions, one in the backwoods of Honduras, and Tourmaline Jacomine had asked them to send her there. It was the least they could do to oblige. Mary Lou, the bossy secretary for the Community, swore there was not only not a phone, there wasn't even a fax machine. Skip doubted that, but her efforts to find a number had failed.

The good news, the Community said, was that Tourmaline had only another year to serve.

After Atlanta, there was no record at all of the Jacomines' grown son—not so much as a Social Security number.

Despite the advice of her therapist to get on with her life, Skip had gone over and over the same old territory. But there was one thing she hadn't done. The only person back in Savannah who really remembered mischievous young Earl (as he'd been called before he was Errol) was his talkative—if totally deaf—aunt Alice.

"I'm going back to see her," she told Steve.

"When?"

"Tomorrow."

"What about Layne's healing?"

"What?" But she knew what he meant—she was just astounded that he remembered, given the way he'd scoffed.

Layne Bilderback was the lover of her neighbor, landlord, and best friend, Jimmy Dee Scoggin, who lived in the Big House along with Kenny, Sheila, and Angel.

Jimmy Dee had had no one but Skip until his sister died—he literally inherited Kenny and Sheila. About the same time, after many years of solitude, he met Layne, necessitating much emergency education for the children on gay lifestyles. As it turned out, they were great fans of the relationship—two uncles were a lot better than one, in their opinion. "Especially," as Jimmy Dee put it, "when I'm one of them."

Then came Angel. Everybody loved her, Jimmy Dee included. In no time, he was fond of saying, he'd fallen in love with three people and a dog.

The problem was, Layne was allergic to the dog.

No remedies, conventional or alternative, had the least effect, but Skip had an idea—she happened to know a coven of witches who'd agreed to try their hand at a healing. Layne could have managed without her, but she had promised to take Kenny, who was just dying to see witches at work.

"Maybe I'll stay overnight," she told Steve. "You can take Kenny to the healing."

"Is it okay if I wear a garlic clove?"

"Oh, forget it. I'll be back."

● ●

Aunt Alice liked her—Skip felt this was due mostly to the fact that she offered the simple courtesy of not treating deaf as stupid. And Skip liked Aunt Alice—she liked her exuberance and her courage. When she visited the first time, Aunt Alice had talked candidly about a relative she thought was dangerous, though everyone else in the family had decided to find him amusing—Earl Jackson, aka Errol Jacomine.

She greeted Skip this time in a lavender windsuit with gray trim. It was meant for walking, but Aunt Alice was heavy and moved slowly, as if what walking she did was done under duress. Her gray hair was short, upswept in front, curled on the sides, and rigid with spray—she'd just been to the hairdresser.

She held both of Skip's hands and looked at her like a long-lost relative. "Hey, precious. You look so pretty." Instantly Skip recalled the way she had taken to Alice the first time they met, partly because of the woman's warmth but also because of her intelligence—and the sense that Alice, because of her deafness, was much underestimated by her relatives.

Skip came and sat down. She was presented with a writing pad— Aunt Alice could talk to you, but you had to write to her.

"Did you get my letter?"

Skip nodded. She wrote, "Thank you. That was sweet of you."

Skip's encounter with Jacomine was national news. Aunt Alice had written to say she knew Skip was just doing her job even though Earl Jackson was a blood relative, and she, for one, not only applauded, she was real sorry the bastard got away.

"It's good to see you again, honey. What can I do for you this time?"

"I know it's stupid to ask," Skip wrote, "but has Jacomine been in touch with anyone in the family?"

"Now, honey, you know I would have let you know."

"Just thought I'd ask," she wrote, and pulled out a list of the things she'd already done to trace Jacomine: looked for his wife, looked for his son, badgered the Christian Community. "Can you think of anything else I could do?"

Aunt Alice's index finger, under a layer of ladylike pink nail polish, flicked at the list. "Didn't even know he'd married again."

Skip's stomach flipped over. Blood pounded in her ears: this was something. She wrote, "Again? You mean this wasn't his first marriage?"

"Oh, lordy, lordy. How would you know? Yes, ma'am, he was married, and thereby hangs a tale. Now where'd I put that thing?" She got up and left the room. Skip wanted to chase her, grabbing at the flapping folds of her purple windsuit.

But there was nothing to do but wait, drumming her fingers, swinging her leg, all but biting her nails.

"Here it is." Aunt Alice handed her a clipping from *People* magazine, about a Texas millionaire who'd just married a nineteen-year-old fashion model who looked like she'd probably suck her thumb if she got to feeling insecure.

Skip stared at it. "I don't understand."

"See that other picture? *That* was Earl Jackson's first wife." She nodded, caught up in the utter satisfaction of having a good story to tell. "Course, she was Mary Rose then."

The inset at the bottom was a head shot of the woman scorned—Rosemarie Owens, a hard-looking blonde with helmet hair, very much in the Ivana Trump mode. She'd gotten an eight-million-dollar settlement, and was suing for more.

Skip was flabbergasted. But then everything about Jacomine flabbergasted her—to her, he was a weedy-looking, slightly ferrety, crepey-skinned, slimy little salamander, hardly capable of inspiring mother love, much less the devotion of hundreds of followers.

"How on Earth . . . ?" she wrote, and then she added a series of exclamations and question marks.

Aunt Alice chuckled, thoroughly enjoying herself. "Well, she was too young to know better. 'Bout fourteen, I think—maybe a little more. She and Earl ran away together."

"She's from Savannah as well?"

"Oh, yes. Oh, it was quite a story. They ran away and then later he came back by himself. And then way, way after that, she came back and brought him a baby."

Skip wrote, "A little late for that, wasn't it?"

"It wasn't a baby exactly, it was a seven-year-old."

The Christian Community records had indicated only one son—Skip wondered if there were two children instead. "What was its name?"

"You know, I can't really recall." Aunt Alice nodded again. "Haven't heard of Rosie since. Can't imagine how shocked I was when I picked up this magazine and there she was staring up at me."

"You're sure that's her?"

"Course I'm sure. Mary Rose Markey always did look like some little animal likely as not to bite you. Look at her picture—you ever seen a nose like that one? It's not the kind of thing you forget. Besides, her age is right, her name's right, and the article flat out says she's from Savannah. Now I may not be a detective, but I can add two and two as well as you can." She chuckled. "Besides, after this ran, the local papers picked it up. No mention of Earl, though. That probably goes back too far for 'em."

"What happened to the boy?"

"Oh, Earl raised him, I reckon. Or—I guess—got him another wife who did. He moved out of town shortly after Rosie came back. *Begged* her to stay with him, I heard." Alice shook her head. "Guess she was already off to catch her a Texas millionaire."

"He begged her? You mean he didn't dump her when he came back without her?"

"Oh, I b'lieve she had *quite* enough of Mr. Earl Jackson right quick. But Earl now—he was crazy about that girl. Always made me suspicious of her. They say like attracts like—you know?"

Skip wrote, "I thought opposites did."

"I'll tell you somethin', precious. Earl Jackson acted like he was the spawn of the devil himself—I never in my life seen a *mean* child but that one. Bad, yes; up to no good; mischievous. All that stuff. But *mean*? Only once. And I just got a feelin' Miss Rosie ain't no angel, either."

Skip left feeling elated—it was her first lead in six months.

She just had time to catch her plane—or so she thought. In fact, it was half an hour late, so that she was late making her connection in Atlanta. As she trotted through the airport, she saw a tangled knot of people crowded into a bar—apparently staring at a television. For a moment, she was confused—was it football season? Definitely not. It was getting longer every year, but didn't yet extend into spring.

Her seatmate on the plane seemed nervous—finger-drumming, knee-swinging nervous, the way she'd been at Aunt Alice's. Finally, he turned to her. "Hear any more about Billy Hutchison?"

"Billy Hutchison? I don't know what you mean."

"Somebody shot the son of a bitch. What goes around comes around, don't it?" He had a red face and a country accent. He probably opposed abortion and kept an arsenal handy in case any blacks wandered into his neighborhood. She didn't need a psychic to tell her he'd revel in something like this—something with the potential to set off race riots. (That is, assuming a white man had shot Hutchison.)

But there was something about what he said—"what goes around comes around"—that had a certain fearful symmetry.

3

• •

Lovelace Jacomine was about to hit her snooze alarm for the fourth time when the clock was wrenched from her.

"Hey, L. Not okay." Her roommate, Michelle, was standing over her, in T-shirt and Calvin Klein briefs, hair sticking straight up, bossy as always.

"I'm not going to class."

"Fine. Dandy. Just quit hitting the alarm, okay? I can sleep another hour."

"Oh, hell." Lovelace got up and grabbed the shirt she'd worn the day before, pulling it over her head on the way to the bathroom. She splashed water, ran a comb through, pulled on jeans. She'd be late to class, but not that late.

Philosophy. It didn't make sense. How could you think deep thoughts before nine A.M.? She didn't like doing anything before ten, but she'd wanted to take the damn class, God knew why.

She shrugged into her jacket—these early spring days were still cool, especially this time of day—and grabbed her backpack. As she walked out of the building, she noticed the coffee stain on the front of her Henley shirt.

Damn.

But there was no time to change. She glanced at her watch and started to run. By now, just about everyone who was going to class was already there. She felt suddenly panicked. What was the point of going to college if you couldn't be more conscientious than this?

She had such a long way to go, she slowed for a while to get her breath. She heard something behind her, not footsteps but something.

And that was all. A hand went over her mouth, another around her waist. She never resisted, never had a chance.

He must have done some carotid-artery knockout thing, or maybe she was so deeply in shock that she lost her memory. Whatever it was, the next thing she knew, she was in a car, gagged, lying down on the seat, hands and feet bound.

The last time she had felt so helpless she'd been eleven, at her dad's cabin in some forest in the middle of nowhere. He had shot a deer and wanted to show her how to clean it. Horrified, finding no words to describe how dreadful she found it—the dead animal, the prospect of defiling it—she ran away.

He chased and caught her, and made her sit and watch. He hadn't needed bonds, but she might as well have been tied tight as a calf, so much a prisoner was she.

The place was awful. Her dad was awful, with his damn lifetime supplies of everything (including ammunition), his tobacco-chewing friends with their camo fatigues and their doomsday scenarios. So far as she could tell, they pretty much thought everybody was stupid except them, and the world was probably going to crack apart any minute, causing black people to storm these pathetic cabins in the woods.

She chided them for being racists, and they said if she had any sense she would be, too. In fact they made fun of her, called her Little Miss Yankee Liberal, and she shrank further and further into herself. That was the summer she made it through about half of Dickens and a little of Dostoyevsky.

She would get a Coke and some Oreos and retreat to her closet-sized room with one of the books she'd brought. Then she'd dunk the cookies in the Coke, lose herself in stories of people—some of them kids—worse off than she was, and she'd feel almost happy. She gained weight just when she was supposed to be having an active outdoor life, and her dad was cruel about it. He called her names she couldn't remember without feeling the heat and shame of tears, even now, and so she never thought about it.

The little room—she thought it really had been a closet—had been okay, though. All it had in it were two things—a narrow built-in platform fitted with a mattress and, perpendicular to that, a sort of wide shelf with a mirror over it that served as a dressing table. That left about enough room to stand up and undress, and no place to put anything other than a couple of stacks of jeans and T-shirts, which was how she kept her clothes—in stacks on the floor. Her books she tucked under the shelf, and she put her panties on top of them, decently out of sight.

Her dad had built the bed and shelf just for her, so she could come visit. Much as she wished he hadn't bothered, she did love the room. It was her only refuge from her opinionated, nasty, gun-toting dad—and from the place itself, with its dead animal heads, off-putting noises, and primitive appointments.

There was indoor plumbing, but everything leaked. There was a gas stove, but it was about fifty years old and didn't always light. There were naked bulbs for light.

The only bedding was worn sheets and army blankets. The sheets were soft and nice, but she couldn't hack the sandpaper wool of the blankets—indeed, had pitched a tantrum until she was allowed to bring her own twin-sized duvet, which her father had ridiculed and called her "sissy cover."

Pretty soon, he was calling her Sissy, and so were all his friends. Of course it beat Blubberface, but that came later and didn't last. Sissy stuck.

She was so unhappy that summer, she actually missed her mother. God, her mother! Jacqueline the Queen. If her father was a minimalist, Jacqueline was his antithesis. Her apartment was so full of frills and pillows and lace and fuss, you had to struggle for breath. She had more clothes than Macy's and more makeup than Maybelline. She loved to go partying with her boyfriends, and she stank of gin on weekends.

Her dad hated to party, hated almost everything, Lovelace included, and Jacqueline was way at the top of the list. But he did love to drink. Her mother said she worried about it and even asked Lovelace if he'd ever "touched" her.

She'd answered, "Of course, Mom—what do you think? How's he going to hit me if he doesn't touch me?" and her mother had laughed. Lovelace hadn't figured out why until years later.

Actually, Lovelace liked it when he drank—he tended to get woozier and woozier until finally he'd just fall asleep, which left Lovelace more time with the Cokes, Oreos, and books.

The feeling she had now was similar to the one she'd harbored that whole summer—trapped, but not hopeless. She'd get out, that much was certain, but she had to bide her time. She had to wait, and get through. Just get through.

"You have to pee or anything?"

She didn't know how to answer, but she was damned if she was just going to lie there. She made some sort of hum through her gag.

"Baby, I hate having you tied up like that. You want me to take the tape off?"

She hummed again, as loudly as she could.

"Well, let's stop up here. You can go behind some bushes."

He stopped the car and cut the tapes, even rubbed her wrists.

"Now you go pee, but don't try to mess with me. I'll just catch you."

She knew he would. Besides, it was better to gain his trust a little, hope he'd let down his guard. Maybe next time she could talk him into a gas station bathroom, and that would be it—she'd be free.

When she came back, he was holding out a Coke to her, its top already popped. It was cold, and she needed it.

"Can I sit in the front—with you?"

"You know I'm different now, Lovelace."

She made her eyes go wide. "Really?"

He opened the door for her—she'd won a concession.

"I'm not conservative anymore—I'm a liberal."

She didn't know what she'd been expecting to hear, but it wasn't that. Even in her confused state of mind, she recognized that it was an extremely odd thing for a kidnapper to say.

What the fuck do I care? she wanted to shout. *You're a sickie and a weirdo and I hope you rot in hell. Why the fuck do I care what your damn politics are?*

"Nooo!" she said, drawing it out, as if shocked out of her mind. "I don't believe it."

"Hey, I saw the light. I bet you thought it would never happen."

"Did it—" she couldn't think of the phrase "—Did it . . . uh . . . come in a flash of . . ." *Of what?*

"You making fun of me?"

She was feeling a little odd, as if she couldn't quite follow the conversation.

"Making—uh—fun? Of course not, I wouldn't . . ." Her hands felt slightly numb and her brain was just . . . not . . . revving . . . up.

At the last minute, she got it: the Coke.

The can slipped through her fingers and started dribbling out its contents as a flicker of fear passed through her. Till now, she had thought only of making her move, of biding her time until the right moment.

She saw that she had underestimated her adversary.

The fear left and as she went under, she felt a darkness, a heaviness, a cottony weight descend upon her, and she recognized it.

She knew it.

It was her old friend Depression.

●　●

Skip arrived home to find Steve glued to the television like the people in the airport, riveted by news of Billy Hutchison's assassination.

"Oh, no. Not you, too," she said.

"Hey. Me and the whole world. You mean you *don't* want to know about this stuff? It's not every day the good guys get somebody. Refreshing for a change."

She sat down. "You're kidding. Right?"

He laughed and pulled on a long-neck Dixie. "Reality check here. This is me, Steve. Not some raving redneck."

She got up again, breathing easier. "Yeah, well," she muttered, "lines are getting a little blurry."

"Tell me there's not a piece of you that's going, 'Nyah nyah nyah nyah nyah.' "

28

She winced.

"See. There is. You don't want to think about it, but there is."

"It's creepy. It gets you on a real childish level."

"I know. I think I'm going to go make a peanut butter sandwich."

"I've got to get ready for a healing."

As she stood in the shower, it occurred to Skip that Steve hadn't even asked her how it went with Aunt Alice. When she came out, the phone was ringing.

It was Layne: "Do we have to wear, like, black robes or anything?"

"They didn't mention it."

"Okay. I'm at the Big House. Kenny's dressed up in a little suit and tie, all ready for weirdo-church."

She heard Kenny in the background: "Hey, man, come on."

He was probably wearing jeans but Layne had hit on a central truth about him: Kenny was a born Good Boy. He just couldn't help it, which Skip thought must be impossibly annoying to his rambunctious sister, Sheila. Yet he wasn't a goody-goody at all.

Somehow, he instinctively understood grown-ups' rules, and for some reason had no wish to break them. She didn't get it, having been not a bit like that as a child. Either she'd instinctively gotten everything wrong, or she was so appalled by what she was expected to do that her subconscious simply filtered it out, with the result that she felt like an alien in her own family. She was the child of brazenly social-climbing parents who used their children to get them into the right parlors. Skip had a way of becoming embarrassing once her parents were in—knocking over the ancient porcelain, perhaps, or innocently asking little Eugenie's mom why she didn't put vodka in everyone's iced tea, since she always took hers that way.

She still hadn't mastered the mores of Southern womanhood and probably never would.

Being a police officer took up a lot of the slack, since she wasn't expected to spend all day backbiting or arranging flowers. Also, it was so eccentric a job for an Uptown girl, she could more or less march to her own tune.

Sheila was a lot like Skip. She meant well, she was just clumsy.

Beyond all that, Kenny had something more than social instinct—he had an abiding sweetness and openness—not exactly innocence, he was a French Quarter kid, after all. But he didn't condemn any human activity on the basis of being different—a convenient attitude for a child whose only "parent" was a gay uncle—and he wanted to experience things. He'd insisted on going to the witches' circle, though Uncle Jimmy had scoffed and Sheila said the whole thing gave her the creeps.

"Good-bye, chickens," said Dee-Dee when the three piled out the door. "Bibbity-bobbity-boo, now."

Kenny said, "They say, 'blessed be,'" and Skip had no idea how he knew.

"Well, blessed be the free-of-sneezes."

Dee-Dee was like that—the perennial joker. But the simple fact was, Layne's allergy threatened the relationship. After what the kids had been through—their father had first deserted, then their mother had died—he truly would sacrifice his first love in years before he'd find Angel a nice home in the country.

The witches, whom Skip had met on a case, were having the ritual at the home of a new member who lived in Old Metairie, about as nonthreatening a neighborhood as existed anywhere—the kind with bikes parked in the driveways and shaggy sheep dogs lying on the porches.

The new witch was named Melinda, and nothing, to the best of Skip's memory, like anyone else in the coven. She was a chirping, bird-boned woman in her thirties, with short blond hair and tiny features. She wore white shorts and a black T-shirt that looked as if it had been ironed.

The other witches—all women—awaited in a living room full of Hurwitz-Mintz furniture. There wasn't a single thing to indicate an affinity with the occult, until Kit, the high priestess, started unpacking small objects from a basket.

She spread a scarf on the coffee table to serve as an altar cloth, and placed on it candles, a chalice, a knife in a case, and a few other more-or-less commonplace items, including a plate of cookies.

She said, "Kenny and Layne, do you know anything about all this?"

Kenny nodded, all eagerness. He had said something once about learning about paganism in school, and Skip suspected he'd also read up on it.

Layne, in contrast, blushed and shook his head.

"Well, don't worry. It's not spooky or anything. Every coven's different, but in ours, which we call the Cauldron of Cerridwen, by the way, we wear different-colored robes at different times of the year."

"Why?" It was Kenny, of course.

"You know about the three aspects of the goddess?"

He shook his head.

"Maiden, mother, and crone—and the year follows the goddess's phases. In spring, we think of the maiden, and so we wear white—then red in summer, and black in winter."

They left to put on their white robes, and when they returned, the atmosphere had subtly changed, grown more contemplative.

Kit said, "Everyone ready?"

They were silent a moment, and then Melinda lit a white candle, saying what appeared to be a prayer to the East. Then someone lit a red one, for the South, and so it went until all the directions had been invoked.

Skip had seen this before, and she found it calming and energizing at the same time. She looked at Layne and Kenny. Kenny, wide-eyed, might as well have been at Disneyland. And Layne, the sophisticated, hyperintelligent pal of Jimmy Dee Scoggin, was soaking it up, though slightly wary.

Kit picked up the knife and used it to cut out an imaginary circle to serve as a temple. And after that was done, Skip thought she felt the atmosphere change again. She couldn't have described it, really, except to say it felt cozier, as if a real circle existed.

The high priestess lit two more candles, invoking deities associated with the healing arts, Brigid and Asclepius.

"In Cerridwen's Cauldron," she said, "we sometimes plan the ritual and sometimes we invent it on the spot. We thought since we didn't know Layne, we wouldn't plan this one. So we can't tell you what to expect."

"You mean anything can happen?" Layne sounded nervous.

Kit spoke almost sharply: "I'll tell you what's going to happen—we're going to heal you. Now tell us about your allergy."

"I—uh—sneeze around Angel. And I can't breathe, and my eyes water."

"And what helps? Anything?"

"Being away from the dog. And of course—from Jimmy Dee."

He almost cringed as he mentioned the last part. Kit said, "Anything else?"

"Hot soup. That's about it—but of course, it only relieves the symptoms."

Kenny said, "I brought some," and reached into his backpack. He pulled out a soup can: "Chicken. Magic works by metaphor, doesn't it? I just . . . thought I'd bring this. I brought a picture of Angel, too—in Layne's lap."

He passed the picture around, showing it first to Layne, who rubbed his nose as he took it. "I think I'm going to sneeze just looking at it."

Melinda said, "Why don't we just—you know—set up an astral cauldron and make some allergy-curing soup?"

A couple of coven members said "Yeah!" Apparently this was something they'd done before.

But Kit looked hard at Layne. "I want to touch him, too. Anybody else?"

Layne blushed and drew back.

"It's okay. You'll be fine if you just do what Kenny said. Think of it as metaphor."

Skip noted privately that that wasn't exactly what Kenny had said.

"Do you mind?" said Kit.

Layne said, "No. Of course not." But he looked scared to death.

"Here." Kit placed a chair in the center of the circle. "Sit here and close your eyes if you like."

She passed her hands from his head to his feet, close to the body, though not actually touching, despite what she'd said.

"I don't feel any energy blocks. Janna?"

Another woman did the same thing. She let her palm hover

between his shoulder blades. "There's something here." She began pulling at air, hands working as if pulling a rope out of Layne's body.

Each witch took a turn. Some pulled the rope out—toxins, maybe, Skip thought—some laid on hands, some didn't touch, but held their hands for a while in front of a certain part of his body, and breathed loudly, as if through their palms.

When the last one had had a turn, Kit said, "Skip?" Skip passed and she turned to Kenny.

Without a word, almost in a trance, Kenny did exactly what the witches had done—checked Layne's aura, if that was what it was—with his hands, and then, suddenly, he began making sweeping movements an inch or so from Layne's body, and flinging out his fingers, metaphorically removing something.

He said, as if he'd written it in advance:

> *Allergy, go!*
> *Allergy, leave!*
> *Heed the spell*
> *That I now weave!*
> *Angel be pure!*
> *Layne be cured!*
> *Allergy, go!*
> *Allergy, leave!*

"So mote it be," said all the witches in unison, as if the whole thing were scripted.

"So mote it be," Kenny repeated, leaving Skip flabbergasted and wondering if Layne was, too.

This is too weird, she thought. *Here I am with a thirteen-year-old boy trying to cure his gay uncle's lover with witchcraft. No wonder I didn't fit in on State Street.* Where she grew up.

It was weird, but it was making her feel good—oddly elated, as a matter of fact.

Kit said, "Kenny, will you help me smudge him?"

The boy nodded, as if he did this every day, and took the smoking twig of sage she gave him. When the two of them had ritually cleansed Layne's body with the smoke, they sat down. "Shall we do the meditation? Everyone close your eyes and get comfortable. Let's fire up the cauldron now, and make a nice, healing soup for Layne. I think it needs some love in it, so I'm putting that in first."

"I'm going to put in aspirin," said Melinda. "Can't hurt."

"Mushroom pizza," said Kenny. "Layne's comfort food."

Janna said, "Eucalyptus keeps fleas off dogs, and in this soup it keeps allergies off humans. Also fleas, if Angel has any of those."

"I'm putting in patience," said a woman named Suby. "It might take a while, but that allergy's out of here."

"Stinging nettles," said Kit. "An herbal allergy remedy."

Skip was trying desperately to think of something when suddenly she remembered: "We forgot the chickens. Here go two. And some carrots and onions for flavor."

"Mmmm. Lots of thyme, to make it savory."

"A dash of white wine."

"Some dumplings."

And so it went until the brew was thick and nutritious. "Now, Layne, take as much as you need. And everyone else have some, too—maybe you have an allergy also, or maybe something else is bothering you—a hangnail, a backache—chicken soup will cure it. Everybody have as much as you like, and when we're done, we'll send the rest home with Layne."

It was silly—Skip knew it was silly—but she took plenty of astral soup for her fear—the fear she had about the kids, about Steve and Jimmy Dee—the fear that wouldn't leave her until she got Jacomine. Unless the witches' brew worked, of course.

Oh, well, as Melinda said about the aspirin—can't hurt.

They were back in the car before Skip thought to ask Kenny about the rhyme he'd made up.

He shrugged. "I just thought I'd write a spell," he said, as if it were the most natural thing in the world.

She looked at Layne, who touched the top of the boy's head, awkwardly trying to say thanks. Skip could almost see him biting back whatever he'd really thought about the ritual.

Instead he asked, "What'd you guys think?"

Kenny said, "Cool," more or less his only positive adjective.

"But what was cool?"

"Well, the rhymes for one thing—especially mine."

"They don't strike you as . . . childish?"

"Well, sure they do, Layne. That's the point."

"Oh."

Skip had to laugh. "Yeah, I like that, too. I really do." There was something else she liked that she couldn't put her finger on—it was the second time she'd been to one of these things, and she'd noticed it before. Both times, a kind of peace came over her afterward. She wasn't the type who craved religion, but this stuff was sweet.

Kenny is, too, she thought. Sometimes she worried about him—she was afraid he was so nice he'd get hurt.

4

• •

Steve opened the door, a drink for her in hand.

"What's this for? Think I need it after a hard day conquering allergies?"

"Nope." He smiled and sat on her striped couch, pulling on his own beer. When he put the bottle down, she saw he was smiling again. "This is a celebration."

She flopped into a chair. "Well, I know we're not pregnant. So tell me more."

He kept smiling.

"What? You're driving me crazy."

"You got a new boss."

She leaned forward, suddenly all ears. "Somebody good?"

"Somebody Goodlett."

"Albert? No. Impossible. Too nice." Like Kenny.

This was way too good to be true. Albert Goodlett was an assistant chief she knew very slightly, but one who had the respect of nearly everyone in the department.

He was black, but whites liked him.

He was male, but women liked him.

He was intelligent, but dummies liked him.

He was educated; the streetsmart liked him.

He was a stickler; the lazy liked him.

He was so well qualified, it was hard to believe anybody didn't like him. But he was so nice there might be some who didn't think he was tough enough (though there was no doubt in Skip's mind he was).

And he was honest. That made it doubly hard to believe he'd really been appointed superintendent—an honest cop could be appointed, but it was usually thought that he had to come from outside the department.

"This is no joke?"

He raised his Dixie. "Here's to Chief Goodlett."

"Let's catch the ten o'clock news."

It was the lead story.

"See?" said Steve. "Would I lie to you?"

He was so genuinely happy for her she was touched. And she was absolutely elated about the new boss—an outsider would have been fine, but someone from home stood a better chance of working out, she thought. At least he knew what he was dealing with—or, more important, whom.

She went to get Steve another beer and when she came back, Billy Hutchison's picture was on the screen. Steve said, "Listen to this."

Suzanne Nickerson, the current fave anchorwoman, was reading a letter to the press, purportedly from a group calling itself The Jury:

It is impossible for an ordinary, honest person to get justice in America today. Those who are successful in court are those who are able to buy their freedom—or conversely, another person's conviction.

Corporate America can buy "justice." Billy Hutchison can buy "justice." You and I cannot. Justice is not the concern of the American judicial system today—it has bigger fish to fry. It is interested in maintaining its pathetic, perverted self. It is interested in its own sick values—and we do not necessarily mean the values of the fat-cat judges and the incompetent bureaucracy—we mean as well the values of the juries so blinded by fame and money that they no longer have a conscience.

Someone must draw a line somewhere. Billy Hutchison killed a woman. Is there no justice for that woman? The woman was his wife. Is there no justice for all the abused and murdered wives of all American men who believe they are entitled to whatever crimes they wish to commit within a marriage?

And yet, all that is beside the point. We can do no good for Mrs. Hutchison or for her many sisters. We can only vent our own frustration. This time, we have declined to let a guilty man go free.

Yes, this is vigilante action! Yes, we have taken the law into our own hands! Why? Because someone must. Because we are tired of talk, tired of frustration, tired of rage.

In America, we each have a right to be tried by a jury of our peers. Yet juries today are composed of those people too weak and too poorly connected to get the judge to excuse them, people whose jobs are considered so unimportant they can be spared, retired people—those at the bottom rung of society—in short, people who hope the glitz and glamour of a Billy Hutchison will rub off on them, not people who have the slightest idea of justice.

And so we have appointed ourselves a Jury of Mr. Hutchison's peers. A Jury of your peers. We have committed this crime—knowing full well that it is a heinous crime by American standards of so-called "justice"—because it is the only way.

The only way to bring a criminal to justice. And the only way to force on overhaul of our legal system.

The letter, Suzanne Nickerson said, was signed simply "The Jury."

"My God."

"Yeah. Creepy. I heard it earlier."

"Creepy because it's what you think. In your heart of hearts you agree."

"I'm telling you, it gives me goose bumps."

"Jacomine—"

"Oh. come on. You're not going to blame this one on Jacomine."

"He used to say, 'bigger fish to fry.' "

"Not much, as you people say, to go on."

"No. Anyway, it's too literate for him."

"Yeah, but his trick is having people around him."

"Don't you start, too. Let's go to bed."

"Can't. I have to walk Napoleon."

"You know what? They're right. There's no justice."

• •

Her head was splitting, and it cost her to pry her eyelids open. Some-one was in the room with her, and it wasn't Michelle. Michelle didn't snore.

But Lovelace was still too woozy to be frightened. That came in a moment when she saw that it was a strange room. She felt her heart speed up, heard its pounding even before she remembered that she'd been kidnapped, that it was her kidnapper sleeping in the next bed, fully clothed, lying on top of the bedclothes.

As her eyes became accustomed to the light, she could see him, could see everything perfectly well. They were in a cheap motel room and there was a crack in the curtains. Light from the parking lot illu-minated the room—and, unfortunately, Lovelace's sorry condition.

My hands, she thought, and flexed them, looked down at them. They were numb, bound with duct tape.

She wiggled her toes. Also numb; feet bound.

Like her companion, she was dressed and lying on the made-up bed, still in the jeans and shirt she'd been wearing that morning when she left for class. At least she thought it was that morning. The poisoned Coke was the last thing she remembered, so she probably hadn't awakened since she drank it.

Especially since she was desperate to pee.

She scratched her face with her finger, just to see if she could get it to work. It was fine. She grabbed a hunk of her T-shirt, at the hem, and wadded it up. Feeling or not, her fingers worked.

She looked around the room and saw something that heartened her—a Jack Daniel's bottle on the nightstand, about a third empty, and a glass with some amber liquid still in it. He had probably watched television, drinking, until he fell asleep.

Whew. I must have really been out.

She hoped he was now. She thought perhaps she had a chance, in fact she was pretty sure she did, if she could just work the tape off gradually, so that it didn't make a tearing sound.

She worked on her hands first, with her teeth, but she couldn't get any purchase and gave it up.

She turned on her side and got into as tight a fetal position as she could, hands as close to her feet as possible. Almost immediately, she found the end of the ankle tape.

Painstakingly, she peeled it, despising the very action, with its minute hopeless movements, despising her fear as well.

Her hatred of it, in fact her total concentration, served to displace the fear and hopelessness that surfaced in flashes now and then. If she just peeled, peeled, peeled, slowly, slowly, slowly, she couldn't really think of anything else.

Peel, peel, peel. Try not to let the springs squeak. Don't rustle the covers.

Except for cooking, which she adored, Lovelace loathed little delicate hand chores. She hadn't the patience of a monkey. She had stopped her piano lessons because practicing was tedious, never could learn to knit or sew because the tiny hand movements frustrated her so badly.

And now she was condemned to a life of peeling motherfucking duct tape nearly upside down in a Motel Six in . . . where?

Right now it really didn't matter.

The tape was off.

Should she try to get it off her hands? No. *Massage feet.*

She tried, but couldn't do it without shaking the bed. The kidnapper stirred a little.

Okay, then. Go back to getting the wrist bonds off.

She chewed at them while feeling returned to her feet, but in the end got nowhere. All she had to do, really, was get off the bed, walk quietly to the door, open it, and go to the manager's office.

No, she couldn't do that. Even her bound hands wouldn't get her out of this.

Okay. Open the door and run like hell.

She hoped that, wherever she was, it wasn't too cold out there.

Okay, this is it.

She still lay there.

In the end she didn't have the courage just to sit up, swing her legs off the bed, and split.

Instead she did it inch by inch, slithering to the edge of the bed and then lowering her legs. She had to do it slowly, let them unkink themselves—in the end, slow and steady might win, no matter how much it got on her nerves.

She slid off the bed, and the mattress did creak, there was nothing she could do about it, but the man moved at the same time, turned over or something, so the sound was masked.

She hadn't really planned it this way, but it seemed easier to stay on the floor, simply to crawl to the door.

Good. This way she could use the door to brace herself as she stood for the first time. That was lucky—she was a bit unsteady on her pins.

She worked the chain lock out of its mooring.

Bingo, that was all there was to it. She opened the door and slipped out.

No way to avoid that telltale click, though. A car was pulling into the parking lot—if she left the door open, the noise might wake him.

She closed it and started running. Almost immediately, he was out the door, after her.

Damn!

She had to play it out. She was in the light now, and held up her hands, so anyone, surely the person in the car, could see her bound hands. She yelled as loud as she could, "Help! He's going to kill me. Somebody help me."

The car, which had found a spot, reversed, turned, and sped out so fast it nearly knocked Lovelace over, and did hit her pursuer, who rolled over the hood and fell on the asphalt.

The driver leaned back, opened the back door, and said, "Get in. Quick."

She did and he peeled out of there.

He was young and he wasn't alone. He was very young, in fact younger than she. The girl in the front seat looked about sixteen. Her back was glued to the seat and she stared rigidly ahead. They were on open highway now, burning rubber.

The boy looked like Woody Woodpecker. He had a shock of red hair, thick and wild, a pinkish face, and he wore a rust-colored shirt, no doubt picked by his mama, who thought it flattered him. The girl

41

was a Barbie blonde. Her nail polish and lipstick probably matched and were called "Candy Apple" or "Sugar Frost."

Lovelace noticed one thing that pleased her—the girl wore shorts. She hadn't even thought to notice the weather, but she did now. It wasn't freeze-your-butt weather, which might mean she wouldn't die of exposure if she ever managed to get away.

She said, "Where are we going?"

Nobody answered. Apparently, they hadn't thought it out. The girl remained rigid.

Lovelace touched her shoulder. "Are you all right?" The girl turned to her, her face an odd mask of fear and confusion, her painted lips twisted. "What happened to you?"

Lovelace hadn't had time to think about what to do once she got away. In fact, she was still dealing with the odd sensation of being free—in her heart of hearts, she hadn't thought she'd make it.

"I wonder," she said, "why he isn't chasing us."

She was sorry instantly—the girl looked terrified.

"Oh, don't worry," she said. "He isn't dangerous."

Woody and Candy both spoke at once. "You know him?" "He didn't hurt you?"

Lovelace thought fast, and she was amazed at the clarity and speed with which her thoughts came.

These two probably want to keep a low profile as badly as I do.

The last thing she wanted was to be taken to the cops. She didn't know where she was, but so far it showed no signs of being a big city. These two had been in a motel parking lot, probably having just checked in, and they were both babies. More important, the girl was probably well under eighteen.

She told them a blend of truth and fiction, inventing as she went along. "He's my dad. See, I've been living with my boyfriend and he doesn't approve. He's like . . . I don't know, some kind of family-values freak, I guess you'd say, and he just . . . came and got me."

"Oh, you poor thing."

Lovelace would have smiled if she hadn't been so scared—it was certainly the right story for Woody and Candy.

"Could you help me with my hands?" She thrust her taped wrists in the space between the neck rests.

Candy gasped, but she began rummaging in her purse. "Your dad did that?"

"Yeah. My own dad did that." She tried to keep her voice tight and contained, but it got away from her. "My own father, god-dammit!" She couldn't even wrap her own mind around it. What kind of father kidnapped you and drugged you?

Candy fished out some nail scissors and hacked at the duct tape. Woody kept glancing in the rearview mirror.

"See anything?"

"Not yet. Look . . . are you a minor?"

Ha. Woody's not dumb. But maybe he'll think I am. "Why do you ask?"

"Because if you are, the cops are just gonna send you home."

"Cops? Omigod. I didn't think about that. What am I gonna do?"

"I'm thinkin'," Woody muttered. "I'm thinkin'."

"Uh . . . could I ask something? Where are we?"

"You mean what town? Jackson, Mississippi. That is, near it, sort of."

A long way from Evanston, Illinois. Why? she wondered. And where had he been taking her?

Candy said, "Where do you live? I mean, with your boyfriend?"

Something told Lovelace to lie about the place, too—to lie about everything.

"Austin," she said.

"Well, do you want to go back? We could take you to a bus station."

"Would you? That would be great. I mean, that would be *really* great."

It had drawbacks, though, not the least being that she had no money. She thought of saying it, knowing they'd give her some, but in the end she just couldn't mention it—she'd rather steal than sink that low.

They drove for a while in silence, Lovelace getting more and more nervous as various scenarios crowded into her head: They dropped her at the bus station, and he was waiting for her. She tried hitchhiking, and he picked her up. She checked into a hotel, and he broke into her room.

Woody broke her reverie. "Shit! That was Pearl Street."

"I don't understand."

"It's okay. I can get off at Lakeland Drive and double back." He swung off the Interstate, and in a moment they entered an area with a lot of street life—young people, bars, coffeehouses. She might be able to get lost in the crowd.

"Hey, listen . . . you know—you could just drop me here."

"Here? Why?"

"I think . . ." she leaned out the window. "I could swear I see someone . . . Hey, Michelle!" Lovelace yelled loud enough to grate on their nerves—bad. A girl turned around. Lovelace waved madly.

Woody slowed to a stop.

"Hey, thanks for the ride." She leapt out of the car and bounded in the opposite direction, just wanting to lose Woody and Candy, not really having any plans.

As soon as she dared, she slowed to the prevailing pace, trying to make herself invisible. She went into a bookstore and pretended to look at magazines, mind racing.

What did she do now? Where could she go?

Woody had been on the money—she was not only a minor, she'd spent a little time locked up once, courtesy of her old pal Depression.

She just wasn't going to win any argument about why her dad shouldn't kidnap her if he wanted to—he could always say she was suicidal; she'd phoned and begged him to pick her up. And now she was irrational, she needed her meds.

Michelle would vouch for her, but not much good it would do. Her dad would say she was a pathological liar, Michelle didn't know . . . she was a danger to herself and others.

Her mother might help her if she could find her. But Jacqueline was in Mexico living on a beach or something, probably stoned out of her gourd.

What a couple of pieces of work. Why isn't there anybody nice in my family?

A flashback of her uncle Isaac's Christmas card popped into her mind. It was a drawing of an old streetcar loaded up with holiday packages. On its side was written DESIRE, and the caption was in red, a holiday wreath around the streetcar: "Here's wishing you loot, and many a hoot."

Inside was the usual lovely letter. She got them twice a year—on her birthday and Christmas. Uncle Isaac never forgot. He nearly always made the cards himself—he was an artist. He always told her what he was doing—painting and drawing, lately—and where he was living—New Orleans these days—but mostly he went off on poetic tangents he thought she might enjoy, and she always did.

They were a little sentimental, sometimes a bit embarrassing, actually, but they were as sweet as maple syrup. She wrote him back as regularly as he wrote her—twice a year—and never talked to him, hadn't since she was ten or twelve—but she felt close to him, truly felt he cared for her and would help her if she got in trouble.

She'd gotten in trouble.

She reconnoitered: He was her father's brother, not her mother's, but she didn't really think that was a problem. Neither of the brothers had ever mentioned it, but she had the feeling there was some bad blood between them.

She'd call him.

But she broke out in a sweat when she remembered she hadn't a cent.

Where to get money?

In a bar or restaurant, she thought: an unclaimed tip, a careless tray of change, something like that.

She cruised a couple of places and couldn't bring herself to do it.

Finally, at a particularly busy coffeehouse, she saw a line for the phone and stood in it. When it was her turn, she made a show of looking up a number, fumbling, taking more than her share of time before "discovering" she had no change.

The girl behind her was only too glad to speed up the process.

Lovelace deposited the girl's quarter and asked for information in New Orleans, intending in the end to reverse the charges and pay back her benefactor. But it never came to that: Isaac wasn't listed.

She found a table and sat, thinking to move on if anyone asked her to.

Well, no problem: she knew his address. She had answered the Christmas card by continuing his gag with a play on the street name—something about the streetcar named Desire rolling down

45

the street called Royal. The number was the year, with a "20" in front—Lovelace didn't forget things like that.

All she had to do was get there.

A guy paused at her table. "Excuse me. Would you mind having my baby?"

Seize the day, she thought. She said, "I've got a better idea. Let's go to New Orleans."

"When you wanna go, sweetheart?"

But it wasn't going to be that easy. Half an hour later, she realized he was just flirting, but at least she had a plan.

She was tall (very tall—five-feet-ten) and had a pretty good figure (though she wouldn't mind losing ten pounds) and reddish sandy hair. She'd just ask people if they'd take her—nonthreatening-looking male people. Surely someone would bite.

The first one had bought her some coffee, so the coffeehouse people let her keep her seat awhile longer.

But finally, she went out to the street and simply stood, grabbing any lone male or two males she saw. Her approach was simple and straightforward: "Hey, I'm looking for a ride to New Orleans. You wouldn't want to go, would you?"

They all wanted to go. But, alas, they all had previous engagements.

She had about given up and was blinking back tears, trying to think up a new plan, when a blond man spoke to her, one she'd barely noticed, he looked so conventional. "Well, hey, pretty thing, why're you so sad?"

Make it good, she thought to herself.

Instead she blurted, "I want to go home," which wasn't even true, and started to sob. The man opened his arms, gathered her against his polo shirt. She felt the sturdiness of him, the thickness of his chest, and it was comforting.

"It's okay. That's right. Cry now, baby. Go ahead and cry." He was like some great male mom.

What a weird thing, she thought. *I must be really fucked up—there are no male moms. You call them fathers, right?*

She realized she was starting to calm down.

"Now tell Sam about it. You tell ol' Sammy all about it. Let's just sit on that bench over there and we'll have a little talk."

46

"I can't. I mean—do you mind if we walk?" The bench faced the street, and the last thing she wanted was to be conspicuous to cars driving by. What she really wanted was to go inside someplace, but she didn't want to ask for anything—not yet.

"We'll just do any little thing you want." He put an arm around her waist and started to walk.

She knew it wasn't right. It was way too familiar—taking advantage, at this point, rather than offering sympathy. But two things about it—it felt good, and Sam was all she had right now. He might be dicey, he might even be dangerous, but she sensed he had a heart.

He had a baby face, one of those more or less Irish visages with a smallish pink nose, chubby cheeks, blue eyes, usually a dimple (Sam's was in his chin), and a curl of blond hair dripping down a broad brow.

He was a little shorter than Lovelace, but he had heft. Lots of comforting heft. Maybe he worked out, maybe his ancestors had been built like barrels, or maybe it was a combination, but the result was plenty of beef inside his now-damp Ralph Lauren pullover. The shirt was faded purple and he'd tucked it into faded jeans, which in turn topped a pair of running shoes. He might have been twenty-five or he could have been a little older—at any rate, she got the feeling he was a little old for the neighborhood.

She had the vague feeling he didn't smell quite right, but it was sufficiently vague that she dismissed it.

"First of all, we should probably meet, don't you think? I'm Sam Marshall."

"I'm Michelle Jackson," she said, thinking she probably wasn't fooling him, but at least she hadn't said "Smith."

"Ms. Jackson from Jackson," he said, and she wondered if he was mocking her.

She couldn't be bothered worrying about it. "No, I'm not from here. That is—I was going to move here, but things didn't work out. Oh, God, I can't believe I've been so stupid!"

"Easy now. Just take your time."

"I came to visit my boyfriend and we had a fight."

"Umm-hmm."

"And he said he was sorry he'd ever spent a penny on me and I wasn't worth a penny and he was taking his own back. And he took all my money out of my purse and stuffed it in his pocket and threw my purse out the window. And then . . ." she thought fast, trying to make it believable that there was no going back ". . . he leaned over and smacked me across the mouth."

"You've got to be kiddin'."

"And he stopped the car and said, 'Get out, whore.' And I just sat there stunned, and he gave me a shove, and I landed on my butt in the street, and he peeled off with my suitcase."

"Well, no wonder you're so shook up."

She turned her face and looked into his, about six inches away. *Oh, God, I hope he doesn't try to kiss me.*

Instead, he said, "Where you from, Ms. Jackson?"

"New Orleans."

"Well, I'll take you home."

"You will?" *Finally.*

"Hell, yeah. Been wantin' to go there myself. Just got to take care of a little business. You wait for me?"

She nodded, feeling numb. What else was she going to do?

"Back in ten."

She went back in the coffeehouse and found the bathroom. One glance in the mirror convinced her that wasn't something she should try again.

She had no idea if Sam would show, but for the moment at least, she didn't have to think of a new plan.

He came up behind her. "Hey, Miss Michelle. I want you to meet my friends—Chip and Mimi. They're going with us."

They looked okay—a little rednecky, but not bikers or anything. Both wore jeans and T-shirts, which now made four of them. Mimi had a lot of long curly hair, cut in layers. Chip was tall, had a gut, and he was gray at the temples. She wondered if Sam was even older than she'd first thought.

"Hey, Michelle. Sorry about your hard luck."

Sam said, "Y'all ready?"

Later, Lovelace couldn't remember getting to the car, which was a four-by-four, a Blazer or something, and getting in, and taking off. She did remember that once they were in the thing, somebody fired up a joint and all three of the others cracked open beers and offered her one, but she was so tired by then she could barely shake her head no.

She must have fallen asleep right away.

The drug her father had given her had probably never really worn off, but she had operated on adrenaline for a couple of hours, as long as she needed to, and the minute she could, she crashed.

She fell asleep sitting up, strapped into her seat belt, Sam driving, the other two in the back.

She awoke to find someone's hand between her legs, stroking her. She was aware that that was what had awakened her; she had dreamed about sex with someone—a stranger, perhaps, or an old boyfriend; just a fragment of a dream. She opened her eyes a crack, saw the car, remembered where she was, and closed them again while she tried to think what to do.

No thoughts came.

Finally she simply sat up straight, opened her eyes, and looked around, preparatory to any sudden moves.

To her horror, she saw that the owner of the hand was not Sam but Chip, who was now in the driver's seat. She stared at him, wild, riveted. He smiled, puckered his lips, and kissed the air in her direction, jamming his hand tight against her crotch.

She shook her head and pushed at his hand.

He smiled, not budging.

What the hell was this? A cat playing with a mouse, smiling because he'd won? Or his idea of seduction?

And there were other issues—why Chip, not Sam? Had they flipped for her, or what?

The air was heavy with beer breath, and she realized that was why Sam hadn't smelled right—he was probably half-loaded when they met (as were Chip and Mimi), and now they were no doubt fully tanked.

She felt fear trying to close her throat and forced it back down. No time for that now.

She said, "Where are we?"

"Almost there."

"Almost to New Orleans?"

"That's where you want to go, idn't it?"

Which wasn't the same as a yes. And she thought she heard a slight edge to his voice.

Still, she nodded. "I'm tired."

He said, "Want to go to bed?"

Men are so damn predictable, she thought, and she nodded again. "I'm pretty tired. Could I have a beer?"

"Sure." He smiled, as if happy to see her entering into the spirit of things, and when he removed his hand to give her the beer, she seized her advantage and changed positions.

The sun was coming up when they entered that long, lonely stretch of Highway 55 that seems more like a bridge over a swamp than a highway. Lovelace was still holding her barely touched beer and thinking. She couldn't come up with a plan that didn't involve the police, but she wasn't too worried—yet.

Sam woke up. "Yecch. I feel horrible. What'd we do last night?"

"You did a little speed, ol' buddy. Little booze, too."

"Well, lemme have some more speed."

Speed. Did that dull or enhance the sex drive?

She couldn't remember.

"We better find a place to crash. There's gonna be nothin' within miles of the French Quarter."

Lovelace said, "Why not?" before she caught herself.

"Never is on the weekends." Sam sounded offhand, but a moment later he put a hand on her shoulder. "Hey. Thought you lived there."

She turned to the backseat. "That's why I don't stay in hotels."

"Wait a minute," said Chip. "Why don't we just stay at your place?"

"Are you kidding? I live with my parents."

Sam said, "Well, why are we giving you this ride, anyhow?"

Lovelace thought, *Oh, boy.* But she was starting to feel like herself again, the shock and numbness of her experience receding, the drug wearing off. She said, "Because you are fine Christian men helping out a damsel in distress."

Chip laughed in a way Lovelace really couldn't construe as anything but evil. "Oh, yeah, right."

It occurred to her that she should have wondered herself why they were giving her the ride. But the answer seemed obvious and not even sinister—they were drunk and it seemed like a good idea at the time.

Sam winked at Lovelace, who had noticed by this time that Mimi was stretched out with her head in his lap. "You two gettin' along?"

She smiled with her lips together, hoping they hadn't thinned into a telltale line. "Just fine."

"Hey, ol' buddy, gimme another hit of speed, okay?"

Chip pulled some pills out of his pocket, passed them back to Sam, and offered one to Lovelace. She took it, thinking she could use the rush.

The two men looked at each other. Chip said, "Aw right!"

Apparently, they thought they'd found a kindred spirit.

Sam said, "Gimme a beer."

"Want to go to the French Quarter? I mean, y'all don't really need to sleep now, do you?"

"Who said anything about sleepin'?"

"Listen, I kind of need to get home."

Chip grabbed her leg again. "Aw, come on. Just have breakfast with us. Then we'll take you home."

Lovelace noticed Chip hadn't availed himself of the speed, and her only hope was that he wouldn't. She needed him to crash. Breakfast might make him sleepy.

"Whatever." She shrugged and smiled at him, just a bimbo along for the ride.

They got off the Interstate and found a McDonald's, where she promptly excused herself to use the ladies' room, thinking home-free thoughts. But two things went wrong—Mimi came with her, and there was no window.

The guys had ordered her an Egg McMuffin. *If I eat it*, she thought, *does that mean they'll think I owe them? And if I don't, are they going to get ugly?*

In the end she nibbled, and when they urged her to eat up, she said she wasn't hungry. Sam said, "I know what you mean, man. I got other nourishment in my bloodstream."

Chip was starting to behave like a kid who hadn't had his nap. "Come on. I'm draggin'."

51

Sam said, "How about I drive for a while?"

"Are you kiddin'? You nearly wrecked us last night. Hey, I saw a Quinta Inn—let's go check in for a couple of hours."

"I want to get to New Orleans, man."

"Hey, man, we're there. This is Veterans Highway. We'll just stop for a nap, okay? Everything in the French Quarter's gon' be booked."

Mimi was nuzzling Sam. "Come on, Sammy. Let's stop for a little while."

If Lovelace had had any questions about the sleeping arrangements, they were answered.

So here's the problem, she thought: *The lady or the tiger? The devil you know or the devil you don't? I could just start hitchhiking, but maybe the new Ted Bundy'll give me a ride.*

She opted for her new best friends.

As soon as the door closed, Chip was upon her, beery, eggy breath in her face, tongue between her teeth.

She kissed him, but with her hands on his chest, pushing gently even as she opened her mouth, teasing a little. She broke away and whispered, "Let me take a shower first."

Once again there was no window. Still, she knew she wouldn't have used it. She was getting bolder by the moment, and more and more reckless. Later, she knew that she'd known in the back of her mind what she was going to do, but she never put it into words, never admitted it to herself—she just did it.

First, she did take a shower—a long, leisurely, delicious one. Then she put all her clothes on, stepped back into the room, and observed a dream come true.

Chip had stripped in anticipation, turned on the TV, and crawled between the covers, leaving his wallet and car keys on the dresser. He was snoring.

The keys were tempting. Really, really tempting. But the goal was staying away from her dad, and if she got busted for car theft, she'd be stuck with him for the next million years.

Besides, Chip had five or six twenties in his wallet—he probably didn't know how many himself. He'd never be sure if she took one or not. In fact, he wouldn't know if she took two.

She asked the desk clerk to call her a cab and was waiting in the lobby, big as life, when Chip came in loaded for bear. He was so mad he clenched his fists as he walked; his face was close to purple. She'd probably have wet her pants if there hadn't been two or three other people around.

"What the fuck do you think you're doing?"

She smiled as if he was her long-lost lover. "Hi, Chip. I realized I've really got to get going—my mom's going to be frantic if I don't get home soon."

At the mention of her mom, his anger turned to confusion. She knew what she looked like—a well-scrubbed college girl. If he tried anything here, these people would call the cops—fast.

"Well, why didn't you say so? Listen, I'll take you home. No problem."

"Oh, that's okay. Here's my cab."

He followed her out and spoke through clenched teeth: "Give me my money, you little whore."

She said as if she didn't hear: "Listen, I really appreciate the ride. Tell Sam and Mimi good-bye."

She gave the driver her uncle's address.

5

• •

The White Monk pulled up his hood and began sweeping the patio, counting each stroke as he did so. He sometimes did this three times a day, sometimes six or eight. Because he worked practically for peanuts, his boss, Dahveed, thought he'd died and gone to heaven.

The Monk could count and think at the same time. It was a form of meditation for him. On a beautiful March day like this—crisp and windy, but bright as copper—he could contemplate theology all afternoon. But there were other things to do—some dusting, some heavy cleaning, some framing. Even his own work.

He looked forward to it all equally, would as soon be doing Dahveed's work as his own.

He was as close to peace as he'd ever been; except for the doubts. He still couldn't be sure he hadn't killed someone. Or wouldn't, sometime in the future.

"So then," said Revelas, who was painting in the courtyard, "I says to the guard, 'You blink your eye, I'll cut your eyelids off.' Meanwhile, Skinny and Poss are lyin' there bleedin', see . . ."

The Monk was conspicuously not in the mood, but there wasn't a damn thing he could do about it. "See, I got a philosophy—long as

I'm not dead, I'm ahead. So I know if I can get through this, I'm ahead. If I don't, well, then, I'm only dead and who's gonna care about that? Not me, I can handle it."

I love him, The Monk thought. I swear to God I do. The guy's a thinker. "Long as I'm not dead, I'm ahead." It's a version of "Whatever doesn't kill me makes me stronger." And I love his courage! Talk about nonattachment. "If I don't, I'm only dead and who's gonna care . . ." What would it be like not to be afraid?

Yet The Monk was in a good place right now. There had been times—lots of them—when he absolutely couldn't have listened to this. Every single negative thought would have had to be counter-acted. Every time Revelas said "dead" or "die" or "kill," The Monk would have had to wait until he said "live" or "life" before he could leave his presence, and then every time he thought one of the words himself, he would have had to counteract it in his own mind. But that wasn't plaguing him right now. At the moment there were only two really forbidden words, and they were a name, a name that Revelas probably didn't know, thank the gods.

He had to count right now, and some other things, but the word problem had receded for a while—a good thing, too, or he couldn't work with Revelas, who was his best friend at the moment. It could pop up at any time, though. He never knew what would trigger it.

Damn!

He swore because he'd lost count and he had to start all over again.

He tapped Revelas on the shoulder and crossed his index fingers in an X—their signal that The Monk was meditating.

Revelas was so black he looked painted. Though he was technically unable to blush, he looked so distressed, so truly embarrassed at disturbing The Monk, he might as well have turned pink. He was one of the most sensitive people The Monk had ever met, though the wife he had stabbed to death may have had her own opinion.

Everybody knew The Monk counted. That is, they didn't really—they just knew he couldn't be disturbed when he was sweeping or he might never finish. The Monk didn't tell them why.

No doubt they thought he was thinking deep and holy thoughts when he was only counting his broom strokes. In truth he hardly ever thought deep and holy thoughts, or so it seemed to him.

To him, his spiritual growth seemed so slow it was like watching a plant grow.

Today, he could believe in it, though—and in God, or the gods, in Kali or Coyote, in Jehovah or Allah.

He just plain felt good, almost as if his life was about to change—though how it could, he couldn't imagine.

Maybe it was the painting he was working on—the angel who was half-white, half-black. He called it *Pregnant with Possibility*. Her head was the size of a pin, she had no neck, and her huge belly contained both heaven and hell.

It was a breakthrough for him. Most of his work was crude, raw, obvious as fur. This one was minutely detailed. It terrified him, yet he was obsessed by it and couldn't stop working on it.

He had dreamed of her lately, the lady with Pandora's Box so neatly juxtaposed with Valhalla.

Dahveed hated the painting and said he couldn't sell it, it wasn't the sort of thing he handled, and maybe The Monk ought to try his luck over on Julia Street. This was Dahveed's greatest insult. Though his gallery was in a high-rent section of the French Quarter—very nearly the highest—Julia Street, in his lexicon, meant effete and la-di-da. The Monk paid him no mind at all. He was painting it because he had no choice, not because the House of Blues might take it. They had taken some of his paintings, and Revelas had acted as if he'd been elected president. This was nothing to The Monk. One of his vows was that of poverty.

He prided himself, if not on poverty itself, on being a true outsider, being able to get along without much money.

His salary here at the gallery, plus the little he got from his paintings, covered the rent with enough left over for food and utilities. He knew how to cook rice and beans and other things—vegetables, mostly—that cost practically nothing and were about the best things you could eat. He burned a lot of candles, which really cut down on electricity, and he needed only white robes to wear. A woman friend had made those, before his vows were complete.

He finished his chores and waved good night to Revelas. He had painted in the early part of the day, and now he could get on his motor scooter and go home and pursue his spiritual life.

Once home, he cleaned his house from top to bottom. This might have been easy, as there was very little in it, but The Monk was a thorough cleaner. He threw off his robe and washed it, along with his towels and sheets from the night before. Then, naked, he pulled up his one tatami, shook it out, and swept his floors—living room, bedroom, kitchen, and bathroom.

He scrubbed the bathroom and kitchen. Then he got in the shower and let the water run till all the hot was gone. Finally, after donning a clean white robe, he could put his tatami back down, light a candle, and sit down to meditate.

On Mondays, he would start with a mantra and then he would stop and simply sit, until he realized a subject had taken hold in his head; and then he would ponder that subject. He would sit with that subject, that idea, for a whole week, and the next Monday a new one would come to him.

It was Saturday now, and for nearly a week the subject had been his mother. This wasn't the first time—far from it—but it was always hard for him. He felt her pain when he thought of her, when he let himself go to her in meditation—such a lovely woman, so sweet, so naïve. So deeply betrayed.

He always cried, and he wondered if it were literally her pain he felt, if he could, by sheer force of his mind and soul, reach across continents and oceans and find her, pluck her pain out, suffer it for her.

She was one of life's true innocents, so vastly undeserving of the thing fate had sent her. After she had gone—and after the incredible perfidy of his sister-in-law—he had left town to become an itinerant seeker, almost literally with a begging bowl, like the Buddha himself.

By a stroke of amazing luck—and because of a woman he met—he ended up in New Orleans, where the river flowed so close you could stick your toes in, where the air was velvet and carried the music of a thousand artists trying as hard as he was to bring order to their own chaos. It was a wonderful place to be in love, and The Monk had been, though he had had a name then, before his woman dumped him. That was when he took his vows.

The art started before that, on the road. He didn't know how, or why; just one day he was sketching on the lined page of an old notebook, and he realized that he'd fallen into a sort of trance. As soon as he was able, he bought some art supplies, and the thing came out of him, he couldn't stop it.

It was better, in a way, than sitting; he felt better afterward, anyway. Sometimes he felt that his meditating, his spiritual practice, was going nowhere—and yet, what would he replace it with? What else was there (other than his art)?

The idea terrified him. It had been confirmed again and again—for some reason, maybe only God could say (or one of the gods), he had not been born to be loved. He was innately unlovable. He did not know why this was—why some people had such an easy time, were loved and surrounded by friends, and others were destined to be alone. It was a subject of deep concern to him, and yet if that were the case for him, so be it. One of the goals of his spiritual life was to learn to accept what was.

He was watching the candle, so caught by the flame, so deep in its hypnotic envelope, that he felt for a moment at peace with the universe and himself, breathing with the tiny fire, and the world. It was the feeling that mystics might mean when they speak of bliss—The Monk wasn't sure—but it was certainly among the top three feelings he'd ever had. It never lasted more than a moment, but this time it seemed barely to arrive before it was literally chased away by a knock on the door.

The Monk had no friends who would visit him—Dahveed or Revelas would probably bail him out of jail if he found himself there, and the woman who made the robes would sew for him, but none of them would come calling. It was probably a Jehovah's Witness.

He ignored it. But the knock came again; and again, louder, faster, a bit staccato. It sounded slightly hysterical to him, though it was only a knock. What could you tell from a knock? Yet he wondered if there was a problem—perhaps his next-door neighbor's house was on fire, or her phone was out and she needed his. The Monk had no idea why he kept his phone—each month when the bill came, he considered having it disconnected, yet he never did and he never knew why. Perhaps this was why. Perhaps Pamela needed it now.

He got up and crossed the room before he remembered two things: Pamela was so fat that he'd have heard her footsteps on the porch. She had come up once before, and he had heard her. And that time she hadn't knocked, she had yelled, "Monkey." That was her nickname for him, though she claimed it wasn't the simian, but the diminutive of "Monk," therefore spelled "Monkie."

It couldn't be Pamela.

As soon as he had the thought, the knocking stopped. He returned to his tatami and resumed his meditations.

He had a breakthrough. It was an image of his mother with her eyes closed, her hands stretched out in front of her, sleepwalking through a busy street.

Maybe it didn't have to be that way, he thought. *Maybe she could have just opened her eyes.*

Tomorrow, he would meditate on that—his mother with her eyes open, and maybe he'd be able to see what she would have seen.

He could have his treat now.

The Monk had a vice, which he permitted himself to indulge once a week on Saturday—Häagen-Dazs ice cream. He had to clean his entire house every day (which he would naturally do anyway) and complete two hours of meditation every day, as well as twelve hours of painting a week, and a few other little things, mostly involving kindnesses to Revelas and Pamela, and then he could have a quart of any flavor he wanted (he varied them), to be eaten over the course of two days. Ice cream could not be eaten on weekdays.

He got a five-dollar bill and picked up the shepherd's crook that Revelas had made for him, a multicolored, intricately carved instrument that Revelas said was supposed to remind him of the Twenty-Third Psalm, though The Monk couldn't get past the fact that it wasn't the narrator who was the shepherd. Nevertheless, he appreciated the gesture and he dearly loved the crook, although he never permitted himself to take it to work and used it only on special occasions.

He opened his door, and nearly tripped over a waif sitting on his steps, her back to him. She turned and said, "Oh. I thought no one was home."

It was his Angel.

He watched fear start at her eyes and spread over her face. "Omigod, I'm sorry. I was looking for my uncle." She got up and started to back away. But The Monk stepped toward her.

She stepped backward again. He needed to speak, but he couldn't. He could only make faces and gesture, waving his crook.

She turned and ran.

He could not call to her to stop, could only pound after her until he caught her.

● ●

For Skip, it had been a great weekend—she and Steve left Napoleon in Kenny's capable hands and drove to Nottoway Plantation, where they spent Saturday night and damn near forgot about kids who shot each other and cops who did, too.

They went hiking Sunday afternoon and arrived home exhausted. It was probably around five A.M. Monday morning when Napoleon started barking.

Steve couldn't be roused to reason with him. Skip tossed for an hour and finally got up. She was on the first watch anyway and had to be at work at eight. Might as well go in early and maybe leave a little early.

She was the first in her platoon to arrive and, coincidentally, the one up for the next case.

The others came in one by one—her sergeant first, Sylvia Cappello, and then the young guy named DeFusco, and Jerry Boudreaux and Charlie Dilzell and Adam Abasolo, also a sergeant, but not hers.

The call came in at five after eight. Later they found out the dispatcher had lost it: "The chief's been shot! The chief's been shot!"

Corinne, the secretary for Homicide, simply gave the call to Cappello, her face white, her lips drawn, but not losing it, not saying a word. Skip couldn't hear what the dispatcher said; she was told later. Still, Corinne's whiteness, her tension were enough—it was something bad. *A policeman,* Skip thought, her heart sinking. But she never thought of the chief.

Cappello didn't tell them till they were in the car. "The call's at Chief Goodlett's house. A man's been shot there."

Jerry Boudreaux said it for all of them: "Oh, shit."

"Sylvia, goddammit. Is it the chief?"

He hadn't even been sworn in yet.

"There were several calls. People said different things."

She didn't speak again during the ride and, oddly, neither did anyone else except Charlie Dilzell, who seemingly out of the blue hollered out, "Fuck!" when they were nearly there. It was as if they were in awe of such a thing, as if it demanded silence out of respect.

In Skip's case, she was simply trying to hold it together, to assimilate the fact that Albert Goodlett, her friend and the only possible hope of a thoroughly decayed department, was really gone. In her heart she knew he was. Cappello was being circumspect, but it had to be that. And yet it couldn't be; it was impossible.

Goodlett lived in a modest neighborhood out in Gentilly. Everyone who lived there was outside. The street was choked with district cars.

The chief's car was in the driveway, and the chief was still sitting in it, the whole area closed off with yellow tape. The car had no rear windshield. The chief had an entrance wound in the back of his head and, as a result, no face left.

Someone had apparently driven by and opened up with automatic gunfire. Or perhaps they had been parked, waiting for the chief to back out of his driveway.

Skip was dazed, wondering how the hell she was going to function. Cappello didn't even bother to take her aside. She said simply, "Langdon, I want you to handle this. You've got kind of a knack with heater cases."

Jerry Boudreaux said, "This ain't no heater case. It's a fuckin' volcano."

Skip's heart pounded. She wanted the case badly, almost as much as she didn't want it.

She sent the other detectives to canvass the neighbors and went in to see the widow, whom she knew slightly. The woman fell upon her chest as if they were best friends—*any old port*, Skip thought—and cried like a child. Skip's eyes filled as well, and she choked up.

I will be calm, she chanted to herself. *I will not cry. I will be professional.*

A lot of officers might lose it in a case like this—it wasn't your everyday homicide—but Skip couldn't. She had once when she should have been cool—it had to do with the man she'd shot, Shavonne's father—and that was how she ended up on leave. Cappello was sticking her neck out, trusting her with this one. For right now, she couldn't afford to show emotion. So she had to comfort the widow as best she could, hanging by a thread, yet appearing stoic as a statue.

She just held the woman tight and mouthed the usual meaningless soothing sounds: "That's right, Bernice—you're okay, Bernice. Everything's going to be okay."

The hell it was.

"I'm going to catch this bastard," she said. "And you're going to help me, aren't you? You feel like you can do that?"

Bernice pulled out of Skip's grasp. "He just walked out the door. He was on his way to work."

"And then what?"

"And then . . . it sounded like the end of the world." Bernice started weeping again, remembering the peppering, drilling hailstorm of the fusillade.

"Where were you?"

"In the kitchen. I was still drinking coffee. Oh, baby . . . oh, Skip . . ."

"What?"

"I hardly even said good-bye. I was just reading the paper, and he came in to kiss me good-bye. I barely even looked up—I just kind of let him peck me. . . ."

"On the cheek?" It was an unprofessional question, but Skip wanted to make Mrs. Goodlett feel better.

"Why, no. On the lips."

Skip had never seen a good-bye cheek-peck. "You see? He knew you loved him."

She thought of the familiarity of the scene—the husband leaving as he had a million times, coming in automatically for an automatic kiss, the two partners going through it almost like robots, they were so used to it. Yet underneath there was a vast canyon of feeling, this enormous pocket of love that the chief's death had opened up. Skip felt her eyes fill again, in sympathy with the widow's regret.

"What did you do?"

"I dropped my coffee. I just sat there staring into space for a minute and by the time I got up, the shooting had stopped. I went to the door and . . . everybody was there."

"Everybody?"

"All the neighbors were coming out. And he was still in the car. Other people got there first. They told me not to go any closer and so I didn't." Her mouth crumpled up. "The last time I saw him was in here saying good-bye."

"Kissing you. Remember that, Bernice."

"The kids . . ."

"Somebody went to get them?"

She nodded. "They don't even know yet."

"Bernice, I know this is hard, but please try to help me for a minute. Do you know anyone who'd want to kill him? Anyone who threatened him?"

"No." She said it as if the idea had never occurred to her. "Everyone loved him."

"He was a tough cop, Bernice. He must have had enemies."

She shrugged. "Racists. But everybody . . ." She stopped, apparently afraid of giving offense.

Skip was silent.

"I mean, there's always the fear . . . when you achieve something."

When a black person achieves something. It was obvious what she meant.

Skip said, "Anything specific?"

Bernice shook her head. "Nothing. No."

Skip wondered if she had something here. Probably not, she thought. More likely some criminal he'd crossed, some gang who thought he was too good a cop, some crazy. Or the mob. If it was mob activity, things were about to come out that she didn't even want to think about.

She made her manners and went outside. Charlie Dilzell was racing toward her. "Langdon! We got a witness. Guy across the street saw the shooter." He pointed at an upstairs window. "Guy went over to the window to tie his tie—checking out the weather, he said. Saw a white Chevy pickup parked in front of the chief's house. Man got out, started shooting, got back in, and drove off."

"Did he get the plate number?" It was more or less a rhetorical question—they weren't going to get that lucky.

"Said the truck wasn't in the right position. But he could see down into the bed of the truck. It was full of painting supplies."

"What'd the guy look like?"

Dilzell shrugged. "White, he thinks, but he can't be sure. Plain, light-colored pants, same kind of shirt—work clothes, maybe; something like khakis. Baseball cap."

"Did the cap say anything?"

"It was turned the wrong way."

Skip drew in her breath and let it out too hard, in a sigh she hadn't meant to make. They still had hardly anything. "Okay. Put out a bulletin, will you?"

"With that?"

"Yeah, with that. I don't care if we have to stop every white Chevy pickup in the state of Louisiana. Let's go with it." She spoke more sharply than she intended. She was angry—not at Dilzell, but at the asshole who'd killed the chief, and the dude with the tie for failing to get the plate, and the chief for dying.

"Charlie."

Dilzell turned around.

"Was it this house?"

Dilzell nodded and turned away, piqued at her for snapping.

She rang the bell and identified herself. The witness's name was Ezra Johnson. He was a light-skinned black in his early twenties, young to have such a nice house—she suspected he lived with his parents.

"Now Ezra, I hear you saw down into the bed of the truck. I wonder if you could tell me what was in it."

"I told the other officer. Painting supplies."

"Paint?"

"Yeah. Cans of something. Looked like paint."

"Brand? Colors?"

"I couldn't see." His body language showed irritation. She didn't blame him.

"Anything else?"

"A ladder."

"Aluminum or wood?"

"Aluminum." He thought a minute. "Not tall, not short. About medium."

"Now, you got it. You got it, Ezra. What else?"

"Drop cloths. Hey! Bed in a bag."

"I beg your pardon?"

"There's this company that puts together these kits—you can buy everything, a comforter, dust ruffle, sheets, pillowcases, everything you need for about a hundred dollars. The whole thing comes in a plastic bag and they call it 'Bed in a Bag.' Cheap, but popular. Real, real popular."

"You sound like you know all about it."

"I should. I work at Macy's in the bed and bath department. I've sold about a million of them. This guy had 'Early American'—the drop cloth."

Skip felt a tingling in her stomach. "What does it look like?"

"Kind of like a quilt. Only it's not, really—it's just a polyester comforter. It's red, white, and blue. I guess that's what the name comes from."

"You're sure?"

"Yeah. I bought one for my sister last week—she just moved into her own apartment." It wasn't a plate number, but it was something. Skip went back to add the ladder and the drop cloth to the bulletin.

The coroner had already come. She was consulting with the crime lab techs, barely listening, mostly just trying to hold herself together when the call came. A district car had the truck in sight.

She took Boudreaux with her, leaving Cappello to supervise the crime scene. Tires squealing, they drove to Earhart Boulevard, where the vehicle had been spotted. They heard it all on the radio: The district officers waited for backup and then signaled the truck to stop. Instead, it went through a light and took off. The officers gave chase. Skip drove like a demon.

In a minute it was all over—the officers lost the truck. The good news was, they had a plate number. The truck was registered to a Nolan Bazemore, who lived in Mid-City. A new bulletin went out.

Skip asked the dispatcher to send someone to Bazemore's house, but she wasn't hopeful. She might as well get back to the crime scene. Bazemore'd have to be crazy to go home. He'd go someplace he felt safe.

But where?

"I don't know," Boudreaux said. "I'd go to my girlfriend's."

"Yeah, or some other friend's. Maybe even a bar."

"Naah, I don't think a bar. He'd want to go someplace with a garage. To hide his plates."

Boudreaux chewed on a toothpick. He'd quit smoking and started chewing. "Bazemore's kind of a funny name. I was in the army with a kid named that—from South Carolina or someplace. Never heard the name again till I read *Beach Music*—you know that book? Same damn part of the country. So I figured, must be some kind of Carolina name—like Boudreaux's a Louisiana name. Guy's probably a peckerwood from the low country. That's what they call it, see . . . what the hell are you doing?"

Skip had pulled into a gas station and put on the emergency brake. "I'm looking him up in the phone book."

"You crazy? We know where he lives."

Two Bazemores were listed, Nolan being one. It sure couldn't hurt to try the second.

She got back in the car. "I thought since it was such an odd name, he might be related to all the others. Guess what? There's only one."

Boudreaux chucked his toothpick and stretched his feet out. "You're grasping at straws, Langdon."

The other Bazemore, Edwin, lived in Lakeview, a modest residential section that didn't have a view of the lake.

As soon as they turned onto the street, they saw the truck. It was making a spectacle of itself, though, in truth, if Skip and Jerry hadn't been there, there'd have been no one to observe it. The driver was backing into a driveway, as if to get the truck bed close enough to load something—though Skip was sure it was to hide the plate number.

Boudreaux had unfolded from his languid slump. He was bolt upright, head swiveling. "Jesus fucking Christ."

The door opened and a woman peeked out—an older woman, with black cotton knit pants pulled over spreading hips. A print polyester blouse completed the ensemble. She couldn't more obviously have been someone's mother if she'd been drying her hands on a dish towel.

"Nolan? What you doing here in the middle of the day?"

The man had stepped out of the truck. Skip slammed on the

66

brakes and hopped out of the car, hand on her gun. "Nolan Bazemore, freeze. You're under arrest."

For an instant, he did freeze, utter amazement written on his dim features. Then he dived back toward the truck.

The woman screamed and started running toward the vehicle. "Don't shoot. Please don't shoot."

In a second she'd be in the line of fire.

"Mama! Mama, no!"

Skip heard Boudreaux calling for backup. She said, "Freeze" once more, but she was acutely aware that for crucial seconds she herself was frozen by circumstance, the other woman controlling the action.

The woman reached her son and knelt beside him. He said, "Get back, Mama. I'll handle this."

Boudreaux shouted, "Back up, Mrs. Bazemore. That's it. You're okay. Everything's okay now."

Nolan Bazemore lifted his chest, rearing up on his arms, obviously flabbergasted. Astonishment seemed his only emotion.

6

• •

She should have known her uncle Isaac didn't live here—the neighborhood was dicey at best, and scary was more realistic. Various dudes had given her the eye, though she had to admit none had actually accosted her until this crazy started chasing her.

She tried apologizing. "I'm sorry, mister. Listen, I didn't know I was trespassing. I thought my uncle lived there."

The footsteps continued. He had that damned, heavy crook thing. Who but a screwball would carry something like that? Her neck prickled as she imagined it around her waist, her neck, even her leg, tripping her. She stepped up her pace, but she was no match for the crazy. He was gaining on her. She tried shouting: "Help! Somebody! Please help me."

Almost immediately a hand went round her waist, at least not the hook, thank God, but still she was being grabbed. She was being kidnapped a second time. A harrowing idea occurred to her—maybe this was some employee of her dad's, sent to wait for her at Isaac's.

A hand went over her mouth. But she wasn't truly frightened. It had to be impossible to get kidnapped by two entirely different men in two days—therefore, this guy had to be working for her dad. So, big deal, she was back to Square One, but she probably wasn't going to die.

The man took his hand off her mouth, spun her around, and put a finger over his lips. Was he kidding? Why in hell should she keep quiet.

"Let me go." She struggled in his grasp. "Let me go or I'll yell some more."

To her great surprise, he did. He simply took his hands off her and held them up in front of his chest, palms out, as if to show he had no weapons.

He touched his mouth and shook his head at the same time, why she couldn't imagine.

"I'm going now," she said. "If you try to follow me, I'll yell so loud they'll hear me in Alabama."

Now he put his hands together, as if praying, and shook his head vigorously.

She began to catch on that he was communicating in some sort of sign language—apparently he was a mute.

Well, he hadn't hurt her yet. In spite of herself, she was intrigued.

He made writing motions. She shook her head—she had no pen or pencil.

He scratched something on his palm, but she didn't get it. Finally, he pointed to his chest.

"You," she said.

He shook his head and pointed at her.

"Me."

He looked so chagrined that for a moment she felt sorry for him. Finally, he pointed to his eye.

"Eye."

He nodded, and made a curve in the air.

"S. Is." She was puzzled.

He made an *A* in the air, and another one. Finally she got it—he was drawing his air *C* when the police car arrived.

A young black cop got out of the car, heavyset, a little sullen. "Everything all right?"

She realized they must look friendly, just standing there staring at each other, no matter that she'd been screaming for her life two minutes ago. Someone must have heard her and dialed 911.

"Everything's fine. We were just having an argument. He's my boyfriend and . . . I got mad."

"About what?"

"Another woman." She tried to look philosophical, as if this kind of thing happened all the time.

The cop didn't look convinced. He stared back and forth, first at one, then the other, and finally said, "You got any ID?"

"Sure. Back at the house. I got mad and I ran out and he chased me. But we can go back and . . ."

He gave her a half smile. "Don't worry about it. Y'all just try to be a little quieter next time. Don't upset the neighborhood."

"Oh, gosh. I'm really embarrassed."

The cop went back to his car, and Isaac thumped a hand against his chest. When Lovelace didn't react, he drew a heart in the air.

"Love. Oh—my name."

He pulled on his shoelace, to prove he really knew her.

"Uncle Isaac? It's really you?"

He nodded.

"Why can't you talk?"

For answer, he beckoned her back to his house.

Inside it was white. Walls, ceiling, floors, trim, and furniture, what little there was of that. It wasn't sterile or grim, however, and it took her a while to figure out why. There were ceramic bowls on tables, some filled with fruit, and the walls were covered with paintings, mostly in primary colors. The figures in the paintings were flat, two-dimensional, offhand almost, as if they'd been drawn by children. Some were on pieces of wood rather than canvas.

The place looked very, very clean, almost painfully so, and could certainly have used a rug, but she couldn't say it didn't have personality. Isaac went to the wall, plucked a picture, and brought it to her. It was an angel, rendered in colors that probably weren't allowed in heaven. Puzzled, Lovelace took it and stared at it.

It took a few moments, but she let out a little cry when she realized the angel's face was her own. She saw another angel across the

70

room and went to examine it—it, too, had her face. Feeling as if she were in a dream, completely ignoring Isaac, she walked around the room, looking carefully at the paintings. She saw that they were signed by several different artists, two of whom were represented in large numbers—someone named Revelas and someone who signed simply "W.M."

W.M. was the one who painted the angels—it had to be Isaac.

"Why W.M.?" she asked, and he wrote on a yellow pad, "They call me the White Monk. In answer to your previous question, I have taken a vow of silence. Welcome to my house. I'm happy to see you."

"Thank you," she said, and he wrote, "Why are you here?"

"Oh, God." She sat down in an old rocking chair her uncle had painted white. "May I sit?"

He held out a hand in the "please" gesture, rolled out one of those Japanese mats, and sat down himself.

"My father kidnapped me. And my mom's—I don't know—in Mexico, I think, with one of her boyfriends."

His face twitched a little, she thought, in sympathy. He had longish brown hair and a neat brown beard—very much the cliché image of Jesus—and enormous blue eyes that made him look vulnerable and sweet. Also, she noticed, he had a great smile. He was oddly attractive. The thought shocked her—he was her uncle.

And he was weird.

But it was so sweet the way he seemed to have perfect empathy—not, she thought, that it should have been surprising. He came from the same screwball family she did.

He seemed to wince again when she came to the part about the drug. And why not? she thought, understanding again that this was an extraordinary thing for a father to do.

It wasn't a custody thing—she was grown.

But in the back of her mind, she knew. She knew what it had to be.

When Isaac asked, she said, "I'm pretty sure he's with Grandpa."

He nodded as if he'd already deduced that.

"But I still don't get it. What do they want with me?"

"Your father and my father are two of the most—" He spoke

71

loudly and he sounded furious—absolutely furious—yet he was speaking. She was more frightened than surprised. Watching his blue eyes cloud over with anger, she felt her own fear get bigger, felt herself shrinking, drawing away from him.

"The most what?" she asked.

He shook his head, grinning, and started writing furiously:

"This is the point of my vow of silence. I get mad and say too much and half the time I don't even know what I'm talking about. Anyway, that's one reason, the rest is that I just plain don't understand anything anymore and therefore I have nothing to say. If I ever do figure anything out—just one thing, that's all, even one—I'll speak again. Are you hungry?"

Lovelace said, "Starving."

He nodded.

She said, "Listen, I love to cook. Let me make something, why don't you?"

He wrote, "Nonsense. You're my guest. One thing, though. Just don't mention my father's name. You can call him 'grandfather' or 'grandpa'—but don't say his name, okay?"

"Why?"

"Humor me," he wrote. "Just please humor me."

He sent her to freshen up while he put on some rice and started cutting up carrots, celery, green pepper, zucchini, onions, tomatoes, mushrooms—everything he could think of for a nice stir-fry.

Isaac was one of those people for whom cooking is like a meditation. He used this time alone to figure out what he thought about this peculiar situation. He was crazy about the girl, he always had been—that he was glad to see her wasn't in dispute.

But he was trying to hold his fear at bay. His father was a dangerous, dangerous man, and his brother was nearly as bad—Lovelace had no idea, really. And what the hell did they want her for?

His father was always getting together some crackpot following—perhaps his ego demanded that he be surrounded by family, however unwilling.

But that didn't hold water, or he'd have come after Isaac, too.

Would have if he could have, Isaac thought. *Nobody knows who the White*

Monk is—just another street-corner weirdo. And anyway, New Orleans has to be the last place he'd look for me.

He had other problems with Lovelace. She was grown-up and attractive, for one thing—that was dangerous enough in any woman, considering his vow of celibacy, but this woman was his niece. Being attracted to his own niece wasn't a crime, but *considering* his vow of celibacy, he was probably more frustrated than the average uncle, and having her around might be something of a challenge.

Then there was the dirt. He never let anyone into his house because of possible contamination. He wouldn't be able to take a shower now without bleaching out the tub; if he let her use his bed, he'd have to find a way to sterilize everything afterward.

Actually, he'd known all that when he went after her, and bringing her here had simply seemed to outweigh it. Now he was getting scared. He chopped a bit of his finger off.

Not much, just enough to bleed a little. Blood carried contamination. He needed a Band-Aid, only Lovelace was in the bathroom. What was he to do? He started to hyperventilate and wondered if he was going to get hives.

Better sit down. He grabbed a paper towel and applied pressure to the cut, rocking in his white rocking chair.

He'd taken the same vows he'd always heard that priests took—poverty, chastity, and obedience—but the vow that really mattered to him was silence. If he couldn't have the others, at least he'd want that one. Poverty was his next favorite. Being an artist, he was bound to be poor; it added up nicely.

Chastity wasn't too hard, usually, till Lovelace came along, and it wasn't as if the vow was in danger even now—he wasn't about to try to seduce his own niece—it was just that it was going to weigh on him.

Obedience, however, required that he take her in. Since he didn't have the Catholic church to tell him what to do, his form of obedience was a little loose. The way he saw it was the way somebody else might see flowing with the river or rolling with the punches, something like that. He was working on acceptance—whatever the gods sent him, he wanted to accept, even embrace, and nurture if it needed nurturing.

They had sent him Revelas, a convicted murderer, and he'd accepted him. Now they'd sent him his own Angel—surely he could accept her.

Little Lovelace. A name so ironic . . . given to her by her parents, maybe because it had "love" in it, yet considering Daniel and Jacqueline, what a life she'd probably had.

Certainly had.

She was here now because her mother was out of pocket and her father had done violence to her.

His heart surged with pity and affection for her. And fear. This was a girl who had to be protected.

If she was an angel, he'd be an archangel—Michael, the defender. He'd keep her from her enemies.

He needed to make her feel welcome. What could he do?

Flowers. That would be good. His were white only, but there were some nice ones—plenty of calla lilies, for instance. He got a pair of scissors and was halfway out the door when he felt his feet dragging. Did he really want to do this?

No!

He did not.

He wanted to do the minimum so that he could feel as if he was keeping his vow, yet she'd get the hint that he wished she'd be on her way.

Cold, nasty bastard, he thought, so disgusted with himself he clipped half his Confederate jasmine to go with the calla lilies.

7

• •

Daniel went before his father with the knowledge that he was a grown man, much larger and stronger than the other man, more imposing in every way. He could handle whatever Daddy was dishing out.

"She got away," he said.

"She got away. Daniel, you don't mean that. You're a grown man and she's a little girl. What do you mean, she got away?"

Daniel began to sweat. How was he going to say she'd just walked out while he was asleep? When he was a kid, his father would rage. "Son, you left the plug in the sink and the water ran over. How could you do that?" It would start out that way.

Daniel would think his father meant it, that he was really asking him how it happened, and his father would say, "You don't mean that, Daniel."

He'd try to explain that he did, and then the name-calling would start, and the ridicule. And then the blows, always on the head or face. His father would simply let fly, sometimes knocking Daniel's whole head around, sending it wobbling on his neck, leaving him sore for days; sometimes giving him a bloody nose or a busted lip;

75

he didn't care if he made marks, indeed, seemed to prefer it that way, and Daniel dared not cry, because the punishment for that was "something to cry *about*."

Things were different now. He'd come back partly to resolve things with his father, to work with him as an equal. But also because he agreed with him on this one. His father was onto something important, something Daniel believed in.

Whatever problems he'd had with his father as a child, whatever fear he'd had of him, he could put behind him now, because Errol Jacomine was a formidable ally. The papers called him "the disappearing preacher" because of that thing he'd pulled in southwest Louisiana. He was a legend, the D.B. Cooper of charismatic religion.

Daniel's relationship with religion was problematical, but his dad had moved on. The thing he was working on now was what America needed, and if anyone could pull it off, Errol Jacomine could—with Daniel's help.

There were other reasons Daniel was here—one good one anyway. Things hadn't worked out that well elsewhere. He knew why, too. He knew exactly why.

It was Jacqueline's damn fault.

Everything was fine until he married the bitch. He was a Christian, his mom and dad were Christians, Jacqueline was a Christian; things were just fine.

Then Jacqueline went weird on him.

She started with that feminist shit. Wouldn't stay home, had to have a job—stupid job, too; receptionist somewhere. Wouldn't take care of the kid. Wouldn't, wouldn't, wouldn't.

Wouldn't do a damn thing, is how it ended up.

Fucked up Daniel's life in the process. Got him started on marijuana, which didn't lead to heroin, but most certainly did to alcohol, which had turned out to be his personal demon.

Only good thing came out of it was Lovelace. Bright kid. Real bright kid. He might not have Jacqueline—he wouldn't want her anyway—but he'd fallen in love with his own daughter, and that was good enough to get him through. Even in the years when he was in Idaho, stockpiling food and living off the land, he'd get a job now and then—in "agricultural imports," he liked to say. It might not be banking, but he had enough socked away to get the kid through college.

Meanwhile Jacqueline had gone and joined the New Age. If she wasn't off doing a firewalk or something, she was flying somewhere with one of her twenty-five-year-old dope dealer boyfriends. Which was where she was now, and maybe under the circumstances that was more a good thing than otherwise.

He'd had a whole lot of second thoughts about bringing Lovelace to his father. He loved her so much he'd let something slip about what The Jury was doing—nothing much, really, just a hint that maybe he knew where her grandfather was, and his father had decided that made her dangerous.

That was what he said. He knew his dad—actually, he wanted her. He wanted her brain and her spirit. He wanted her for the movement, and so did Daniel. So he'd gone to get her. He'd done it his dad's way, but he was sorry now. He wouldn't hurt her for the world, but he'd certainly scared her—that was a way of hurting her.

He wondered if he had let her get away, if subconsciously he hadn't wanted to kidnap her, and he'd been careless accidentally on purpose.

He said to his dad, "You're right, I don't mean it, she didn't get away. I decided not to bring her."

His father threw his arm back, and Daniel saw what was coming next, but he was frozen. Errol Jacomine whacked him as hard as he could on the side of the head.

"What's the matter with you, Daniel? Are you crazy? You get that little girl back or we're *all* gonna fry."

It didn't really hurt. It wasn't a big deal at all. Though he'd just been hit, Daniel was elated. This was what he'd hoped for—he was over all that.

"Come on, Daddy. Tell the truth. You just want to see your granddaughter."

"Yeah. Maybe I do."

Daniel grinned, and his dad grinned back.

Errol Jacomine said, "Now, is what we're doing important work, or are we merely spinning our wheels?"

"It's real important, Daddy."

"Are we going to save the world, Daniel?"

"We're sure gonna try." For the first time in his life, he actually felt close to his father, felt they shared a mutual respect.

"Well, let me tell you something. It won't be because of your brainpower if we do. You don't have the sense of a rhesus monkey, do you know that? I swear to God I wish I had time enough to send you back to school. What were you doing all those years in Idaho? Lettin' your brain atrophy? Is that what you've been doing?" He let his voice rise.

"I haven't got *time* for this crap, Daniel. I just haven't got time for it. What we've got going is big, and what we're going to get going is bigger. Do you understand me, son? Do you actually get my drift, or is it too complicated for your tiny brain? We have to move fast. We have to move *very* fast. You get that young lady back and you get her quick. *Double quick, goddammit.*"

He shouted so loud Daniel felt like running. Simply turning tail, slamming the door, and hightailing it down the street, exactly as he'd done a thousand times when he was growing up.

This time he didn't. He thought to himself, *He's right. He's acting like an asshole, but there's nothing wrong with what he's saying.*

He felt proud that he could separate the two. Working with his father was hard, the hardest thing he'd ever done, but what he thought was, the man was smart, the smartest man Daniel knew, probably, and he'd taught Daniel good values.

Daniel liked what he was trying to do, and deep in his heart he knew his father was proud of him and trusted him or he wouldn't have come to Idaho to get him, revealed himself even though he was wanted for half the crimes in the universe, recruited his older son to be his first lieutenant.

A woman came into the room, shaking wet hands and looking worried. "Daddy! Everything all right?"

"Well, Miss Bettina. However are *you* today?"

"Daddy, I heard shouting. . . ."

"Were you worried about me? Were you worried about your old daddy? You know, you are absolutely the sweetest woman I've ever met in my entire life. You're going to make someone a wonderful mama."

The woman looked about nine months pregnant. She smiled. "I just wanted to make sure you were okay."

"Well, that's not the point. The point is, how are *you*? You still getting sick around cigarette smoke?"

She kept smiling, obviously reveling in the attention. "I'm better, Daddy. Thank you."

"Well, you take care of that precious cargo."

The woman left, leaving Daniel shaking his head. Daddy was like that: furious one moment, all concerned about someone the next.

He thought: *Daddy has a style, that's all. He yells and he says things, but he doesn't mean 'em. If he did I wouldn't be here. I'm gonna do my damn job, and the hell with that crap. I really don't care.*

His dad was all business again: "One thing. Before you get my granddaughter I want you to do something else."

Daniel thought he couldn't be hearing right. "Daddy? I don't understand. I thought you just said—"

"You thought. You *thought*! You're not supposed to think, son, you're supposed to do what God put you on this Earth to do."

"But . . ."

Errol Jacomine leaned over his desk and pushed his son's chest with the flat of his hand—a little peanut of a man with fire in his eyes, pushing Daniel, who prided himself on his body, who went to the gym every day. "Shut up, Daniel. I'm telling you, do this first and then do the other and I want 'em both done by tomorrow. Have you got that?"

"But tomorrow I have to—"

"I know what you have to do tomorrow. Don't sleep. Work round the clock. Just get the job done, goddammit. Listen, I'm going to give you some pills." He rummaged in his drawer until he found them. "These'll do it for you."

Daniel took one and made as if to go, testing the waters to see if his father had forgotten what he wanted. But Jacomine didn't even see him. He was staring at the wall, fingers steepled. "I want you to put together a dossier."

He pulled a *People* magazine article out from under his desk blotter. "I want you to find out everything you can about this woman." He handed Daniel the article, which included a picture of a woman—Rosemarie Owens, according to the caption. She was a blonde who wasn't quite pretty and who looked hard as nails, more or less in the Ivana Trump mold—or maybe Daniel just thought that because of the article.

It said she was at the center of some nasty Texas scandal, the scorned woman in a divorce involving giant bucks and a younger woman. She was suing.

Of course she was suing. That was the way she was made. Daniel said, "Ball-busting bitch," and his dad backhanded him. Smacked his right cheek as if it had a mosquito on it. No warning, no nothing.

"Get the fuck out of here."

Daniel didn't even bother to analyze this one. He turned his left side toward his dad. "I'm turning the other cheek."

His dad smacked that one, not quite as hard. "You know what Jesus said about his tormentors? 'Father, forgive them for they know not what they do'? Remember that, son? That's what I'm praying for right now. You know not what you do, Daniel. You know *not*, boy." He was standing up, roaring.

• •

Dorise had gotten her sister to take care of Shavonne—her sister and her sister's television set—and here she was at a movie with Troy. Holding hands.

She wondered if he was going to ask her to get something to eat afterward. Or maybe have a drink. She hadn't dated in so long she didn't know what people did after a movie.

One thing, if he didn't take her somewhere, she wasn't going to bed with him.

She bit her lip. *Going to bed with him.*

Was that really what she was thinking of? *Am I going to bed with this man?*

She found the thought gave her a funny feeling in her pussy, a good kind of funny feeling, one she remembered as if she had it every day. The truth was, she'd had a good sex life with Delavon. Real good, if you didn't count the way he made her feel bad about herself, and he hadn't done that until after she gained weight.

And there was something else—even as he said those things, all those nasty things about her body, he used to act like he couldn't get enough. He'd take her great pendulous breasts in his hands and then in his mouth and he'd squeeze and bite and suck. Sometimes he'd do the same thing with them she'd do with his cock when she sucked it—he'd kind of go up and down and all around, as if he were expecting her to spout white stuff. Then he'd put one hand on each breast and just squeeze and squeeze.

He'd do the same thing to her butt. Grab great hunks of brown flesh and hold them tight and shake them; then he'd grab more hunks and do it some more. He'd grab the extra flesh around her midriff and around her thighs and feel it good. He'd do it like he loved it.

That was how it was when they were in bed. Now when they were out of bed, he'd say mean things, but she didn't care that much, long as he kept on grabbing her.

She wanted that again.

The lights came on. "So what you think?" Troy said.

"I don't know. Didn't see what they saw in each other, 'cept they both movie stars."

"Well, ain't that enough?"

He meant her to laugh, but she chose to answer him seriously.

"No. No, that ain't enough, Troy Chauvin. You need to have somethin' in common."

"You think you and me have somethin' in common?"

"I don't know." Her nose was out of joint and she didn't know why.

"Well, I think we do. I think we both like to have fun. That's true, ain't it?"

"I don't know." Having fun had been hard for her ever since Delavon died.

"Let's go hear some music. I'll show you."

They danced, eyes locked, and then they danced slow, and he kissed her.

He'd kissed her good night before, but this time she had a few drinks in her, and he *really* kissed her.

She wanted him bad. She must have all the time, because she'd gotten her sister to take Shavonne for the night.

She took him home and got into bed with him, and he played with her body like Delavon did, gloried in her copious flesh like she was some kind of goddess.

But he did one thing different from Delavon. He talked to her real nice while he was making love to her. He'd say things like, "Oh, baby—man, you beautiful. You so beautiful, baby. I ain' never seen nothin' that pretty in my life. Oh, *man*, look at those titties. Oh, *man*."

Like that. It made Dorise feel shy and strange, and she woke up with her nose out of joint again. She got up and pulled on a robe and went in the kitchen.

She was standing at the sink, drawing water for coffee, when Troy came up behind her and grabbed her round the waist. "Baby. I thought I'd lost you."

He wore only his jeans, his big, good-looking chest hanging out for anyone to see. He was built like Delavon, sort of—both of them had good big shoulders, handsome torsos. His skin was light, too, much lighter than Delavon's.

"Whatchew mean?" Her tone sounded harsh, even to her. She didn't know why.

He put his hand gently on her head and stroked her hair. "Hey. Hey, look at me, baby."

She didn't want to.

He dropped into a chair and took her hand, so that she had to look down on him. "Wha's wrong? Now tell Troy wha's wrong."

"Ain' nothin' wrong." Once again, she heard the snap in her voice.

"Baby." He stared up at her, adoringly, she thought, but that was impossible. He barely knew her. "Baby, you cain't be this way. You tryin' to break my heart? Huh?"

He looked so sad she smiled, to see if she could make him smile. "I'm not tryin' to break your heart."

"No? Well, then whatcha doin'? Whatcha think ya doin'? Baby, I need you. Don't do this to me."

"Don't do what?"

"One-night-stand me. Love me and leave me. Suck me dry and throw me out."

She had to laugh. "Suck you dry? I ain' even started yet."

He grabbed her around the waist again, and then leaned toward her. He dropped to the floor, to his knees, and slid his hands down over her hips, around to the front of her thighs.

He opened her robe and thrust his face inside, licking her pussy.

She thought she was going to die. This man was on his knees, licking her pussy. Delavon wouldn't do that in a million years.

Wouldn't do either thing, she thought.

She wasn't sure she really liked it.

But they ended up in bed again, and she was damn sure she liked the rest of it.

How did I ever do without this? she thought.

He said, "Man. I could sure use some eggs and grits."

"I'll make you some." Automatically, she swung her legs over the side of the bed.

"Uh-uh. I'll make 'em."

"You know how to cook?" This was too much.

"No. But I can make eggs and grits."

She took a shower while he made breakfast, and it was a new experience for her.

This a day for firsts, she thought. *I never see a man go down on his knees, and I never had one cook me breakfast. I sure am gonna enjoy this.*

They were having coffee when he said, "What you doing this week, baby?"

"I'm—well, I got Shavonne and—"

He looked impatient, made some kind of quick gesture, like brushing away a mosquito. He said, "We work somethin' out. I mean, who you workin' for?"

"You know who I work for. What you mean?" She'd flared again.

"Now don't get mad. Course, I know who you work for. Uptown Caterers, right? Am I right?"

She nodded, wondering where this was going.

"I meant what *ladies* are you workin' for?"

"I don't know. I never know till I get there."

"Sometimes they perfect strangers, right?"

"Umm-hmm. Usually they are."

"And they real rich, right?"

"I don't know about that. Some of 'em just have stuff they inherited, ain't made no money their own selves. But they got stuff. They got stuff piled up on top of stuff. They got antiques covered up with real nice linen scarves and they got more antiques sittin' on top. Like maybe a jewelry box worth as much as the jewelry they got in the box. Then they got a silver candleholder on top of the box. You know what I mean? They got so much stuff they can't keep track of it." She went off in one of her dream states. "Wonder what it'd be like to have that much stuff?"

Troy pulled her back. "I could maybe help you."

"Help me what?"

"Help you get some stuff."

"Now how you gon' do that?" Dorise leaned back in her chair, her robe gaping open, showing the tops of her breasts, but she didn't mind, at the moment didn't feel the least bit modest. She felt light-headed and a little bit in love. The flaps of her robe could fall where they wanted. She felt like running through a field of flowers with Troy, or maybe down a nice beach.

"Well. You'd have to help me help you." He had a come-hither grin on his face, real flirtatious.

Dorise took his hand and started licking his fingers. "What you want me to help you with, baby?"

"Well, you know. You don't have to do anything. Not a damn thing. All you do, you look at where everything is, and you tell me. Tell me what you want, specially. Then you tell me about all the doors and windows, when the family comes and goes, how the alarm system works . . ."

Shocked, Dorise jerked his fingers away from her lips. Still holding his hand, she stared at him, trying to read his face, to figure out if she'd heard him right. Up till the word "alarm," she hadn't got his drift at all. She thought he meant he'd buy her something she wanted. The "help me" part was something about getting in the mood, the way she heard it.

It occurred to her now that she was sitting across the table from a burglar. She, Dorise, who'd been married to a big-time drug dealer and hadn't even known it. She was a Christian now. She'd found a lot of comfort in the church. She couldn't believe this was happening to her.

"Dear God," she said. "Dear God, what have you sent me?"

Troy took it the wrong way. He said, "Your salvation, honey," and chuckled. "Your salvation."

"I don't need no salvation and I don't need no criminal in my life, Troy Chauvin. You better go."

He grabbed her cheek and a little bit of her hair. "Aww, honey, you didn't think I meant it, did you?"

Slick as shit, she thought. *Just slick as shit.*

He lit a cigarette and leaned back. "I almost had *me* fooled."

She gave him her evilest look, mean little eyes like racists have— old guys out in the country who hate everybody they aren't related to and everybody they are as well.

"Oh, come on, baby, don't tell me you never think about it. I know different 'cause you already told me you do." He shrugged. "So I was just doin' it, too. Just playin' the same game you already told me you like to play yourself. What if I was lord of the manor? What if all this was mine? What if I could give it all to the sweetest woman on the face of the Earth? With the most beautiful ass I ever saw in my life?"

God, he was good-looking. She thought about it. Troy had a good job and no dependents. Why should he be a burglar, and when would he have time anyway?

"Well, it *would* be kind of fun to just pretend Cammie's house was like a supermarket. To just go shoppin' for anything you want."

"Tha's what I mean."

"She got silver! Whoa. Silver coffee things and silver tea things and—you know what? She keep her hairbrushes in some old silver vase-lookin' thing."

"She got jewelry?"

"Yeah, but I don' like it much—mostly little bitty pearls and shit. Too *dainty*—you know?—for somebody like me. She got nice ear- rings though. Rubies that hang down. Think her mother left 'em to her—can't imagine her wearin' anything like that."

"Know what I'd like? A real nice stereo. She got anything like that?"

"Oh, man, a whole room full. They got this great big room on the second floor they call the music room—got a piano in it and everything. But mostly stereo stuff. And a TV. *Great* big screen."

"VCR?"

"You kiddin'? They got three kids. They probably got three VCRs." She giggled. "Adult movies, too. I seen those."

"Wish she'd sell tickets to her house. You and me could have a bunch of fun in there, just for one afternoon, maybe."

"Too bad she so little. No fun to try on all her clothes."

"She got furs? Bet those'd fit."

"Wooo, I bet they would." She leaned back and laughed, at peace again. Enjoying the game. He was right, it was her game. She played it all the time, she just didn't approach it quite the same way he did—like it was halfway real.

8

• •

Skip planted her foot hard and nasty on Nolan Bazemore's spine as she cuffed him. She put her weight on the foot and almost enjoyed watching him wince, though in the end her own cruelty gave her the creeps.

Internally, she shuddered at herself, but she said calmly, "Okay, stand up."

Bazemore wasn't hurt and he wasn't armed. But there was an MP5 on the floor of the truck that made Boudreaux grin. "That's it, Nolan babe. Your ticket to Death Row."

"What are you talking about?" The older woman had her hands on her hips. She had a wash-'n'-wear perm and carried about sixty pounds of extra weight. Eighty, maybe. She looked as if she hadn't exercised in a couple of decades.

Bazemore said, "Mama. Go inside."

Nobody's all bad, Skip thought. *Everyone's got a mama somewhere.*

But in the next few hours, during which she got to know Nolan Bazemore a great deal better than she wanted, she concluded he came close.

While they waited for backup, Mrs. Bazemore cried and tore at a

Kleenex. "My boy's never done nothin'. It's that trashy girl's fault—that damn Joelle. I rue the day he ever met her."

Skip didn't know that she'd ever heard the word "rue" spoken aloud. She said, "Why is that, Mrs. Bazemore?"

"That whole stupid thing was her idea. She didn't have the faintest idea what these Bazemores are like—Nolan and Edwin, both of 'em."

"What was her idea?"

Bazemore said, "Mama, don't you say a word. I don't want you in trouble, now."

"Neither you or your daddy ever had a lick of sense." She turned on her heel and went inside, leaving her son to fend for himself.

Eventually they pried the story out of her.

Nolan and his no-good girlfriend, Joelle, had come over for dinner the night Albert Goodlett's appointment was announced. One of them—Mrs. Bazemore couldn't remember which—said it was "time to give this town back to the white people."

She said, "Since niggers are responsible for the crime, it's pretty stupid to go and give a nigger the job of stopping it, innit? Now, how hard is that to figure out? I mean, it don't make no sense. Time after time, too. I think we're all just damn tired of this, don't you?"

Skip said, "Go on."

"So Nolan said somebody ought to stop it. And that dumb Joelle said, 'You think you're man enough to do it?' And his daddy said, 'You better watch Nolan. You don't know how crazy he is.' "

The rest of it came out in the interrogation room, and it appeared everything his mother had said about Bazemore was true, and more: You couldn't imagine how crazy he was, or how reckless, or how twisted and dim-witted. He was more like a stray bullet than a loose cannon, faster and surer and scarier and a lot more deadly.

First he waived his rights, saying the Miranda decision was a liberal tool for coddling criminals, and a white man couldn't get a fair trial in this country nohow. Then he lit the cigarette Skip gave him and grinned. "I done it," he said. "I done it and I'd do it again. I'd mow down every goddamn jungle-bunny cop and judge and politician in the country if I had time, and when I got done with that I'd start on the Jews. Anything else you want to know?"

"Oh, my God." Skip had spoken involuntarily. He sounded so nuts, she worried he'd get off on an insanity defense.

Still, she and Jerry Boudreaux led him through the details, trying to pick holes in his story, making him fill in every gap. They ran his rap sheet and found he had a history of assault and one attempted rape.

Then they brought Joelle in and questioned her. If anybody was ruing the day, it was she. Nolan beat her routinely, and also beat her four-year-old son; she wanted to leave, but didn't have the money.

Cappello called Skip into her office. "You're not going to believe what they've been running on TV—his dad's been giving interviews saying he supports his son no matter what he did because somebody has to stand up for white people."

Skip plopped down in Cappello's extra chair. "Nobody's that stupid. Everybody knows how that sounds—even the worst racist knows in his heart of hearts it won't fly in public."

"Ed Bazemore says it's time to blow the lid off all that."

"Hold it. His son gunned down an innocent man in front of his house. Surely he knows the kid's gonna fry for it."

Cappello shrugged. "These are not normal people. Have you noticed that? Abasolo went to execute the search warrant on Bazemore's apartment—said it was filthy, by the way—and found it full of white supremacist tracts and newspapers. Quite a few weapons, too."

"Great. I'm thrilled. Or I'm going to be thrilled as soon as I'm through throwing up."

"The brass want a Hollywood walk."

Skip made a face. "Oh, no."

"Buck up, Langdon, it's your big moment. The media's all notified. When do you want to do it?"

Skip shrugged. "Oh, well. What can it hurt? Give me fifteen minutes to put on lipstick."

She was kidding about the lipstick, though she figured Cappello probably took her seriously. In her shoes, the sergeant—ever image-conscious—would have meant it.

A Hollywood walk was basically a photo op. The prisoner had to be taken from Headquarters to what was now grandly called the Intake and Processing Center ("central lockup" in simpler days). This could easily be done without going outside, but that wasn't sexy.

When the superintendent of police got shot, the department damn well wanted everyone to know it got its man. Hence, a short walk from the garage door at the rear of Headquarters, about half a block up White Street, and over to the booking facility on Perdido.

A short walk with more media people in attendance than there were cops in the building.

Bazemore's hands were cuffed behind him, Skip at one side, Boudreaux at the other, cameras everywhere. People eddied and swirled, shouting inane questions. Skip felt as if she'd been up for two days.

Perhaps, she thought later, she should have been more alert. In retrospect she had no idea where her attention had been when she heard the shot.

Bazemore stumbled and went down.

Reporters scrambled, some tripping over wires and falling as well.

Skip stared down at her prisoner for no more than a second—a split second, it couldn't have been more—and immediately jerked her head up to the Broad Street overpass. A man was there, running. Traffic had slowed. But she had no shot, given the number of civilians both here and there.

She simply watched, frozen, unbelieving, as the man ran, holding what was apparently a high-powered rifle.

When they turned Bazemore over, his nose was gone.

• •

Skip spent the next morning giving statements to other officers and avoiding giving any to the press. Cappello was handling that.

The letter came with her other mail—the only piece that wasn't junk, but she would have noticed it anyway. It was in a plain white business envelope, with her name and address neatly typed, plain as you please. The arresting part was in the upper left-hand corner, where the return address should have been. It was only two words: The Jury.

It had been mailed the same day Nolan Bazemore was shot.

Skip called Cappello. "Sylvia, come over here."

Cappello took one look and immediately came to the same

conclusion Skip had. "Omigod. Let's get the bomb squad. And the crime lab."

They left it there, not touching it, till the bomb squad had pronounced it safe and the lab had dusted. Then, carefully, and in the presence of witnesses, Skip slit it open and read.

Dear Detective Langdon:

We wish to congratulate you on your swift and excellent work in apprehending Nolan Bazemore, a blight on the city of New Orleans and indeed on the entire country, which used to be worth something. That's right—used to be. This used to be a country where it was safe for old ladies to walk down the street in the middle of the day, where public schools were excellent and every child assured a good education, where neighbors took care of each other, cared about each other, and where crime was negligible. In the event a crime was committed, the criminal was entitled to a fair and speedy trial by a jury of his peers, twelve good men and true, and more often than not, justice was done. At any rate, we certainly expected it to be, and if it was not, we were surprised. We were shocked and we were outraged.

To our eternal sadness, this is no longer true. We no longer permit our grandmothers to walk alone (or our children, for that matter), we accept the decrepitude of our schools, many of us carry guns against the rising tide of crime, and we do not expect justice. We have become a nation of cynics. We expect judges to sleep on the bench, juries to acquit, and lawyers to get rich.

Why is this? It is because we do not care anymore. Because we are beyond caring. Because we do not see why we should care because we know the situation is hopeless. Our situation is hopeless.

We are too defeated to have any hope.

We know that the people selected to serve on juries will be poorly informed, poorly employed, possibly below average intelligence, and easily influenced by unscrupulous lawyers. We believe this is how the system has evolved. Yet we do not care enough to try to correct it.

Are we willing to serve on juries ourselves? Certainly not. We have bigger fish to fry. We have our jobs and our families—we cannot be troubled by a little thing like justice. And so the system has been subverted. And so we are without hope.

In Chief Albert Goodlett we had a chance at a real change in one of our major cities. In the only city in the world, possibly in the history of the world, that currently has two officers on Death Row. In what is possibly the worst police department in, once again, the history of the world.

There is much in a name. Chief Goodlett was a good man. An honest man. A competent man.

And he was shot to death by an unworthy enemy, an enemy of the church, the state, the Lord—of our very system of justice and the only decent chance it has had in years.

Nolan Bazemore was scum. He was not fit to lick the boots of Chief Albert Goodlett, and there will not be a single detractor among those who read this letter, black or white. This is not a racial issue. Yet Nolan Bazemore was a racist—an ignorant racist peckerwood who deserved to die. Nolan Bazemore was guilty of cold-blooded homicide and he was guiltier still of another outrage—of destroying our Hope! Just when we had Hope, he destroyed it.

Had he stood trial, Nolan Bazemore, poor as he was, ignorant as he was, would have had a lawyer, and that is right and good. But that lawyer would have had that courtroom full of psychiatrists. They would have presented a defense that would have shamed us all as Americans and there is not a one among us who is not aware of it. We would have heard that Nolan Bazemore was deprived of love, he ate too many sweets, or he had a rare disease that caused hatred of people of color, and we would have watched helplessly as he was found innocent of the murder of a good man.

This is the truth, fellow Americans—there will not be one who reads this letter who expected him to be convicted, any more than Billy Ray Hutchison was convicted. Because we do not expect our system of justice to work, and we are not disappointed. IT DOES NOT WORK!

And so we The Jury claim responsibility, as the newspapers say, for the trial, conviction, and execution of Nolan Bazemore. It saddens us deeply that such action is necessary and yet we know that it is, and you, Detective Langdon, know that it is, and you, fellow Americans, know that it is.

We refer you to the Bible:

> Vengeance is mine, saith the Lord.
> Romans 12

> In anger and in wrath I will execute vengeance.
> Micah 5

If I whet my glittering sword,
and my hand takes hold on judgment,
I will take vengeance on my adversaries,
and will requite those who hate me.
I will make my arrows drunk with blood,
and my sword shall devour flesh.

                                    Deuteronomy 32

He said, I will rise, I will cover the earth . . .
That day is the day of the Lord God of hosts
a day of vengeance,
to avenge himself on his foes,
The sword shall devour and be sated,
and drink its fill of your blood.

                                    Jeremiah 46

The letter was signed, "Very sincerely yours, The Jury." A "c.c." note indicated the New York Times, Washington Post, Los Angeles Times, San Francisco Chronicle, Chicago Tribune, and New Orleans Times-Picayune had also received it, along with various television stations.

Sergeant Adam Abasolo had come up behind them as they were reading it. "Well," he said. "Gets my attention."

"That," said Skip, "says it all." She felt her lips tight against her teeth.

She hated this. It terrified her. It scared her a great deal more than mindlessness, or simple craziness. This was complicated craziness. This was a very effective mind at work. And it made her want to run screaming into the woods.

She felt her heart beating, her pulse racing, and realized that part of what she was feeling was anger.

We might expect our system to be falling apart, but we've got other expectations, too—criminals are supposed to be stupid. I don't need goddamn Professor Moriarty here.

Part of it was irrational anger, but part of it was rational—she was pissed off at anyone who had a brain that functioned as well as the letter-writer's and still went around killing people. A person who most assuredly knew right from wrong, and who had chosen wrong.

93

Chosen evil.

She shivered. It gave her goose bumps. And made her think of Errol Jacomine.

Her heart pounded faster as she scanned the letter again.

Maybe there's a reason it makes me think of Jacomine.

"Bigger fish to fry." That phrase again.

And the cadences. The rhythm—so like a sermon. The Bible verses at the end, as if tacked on—first the rational mind, then a little glimpse of craziness, as if the writer couldn't stop himself.

And New Orleans—why focus on New Orleans?

I'm crazy. I'm not thinking like a cop.

But the idea wouldn't leave her. She let it be for a while, decided to go home and sleep on it. And an hour later found herself wandering back to Abasolo's cubicle.

Abasolo was someone with whom she'd partnered up a number of times and if truth be told, she'd probably rather work with him than anyone in the department—not that she'd rather have him for her sergeant than Cappello; this way she felt a little more free to run crazy ideas by him. Like her bizarre notion that The Jury was very likely a group instead of one crazy person—because that was the way Errol Jacomine worked. He always managed to draw people into his schemes, get them blind-loyal; he had a dark charisma that was lost on her, but which it was dangerous to underestimate. Because he was crazy—and she was quite sure he was—he didn't mind looking like a fool, or asking others to do crazy things.

He had once mounted a letter-writing campaign against her that was so transparent a seventh grader would have been ashamed of it. Yet it worked—most of the brass took his side against her.

"Adam, tell me if I'm crazy."

"You are. We all are. Nothing that happened today could really have happened. We hallucinated it."

She slipped into the chair across from him, chewing on a pencil. "I've got a bad feeling about this Jury thing."

"Well, yeah. Sure you're crazy. All right-thinking people are thrilled about it."

"Now, don't laugh. The letter reminded me of Jacomine."

"Well, look, all these nuts—" he broke off. "How, exactly?"

"Well, he quoted the Bible."

"Yeah." Abasolo looked interested.

"And he wouldn't stop. That's exactly what Jacomine did. He'd get started and he'd go on and on. Like he'd memorized a lot of verses with a particular word in them, but that didn't really make much sense when you put them together."

"Well, yeah, but it's the kind of thing a nut would do, right?"

"This is a reality check—you tell me." She put out her hands, palms up. "I never saw anyone else do it. Did you?"

"I don't know."

"And there was this one phrase he used to use—'bigger fish to fry.' "

"Yeah. Yeah." He was biting his lip a little.

"And then there's the way the thing reads like it was done by more than one person—like a ghostwriter did the real work, and then along came the boss and screwed it up with Bible verses. I mean, it seems so normal except for that." She felt her face twitch with embarrassment. "I don't mean normal. I mean . . ."

"Yeah, yeah, I know what you mean. Lucid, I guess. Like nobody but a crazy person would do this, but he doesn't talk so crazy." He sighed and leaned back. "Have you talked to Cindy Lou at all?"

"No."

"Well, I think she's in the building. I had to take something down to Juvenile and she was coming in when I left." He picked up the phone without waiting for Skip's concurrence. "Hey, Cece. Is Cindy Lou still down there?"

Cindy Lou was the department's consulting psychologist and co-incidentally Skip's best woman friend. She was black, she was brilliant, she was breathtakingly beautiful, and—what had drawn Skip to her—she could handle hotshots who liked to put down women.

Though the two women had been close, their friendship had suffered when Errol Jacomine ran for mayor and Skip tried to expose him as a psychopath. Because he was strong on minority rights, Cindy Lou supported him. And because she knew Skip wasn't any too stable at the time, she was inclined to dismiss her friend's fears about him. The friendship was more or less healed, but inwardly Skip winced at the notion of opening up old arguments.

Waiting the five or ten minutes for Cindy Lou to show up, she remembered the other times they'd been through this—except Skip hadn't needed a reality check. That time she was sure she was right, and Cindy Lou was equally sure she was wrong.

"Adam," Skip said. "You present the problem, okay?"

Cindy Lou—Lou-Lou to her friends—was dressed in lime-green, a color that would turn most people pea-green. But on her it looked great. It was funny—she was tiny, but had such presence that the first time Skip met her, she thought Lou-Lou was almost as tall as her own six feet. Yet she could make Skip feel clumsy and lumbering.

Adam ran the question past her, and before he was done, Skip knew how Cindy Lou was going to respond—with extreme caution, because she'd been wrong before.

"It's possible," she said, and Skip almost said it with her. But then she started to pick up steam. "In fact, it's a perfect role for Jacomine in lots of ways. It's anonymous, and he certainly can't be public again—being wanted for murder is pretty awkward for most people's careers. It may very well use the services of other people, which we know he's good at getting—in fact, if he really has followers, they could be some of the same ones from before. Most of all, though, it seems to be about power."

"Power," said Abasolo, mulling it.

"Well, Jacomine certainly isn't after money. I mean, being mayor isn't a high-paying job—of course, some say it's a license to steal, but that's not Jacomine's thing. We know that from the tight control he kept on his followers.

"I mean, we know that's his thing—tight control. Anyhow, it's always the same with these gurus—they think they're God and they set themselves up as God." She started to get excited. "Look what's in the letter: 'Vengeance is mine, saith the Lord.' That's usually interpreted as 'don't take the law into your own hands.' So The Jury's taken over the Lord's job by their own admission.

"Then there's New Orleans. He picked us to operate in, for openers. He can't have been too far away, because there wasn't enough time . . ."

"Or more likely he got someone else to do the shooting for him. That's completely Jacomine's style. I mean, but completely."

Cindy Lou nodded. "That's his M.O. *And* he'd have known about the Hollywood walk—that we do that, I mean. And nobody, but nobody could know that who hasn't spent time here." She nodded again, adding things up and getting answers. "The gunman knew exactly where to stand . . . he was definitely someone familiar with the layout."

Abasolo said, "Let's get Cappello in on this—and then let's go talk to Joe." Lieutenant Joe Tarantino, in charge of Homicide.

The rest of the day was dizzying. They went from Tarantino to the captain in charge of the detective bureau, right up to the acting superintendent. It was only about three hours before Skip found herself at FBI headquarters.

She'd worked with one of these dudes before—Special Agent Turner Shellmire. "So you figured it out, too," he said.

"Figured what out?" Skip said, knowing she hadn't figured much out at all.

He pointed out the window, somewhere in the direction of the river. "The Crescent City Connection."

It was the name of a bridge across the Mississippi. "This dude knows us."

9

• •

The whole thing had happened so fast, Daniel was a little woozy.
He'd lived a long time in Idaho with people who didn't give a damn;
he'd seen a lot of things, but he'd never seen anything like this. Anything remotely like this.

He was feeling kind of schizophrenic about it. On the one hand,
exhilarated, a little dizzy. On the other, a little down. Like somehow
it shouldn't have been so easy. Like it's the kind of thing people talk
about but don't actually do. Because for one thing they wouldn't
know how. For another . . .

He didn't quite know what the other thing was. That path made
him feel kind of wiggly and crawly, like he needed to get away,
quick. He knew what it was, deep down, but he couldn't bring himself actually to think the thought: *Maybe this wasn't such a hot idea.*

Also, it was making him feel strange new ways about his father
that he hadn't sorted out yet. Respect was way high on the list. The
man had actually pulled it off. He couldn't get over it.

And he had done it with such *ease*. It was as if he had snapped his
fingers, and—poof!—the asshole was dead.

It made Daniel feel weird, no question about it. Like his dad was

98

different, or maybe even more than the person he knew—wasn't really his dad, but some kind of evil magician.

Truth to tell, Daniel was a little in awe.

He thought: *You can think and think about a thing and still not have any idea what it is until you actually do it. Like sex. Or being a father. Or killing an animal.*

For some reason he hadn't thought killing a person would feel like getting broadsided by a truck.

It had happened so *damn* fast.

His father had called him into the office in a kind of excited rage, almost frothing at the mouth, furious but getting off somehow. Daniel could see he was getting off.

"The bitch is out there again, son. The bitch is on the move. It's like God sent her to torment me." He grinned all of a sudden. "But we're gonna get her, Daniel. We *are* going to get her."

Daniel sighed, sitting down without waiting for an invitation. His dad ran a formal office even though it was in the living room of an apartment. He sat at a desk and if you were called there, you sat across from him. "What's up, Daddy?" He had his dossier to do.

"Listen, we have to do another one." His dad's mouth was tight, but his muscles fairly rippled under his polyester shirt. His body was a coiled spring.

His dad had done Billy Hutchison, yes. Daniel knew it in some part of his brain, but he hadn't been in on it—it was a California operation, and Jacomine had used California people, loyalists from his Blood of the Lamb days. Half the cops in the country might be looking for Errol Jacomine, but he still had quite a little underground following.

His dad had told him how he did it, too. He had picked only the most loyal lieutenants. He had been sure that the people at the top were absolutely trustworthy. And those people now formed the network that had become the Jury.

Daniel knew all that perfectly well, but it still seemed rather abstract; kind of exciting, yet distant.

Now they were going to do someone, and Daniel had proof they could—the Hutchison proof. His stomach fluttered.

"You know that good police chief they almost got in New Orleans?" Lightning had shot out of his father's eyes.

"Yeah. I think so." Daniel wasn't all that sure what he meant—
he'd been too busy with the Lovelace problem.

"Some asshole killed him." He pounded a fist on his desk. "I will
not have that. 'Vengeance is mine, saith the Lord.' I will not have it!"

"Oh, shit." He remembered now. An honest cop. You didn't see
that every day in Louisiana.

"We are going to do the asshole that did him. We are going to *get*
the son of a bitch."

"Hold it, Daddy. Wait a minute. It was a woman?"

"No. Where'd you get that idea?"

"You said we're gonna get the *bitch*."

His father chuckled. "I certainly did. Well, I certainly did say
that. Because this time we are. Detective Skip Langdon's who I
meant. Mine enemy. Every time I turn around the bitch is out to get
me. Always has been, right from the first time she laid eyes on me.
Some kind of weird grudge, probably about something simple like
sexual repression—nearly always is. Hell, I can't figure it out. You
ever have anybody hate you, Daniel? For no reason? It's a baaad feeling. I never did a damn thing to piss her off, so I have to conclude
she was sent by the forces of Satan to torment me."

"I thought you said God sent her."

"Why would I say that? She couldn't have come from God. If
she'd have come from God she'd have been on our side." His father's
voice had the slight edge that Daniel was getting to know—it seemed
familiar, as if he remembered it from childhood, but at first he
hadn't recognized it as a danger signal. He did now and he kept his
mouth shut.

"Detective Langdon made the arrest," his father said. "Some
peckerwood crazy who's going to get off on an insanity defense." He
shook his head. "Worst thing that ever happened to justice in this
country."

Daniel nodded. "Amen to that."

"So we're just going to shoot her prisoner right out from under
her, thereby savin' the taxpayers the cost of a trial."

Daniel nodded again.

"See, this is the way it's gonna work. Later on today, when they finish beating him with rubber hoses, or whatever they do, they're taking him on a Hollywood walk. That's where they trot out their prize criminals on the way to be booked. So the media can get some nice footage and make the cops look good." He sat back in his chair, hands folded in his lap, a contented, happy man, the fury and frothing only a memory. "And that's when we're gonna get him."

"How're we gonna know when it is?"

"We have contacts, son. We have some real good contacts."

"In the police department or the media?"

"Both."

Daniel never knew if these things were true. Probably his dad had one contact in either the police department or the media. But who cared? He always seemed to know the right person in the right place. Either that or he had a lot more followers than Daniel imagined.

"Now here's a map of the area. The beauty of it's that nobody, absolutely nobody's going to be watching the Broad Street overpass. Assholes'll be falling all over themselves to get their smug little faces on TV." His dad pronounced it TEEvee, on purpose, Daniel thought, to belittle it. "You'll have time for one shot. Just as they clear the edge of the building."

This was what he had come here for and what he wanted to do. All the same, Daniel felt his breathing go ragged.

"And another thing," his dad said. "In three days we're moving all operations to New Orleans."

"*What?*"

It was a rhetorical question that his father didn't dignify with an answer.

"Now get down the road, son. You've got plenty of time to find us a place before you have to get up on that overpass. Okay, let's think now. We need something big enough for a lot of people—the four of us here and three or four more, say. And it has to be in a neighborhood where you wouldn't notice white and black people together, all coming and going at the same address. And I guess that means a place with a lot of foot traffic, since we're going to *have* a lot." He closed his eyes. "Magazine Street. A nice duplex on Magazine Street. Or just off it. Irish Channel, anyway."

101

Daniel was getting into it. "No. Is Magazine Street a main drag? That's the best. Nobody'll notice a thing."

How am I going to find it in one day? he wondered.

In the end he hadn't. He didn't know New Orleans, for one thing, and for another, he didn't want to miss his appointment on the overpass. He ended up staying overnight at a Holiday Inn.

Holed up in his room, drinking some beer he'd bought, he watched himself on television, shooting Nolan Bazemore.

Or rather he watched Bazemore fall dead and then saw himself leaving the scene, as the police would say. Some cameraman had been quick enough to catch him. But you couldn't begin to see who he was—he was just another dude in a baseball cap and shades. He was cool, too, hardly even running, just walking fast.

Still, it wasn't nearly as much fun as television the next night—watching the reactions to the letter. He'd mailed it in New Orleans right before he did the hit.

Various public officials said sober things about vigilante action and taking the law into your own hands—a shrink had opinions on the kind of crazies who'd do a thing like that. And one reporter had had a great idea. Gal named Jane Storey.

Jane had done man-in-the-street interviews. A man in a business suit said, "These people are scary because they're doing what a lot of us would like to."

A dignified black man dressed in a waiter's uniform seemed as mad as Daniel's dad had been: "This man, this Bazemore killed our only hope of gettin' out of this mess we're in." He snapped his fingers. "Like that, it's gone. I'm sorry, I think there's a lot to what they're sayin'. I'm sorry, I can't say I disagree with 'em." He shook his head, a sad look on his face that made Daniel think of the old expression "more in sorrow than in anger."

A woman in a pink power suit—Daniel was sure she was a liberal-assed lawyer who'd benefit mightily from a good fuck—said, "I thought it was just another group of racists when they killed Billy Hutchison. But . . . you know . . . the ACLU defends everyone from pornographers to Nazis if it has to, to protect the First Amendment. These people are like that—they couldn't have picked more different enemies. They've proved to me, anyway, that they're not racists and they're making a point. I mean, you can't say they're not making a point. They've got something to say."

The camera turned to Jane, who said to the audience: "Too bad they felt they had to kill to be heard."

"Yeah!" Daniel shouted. "You got it, Jane, baby. Too damn bad, ain't it? But, listen—otherwise, who's gonna listen?"

He couldn't believe The Jury had so much support.

That day, the day after the hit, Daddy called him into the office.

"Okay, Daniel. Goddammit, okay. The Lord's work is getting done, even if ours isn't."

Daniel grinned. He couldn't be in that bad a mood, not after what they'd accomplished.

"Have you got the dossier?"

"What?"

"On Rosemarie Owens."

He'd all but forgotten. He'd put it on a back burner. His father hopped around so much, Daniel wasn't even sure he'd remember it.

He said, "I'm working on it."

"All right, boy. All right. You work on it." Jacomine sounded vague. "What about the girl?"

"Lovelace?"

"Of course, Lovelace. Goddammit, who the fuck else are we looking for?"

"I've kind of had my hands full, Daddy."

"Now is when we're going to get her. Have you got that?" He was intense today; his eyes were lasers, but he hadn't raised his voice and he hadn't hit his son.

After the session in which he'd been struck three times, Daniel had given some serious thought to leaving The Jury. Prayed about it.

In the end the whole hitting thing seemed stupid. Daniel could lay his father out any time he wanted to. If it bothered him so much why didn't he just do it? Or else quit the movement and go back to Idaho. He asked himself and he asked God. And the answer he got was: It doesn't bother me that much. In fact, it's kind of humorous.

But the hitting was a signal—it meant his dad was under stress. And he wasn't under stress today. He was mellow as a Buddha.

"Okay," said Daniel. "You bet. I thought maybe we could put

our heads together on it. Brainstorm, maybe." He didn't pause for an answer. "I've been racking my brain wondering where to look for her. Where would she go?"

His father was steepling his hands again. "To her mother."

"Naah. Jacqueline's off with one of her crazy boyfriends—climbing the Andes or some kind of shit."

"Well, then it's obvious. Isn't it, son?"

"I don't know. Does she have a boyfriend I don't know about?"

"Hell, you're her father."

"I just thought she might have written you."

"Written me? Did you forget I'm a wanted man, boy? She can't write because she doesn't know where I am. Unless you told her, like you told her everything else."

"Okay, no boyfriend. Her roommate's her best friend and she's still at school."

"Well, bully. So who does that leave?"

The answer came to him like a visitation from an angel. "Isaac. Her only uncle." He snapped his fingers at the realization. "She's with Isaac."

"And where's he, son?"

"I don't know, sir." Daniel was so humbled at realizing how simple it all was, he forgot to be on the defensive.

"Well, I do. He's in New Orleans. Least he was last time I looked."

"*New Orleans? Where we're going?* How could he be in New Orleans?" It was the last place Daniel would have thought of. Yet it made sense; New Orleans was easily accessible from Jackson, where Lovelace had disappeared.

Sure she'd head for New Orleans.

"He didn't go there because I was there, that's the only thing we know. I didn't pay much attention, because what was the point? But we kept loose tabs on him, and that's where he was."

Daniel went to Daddy's reference shelf and plucked a New Orleans phone book. "He's not listed."

"I could have told you that."

"Okay, help me, Daddy. Help me. You know where he lives, don't you?"

"Nope, sure don't."

"If you kept tabs on him, what do you know?"

"We know he used to work at a juice bar. Juicy's Juice." Errol Jacomine smiled, and in the smile there was something of the wolf. Daniel got the feeling his father enjoyed watching him run in circles.

He looked up Juicy's Juice, and it wasn't there either.

His father shrugged. "He just sort of disappeared."

Daniel sat down, aware that something felt funny in his chest, but not knowing exactly how to talk about it. "Well, Daddy, he's your son. And I'm your son, right?"

Jacomine nodded. "What are you getting at?"

"This is making me feel kind of funny."

Jacomine laughed and reached across the desk to give Daniel an affectionate cuff, something he'd never done before. "I didn't follow you to the wilds of Idaho, did I? Didn't mean I didn't love you. If a son wants to disappear, he's got a right."

"That's what he wanted? You think that's what's going on?"

This time his father made his smile sheepish. "I think I embarrassed him a little. Anyway, Isaac's got problems."

"Hell, Daddy, we all got problems."

"Not like Isaac has."

"What do you mean?" Daniel felt a thrill of alarm. Though he hadn't communicated with him in years, Isaac was still his baby brother. He thought it odd that he felt frightened on his behalf.

"He's got demons. The boy's got demons."

He hoped his father didn't mean his brother would harm Lovelace. "I'm going back to New Orleans."

It was a short drive from Baton Rouge, but once there, he hardly knew what to do. For want of a better idea, he went to the registrar of voters—and found no Isaac Jacomine.

Daniel sat in his car, gripping the steering wheel. It shocked him that he knew almost nothing about his brother, had no idea of his interests, marital status, even his educational level; hadn't thought of him in years. But then there was so much difference in their ages.

And we were never a close family, he thought.

Isaac had been a child preacher, coached by his mom and dad; but then he'd had something else as well. Not faith, exactly—all kids believed in God and Santa Claus. More like a radiance. Some kind of thing that actually made you believe.

For the first time in memory, Daniel felt moisture in his eyes. Isaac had been a damn cute little boy.

What a weird thing to remember. What's wrong with me?

•　　•

The FBI would have got to Skip sooner or later if she hadn't acted first—Jacomine or not, she was a pretty key witness. She hoped this way they'd take her more seriously, be more inclined to include her in their investigation.

Working with the feds had advantages—like better equipment, more and better manpower. For instance, they already had data on the other letters The Jury had sent. Each one had been mailed in the city to which it was addressed, or one close by, but big deal—one person with relatives and friends could have done it. It wouldn't take an army of fanatics.

Another good thing about the feds—they had the means to get to the wife, the one in Central America. Within a day, they'd subpoenaed the pertinent records from the Christian Community, figured out where she was, and talked to her. Naturally, she said she didn't know anything, but there'd be follow-ups.

The other thing was, Skip needed all the help she could get in any form she could get it. The brass was so desperate for a sucker for their new heater case that she was assigned to work full time on it, with Abasolo detailed to help her as she needed him. Skip asked for a task force and was almost laughed out of the captain's office: "Wait a minute, Langdon. Things moving too fast for you here? This isn't the chief's murderer we're looking for—we're trying to find the guy who *shot* the chief's murderer. You unclear on the concept or something? Listen, don't knock yourself out on this one—you don't solve it, nobody's gonna get bent out of shape. Just make it look good."

Skip was so mad she could feel the blood rush to her face. She literally couldn't remember feeling this angry. She spoke without watching her tongue: "Unclear on the concept! Captain, please.

The Jury is a huge national case. The whole country's eyes are on us."

The captain leaned back in his chair. "I don't know, I kind of like these creeps. Makin' our job easier, aren't they?"

"He was just blustering," Joe Tarantino said as they walked back to Homicide. "He's what I call a 'goat-getter'—baits people for no reason."

She was still smoldering: "He didn't give me the task force."

"Skip, you're got to look at it from the point of view of the department. If you hadn't caught that asshole Bazemore, you'd have your task force right now. Because he got us where we live. We can't afford to expend a lot of manpower on what's really just . . . a principle."

"Surely you don't believe that."

Tarantino shrugged, apologetically, she hoped.

In a way, she could see it. If Jacomine weren't involved she wasn't so sure she'd give that much of a damn herself.

Cindy Lou was waiting in her office. "Come on, girl, let's go to lunch."

Skip looked at her watch. "I don't know if I can take the time."

"Come on, now. We've got business. And let's get that good-looking pal of yours, too."

Abasolo was two cubicles over, and listening. "You must mean me," he said.

They went for pasta at Semolina. "Look," said Cindy Lou when they'd ordered about three times as much as they'd ever be able to eat. "Jacomine's a paranoid. All these half-baked gurus are the same."

Abasolo said, "I just love a psychologist with tempered and cautious views."

"Well, look—they are. The way cults work is pretty much the way police departments work—on the us-and-them principle."

Skip started to protest, but Abasolo held up a hand and mouthed something at her. It could have been, "Humor her," she wasn't sure.

"If you're in the cult, you're on the side of righteousness against the forces of evil. If you're not, you *are* the forces of evil. When things are that black and that white, you get a very volatile situation.

"These guys operate on fear. Even their former followers can't get over it—it's hell getting them to come forward."

"Hey," said Abasolo. "I just got an idea. Why don't we set up a tip line. Ideal for the faint of heart."

"More to the point, for the scared shitless."

"O Bodhisattva of Compassion, forgive my callousness."

Cindy Lou never, but never, took crap from anybody. Skip adored Abasolo, but all the same looked forward to her deliciously acidic retort. Instead, Lou-Lou gave Abasolo a look that Skip could only describe as appraising. All she said was, "I'm no bodhisattva, baby."

It was almost as if they were flirting, but it couldn't be—Cindy Lou would never waste her time on so solid a citizen as Abasolo, despite the fact that he also happened to be the owner of black hair, blue eyes, and a long, wiry body. Skip had always thought he looked a little like a thug and a little like a movie star—something for everyone. In addition, he was a longtime member of AA, which might mean he'd achieved some measure of spiritual growth. Lou-Lou, however, was famous for her execrable taste in men.

Could this be happening? Skip thought. *Well, hell. Maybe it is. I'll give 'em a break.*

She said, "I'm going to go see about that tip line."

It was easy enough to fix it—the *Times-Picayune* was voracious for news, and this was all she'd had for them in two days.

She called Special Agent Shellmire. "Think of the devil," he said. "I've got a little present for you. Jacomine's ex-wife's flying in tomorrow. From Honduras."

• •

Skip and Shellmire flew to Atlanta together. The Christian Community, having finally seen the handwriting on the wall, had decided to bring Mrs. Jacomine in from the field. She'd agreed to be interviewed at church headquarters.

Tourmaline Jacomine was a tall, almost colorless woman, with slightly fuzzy blond hair—poorly permed, probably. She had once been slender and rather stately, Skip imagined, but she was now a bit lumpy and stooped over. Her hair and skin were beige on beige and her dress was tan. She looked tired, and it wasn't only her eyes and body—there was something about her that bespoke a spiritual tiredness, a need to escape even farther than Honduras and just lie down for a while.

But she also had a jumpy feel to her, as if she expected something to spring from the bushes and bite her.

"Mrs. Jacomine?"

"Yes?" Her mouth pulled tighter as she admitted it. "Call me Irene," she said.

"I thought it was Tourmaline."

"He gave me that name. I always hated it."

Skip and Shellmire identified themselves.

Irene nodded. "I'll be very glad to do what I can. I had no idea all this was happening. I'm afraid the church was protecting me."

"We'd be grateful for anything you can tell us about your husband's activities."

"I don't know anything about his activities and I don't want to know. I really don't know anything about him at all except what I read in the paper. You know what happened with the church, of course."

Skip and Shellmire nodded. "There was a scandal," Shellmire said, "involving women."

She lowered her head as if he'd said, "Take that, Irene!"

"I'd been married to a stranger," she said. "I had to learn to live with that."

"You didn't have any clue as to what he really was?"

"Oh, yes. Oh, yes, I did. But I just didn't know I did. In retrospect I see what a perfect fool I was, but there was no understanding it at the time. Not when I was married to a man of God." She paused. "He used to beat my children and me."

"I'm sorry," said Shellmire.

"Now just why did I think that was all right?" She looked at her lap again. Skip could see why she'd requested the missionary outpost as soon as news of her ex-husband's criminal activities became public. She was a wreck and must have been worse then. "I was married to a psychopath and I didn't even know it."

"Why do you say he's a psychopath?"

109

She lifted her chin and stared at a place far outside the office. "A million little lies. Two million cruelties without meaning—except to him, I suppose. That's what I know about him. But what's he doing now? I couldn't tell you. I haven't spoken to him since the thing broke in Atlanta. We have a child together, you know."

"I thought you said 'children.' "

"Did I? Daniel was his son by a first wife, but I guess I think of him as mine."

"Odd—he wasn't mentioned in the church records."

"What records? Oh, I know—we filled out insurance forms. He hasn't been a dependent in—oh, twenty-five or -six years I guess— he's much older than Isaac."

Skip said nothing, hoping she'd expand without prompting on Jacomine's life story. When the silence had gotten too long for comfort, Irene Jacomine said, "It was rather ironic. That first wife is probably the only human being who ever got the best of him. Maybe it's part of the reason he's the way he is."

Irene spoke very precisely, almost formally, as if expecting to be judged. She was a timid woman, Skip thought. She spoke kindly. "We really don't know much about his background. Maybe you can fill in some of the blanks."

"Evidently I didn't know enough myself. I think there's a lot I still don't know." She took a deep breath. "But I do know how Daniel came to be. Errol got a girl pregnant when he was fifteen, and married her. He was married at fifteen—I can't even imagine that. Can you? They ran away together, those two, and in two years Errol was back—without Rosemarie. He told me that she left him, he didn't leave her. If she did—" Skip thought she saw admiration on Irene's face, but the older woman quickly remembered she was a church lady. "She probably didn't. Errol is an inveterate liar. However, what seems certain is that she arrived back in Savannah some five years after that, bringing the child, whom she dumped on Errol. I married a criminal, I know that, but sometimes—I don't know, sometimes I think *he* might have, too."

For a second Skip wondered if she meant herself, but she said, "The first time around.

110

"Imagine that—abandoning your husband and *then* your child."
She shook her head. "Mmm. Mmm. Mmm.

"And then he left Savannah. I guess he didn't want to be found
after that." She tried out what was meant to pass for a chuckle. "He
was preaching even then. And finally he got a church from the Community and then another one, until he got the big one in Atlanta. We
met in a small town in Alabama, where he had a church at the time. I
was younger than he was, and flattered when the preacher took a
shine to me. I guess he dazzled me."

Skip kept a poker face but she wondered, as she often had, why
Jacomine's particular charisma was invisible to her. She supposed she
had an overdeveloped bullshit-detector.

"I guess I thought he must have an interesting past, this preacher
man with a teenage boy—I met him seven years after Rosemarie
came back. Daniel was fourteen then, and so shy he couldn't look at
anything but the floor. If ever a boy needed a mother, it was that
one."

"And so you married his father."

She looked astonished. "Well, that wasn't why. I was in love
with him."

Skip thought perhaps she hadn't managed to keep the perplexity
off her face, because Irene seemed to have a need to justify herself.
"He seemed such a *principled* man." For a moment her features cap-
tured that early passion, and then gave way to irony. "*Seemed* is right.
I guess I fell into the trap of listening to what he said rather than seeing what he did."

"What did he do?"

"Oh, he was horrible to the boy. He beat him, but I didn't even
know about that. I did see him speak harshly to Daniel, and humili-
ate him." She shook her head again. "I just don't know why I
thought it was all right. He said the boy was a behavior problem, and
it hurt him a lot to do that, but he had to, a psychologist had told
him to; and he said the school counselors were always telling him he
was too lenient. I thought if *they* said to do it . . . now I know. Now I
know."

Skip said, "I beg your pardon?"

"Well, I'm sure they said something. Errol just had a habit of interpreting things his own way. I mean, one thing I know happened. A neighbor's cat died mysteriously. After that, maybe they said something like Daniel really needed some attention, or guidance, maybe—something like that." She shrugged. "What they meant was, a kind word, maybe—or a few sessions with a shrink. Errol read it as 'punishment.'

"Well, anyway, I might have been crazy, but I married him. And Isaac was born three years later, when Daniel was seventeen. I had my hands full for a while, I sure did."

"How old is Isaac now?"

"Twenty-seven. And Daniel's got a grown girl. In school at Northwestern."

Skip tried not to show surprise. She hadn't known about the girl.

"Daniel came out kind of strange after all. He drank too much for a long time—for all I know he still does."

"You're not in touch with him?"

Irene looked surprised. "Oh no. None of us have been for a long time. He went off to Idaho to be a survivalist."

"What about his wife?"

"Jacqueline? They got divorced before that. Now, she never was any good."

"How's that?"

"Drinking. Drugs. Anything you can name. It's like Daniel married his mama without even knowing her. Jacqueline left Daniel when Lovelace was ten—ten years ago."

"Did you know Rosemarie?"

Irene blushed slightly. "I've been told about her."

"Where is Isaac now?"

"I don't . . . really know. When the thing happened with Daddy— I mean Errol . . ."

"Wait a minute. Which thing? Atlanta or Louisiana?"

"Atlanta. When the thing happened in the church and I left his father, Isaac just . . ." she paused ". . . he just stopped writing. Or almost did. I got a postcard once saying he was all right and healthy." She smiled. "So healthy he was working in a juice bar. That's what he said."

"Where was it mailed from?"

"Mailed from?" She looked puzzled, then seemed to catch on. "Oh. New Orleans."

"Is his dad in touch with him?"

"Well, I don't know. I suppose . . ." She was clearly going over the events of the last few months in her head. "I suppose he could be. They were both in that part of the world."

"Do you have an address for Isaac? Or the name of the juice bar?"

"No." She crumpled a little, and Skip felt she had just torn off a bit of the woman's scar tissue, exposing the wound beneath. "Isaac will . . . Isaac was an unusual child. A fragile child. He can only do what he can do. For some reason he doesn't feel he can be in touch with me right now. When he can be, he will be."

"What do you mean, Irene? Does he have mental problems?"

Irene stared at Shellmire, angry now, for the first time showing an emotion other than despair. "He's fragile. I told you that."

"Are you in touch with Daniel's daughter?"

Her face changed course completely, was suddenly radiant. "Oh, yes. Lovelace. We're all so proud of her."

"All?"

"She's such a lovely girl."

"I meant . . ." Skip decided not to continue. She had meant, how could Irene know if she wasn't in touch with any member of her family, but that didn't really matter, she thought. In this case, "all" was probably a euphemism to make herself feel better about their loss. Only one person really mattered.

"Irene—I have to ask you directly—have you heard anything from your ex-husband?"

"No, I have not." Her washed-out eyes burned briefly—weak blue flames in the wilderness.

"Do you know where he is?"

"I do not."

"Do you know if he's in touch with anyone else in the family?"

"I would have no idea about that."

She had suddenly gotten on what Southerners call her high horse—why, exactly, Skip wasn't sure.

"Do you have an address for Daniel?"

"I do not. Jacqueline might, but I couldn't tell you where to find her. Or Lovelace might. Oh, yes. Lovelace would. You can find her at Northwestern."

Skip thought that in Irene's shoes, she, too, would have asked for some time off in the boonies. If her sons had cut her off, they might have a very good reason—those beatings, perhaps. By her own admission she had "thought that was all right." She must have gone along with Jacomine's sadistic ideas of discipline as if they were hers as well.

She was paying the price now, and Skip felt sorry for her. She stood and said, "Thank you, Mrs. Jacomine. I'm sorry for your trouble," as if someone were dead.

Surprise filled the woman's eyes like tears, and Skip was reminded of an animal that expects, from long experience, a kick instead of kindness.

10

• •

Dorise hadn't liked these white people from the minute she arrived, though they were friends of Cammie's. She came to set up for a Sunday brunch—a job she damn well knew how to do as well as the next person. All you had to do was tell her where you wanted the food and where you wanted the bar and then enjoy your party.

She walked in and this Meredith, who introduced herself as Mrs. Clemenceau as if it were the nineteenth century, started in with a checklist. She, Meredith, had made a list of what Dorise was supposed to do!

Dorise said, "Don't you worry, darlin'. I've done this a hundred times. I'm gon' take care of everything and you're not gon' have to worry about a thing. Those sure are pretty earrings you're wearing."

Diamonds. First thing in the morning.

Every now and then she ran into an uptight one and she always said that, or something like it, and you could just see the little wrinkles in their foreheads straighten out. And then they would show their pretty teeth and they would whisper, "thank you" or some such, and leave in a cloud of perfume.

Dorise moved slowly and confidently. She didn't race about

creating more panic. She just did what had to be done, in about the time it took these ladies to put on lipstick.

This one didn't respond. Her eyes squinched even closer together, as if she considered Dorise impertinent, and she snapped, "You haven't done it a hundred times at my house."

And then her husband came out and when Dorise smiled and said hello, he didn't even respond, just looked right through her as if she didn't exist.

Dorise had no choice but to waste her precious time listening to what this Mrs. Clemenceau wanted her to do and then do it in the order that Mrs. Clemenceau wanted it, with Mrs. Clemenceau standing over her the whole time, practically daring her to do something wrong, which she did. Being supervised affected her that way.

And naturally everything took twice as long, doing it Mrs. Clemenceau's way, and so she wasn't even completely set up before the first guest arrived, though she was only five minutes away, and though the next guest didn't arrive for another twenty minutes. Still, it hurt her pride.

She served mimosas and Bloodies for a good half hour after she judged it was time to eat, but Meredith had told her not to start serving until she told her to. And then she forgot to tell her, and clicked in on a cloud of ruffled feathers: "Dorise. It's twelve-thirty."

As if that were something to Dorise.

Dorise didn't even like her guests. The men were overweight and a little too loud, especially after a few drinks, and they had quite a few. The women all seemed to have those same wrinkled foreheads Meredith did. Dorise would catch snatches of the conversation and they were all talking about crime. Crime and who did it. The people who did it were called "they" and it was abundantly clear from the way the guests cut their eyes to see how much she heard that "they" were invariably African American.

Going through the house to collect the glasses, Dorise noticed that Mr. and Mrs. Clemenceau, despite their obsessiveness, poor manners, and general sourpussness, had some pretty nice things.

They had those good, nearly threadbare Oriental rugs. They had gold leaf mirrors that had cost more than Dorise's car. They had silver and jewelry and stereos and all the things she had talked to Troy about.

Thinking of Troy, it occurred to her that if the Clemenceaus lost some of their nice things it wouldn't completely break her heart. Playing that game with Troy had made her uncomfortable that time, but here, in her head, there wasn't any harm in it and as it turned out, it was lots of fun. These people talked about crime all the time and didn't even have a burglar alarm. They didn't have decent locks on their windows either, and they sure didn't have a dog that was going to do them any good.

Now they did have a dog—a little yappy white thing that had been trying to get a grip on Dorise's ankles ever since she arrived. But its nasty little mouth was too small.

When she got home, she needed something nice and real to get the taste of that place out of her mouth, so she put on a pot of red beans and called Troy to come over and help her and Shavonne eat them.

He didn't stay over that night because Shavonne was there, but when she went off to do her homework, Dorise told him about Mr. and Mrs. Clemenceau and their delightful personalities. She told about the guests and their opinions on crime and the windows without locks and the little canine dustrag, and everything.

The other way they'd played the game had had an uncomfortable edge to it—a kind of greediness, and longing, a sadness, maybe, that they couldn't be lord and lady of the manor, no matter how odd the role. This way was just funny—they laughed themselves silly planning a fake robbery of Mr. and Mrs. Sourpuss Clemenceau. She said, "Least you wouldn't have to worry about that little kitty-cat of a dog. You could just pick him up and throw him against a wall."

They got so carried away, Shavonne came out and said, "Are y'all gon' let me do my homework or not?" and she was so funny saying that, they started laughing again. She stuck out her lip and turned and ran. Dorise knew she was going to cry, so she ran after her. Shavonne had been as fragile as a butterfly since Delavon died.

Troy was gone when she came back.

•   •

Two days later Dorise did another Uptown lunch, and the ladies were all abuzz about the burglary of a friend. The burglar had apparently done something unbelievably brutal—had picked up the couple's little white dog and thrown it against a wall—or so it seemed from the dog's injuries. It was still alive when they came home, but it had to be put to sleep.

The story knocked the breath out of her. Surely they couldn't be talking about Meredith Clemenceau. She and Troy had made up that story about the yappy little dog—it wasn't real, it was something they imagined, just to have something to laugh about.

She wondered, *Can you make something happen, just by talking about it?*

She didn't tell Troy, didn't tell anybody—it was too creepy. The coincidence, for one thing, but also that someone would actually do that to a dog! She didn't want to think about it.

It was another two days before Troy called and came over and presented her with Meredith Clemenceau's diamond earrings.

●　●

That first night Lovelace lay awake in Isaac's bed (Isaac having insisted on sleeping on pillows on the floor) and assessed her position.

She felt bad for her uncle, for a lot of reasons, but most immediately because he had to sleep on the floor. She had to get him an air mattress of some kind.

It surprised her that she thought that—it must mean she wanted to stay.

She didn't want to deal with that—whether she did or didn't want to stay—but one thing she knew. She was happy. Lying in this hospital-clean bed, squeaky clean herself from the shower, full of Isaac's inconceivably healthy vegetable stir-fry, she was absolutely euphoric.

Of course it's always nice, she thought, *not to go to bed with your hands bound, and with no knockout drops in your bloodstream. Damn! I still can't believe my own dad did that.*

She certainly wasn't afraid of her dad in the sense you'd be afraid of a criminal—he wasn't going to rape and rob her—but this had to have something to do with her grandfather, who really was scary, and not only to her—this was a man who'd killed people. She hadn't seen him at all in recent years and really had no idea who he was.

When she was a kid she'd hardly noticed him, and she was pretty sure he'd hardly noticed her. She tried to think back, to get anything at all, and she drew a blank.

Michelle knew about him. When Lovelace told her, her roommate had all but fallen out of bed. "You mean your grandfather's a killer? But what's that like? What's *he* like? How on Earth could you have a grandfather who's a killer?"

She didn't know. Try as she might, she couldn't conjure up the least image of him, except preaching. She'd been made to go to church and hear him.

He sounded like a preacher. That was really the only impression she had. But it frightened her that she hadn't noticed anything odd.

What a weird family, she thought, thinking of poor Isaac.

All the warm feelings she'd ever had for him had come flooding back—and more. They were nearly the same age, she realized. When she was three and he was ten, he was another whole species, and when she was ten and he was seventeen, he was yet another. Now though, when she was twenty and he was twenty-seven, they were close to being contemporaries. She'd had dates with men who were twenty-five.

They might be contemporaries, Lovelace thought, but they couldn't be more different. Lovelace didn't get him at all. There was almost nothing about him she understood, even his obsessive angel art, which seemed to be about her.

Despite that, she adored him. She knew in her bones he had as beautiful a spirit as anyone she'd ever met and that they were deeply connected, the two of them. She felt close to him, drawn to him— *safe* with him. There was something about him she'd never felt with anybody else—she felt he had her best interests at heart. So here she was lying in his bed and feeling like a baby in a crib.

It wasn't as if she didn't have a life. But how the hell did you go back to school when your own dad was stalking you? God knows what he'd told the administration by now—maybe that she'd been in and out of institutions, that she'd threatened to kill herself, that she was so depressed she was suicidal.

If he'd said that—and she knew he probably had—they'd be dying to get her off campus. Blood was *so* embarrassing to a college. Then, too, there was her name—if she did anything that made news, it would make double news because of her grandfather. She'd be a very high-profile suicide. And the school would be putty in her dad's hands.

So there was no going back. Which brought up the problem, In that case, what now?

She slept on it.

And in the morning, the answer was obvious—she'd have to stay here till her mother got back from Mexico. Jacqueline wasn't good for much, but she could probably get Lovelace out of this one.

But how to make it through till then? Isaac obviously couldn't afford to support her, and anyway, she had to have something to do. She'd done temp work before and she could do it again.

She found a coffeehouse, where she perused newspaper ads, and from which she made a quick call to her roommate.

Michelle squealed. "Omigod. You're alive."

"Have you reported me missing?"

"I didn't till yesterday afternoon, but by then I was out of my mind. I hope I did right. They said you'd been called home unexpectedly."

"And you believed that?"

"I've been tearing my hair out, Lovie. I called your house in Florida and nobody answered. Tomorrow I was going to go to the cops—or at least a shrink."

"Well, I'm okay, but this is dicey." She ran down what had happened, and then admonished Michelle not to breathe a word to the authorities even if they tied her up and tortured her.

"Hey, no problem. I never heard of you. The last thing I want is your grandfather in my life."

That done, Lovelace registered at three different employment agencies, and spent the rest of the day prowling around. She hadn't been to New Orleans before, and she found it had a strange, languid air to it, an anything-can-happen kind of feeling. It was a hot day— much too hot for March—but she found herself oddly energized, excited somehow. By what, she wondered? The weather? It made her feel languid and sexy and kind of exuberant, but she didn't think that was what the excitement was all about. It was partly the beauty of the architecture—Lovelace wanted desperately to go to Paris, which she hoped would look like this. It was partly the beauty and the foreignness, and partly the weather, too. But there was also a kind of rife feel—as if every moment was a bud that could open up into some wonderfully unexpected flower, something as exotic as it was irresistible, something lush and bruised and dangerous. She thought it no accident that so many vampire stories had been set here.

She walked by the river, strolled the French Quarter, and explored the Faubourg Marigny. She felt something like an American in Paris and something like a time traveler. Who she didn't feel like was Lovelace Jacomine, conscientious (if not brilliant) student at a midwestern university. This place was nothing like Evanston and nothing like Florida and nothing like anywhere she'd been.

● ●

The next day she was in an ordinary, airless office, filing for an oil company.

By ten A.M. she started to cough; by noon she was sure she was choking. It was the mold, people said—in a city this old, it got to you. If you had allergies, they kicked up; if you didn't, you got them.

She went out at lunch and had an extraordinary thing called crawfish bisque and then, because she was intrigued, the dessert they called bread pudding. Every bite was an adventure and not only because she liked the stuff—because she was trying to figure out how it was done.

Partly because her mother was so lame, Lovelace was a good cook—someone in the family had to be. As she was trying to figure out how you turned day-old French bread into the dessert she was eating, it suddenly occurred to her that there were other ways to make a living besides slaving in an office.

She went back to finish the afternoon's work, feeling not nearly so choked. The frog started to leave her throat, her voice to return to normal.

She finished out the week at the oil company because Lovelace was conscientious by nature—and because she needed the money.

Meanwhile, she read the ads and even applied for a restaurant job or two, but she knew she wasn't going to get them—she didn't know how to fake the references.

She also felt weird about trying to fake the work itself. How did

121

you translate little quantities into big ones? Just for openers. She was sure there was a lot of professional stuff she'd be expected to know that she didn't. But it occurred to her she didn't *have* to work for a restaurant. All she needed was a job cooking. Maybe for an old lady or an old man who couldn't manage anymore. She daydreamed about the kind of house her employer would live in—ten thousand square feet in the Garden District, perhaps; rooms no one had entered for years; dust an inch thick on the ancestral brocades; a garden that was a tangle of ancient climbing roses choking out sedate camellias.

Of course, she'd probably have to cook on a woodstove.

But who else would need a cook?

Maybe a young family with a mom like hers—one who was never home. A divorced lawyer or doctor, somebody like that. White canvas at the windows instead of precious tatters. Maybe she could even live in.

On Sunday the ad ran in the Times-Picayune for exactly the kind of job she wanted: "Part-time cook for family of four. No Louisiana dishes. Low fat."

Her heart pounded like John Henry's hammer. She didn't answer the ad.

11

• •

One good thing about working with the FBI—they were everywhere. Skip and Shellmire stayed in Atlanta while special agents in Chicago checked out Lovelace Jacomine. Skip was waiting in a conference room when her partner came in. "She's not at Northwestern. Her dad told them she'd come home unexpectedly."

"Daniel phoned them?" It sounded far too pat.

"He's her dad, right?"

Skip was irritated. "Well, where's home?"

"Fort Lauderdale, according to their records."

"And have your crack agents been there yet?"

"We should have a report in a couple of hours. Meanwhile, they did talk to her roommate, whom they found uncooperative. They think she knows somethin'."

"What's her name?"

"Michelle Greene."

"They just questioned her a little and took no for an answer? That was it?"

"Not exactly. That's where we come in. Apparently, she never reported Lovelace missing—what does that say to you?"

"She knows where Lovelace is."

"Yeah. She's so hinky they didn't want to let her go, but what were they gonna do? She hasn't committed a crime or anything. They want to know what we want to do about her."

"Are you kidding? I'm going to see her. Want to come?"

He laughed. "I kind of thought you'd say that. But no thanks. You're the Jacomine expert."

She called Cappello to say she was going—didn't ask; told her. There was no question of being sent—the department didn't have the money for a trip like this. Skip would have to pay for it herself, and, given that, Cappello wasn't about to put her foot down.

She got lucky and got a flight almost right away. The agent who met her in Chicago had a report on the Fort Lauderdale end—the neighbors said no one was home, and apparently no one had been for weeks. He took her to Michelle Greene.

Shellmire had briefed her on everything in Michelle's school records—she was from Charlotte, North Carolina, where her father was a banker and her mother was a lawyer. She'd been a straight-A student in high school and president of the student body. At Northwestern, she was doing well, and in her spare time, she did fundraising for AIDS research. In short, she was the kind of girl who probably had no reason to think she didn't own the Earth.

Still, if anyone could intimidate her, it was the FBI.

She was a bit crumpled right now, at least so far as her posture went. But her blond hair still looked shiny, her eyes were bright, and the close-fitting T-shirt that came just to the top of her jeans was fresh as ever. It was chartreuse.

Skip could see the girl's exhaustion, but she didn't have an impression of much else before she introduced herself—all she knew was that something changed immediately. Michelle sat up straighter, seemed suddenly alert.

She had said, "Hi, Michelle. I'm Detective Skip Langdon, New Orleans Police Department."

She wondered if Lovelace had known about her, remembered her from the earlier case involving her grandfather, and mentioned her to her roommate. "You know me?"

The girl shook her head, looking confused.

"I thought Lovelace might have mentioned me."

"No. May I see your badge?"

"Sure."

Michelle examined it in detail. Hardly anyone ever did that. It was New Orleans, then—perhaps that meant something to her.

Playing the hunch, she said, "You know who Lovelace's grandfather is?"

Michelle stiffened, and seemed to grow paler. She nodded.

"He's wanted for murder. You know that."

The girl only blinked.

"He kidnapped my niece and almost had her killed."

Once again, she saw Michelle react. Her body swayed backward slightly, as if she'd been struck by an invisible fist.

"What is it, Michelle?"

The girl shook her head.

"Listen, this is no time to keep girlish secrets. Lovelace isn't in trouble, she's in danger. This is not a guy who messes around."

The last sentence was true, anyway. As for the rest, for all Skip knew, Lovelace was even now cleaning her rifle, having mowed down Nolan Bazemore.

"What sort of danger?"

"Suppose you tell me."

"You know what I hate about cops? You expect everybody to spill their guts and you never give anything away."

"Okay, that's off your chest. It's the nature of the job, and there's nothing either I or you can do about it. I repeat, your friend's in danger. You want to help or you want to waste time we could use trying to get her out of it?"

The girl looked almost sheepish for a second and then regained her composure. "I prefer being treated with respect."

Skip chose to take it as a bargaining point—to give the girl what she asked for, as she might give another witness a cigarette. She had a feeling this one was dying to talk—all she needed was an excuse.

She sat down. She'd been standing, in fact standing close, invading Michelle's space and making her look up. "I don't blame you," she said. "Listen, let me tell you something about myself and what I think. I've had several encounters with Michelle's grandfather and he's slightly less dangerous than Hitler, I'd say, but quite a bit nastier than Charles Manson, whom he resembles in certain ways."

"What ways?"

Michelle was trying to take control of the interview, and Skip was willing to let her have it for a while. There was no harm repeating public information. "He's a nasty little man with a strange charisma I don't understand—but that seems to attract people who want to be told what to do." She smiled. "Nobody like you."

"I don't understand."

"Not everybody sitting in an interrogation room at the federal building is quite so uppity."

Michelle blushed. "Well, I—"

"You're obviously an intelligent person in charge of her life, and you're right—I should treat you like one. So here's the story—he's wanted for murder, and anybody he's close to or who he's ever been close to could be in danger. You could be in danger, just because you know Lovelace."

"What about Lovelace's dad?"

"What about him?"

"Where does he fit into this?"

Somewhere, Skip thought. *Or else why'd you bring him up?* She said, "You asked me to treat you with respect and I'm going to ask the same thing of you. Frankly, I think you mentioned him because you know more about that than I do. Look, Michelle, your roommate's been gone for days and you never reported it to anybody."

"I told your—*colleagues*—" she said the word as if it were "servants" "—that she told me she was going home for a while. To me, she wasn't missing. So why would I report her missing?"

"Why would she go home in the middle of the semester?"

"She needed a break." Michelle looked uncomfortable, as if wondering how far to go.

"About that respect you mentioned—excuse me, how dumb do you think I am?"

"That's what happened." Now she was sullen, a little girl who'd been lectured.

She'd been telling the same story for hours and didn't seem

about to deviate. Skip did what every police officer hates doing almost more than anything else—gave her a piece of information: "No one's home in Fort Lauderdale. Where do you think she is?"

"How would I know?" She flailed her arms, irritated.

That was the wrong reaction. "Aren't you surprised to hear she isn't where she said she was going?"

"She could have gone there and left."

"Look, maybe you think cops are dumb."

"No, I—"

"You aren't surprised because you already knew. You know where she is, Michelle. And she's very likely in danger. *Very* likely. I don't care what she told you about her grandfather, or about anything she's doing—the plain truth is, he's a homicidal maniac. Is she your friend or isn't she? It's that simple. If she is, talk to me."

"You really think it has something to do with her grandfather?"

"You think it has something to do with her dad. He called the school and said she was at home. She isn't. He's a man with no known address. Am I getting through to you?"

"Oh, Jesus."

"She's in over her head, Michelle. She needs somebody to pull her out."

The girl put her hand to her mouth and nodded. "Okay," she whispered. "Okay."

Skip waited, not saying anything, letting the girl gather her thoughts.

"Her dad kidnapped her and drugged her. But she got away. She's okay."

"How do you know that, Michelle?"

"She called and told me. And said not to tell anyone. To keep it quiet."

"Why do you think that is?"

"She had . . . problems, once. She was depressed. Spent time in a psychiatric hospital. She thinks her dad can use that against her any time he wants—he can just say she's suicidal or something, or she's crazy, and people'll believe him instead of her."

"Look. The FBI isn't trying to track her down because her dad says she has mental problems—that should be obvious, shouldn't it?"

"Yeah. Yeah. It doesn't make sense." She was finally working it out.

Skip said, "Where is she, Michelle?"

"She's with her uncle Isaac. In New Orleans."

"Her uncle Isaac?"

"Yeah. Is he—uh—involved with her grandfather?"

God, I wish I knew. She said, "Do you have an address for him? A phone number?"

Michelle shook her head, holding her shoulders with arms crossed over her chest.

"Tell me about him."

"Tell you what?" She evidently didn't know where to start.

"What does Lovelace say about him? Does he live alone? Is he married?"

"I think he does live alone. She hasn't mentioned anyone else."

"Go on."

"He's an artist. He wears white all the time."

"What kind of artist?"

"Well, now, I don't know. That's funny, she didn't say—but then she was talking so fast. Like she didn't have much time."

"What's the white about?"

"Some kind of religious thing, I guess. Lovelace says he meditates a lot, and everything in his house is white. Also, he cleans house a million times a day and take showers all the time. Maybe he's got some kind of thing about purity. He doesn't talk. I forgot about that."

"Doesn't talk? He's mute?"

Michelle frowned, apparently puzzled. "I'm not sure. All I know is, crazy Uncle Isaac doesn't talk much."

"Much? Or at all?"

She bit her lip. "Not sure."

"Has she only called once?"

"Yes."

"If she calls back, call us instantly, and try to talk her into calling us."

"Okay."

Skip asked a few questions designed to reveal Isaac's living arrangements, but Michelle didn't seem to know whether he had an apartment or a house, or what neighborhood he lived in.

And then Skip asked the question that was really bothering her: "Why did her own father kidnap her?"

"That's what I'm wondering. She doesn't know."

• •

Skip was fitful on the plane going home. She stared at the picture of Lovelace and Michelle the feds had given her, Michelle at least having cooperated to that extent. Lovelace was quite a bit taller than her friend, and somewhat heavier. She had almond-shaped eyes and a conventionally pretty face, except that it was still round with baby fat. Her hair was light red, pulled back on the sides with a barrette, left hanging in back. More or less a Campbell Soup kid. She looked nothing like the granddaughter of a homicidal maniac.

This thing was gnawing at Skip. Her mind raced the way it used to when she was new in the department. There were hardly any threads to pull at. And when she had pulled them all, she might have nothing. She might race around like some kind of Type A and still come up with nothing.

That night she barely slept. She would doze, and then she would dream of something chasing her, and she would scream and Steve would wake her up—she wouldn't have screamed at all, just made the little gasps of nightmares.

Around seven she fell into a sweaty torpor and awoke two hours later—it was Saturday and Steve had taken pains to let her sleep. It was Napoleon who woke her, barking at birds in the courtyard.

She turned over grumpily and tried to go back to sleep. She was too groggy for mind-race now, but she had a residual panic. She was almost afraid to try anything lest she run out of things to try. She felt paralyzed.

How in the hell to find a man who was "an artist," whatever that might be, and about whom she knew nothing else except that he liked to wear white. What kind of white? Jeans? Ice cream suits? Robes?

She looked him up in the phone book, and then threw it across the room, frustrated.

Who knew him? Other artists, maybe. That was a thought.

His parents and siblings. Only, two of those were missing and he didn't talk to the other one.

It might be Saturday, but she was going to work on this thing until she dropped—which would probably be about noon, the way she felt now.

She opened her home Jacomine file and fingered the *People* magazine piece Aunt Alice had given her—the one about Rosemarie Owens. After talking to Irene Jacomine, Shellmire had said he'd send someone to interview her.

But had he?

Skip thought, *I hate this national case shit. I'd rather do it myself.*

Idly, she dialed Dallas information and asked for Owens. You could have knocked her over when the robot spat out a number. Frantically, she scrambled for a pencil and ended up having to call back.

She got a recording: "This is the voice mail of Rosemarie Owens. If you are interested in the rights to my story, please call Natalie Rosenbusch at ICM in L.A. I am not giving interviews at this time. I am not investing any money, nor am I contributing to any new non-profit organizations, nor am I able to raise my usual contributions to old charities, nor am I interested in discovering any new relatives. This is an informational tape only. It will not be checked for messages."

Even in her nasty humor, Skip had to chuckle. "These Texans," she said to herself and dialed ICM in L.A.

Failing to rouse anyone, she checked information for Natalie or N. Rosenbusch and came up with an "N."

It was two hours earlier in L.A., and N. Rosenbusch was obviously still out cold.

"Sorry to wake you," she said. "But this is Detective Skip Langdon in New Orleans and I have an emergency. I need to call Rosemarie Owens about her granddaughter."

Suddenly Natalie got a lot more lucid.

"You're really pissing me off. She doesn't have a granddaughter—you heard her message. She doesn't want to talk to you, and I don't appreciate being woken up with bullshit stories."

"She has a son named Daniel and a granddaughter named Lovelace who may be in grave danger." She considered using the Jacomine name but decided that would make Rosemarie too angry. "Her ex-husband is wanted for murder and may try to contact her. She really needs to call me right away."

"Lady, you are so full of shit. . . ." She hung up.

It had all happened so fast, so unexpectedly. *I should have done it from the office,* Skip thought, and called Headquarters to say she was expecting a call from Natalie Rosenbusch, just in case.

Fat chance, she thought, throwing on a pair of slacks barely passable for office wear.

It took her less than half an hour to get there, and Natalie hadn't called—but she was probably still home in bed. Skip called back and left a message for her: "I forgot to leave my phone number."

In a moment her phone gave a little half ring, and she had to smile, figuring Natalie had done exactly what she would have done—dialed Headquarters, asked for Detective Langdon, and hung up quickly when it turned out she was real, the call was going through. Ten minutes later Rosemarie called.

"Detective Langdon, I got an odd call from Natalie Rosenbusch." Her voice was lightly accented—Southern but somehow almost British—one of those unplaceable accents self-invented people have. It sounded stiff, almost starched, as if she were holding it tight, keeping it from trembling.

"Ah, Mrs. Owens. I'm sorry to bother you, but your granddaughter, Lovelace, has disappeared and I thought . . ."

"I beg your pardon, could you say the girl's name again, please?"

Oh, Christ. I wonder if she even knows she's got a granddaughter.

"Lovelace. Daniel Jacomine's daughter."

Rosemarie made some kind of a sound—something midway between a sob and a gasp—but said nothing.

Skip said, "Look, it sounds as if you're pretty surprised. I wonder if you even knew you have a granddaughter."

"I really don't . . ."

"We have a situation here. The girl may be in grave danger. Your ex-husband, Errol Jacomine, is the subject of an intense investigation both by our department and by the FBI. I need you to cooperate with us. Now. There isn't time to think this over."

"My God. That must be what the FBI wants. What's happening?"

"Your granddaughter was kidnapped—"

"Kidnapped? From where?"

"From Northwestern. Where she's a sophomore."

"Jesus. She's grown up."

"Mrs. Owens, could you hear me out, please?" Skip started from the beginning. "Your son, Daniel, has one daughter, Lovelace, who's twenty and a sophomore at Northwestern. He's divorced, but there's no custody question—that's long since been settled. However, several days ago, he kidnapped Lovelace and drugged her. Lovelace escaped and we have no idea where she is. We also have no idea where Daniel is, but we suspect he's with your ex-husband, Errol Jacomine, who I'm sure you know is an extremely dangerous man, wanted in at least two murders. We believe your granddaughter is in a great deal of danger."

"Well, this is quite a bit to swallow." Indeed, she sounded choked.

"I'm sure you understand we wouldn't call you if we could possibly have avoided it."

"Detective Langdon, all I can say is you must be a mighty desperate woman. I haven't seen my son Daniel since he was seven years old—I believe he'd be over forty by now. And I certainly haven't seen or heard from Errol Jacomine. To answer the only question you've actually asked me so far, no, I wasn't aware I had a granddaughter. What on Earth can I possibly do for you?"

You're right, she thought. *I'm as desperate as they come. And you sound like one cool customer.* She said, "Well, you've answered one of my implied questions, which was 'Have you seen Errol Jacomine lately?' Let me expand on that. Have you any idea where he is?"

"None whatsoever. When we left Savannah together at the respective ages of sixteen and fifteen, we didn't get any farther than Alabama. I was a young mother waiting tables while trying to take care of my child. Daniel's father didn't care any more about him than he did about that poor dog he killed that used to bark all night and keep him up."

"Your dog?"

"The neighbor's. Earl took care of Daniel while I was at work, which usually meant he invited his buddies over to play cards and threw the kid a peanut butter sandwich now and then."

"Did he work?"

"Well, he brought in a little money. Yes, he did. I have to give him credit for that."

"What did he do exactly?"

"Why, he preached in a garage. And passed the collection plate. He had fliers printed to advertise himself—just like he was putting on a play."

"At sixteen he did this?"

"For a while he did what I did—waited tables—and I swear I believe he robbed a store now and then, although he never admitted it. But he did have sudden influxes of money. Meanwhile, he met a very interesting charismatic preacher—he's dead now, I heard—that Earl kind of learned his trade from. And I'll tell you something, Detective. Earl was good. Not-a-dry-eye-in-the-house kind of good. That man could preach the pants off the choir—and did, too. Why, yes he most assuredly did."

"Is that why you left him?"

"Oh, no. That's not why I left him. You have no idea why I left him, young lady, and you don't want to."

Oh, I do. I do. She said, "Actually, I had a few encounters with him and I'm a lot more puzzled about what anyone would be doing with him in the first place."

"Well, I can tell you about that. I can tell you a lot about that. You've probably read about me in *People* magazine and the *New York Times* and all those kinds of things and what you see is the Rosemarie of today. When I think back to Rosemarie at fourteen, I could just cry." The words were pouring out of her so fast she was tripping over them. Skip suspected her life with Jacomine was something she didn't often think about and couldn't talk about—with anyone.

"Rosemarie in those days was a plain little thing—to look at me today, you'd never believe it. Plain and scared. I lived completely in my head, was what I did. I read a lot. I'll bet that surprises you, doesn't it? You probably think I'm just some brassy blonde who marries rich men, but let me tell you something, honey. You don't get out of Savannah unless you've got some idea what the outside world is like. You die of claustrophobia or become a drunk. I knew the world through books, and I wanted to see it. I wanted to go places and meet people!

"But I was this plain little pudgy girl from the most ordinary family you can name—my daddy was an accountant, and my mama was a cashier in a drugstore. They were Southern Baptists, and they made me go to church twice a day on Sunday and once on Wednesday night. Now, how was a girl like that gonna go anywhere or do anything? I wanted to see England; I wanted to see France; I wanted to see someone's underpants. How old are you, Detective?"

"I'm, uh—"

"I'm sorry, I didn't mean to be rude. You're under thirty, aren't you? Or maybe around there—you've already made detective. However old you are, you have no idea what the world was like then. My mama told me that people didn't have sex outside of marriage unless they were very, very low-rent. But you see, I read novels, so I knew they did—outside Savannah, of course. I bet you think *Peyton Place* never existed before the TV series.

"My mama never touched me that I can remember. Now, isn't that pathetic? I don't even remember her hugging me. Are you getting a picture, here, Detective?"

Rosemarie had become so excited Skip had to hold the phone an inch from her ear. "Are you saying the combination made you— uh . . ."

She was about to say "vulnerable," or something like it, but Rosemarie finished for her: "Hot to trot. I was easy prey for somebody like Earl Jackson, who preyed on . . . easy prey. I remember the first time he touched me, walking me home from school. Put his arm around my waist, and I thought I'd burn up. Is he still as ugly as he ever was?"

"He's not my type."

"Little weasely-looking fellow. I didn't care. I just wanted to be *touched*. By anybody. And then, too, he knew quite a few ways to tap into interesting sensations I didn't know the human body was capable of. Poor a specimen as he was, I always wondered what he saw in me—well, I think I know now.

"First of all, I was a real easy target. Second, I had such low self-esteem he could pretty much push me around any old way he wanted. Third—and maybe this is important—he had this Pygmalion thing."

"I beg your pardon?" Skip hadn't expected to hear her say that— Rosemarie was an odd combination of sophisticated and down-home Southern.

"He wanted to make me into the woman he wanted. Like a Stepford wife or something. I lost weight and got pretty sexy for him, which was his downfall in the end because then I figured out he wasn't the only fish I could catch. But that wasn't why I left him. Uh-uh.

"What happened was I got pregnant and we ran away. I had no more idea what a baby was or how to be a mama than I knew how to fly. I wanted to see the world, and I saw Dothan, Alabama.

"I wasn't a good mama. I was a lousy mama. I had zero patience with my child, and I yelled at him and swatted him sometimes, when he got to be three or four. But I knew one thing—I knew you weren't supposed to suck a baby's penis."

"I . . . what?" *Did I hear her right?*

"I guess I caught you off guard there. Well, Earl got pushier and pushier and more and more abusive, bashing me around, telling me what to do, treating me like a slave, to tell you the truth. And he wanted me to do weird sexual things—I'm not going to go into that right now. But you asked me why I left him. I left him because, when Daniel was a baby he'd cry and keep us up at night, and Earl wanted me to suck his penis to keep him quiet. I told you you didn't want to know. You just don't know what life with that man was like.

"I found myself an older man who was sweet and gentle and didn't mind supporting my kid. But then I screwed up—I found myself a much younger man, and the older one threw me out. I had no skills and no place to go—that's when I took Daniel back to Savannah and dropped him off. I became a flight attendant, and the rest is history."

"You met somebody else?"

"Oh, many. Many, many somebody elses. But the hell of it was, I finally fell in love, and look what happened to me."

Skip was thinking that the younger woman who'd taken her

husband was probably a clone of the younger Rosemarie when the other woman said, "What goes around comes around. I don't blame her. I swear I don't—she saw a chance and she grabbed it. I blame him—I thought the old goat loved me."

"Did you ever hear from him again?"

"Who? My husband?"

"Errol Jacomine."

"I never did and I never will."

"Just in case—it's very important that you contact me if you do."

"You have my word. I'll call you the instant I hear from him, or hell freezes over. Whichever comes first."

Another road leading nowhere, Skip thought. *Still, it answers the question "What kind of woman would marry Errol Jacomine?"*

She could see why Aunt Alice had said this woman was the love of young Earl's life—she had a hard edge to her; might even be as ruthless as he was. And he hadn't yet subdued her.

He wouldn't like that, Skip thought. It would prey on him.

12

• •

After Delavon died, Dorise had gone back to church, and she had found comfort there. In fact, she didn't understand why she'd ever stopped going. When she had a problem, she could put it in the hands of Jesus. But there was another side to it—oh, yes, there was another side. You had to keep up your end—you couldn't let Jesus down because that was letting yourself down.

When Troy brought her Meredith Clemenceau's earrings, she had screamed as if someone died. Shavonne came tearing from the back of the house, where she was watching television, crying, "Mama! Mama, you all right?" and the poor little thing's white shorts were wet, with a trickle of urine still running down her leg.

"Oh, my Lord, what have I done!" she hollered. "I've scared my child so bad she's gone and pissed herself. Troy Chauvin, you get on out of here. You get on out of here and don't you never come back. And don't you worry none about your sorry ass—I ain' gon' tell nobody what you done 'cept the Lord Jesus Christ and he already know. That's who you gon' have to answer to. That poor little dog. That poor, poor little dog. For shame, Troy Chauvin!" She pressed the earrings back into his hand and slammed the door.

Shavonne stood there with her mouth open so wide a bat could have flown in.

Dorise dropped to her knees and hugged her as tight as she knew how. "It's okay, baby. Everything okay now." Shavonne burst into violent sobbing, and Dorise realized that was what she'd said before—that time when it wasn't okay and would never be for Shavonne, ever again.

"Baby, I jus' had a fight with Troy—it ain' nothin' more than that, I promise you, baby. You all right. Ya mama's all right. Okay, baby? Look at me now?"

Shavonne obeyed for about a split second before she ran, and the terror on her face was enough to make Dorise howl again, as she had when she saw the earrings. This time, she held her tongue, though, and fought the impulse to chase her daughter. Shavonne needed a minute alone, she thought, to change her pants and get her bearings.

Dorise sat on the couch and thought about the little white dog, unable to believe the man who had made love to her so sweetly could do a thing like that. She wondered if he took drugs, or if he'd been drunk, or if he was just plain mean and she'd never noticed. The thing was so incomprehensible, her own part in it so over-whelming, she couldn't even cry.

"Forgive me, Jesus," she said to the air. "Forgive me, Lord. I never meant to hurt nobody, even that hateful Meredith and her husband—I shore didn't mean to hurt no poor little animal."

If Troy could do that to an animal, what could he do to a person? she thought. Suppose she'd become involved with him and he'd hurt Shavonne. She went in to comfort her child.

Shavonne was lying on her back in bed, crying. "Mama, I peed myself."

"Honey, you were scared to death. Mama's so sorry to scare you like that."

"Mama, what Troy do make you scream like that?"

"He just surprise me, honey. He say something let me know he got a mean streak, and I felt so disappointed I scream out."

A mean streak like your daddy had, she thought. *But even Delavon wouldn't hurt no animals or children. I mus' be getting worse. Jesus, don' let me get no worse! Please help me find a good man sometime.*

She had got Shavonne into bed and told her a bedtime story and was just beginning to feel peaceful again when the phone rang. It was her boss asking her to come to the office the next morning.

Jesus, don't let the po-lice be there, she prayed.

She prayed all night long she'd be able to handle it all right. When she arrived, she saw that everyone was there who'd worked at Meredith's that day, and they were called in individually. That meant she was probably okay.

When it was her turn, she acted as if she couldn't have been more surprised and said "darlin' " and "honey" a lot and she could tell she was the last person anybody in the company would suspect.

She worked hard at her popularity and it was paying off. *Now I just gotta pray nobody else gets blamed for what I done,* she thought to herself, but she didn't think anyone would. If fingerprints were found, they'd lead to Troy and that trail would lead straight to her. What she had to do was keep him out of her life.

Well, no problem, she thought. *He the last man I want to see.*

Shavonne stayed at a friend's house that night, and Dorise called her sister. She was so lonely and—when you got down to it—so depressed she had to talk to someone. Her sister said, "Girl, you sound awful. What's wrong wit' you?"

"I'm not seeing Troy no more. He didn't turn out the way I hoped."

"You picky, girl, you know that? You just too picky."

Dorise wasn't about to tell her the truth. When she didn't say anything, her sister said, "How's my little sugar-pie?"

"Shavonne sleepin' over at a friend's house."

"She is? Well, let's go, girl. Le's go out."

"I don't think so. I think I'll just sit home and watch the tube."

But her sister came to pick her up in half an hour, dressed for meeting men. "Come on, girl. Put on somethin' show off your nice behind. We gon' go listen to some music."

Feeling more or less like she was in a trance, having very little mind of her own, Dorise followed orders.

Her sister took her to a place outside the neighborhood, a place with a whole new crowd. Dorise had a few drinks and felt better.

A fine-looking man talked to her, too, a man who worked for a painting contractor, but she couldn't get interested to save her life.

She was afraid of him. She was afraid of any man right now.

But it was so hard being alone, trying to raise a child alone. And then there was the specter of sex. She'd forgotten all about that little thing until Troy reminded her so vividly.

It sure was like cigarettes and drugs—once you had some you wanted more and more and more.

She craved male attention and she was nice by nature, so she just didn't have it in her to shine the fine-looking man, and in no time at all he seemed to have gotten it into his head that she was just dying to leave with him.

"Can't do that," she said. "It's a school night."

"You go to school?"

"My little girl does."

"You got a little girl? I love kids—always wanted to have some myself."

"Listen, I gotta go."

"At least give me your phone number."

"Maybe I better get yours, darlin'. I don't want to take no chances you won't call."

She tore it up as soon as she and her sister were in the car.

"What you do that for?"

"I just don't know what to believe and what not to believe these days. I been wrong my only two tries, and I just can't afford to do it again."

"You gon' be a nun or what?"

"I'm gon' pray about it. See what I can figure out."

She entered her empty house feeling more depressed than ever.

● ●

The Monk was in the gallery courtyard painting an angel when he realized he was humming to himself. He had had an uncontrollable urge to abandon his pregnant painting for a while and paint more angels that looked like Lovelace.

And why not? He had to pay for it by dusting every piece of African art in the gallery—because that was the deal he'd made with himself—but painting the angel made him so happy, that was nothing.

She makes me happy, he thought. It's her—having her around.

"Hey, Monk," said Revelas, "I ain' never heard you hum before. 'Zat break your vow or not?"

The Monk smiled and shrugged his shoulders. In his opinion, it didn't, but he thought the idea was kind of funny. He felt light-headed, even a little giddy, as if he were in Paris or something. He felt like humming and he didn't care who heard him.

Revelas came over to look at the painting. "Hey, man. Tha's real nice. These angels different, ain't they? Happier. They got roses in they cheeks."

They really were Lovelace, in a way that the other ones hadn't been. The old ones. Those weren't even meant to look like her—he hadn't known what she'd look like grown-up. He was as surprised when he saw her as she was when she saw the angels.

Now that she was here, he was painting her, and it was only natural the angels were happier. He was happier.

On the way home, he thought of what he'd like to cook for her that evening—a vegetarian lasagna he knew how to do. He stopped and got the ingredients.

When he arrived, he smelled something good. She'd made it for him—the very same recipe, which she'd found in his files.

In a way he was disappointed that he couldn't cook for her, but the coincidence of this utterly delighted him. If he'd needed proof they were kindred souls, this was it.

"Hi, Uncle Isaac."

He smiled at her, unloading the bag he'd brought. She got it right away. "You were going to make this? Cool. You can tell me if I did it right."

He wrote, "Maybe I could just write it."

She laughed. It had been a long time since he'd made anyone laugh.

He went into the bathroom to wash his hands the twenty times it would take to be able to eat, and then he caught the doorknob carefully with toilet paper, thinking that this was something he hadn't had to worry about when he was alone.

Still, she was worth it. He thought: *It's truly a joy to have her. What is a person without family?*

She was tossing a salad when he joined her. She said, "What were you doing in there?"

He felt a hot flush begin at his scalp and travel toward his toes. He frowned to tell her she'd crossed a forbidden boundary, but she was intent on the salad and missed it completely.

Too bad, because it was one of his most eloquent stares. Since his vow of silence, he'd learned to show disapproval in a thousand silent ways, but he was most proud of his stare, though Revelas laughed at it. "Hey, man, you look like a lizard," he said when The Monk turned it on him. But other people got it loud and clear, and even Revelas had taken to saying, "Watch out—he got the lizard look again."

Having taken his best shot and gotten nowhere, he simply walked into the living room, sat on his mat, and folded himself into the lotus position. He couldn't begin to focus, the way his mind seethed with outrage, but that wouldn't show.

As it happened, whether it showed or not was irrelevant. Lovelace apparently had not noticed he'd left the room. In a bit, she came and brought him his version of a cocktail—orange juice on the rocks. She simply held out the glass, expecting him to abandon his mudra and take it.

He did.

She sat in the white-painted rocking chair and moved her arm in a semicircle, taking in the room, taking in his whole universe. "All this . . . white. The hand-washing, the sweeping, all that—it's got to be wearing. I mean, there's got to be—you know—fear behind all that. Surely it can't be easy."

Fear? He hadn't thought of it that way. He was just doing what he had to do. Actually, he lived in a very safe universe, a lot safer than most people's.

He got up and found his writing pad. "Okay," he wrote. "Paint it any color you like."

"Oh, Isaac, come on. They've probably got books about this—they can do something about it."

Once again he wrote. "Hey, I see angels, I don't talk. . . ." *I have no woman*, he thought.

She laughed. "Oh, let's eat."

The lasagna was so perfect he didn't bother to write, just pointed to it and patted his heart, a man in love.

"You like it? You know what I'd like to do? You know what I'd *really* like? I want to cook."

Not getting it, he stared at her.

"I mean, instead of shuffle papers."

He made the "okay" sign—*Good idea.*

"But you know—restaurants—I don't really have any training or anything." She put her elbows on the table and stared past him, out the window. "There was this ad in the *Times-Picayune* for a low-fat cook. . . ."

He gave her the "come-here" sign—*More, more.*

She just smiled and looked at her plate.

He couldn't stand it. He got up and found his pad. "Did you answer it?"

"No. I don't know why. I guess I'm afraid to—I couldn't take rejection right now."

"Why would they reject you?" he wrote.

"I don't have references, for one thing."

He thought a minute, and then drew a picture of himself with a lightbulb over his head. "I used to work in a juice bar and guess what I did? Vegetarian cooking—you know, making guacamole and gazpacho, but still, it was cooking. The owner's a really good friend. I'm sure he wouldn't mind cooking you up a reference."

"Really?"

The Monk nodded.

"I don't know."

He wrote, "It's just a formality—it's not like you can't cook."

She smiled at him, and he knew that she appreciated his caring about her. He was surprised at the way that touched him.

When he meditated and had been sitting quite a while, it

occurred to him how eager each was to live the other's life, Lovelace for Isaac and he for her, and how easy that was. He could plainly see what she could do, what held her back. She could be right about him, too, but she *wasn't* him. It was your own life that was hard.

Later, he thought, *This floor is hard, too. I wonder when she'll leave.*

• •

Things were moving so fast Daniel felt out of breath. They were in the house now, the place he had found on Magazine Street, and there were a lot of them. His respect for his father—his wonder at him—increased every day. He probably had twenty-five or thirty followers in New Orleans with an inner core of a dozen—that was a lot for a man who'd been trashed by the media and was wanted by the FBI. It was enough to really do something.

There were six of them living in the house—all white, so as to draw less attention. The others were couples, and since they had a double, it even looked as if they were two separate households. It was a discreet setup, but a little public. Magazine was a big-deal street and people were so friendly here—or nosy, depending on how you looked at it. They couldn't have anyone dropping in unexpectedly—in fact, couldn't have anyone seeing Daddy at all. It would be dicey, but it ought to work as long as the others shopped for groceries and that sort of thing.

Daniel was in an incredibly productive period, thriving on urban activity after the years of rural isolation. He and one of the women had spent an afternoon finding furniture at various junk stores; another couple had bought linens and dishes. That was really all it took to get settled, except for the two armoires Daddy wanted. That took another afternoon.

Meanwhile, one of the other men had installed the office—computer, fax, copier, everything Daddy needed to communicate with his fellow Jurors.

And Daniel had made phone calls and a couple of trips. He'd made virtually no progress on Lovelace, but he'd filed a full report on Rosemarie Owens that included her unlisted number, which he'd gotten by breaking into her house so gently she hadn't even noticed. She hadn't had her alarm on because she was home at the time. He'd done the research, but what it was about he had no idea. The woman was no exemplar of virtue, but she wasn't someone who needed justice either—not a potential target, to Daniel's mind. Perhaps Daddy saw her as an ally, though why—except for her money—he couldn't imagine.

Or perhaps it was the husband who was the target. Could that be?

No—dumping your wife just wasn't a capital offense. The Jury was a serious organization.

After about a week, when he was satisfied everything was in place, Daddy said, "Let's call that Owens woman. What do you say?"

"Whatever you like, Daddy. You want me to get her for you?"

"Yeah. On the speakerphone. Let's make it a conference call."

"What'll I tell her?"

"Just tell her I want to talk to her."

"Use your real name?"

"Hell, yeah, use my real name."

He shrugged. His father amazed him with how much support he could get, how many people he could rally, but when all was said and done, the old man had delusions of grandeur. Daniel could think of no reason in hell why some rich, gorgeous babe would want to talk to a guy wanted for murder.

A woman answered. "Ms. Owens?"

"Yes?"

"Ms. Owens, I'm calling for Errol Jacomine."

"Well, there's a blast from the past." Her voice had a throaty, been-around quality.

Daddy, normally so tense he nearly twitched, suddenly underwent a metamorphosis. His shoulders relaxed, he grinned like a clown, and his body language conveyed something else—something Daniel had never seen in him before. What was it?

Eagerness, he thought. Almost . . . happiness.

Jacomine said, "Hey, Miss Rosemarie." He dwelt on every syllable of the name, as if making fun of her for putting on airs.

"Hey, Earl. I knew you'd look me up one day."

"How you been, baby?"

Daniel wondered if his mouth was hanging open—his dad and Rosemarie Owens?

"You must know how I've been. I gather you read *People* magazine."

"You've had some real bad luck."

"Well, some good luck, too. One thing—since I became nationally famous I've gotten reacquainted with a lot of old friends."

"You sound like you're almost glad to hear from me."

"You know what, Earl? You were never boring. A girl could do worse."

"You did, sugar. I'm quite sure you did." They laughed like a pair of monkeys. When they had subsided, his father kept talking. "Rosie, I've got somebody I want you to meet. Daniel, say hello to your mama."

She was silent. His father was silent. It was as if Daniel had fallen into a vacuum. His ears roared and it was the only sound in the world.

"Well? Say hello, son."

"You son of a bitch!"

"Daniel Jacomine, is that any way to talk to your mother? You just went from being half an orphan to having a rich, beautiful, internationally famous mama. Now you mind your manners or she's going to think I raised you wrong."

The throaty, Lauren Bacall voice was quavery. "Daniel? Is that you, baby? Oh, Earl, you don't know what a gift this is."

She started crying in earnest and Daniel thought: *What the fuck is goin' on? My mama's not this woman. My mama's Mary Rose Jacomine.*

His father said, "You want to meet him, baby?"

Daniel couldn't stand it any longer. He shouted. "No! Goddammit, no!" Later, he had no idea why he'd said that. He'd simply been too confused to think, wanted time to stand still.

"Oh, Daniel," said Rosemarie Owens. "Ohhh, Daniel, you have no idea. My baby. My little baby I haven't seen in all these years."

Her baby? he thought. *I don't know this woman.*

Memories of his mother began to come back to him. She had had brown hair, not blond, and she was skinny and young and had a different name. Though people did call her Rose because Mary Rose was so hard to say.

Damn! Daddy was so peculiar about this. Why didn't I put two and two together?

And yet he couldn't have, he knew that. Who on God's green Earth could have seen this one coming?

"Daniel. *Daniel?* Your daddy's a shithead, you know that? Always has been, always will be. He didn't tell you what was going on, did he?"

Daniel tried to muster a little dignity. "How about if you tell me."

"Well, I can't yet. It's too much to hope he's had a change of heart and just wants to do the right thing. But for some reason he seems to want us to meet, and that's good enough for me, darlin'. I haven't laid eyes on my boy since you were seven."

"Since you deserted me, you mean."

She started to cry again. "You have no idea why I had to do that or how much it hurt me. Come see me, darlin'. Please promise you'll come see me."

He heard himself saying, "Where, Mama?" Calling her "Mama" as if thirty-five years hadn't passed.

13

• •

Skip assessed her data: Jacomine's younger son was an artist who wore white, who had told his mother he worked in a juice bar, and who meditated a lot. Surely it was all part of a pattern—crummy day job to support painting or sculpting habit, nonconformist clothing, off-the-wall state of mind. A fringe kind of person. Someone, it sounded like, who probably lived close to the edge. Not a bad profile at all, and Skip thought she might be able to add something—since he'd worked in a juice bar, maybe he was a vegetarian.

She picked up the Yellow Pages and turned to "Health and Diet Food Products." There were fifty-three listings, including all twelve Smoothie King franchises—about forty-seven more than she'd expected. She phoned them all and asked to speak to Isaac. When that failed, she enlisted Abasolo to help her call on them. He took twenty-six and she took twenty-seven, both wishing fervently for the task force they'd been denied.

They tried to see managers and owners or, failing that, at least to find out who they were, to call later. And then they talked to the employees about a regular customer dressed in white.

At Whole Foods, the girl at the deli counter raised a finger at

Skip, seemingly pointing at her. Skip looked behind her and sure enough, a man in a white polo shirt and white jeans was perusing canned goods. Another man, not three feet away, stood by the beet and carrot chips in a white linen shirt and shorts.

Neither of them matched the description his mother had given her. The simple truth was, men in white weren't that uncommon at this time of year.

Pursuing the artist avenue, Skip walked around Jackson Square, where street artists could hawk their wares with no overhead; some good artists had started this way. Not-so-good ones also made a living.

They were a friendly bunch, these artists, and they didn't miss much—they all knew a guy who wore white and had a spot a block or so over, by St. Anthony's Garden. Unfortunately, he was African American.

No one knew Isaac, and she wasn't that surprised. For all she knew, he did six-foot metal sculptures rather than French Quarter scenes. *Oh, well,* she thought, *I can talk to Cindy Lou on the weekend. Maybe she'll have an idea.*

It was Easter weekend, when hardly anyone would be working. But Cindy Lou was coming over for Easter dinner, which Jimmy Dee was cooking, "For Layne, darlings, for Layne—our first holiday since the Troubles."

Skip hadn't seen the two of them, had barely spoken to the children, since the Jury case started to break. She said, "Wait a minute. I think I missed a chapter. Does this mean the Troubles are over?"

"The allergy's at bay, anyway. It only comes a little bit now. The odd sneeze or sniffle."

"You've got to be kidding."

"Hey, the witch cure was your idea."

"Hold it. You're saying it worked?"

"Darlin', I can't tell you what worked. Call it the placebo effect, or call it voodoo. All I know is, for the moment, this marriage is saved." Ostentatiously, he knocked on wood.

"But that's great, Dee-Dee. That's fabulous. Why didn't anybody tell me?"

"Tell you? You mean fax you at FBI headquarters?"

She uttered an all-purpose "ummm." "Is there anything else I missed?"

"Let me think. Kenny dyed his hair green. Angel became a lesbian. Sheila's going to church tomorrow."

"Very funny."

"Well, the last one's true. I think she's got a Catholic boyfriend."

"Good. Catholics are still against premarital sex, right?"

"Bad. That just makes them want it more. What are you doing tonight? Rare night out with the Bear?" His name for Steve.

"We're dyeing Easter eggs."

In fact, they went to an early movie first, and then stopped by the Napolean House for dinner. Skip was in a fine mood when they got home, suffused with a feeling much like children get at the start of summer. She put on water to boil, and found herself enclosed in a rear-approach bear hug. Steve said, "Want to make love?"

"Have to, to celebrate the season. Renewal of life kind of thing. Soon as I get my eggs dyed." She wiggled her butt against him and then wriggled out of the hug.

She opened the refrigerator and pulled out a dozen eggs.

"You're serious about this? You're really dyeing eggs?"

"Hey, get in the spirit. It's not Easter every day."

"What the hell." He started getting out cups for the different colors, and she remembered how much fun dyeing eggs used to be. Steam everywhere and the kitchen smelling of vinegar.

When the eggs were done, she opened some brown paper bags filled with the stuff of the season—Easter baskets, fake grass, chocolate bunnies, jelly beans, marshmallow chicks.

"I know that's not for Kenny or Sheila."

"Listen, you're going to think I'm crazy."

"I already think you're crazy, and we've already talked about this—it's for Shavonne, isn't it?"

She looked at him, willing him to understand. "The least I can do is—I don't know—*something*."

He smiled at her, apparently at a loss for what to say. She knew the obvious was so very obvious: *Nothing you can do could make up for not having a father.*

He drove with her to the building in Gentilly where Shavonne lived with her mother, going so far as to creep up on the porch and and ring the buzzer. They left the basket with a note that said: "For Shavonne from the Easter Bunny."

"She probably hates egg salad sandwiches."

"Oh, God. We used to have those for days after Easter."

Napolean barked when they entered their own courtyard and for once she wasn't bothered by it, even rather welcomed it. *A nice, warm animal,* she thought, glad she had a human one to take to bed with her.

She and Steve made love a long time and she went to sleep more relaxed than she'd been in days, the case momentarily out of her head. *Life's too short,* she thought, *to do what I've been doing.*

Easter, as usual, was a perfect spring day. They got Kenny and Jimmy Dee (Sheila being at church) and wandered all day, from one parade to another.

When Sheila joined them finally, and Cindy Lou came over, and Layne, they talked of Layne's miraculous cure and whether there was such a thing as magic. Definitely, said Kenny—he had seen it.

Assuredly not, said Sheila. That was for kids.

"But do you really think you have to see something for it to be real?" asked Layne. "I mean, *something* cured me."

"True love," said Sheila. "Maybe that was it."

Skip was surprised—she wasn't the kind of kid who talked about love; maybe the Catholic lad was going to be around for a while.

"Could have been God," said Steve. "Half the country would go for that one."

"Could have been natural causes," Layne said. "Maybe I just got used to the dog."

"Yes," said Jimmy Dee. "You do."

"You do what?"

"You have to see something for it to be real."

"Oh, yeah? How about viruses. You can't see those."

"How about God?" said Sheila.

Skip said, "For heaven's sake, Dee-Dee. You're the one who sent him to the witches."

"I can't help it—it's too New Age-y. I can't accept it."

"So voodoo would be okay?"

"At least it's part of our heritage."

Sheila said, "I wasn't kidding. How about God?"

"What do you mean, how about God?"

"I mean, you can't see him, but people believe in him. Why is that okay and this other stuff isn't?"

"Because it's in the culture," said Cindy Lou. "And this other stuff isn't."

"You mean, like the majority go for it."

"Just say God's on your side and you're in business."

Skip was starting to hate the conversation. This was the stuff in which Jacomine traded. Because he had used the Judeo-Christian God as a shield, he had quite literally gotten away with murder—and often. Now he was using justice as a shield. She hated the thought that she was going to have to think about him again tomorrow—to have him in her consciousness until she had him in a cell.

She pulled Cindy Lou aside to give her a personality sketch of Isaac.

"Okay, yeah. A little weird," said her friend. "But who isn't? I can't really tell anything from that little data."

"Damn. I've tried juice bars and I've talked to every artist at Jackson Square. He meditates, and there's that white thing—maybe he's in some religious thing. Maybe I need to—"

"Hey, wait a minute. How about galleries?"

"What do you mean how about them?"

"Why stop at Jackson Square? Maybe he's hooked up with a gallery."

"I hadn't thought of that." She considered it. "I guess I just assumed he was a marginal sort of character."

"Even if he is, he might have gone in and tried to peddle his work. Someone might remember him."

"Not a bad idea. Good thing he picked white instead of black for a uniform—in that world, guys in black are a dime a dozen."

It was curious—it had never once entered her mind that Isaac was any kind of legitimate artist—she'd simply assumed he was more or less a street person with ambition.

14

• •

Now this was a house Dorise could live in, all cool and comfortable, without even the AC running; sunlight streaming in the back, though it was late afternoon; prettiest garden she'd ever seen in her life. The party was a fund-raiser for a school called NOCCA—she didn't know what the letters meant, but she knew it was a school for kids to learn music and things like that. Plenty of famous people had gone there, lots of them black, including the Marsalises. And plenty of black people were at the party. She wondered if one of them was Ellis Marsalis, maybe even Wynton.

She thought the people who lived in the house were probably musicians as well, or artists—something interesting, anyway. They had a big old grand piano in the living room, and the walls were covered with paintings—not those stiff pictures of people in old-fashioned clothes that were usually deep browns, real depressing; these were all bright colors, and big as the walls themselves, pictures of leaves or something, except not really leaves, just a design.

The house was in a nice neighborhood, out near Audubon Park, so the people must be rich, but there was something real different about these white folks. The house was different, for one thing—it

153

was real, real big, but cozy, with those same rugs on the floor, the ones that looked all worn out, but these had bigger designs in them, not all those little flower-dy things. And there was some silver here and there, and a little bit of crystal, but most things looked like crockery—ceramic, she thought it was called—or were made out of bright-colored glass, all fancy designs. The furniture was kind of worn, too, like the rugs, and the pillows and things were great, huge, old-fashioned flower prints, like in old movies, or those Hawaiian shirts white men like to wear.

Dorise had just never seen a house like it. She wanted to go get Shavonne and move right in.

And the *people* at this party! Some of them were just regular white folks, little-bitty skirts and great big jewelry on the women; suits and ties for the men; but a lot of them looked like movie stars, or anyway like they just blew in from California. They had on denim vests and they were bare-legged, with good tans, and little catlike glasses, and strange shawl kinds of things, and jewelry that looked as if it had been made by Indians or Africans—turquoise and amber, stuff like that. There were two men with completely shaved heads, one white, one black, and the black one was gorgeous. He could have been Michael Jordan, for all Dorise knew.

Maybe he's my secret admirer, she thought. *Maybe he's seen me somewhere, and he's the one who leaves the little things for Shavonne.*

She smiled at someone across the room and mouthed, "Hello, darlin'," more or less just so she could smile to herself and not look like a lunatic. "Secret Admirer" was just a game she played with herself. She was pretty sure she knew who left the Christmas stocking, and the JazzFest T-shirt, and the little House of Blues souvenir that time. Once she had seen her. She knew it was a white woman, a big one, and she knew the candy wasn't poisoned or anything, because she was pretty sure what it was all about. She just didn't meet it head-on, kept it on kind of a back burner so she wouldn't have to think about it, instead playing this game with herself.

My secret admirer loves me so much he knows the way to my heart is through my child.

My secret admirer is handsome and rich and plays football for the Saints—but he can't declare himself because first he must make me love him for himself.

My secret admirer will buy me the best house in Eastover, and Suzanne Nickerson will come to my parties.

Suzanne Nickerson was here, at this party. She was the gorgeous anchorwoman Dorise had met before and who was more or less her idol. "How you, darlin'?" Dorise said and Nickerson said, "Hello there—nice to see you again," just as if she meant it, as if she remembered Dorise, and she was so nice Dorise thought she really did, no matter what her sister said about her being just the help.

There was dignity in being the help. It was honest work, and the Bible praised honest work.

Just to make the party complete, a fine-looking man even talked to her. She was passing a tray of crawfish beignets, and he said, "You have the prettiest smile. I was noticing the way you say hello to everybody."

"I like meeting people," she said. "It's my favorite part of the job."

He waved a denim-clad arm in a wide, careless arc, nearly upsetting her tray of goodies. "*These* people? My God. You enjoy meeting *these* people?"

She saw he wasn't nice. He was just a bitter white man trying to make himself feel better by talking to a black person, thinking he was giving her some kind of crumb of charity because he probably felt inferior to these people. He was probably an unpublished poet, or a music critic who never made it as a musician. Or—maybe this was it—the husband of somebody good. An artist, maybe, or even a doctor or lawyer. A bitter, pathetic little man who had tried to drag her down with him.

When she got to the Michael Jordan–looking guy, he said, "Hey, baby. Lookin' good," and in its way, it was more polite. He didn't think she looked any better than anybody else, and probably not nearly as good as that skin-and-bones white woman hanging on him, but he said what he said to make her feel good, not him. There was thoughtfulness in that.

And all the women were nice. These weren't those little tongue-clucking flutterbies like at that brunch that made her so mad she'd told Troy about it.

Dear Jesus, is that what I did? Did I tell him so he'd do what he did? Is it my fault that poor little dog died?

"Dorise? Dorise, watch out." The hostess had seen her about to run into a table, nearly bruising her leg and sending little balls of cholesterol all over the living room.

As she caught her balance, got her bearings, she happened to glance out the window and see Troy Chauvin waiting for her in a black Trans-Am.

The hair on her forearms stood up. She thought, *Lord Jesus strike me dead if I ever look at a man again. Any man. Ever. Just get that Troy Chauvin out of my life and I promise to dedicate my life to the church.*

● ●

Lovelace was sitting outside at the Cafe Marigny, working on a cappuccino and trying to get up her nerve when this guy with a puppy came by. It was a little brown-spotted puppy, totally irresistible. She bent down and held out her hand for it to lick, not even looking at the guy. She was patting the puppy's head when he said, "Mind if I join you?"

She looked up at him. Cute. Brown hair, brown eyes. Preppy-looking. Almost certainly gay. "Sure," she said. And they talked.

His name was Larry, he was from Connecticut, and he'd been living with this crazy girl who read the tarot in Jackson Square, but she'd thrown him out on account of the puppy. Not gay, Lovelace noted, and suddenly wasn't sure she wanted male attention. She wondered if the guy was hustling her for a place to stay.

But then he said he'd moved in with his brother, and that was even better because he realized the girl didn't have all her marbles anyway. "Do you have all your marbles?" he asked.

She laughed and then considered the reality, which wasn't even slightly funny. "I'd run like hell if I were you. There's not one sane person in my whole family."

"You must be Southern."

"Oh, don't be so superior." He really had no idea. Nobody could.

"So what are you doing here? Do you work in a restaurant?"

She started. It was like he was reading her mind, almost.

He said, "It's daytime, which is work time. Ergo, you must be a night worker. Like me."

"What do you do?"

"Open oysters at Remoulade. But really, I'm writing a book."

Lovelace murmured, "Aren't they all," and was instantly ashamed of herself. "I'm sorry. I don't know why I said that."

He shrugged. "It's true. Everybody is. What's yours about?" His hair was curly and long, and he had incredible dimples.

"I'm not quite that ambitious. I just want to cook."

"Is this a proposal?"

She felt herself go pink. "More like a plea. They don't have any jobs at Remoulade, do they?"

"Ah. So you just arrived in town. Do you have a place to stay?"

She nodded. "With my uncle. I was doing temp work but—"

"Bleeeah."

"Yeah. I couldn't hack it. And I really am a very good cook. I did it in high school. Of course, that was just a pizza kind of thing, but I'm not kidding, I can do it."

"Hey, I don't own the joint. And I don't think it's the kind of place we could sneak you into with no experience." He seemed to be taking her on as a project.

"Do you know a place where we could?"

He looked off somewhere in the distance. "I'm thinking."

"Why would you help me?"

"Because you're cute."

"Oh, please."

"And because you need me. You have a sad look around your mouth. A little bit sad and a little bit worried. You're too old for a runaway, though. Tell ol' Larry—what's the matter?"

"Well, how about you? You look like some refugee from the Wharton School of Business. What are you doing opening oysters?"

"Trying to keep from cutting my fingers off."

She had met guys like this before. They never told you anything personal—even where they were from, sometimes, and they held you at bay as if with a shield. Like you were the enemy.

It's not a bad way to be, she thought. *I can do it—I'm quick on my feet. I just never needed to. Lovelace Jacomine, Woman of Mystery. That's me.*

As if on cue, Larry said, "If I'm going to rescue you, could I trouble you for your name?"

"I didn't tell you? Jacqueline." Damn! She hadn't had time to think and her mother's name had popped out. "Jackie Daniel." Her mother's and her dad's—at least it was a name she could remember. "Did you say you're going to rescue me?"

"I've got a friend who works in a place near here. Let's go check her out."

It was just a neighborhood restaurant—a pasta and gumbo kind of place—but that would be fine. Larry sent word that he was waiting in the dining room, and in a moment a flushed, harried-looking woman came through the swinging door. She was older than Lovelace and Larry—older by about fifteen years, but very pretty except for a few too many pounds. Her black hair curled in natural ringlets and her face, red with the heat, was round and sensual.

Larry said, "Hey, baby," and his tone was very different from the tone he used with Lovelace. "I brought you something."

The woman looked at Lovelace, and Lovelace knew she was either sleeping with Larry or wanted to be. She wished she could drop through the floor.

"What do I do with it?"

"Wind it up and it cooks."

"You cook, darlin'?" She put one hand on her hip and flashed sharp-looking teeth in what passed for a smile. Lovelace hoped she'd had her rabies shot.

"I, uh . . ."

"Hey, Barb, just give her a chance." Now Larry was uncomfortable, having belatedly realized what a faux pas he'd made.

"Sure, sweetheart, anything for you. What's your name, baby?"

"Jackie."

"Welcome to Marino's. Go in the back and get an apron and meet me in the kitchen. What can you do, by the way?"

Lovelace shrugged. "Anything, really."

It was filthy in the back. She was pretty sure she smelled rat shit, and, worse, something dead. The dead smell was a ripe, meaty odor that reminded her at first of a butcher shop. It was stronger in the kitchen.

She came back, still tying her apron. "What's that smell?"

Barb shrugged. "Damned rat stuck in the walls—it's happened twice this month. You know how to make gumbo?"

"Sure." *With a recipe. For eight people, not thirty or forty.*

"My ... how you say ... *saucier* didn't come in yesterday or today. I was telling Larry at breakfast—I guess that's why he thought of you."

Breakfast. That explained his faraway look back at the coffee-house. He was trying to figure out if he could get away with this.

I could walk out, she thought. But she didn't quite know how.

"We usually go through about fifteen gallons a day. You'll find vegetables over there and everything else. . . . Carlton'll show you. Carlton? Help Miss Priss, will you?"

Carlton was an amiable-seeming guy who didn't seem to give too much of a damn about his job—or about anything else, for that matter. He was smoking a cigarette that had an inch-long ash on it.

Lovelace said, "I'm going to need a recipe."

"Luis doesn't use a recipe."

"He must use a recipe."

"Hell, honey, just cut up all the onions you can find. Then cut up all the peppers. Then we'll talk, okay?"

The smell of dead meat was getting stronger. It had a sweetness to it that she hadn't noticed at first.

"Where are the food processors?"

He looked at her empty hands. "You don't have no tools?"

"No."

"What's wrong with Miss Barb, anyhow?" He looked around to see if Barb had heard, but she was nowhere to be seen. She was probably outside laying into Larry.

"You don't have food processors?"

"Sure, we have food processors. But you gon' need knives, too, aren't you?"

Grumbling, Carlton found Lovelace some knives, while she became increasingly aware of a visceral reaction to the stench. She hoped the onions would drown it out, but it never came to that. By the time she had a nice pile of onions and peppers ready to put through the processors, she was so nauseated she didn't know if she could make it to the back door, which looked like the best bet for an exit.

She ran for it, and stood there retching with the dry heaves.

Carlton said, "You sick, girl? What the fuck's wrong with you?"

The back door gave onto a courtyard where they kept the garbage. The smell was almost worse here than inside, and there was no way out. She had to go back through the kitchen, and then the restaurant proper to escape.

As she streaked through, she was dimly aware of Barb and Larry sitting at a table holding hands.

She heard Barb say, "What the hell?" and then she heard footsteps behind her.

"Jackie. Jackie, stop a minute."

She was running as if The White Monk were chasing her again, crook in hand; as if her dad were behind her. Only this time it felt good because there was nothing to worry about, and she was putting yards between herself and the dead thing.

Larry got to her first. "What's wrong, Jackie? What happened?"

"I got sick. The thing in the wall."

He looked bewildered, but by that time Barb had caught up. "Oh, shit. The rat. I know how she feels."

"What?"

Between ragged breaths, starting to sob a little, Lovelace explained.

"Barb, that's disgusting."

"You brought her over. I didn't ask."

"You said you were desperate without Luis."

"Oh, shit."

Lovelace started walking.

"Hey, Jackie. Wait." Larry grabbed her arm. "Hey, Barb. She just got to town. I was trying to help."

"Yeah? Well, you're a hero. You and Miss Sorority House have a nice afternoon in bed."

Lovelace had to laugh. "You're like Tom Jones or somebody."

"Picaresque hero, that's me. Listen, I'm sorry. I wanted to help you."

"I think you wanted to fuck me."

160

"No, really. How can I make it up to you?"

"You can't. 'Bye now."

"Listen, I was trying to help you. Don't you get that?"

"Nobody can help me."

"What do you need? Just tell me what you need."

He had fallen into step beside her, which meant she couldn't even go back to Isaac's without leading him there. She wasn't sure how to get rid of him, and besides, he was seriously cute. So she told him. "I need a reference. You think Barb's going to give me one?"

"A reference?"

"So I can get a *good* job."

"A reference? That's all you want?" He started laughing.

"What's so funny?" They had now reached the Cafe Marigny, where they'd met, and she sat down again.

"I'll give you a reference."

She stared at him.

"Tell them to call Remoulade and ask for me. They won't know I wasn't your supervisor."

It could work. She was pretty sure it could work.

"You'd do that for me?"

"Of course. I like you a lot."

She wasn't sure the feeling was mutual, but she really did need a reference. She ended up giving him her phone number.

She went home, sat in The White Monk's pristine white living room, and worked up the nerve to call the number in the ad, the one for a family of four that needed a low-fat cook.

"Jacqueline? What a lovely name." The voice that answered, a woman's voice, was husky and warm, almost intimate; one of those voices that might have been trained but probably wasn't; that probably made men propose on hearing it. "When can you come over?"

"I—well . . . now if you like; tomorrow. Whatever's good for you."

"Could you really come now? My husband'll be home and you need to meet him. Oh—I guess I should ask . . . what's your experience?"

"Well, I . . ."

"No, don't tell me. Let's meet first." She spoke slowly and

sounded impossibly sophisticated. Her name was Brenna Royce and her husband was "with" a shipping company, though for all Lovelace knew he was a deckhand.

She lived in the Garden District, which, according to Brenna, could be reached by streetcar. "You know it?" Brenna asked.

"I'm afraid not."

"Good God, you're even newer here than we are. Well, get your passport and hurry on down."

As the streetcar began to pass absolutely improbable mansions, mansions as large as a normal city block, it seemed, Lovelace got an idea what Brenna meant. It was a foreign country and not only on an economic level—it just didn't look like America, certainly not like your average burb in, say, south Florida, where her mom lived.

Lovelace found the Royce home behind an intricate iron lace fence, a gracious, curving, columned structure painted a sort of muted peach color, so that it managed to look both exuberant and stately at once. She was almost afraid to ring the bell.

She expected a liveried maid to answer, someone out of the nineteenth century, but the woman who did was clearly the lady of the house. She was anything but what Lovelace expected, much younger for one thing. She was blond and oddly voluptuous—that is, she had one of those bodies that women of the late twentieth century normally do not allow themselves, fleshy in a sexy way.

She wasn't thin, but she certainly wasn't fat. It's the kind of body, Lovelace thought, that you'd kill for if you weren't already too busy pumping iron. Brenna Royce looked like she'd never pumped iron a day in her life. She was blond and her hair looked as if it simply grew that way, but Lovelace wasn't that naïve.

All that might be expected. It was what she was wearing that was surprising—cotton elastic-waist pants, smeared T-shirt, and some kind of dust; lots of it. Something gooey in the blond hair. Brownish stuff on her nose.

She must be a potter, Lovelace thought.

"Jackie? Sorry, I was in my studio. Come in and I'll wash my face."

Lovelace stepped into the living room. She'd never seen anything like it. Nothing could disguise its stately proportions, but it was painted

162

white, new, and full of wonderful, dazzling contemporary things—art glass and paintings and metalwork and giant ceramics fired in some iridescent, incredibly elegant way. These were Brenna's work, Lovelace knew it.

She sat on a sofa that seemed to let her sink about a foot and a half. Brenna returned, hair loose, face clean, a cigarette in her hand—which partially explained the voice, Lovelace thought.

"The boys are at soccer. They're just under junior high age—not vegetarians, I'm afraid. But Charles and I are. Would you mind making two separate menus?"

"No. Of course not." Brenna was acting as if she already had the job.

"There's Charles now." The door opened on a man who looked as if he drank too much, ate far too much, and smoked. He was losing his hair as well.

Not as beautiful as his mate. Not at all beautiful. But revoltingly rich, probably. He greeted Lovelace in a heavy, syrupy accent, and without further ado headed straight for the sideboard. He poured himself a drink without offering one to Lovelace and Brenna. He sat heavily on the couch, next to Lovelace and a little too close for comfort.

"What's your experience?" he said.

"I've always cooked."

He raised an eyebrow.

"I used to cook at home for my mom, and then I worked in a pizza restaurant, and then a sort of . . . soup and salad place—" this was a bald-faced lie "—and then Arnaud's."

"Arnaud's?" Both Royces spoke together.

"Sorry. Remoulade. Do you know it? It's a kind of spin-off of Arnaud's—a cafe, sort of."

Charles raised an eyebrow. "Why'd you leave?"

"Well, frankly, I haven't yet. I just thought I'd like this better. My boss knows I'm looking—would you like to call him?"

Charles Royce stared at his wife. "I'm intrigued. This one intrigues me."

She nodded. "I thought she might."

Lovelace had an odd moment of sensing something under wraps, as if they were talking about something other than her ability to cook. She thought she knew what it was and she didn't like it. But he turned back to her and said, "You're the first one yet with restaurant experience—could you handle a dinner party for thirty?"

"Thirty? I don't know. How about twenty-five?"

"Oh, hell, twenty's enough." He laughed, and for the first time, Lovelace realized he was young, that they were both young, about thirty-five probably. "We have two goals. We want to lose weight, and we want to feed our friends really well. You look as if you might be able to help us out."

"I'll bet I could. Why don't you give me a week's tryout?"

"We'll call you. We've got a couple of other people to see."

She was shocked. She was so sure she had it. They were acting like she was already hired.

It was only as she walked out the door and stumbled back to the street that that she realized how much she had invested in this. She'd love going to that house, working in those sophisticated rooms, talking to Brenna Royce.

Brenna was somebody she desperately wanted to know, and she even liked Charles, a little bit, kind of admired his lord-of-the-manor act. She was pretty sure there was a sense of humor lurking under it.

She absolutely couldn't believe she had to leave without the job. But, of course, they had to check her reference.

•   •

The Monk woke with an odd sense of foreboding. Foreboding and depression and maybe a little regret—that he'd let this lovely, strange, desperate young person into his life.

He had been so self-contained, so . . . dare he say it? Happy.

You know what? he thought. *I was happy. Now I know what happy is. What I used to be.*

He meditated on it.

Life had been so serene. So lean.

And then Lovelace.

Why hadn't he stayed out of her life? It was he who'd encouraged her to answer the damned ad. Why had he done such a stupid-ass thing?

164

If he hadn't, she wouldn't have gotten involved with that asshole, Larry.

She was glowing when she got home last night, bubbly almost, a condition that normally put him off. But her happiness made him happy—that was the problem. He felt what she felt. It was like he absorbed what was going on around him.

He had forgotten to lay down rules, and so she had given the asshole her phone number, and before he could say "don't," she invited him over and he came.

The Monk had done the only thing he could do—withdraw to his bedroom. But he heard their voices, quiet, normal, and then louder and louder.

"What are you doing?"

"Come on, baby. You know you need me."

The Monk instantly grasped the implied blackmail.

"Are you crazy?" Lovelace said. "I hardly know you."

"Oh, thank you so much, Larry. I think I'll just use you and toss you aside." His voice was like a twelve-year-old's.

The Monk thought it had a dangerous edge, too, but that would have been his own perception. He didn't know if Lovelace could take care of herself, but he certainly didn't want to behave like some interfering older brother.

In the end, he just walked to the door of his bedroom, opened it, and stood there with his crook in his hand.

Larry left, and Lovelace burst into tears.

The Monk didn't know whether she was crying because of what he'd done or not—maybe she was perfectly willing to barter her body—but she came to him and hugged him, and he knew it wasn't that. He recoiled—he couldn't bear to think of the germs she carried—and she was horrified at what she'd done, because she understood, he thought, and that shamed him.

She stepped back, crying, looking bewildered, and he had no idea what to do. He was perfectly clear, however, on what he *wanted* to do, and he did it—stepped back into his room and shut the door. He heard her crying for a long time afterward.

This morning his brain was a tangle of half-baked thoughts, all of them unhappy. He had encouraged her to apply for the job, and therefore she'd allied herself with Larry. But then he'd driven Larry away, and now she wouldn't get the job. On top of that, he'd hurt her feelings.

Yet he had to get to the gallery, he had to paint, he had to do the things he had to do. There were rules, and they were rules he'd made himself. He had to follow them, or the other thing would take over his brain.

It seemed as if a dark, fierce magnet, maybe even a spirit, were trying to hold him to his bed, stick him there like a wad of chewing gum, bitten and discarded.

It took all his strength to get out of bed, throw on a white robe, and slip quietly into the street.

The morning was overcast—sunlight would have been an insult on a day like today.

He was passing St. Anthony's Garden on his scooter when someone hailed him. "Hey! Whitey!"

Only one person called him Whitey—the other artist who wore white; the one who was black. They knew each other because of their clothing. They always nodded.

The Monk raised a hand and lowered it quickly, a salutation of sorts, but one that said, "Not now, if you don't mind."

"Whitey! Come here! I got somethin' to tell you."

The Monk kept going, but the traffic was heavy, and he couldn't get away fast enough.

The other artist was chasing him "Goddammit. Goddammit. Shit, man! I'm too old for this shit—I'm gon' have a heart attack."

Reluctantly, The Monk pulled his scooter over. "Listen to me, man. I got somethin' to tell you. A woman's lookin' for you."

The Monk closed his face and, as well as he could, his brain and his ears. One woman was more than enough.

"She says she's a cop."

He shrugged his shoulders and pointed to his chest. "Me?"

"They want a white dude dressed in white. Think you an artist. Hey. You an artist, brother?"

The Monk stopped and nodded slightly, raising a hand again, like a priest, to acknowledge the warning. It was as close as he got to saying thanks.

"Shit, Whitey, you sho' is trouble. I don' know why the fuck I bother." He headed back to his spot.

The cop wanted Lovelace. The Monk knew hardly anyone, talked to no one at all, and had broken no laws. Therefore the cop wanted Lovelace.

Fear clawed at The Monk's stomach, squeezed at his chest. He ducked around the corner, where no one could see him, and dropped to the curb, taking in air, finding his center.

When he had stopped hyperventilating and could breathe once again from the diaphragm, some oxygen finally got to his brain, along with a good shot of adrenaline. His mind raced.

This was about his father. Daniel had kidnapped Lovelace for his father—why, The Monk had no idea—but somehow the cops had found out. They thought, perhaps, that Lovelace would lead them to Errol.

More likely they'd lead him to her.

It would mean breaking the rules, but he couldn't go to the gallery now. He had to go home.

Lovelace was gone when he got there.

15

• •

Lovelace was humiliated at the way she'd acted. She should never have asked Larry over, should have been more respectful of Isaac's space. And she should never, ever have tried to hug her uncle; she knew how he'd take it, she could sense it. He'd probably had to stay up half the night taking showers.

She was also depressed. She wasn't going to get the job, that was obvious. The Royces were going to call Remoulade and ask for Larry, and he was going to say he'd never heard of her—if, in fact, he worked there at all. It occurred to her that he might not, since he'd tried to collect on his fabulously generous gift before she even had a chance to claim it.

She lay in bed, on the futon The Monk had bought for her, cheeks flaming because she'd been so stupid, tears flowing because she had no prospects, unable to budge. She heard her uncle open the door and slip out, which was unlike him. Usually she could hear him making breakfast. Clearly he didn't want risk her waking up, didn't want to see her or speak to her; probably just wanted her out of there.

She would have stayed in bed all morning, except that she had to pee so bad. Isaac had the only bathroom on his side of the door he had so abruptly closed the night before.

Once she was up, she saw that it was overcast, but there was a lot of humidity, and that excited her, made her blood flow. She might as well go get some coffee—but at PJ's, not Cafe Marigny. The last person she wanted to see was Larry.

As the caffeine entered her bloodstream, she began, against all odds, to feel optimistic. She bought a *Times-Picayune* and looked at the ads.

It isn't the end of the world, she thought. *I can apologize. I can simply say I'm sorry and we can go from there. If he wants me to go, I can . . . what? Borrow money from Michelle. I can just call her up and get her to send some and then check into a cheap hotel. I can go back to doing temp work.*

There were ads for sales jobs, some in good stores; even one in a little gallery. Maybe one of those. That might be better than filing. The Royces' ad was still running. She felt it pull on her. Was there a chance Larry wouldn't sell her out?

None, she thought.

I could do a free tryout. Why don't I just call them before they have a chance to call him? Why don't I say I'd be glad to work a week, free, and see what they say. Who could resist an offer like that?

While the fit was on her, before she had a chance to think it over, she found a phone and called. "Mrs. Royce? Jackie Daniel."

Brenna spoke before she had a chance to finish. "Jackie. We've been trying to call you. Someone picked up the phone, but didn't say anything. Are you home?" She opened her mouth to answer, but Brenna kept talking. "We want to offer you the job."

"You do?" Surely it couldn't be real.

"We like your credentials and we like you. When would you like to start?"

Real or not, she was going for it. "How about tomorrow?" It would take her a day to get some cookbooks, get some recipes together.

"Fabulous. It's Saturday—the kids will be home."

All she could think about was telling Isaac. If he wanted her to leave, she'd leave, but she had to tell him. He was odd; he was a very peculiar man, but she thought that, deep down, he had affection for her. After all, he'd kept in touch all those years. And he was the only one in the world who'd understand what this meant to her. Michelle was the only other choice, and she couldn't possibly relate to it.

The thought shocked her. It seemed about a century since she'd left Evanston. She was a different person now.

Michelle was a cosseted college girl who had parents to take care of her—and who couldn't begin to understand what it meant to have to fend for yourself.

Lovelace hadn't even taken a shower, had just pulled on shorts and a T-shirt (for which Isaac had given her money on her first day in New Orleans). She went home to get ready to face the day, to plan meals, to think about parents who were vegetarians and children who weren't.

Someone had been there. She knew it as soon as she entered the house, though what signals she read she never figured out. All she knew was, the hair on the back of her neck stood up.

She backed out of the house, and when she locked the door, it occurred to her she'd had to unlock it to get in, but she didn't stop to analyze; she just ran.

Isaac wasn't at the gallery. That terrified her still more.

She couldn't call the police. That was the last thing she could do.

Isaac had told her about Revelas. Perhaps she could get him to go back to the house with her. But she found her knees were weak, and she couldn't face it, couldn't talk quite yet. Maybe if she went back to the house . . .

No. Not that.

She went outside to try to get her bearings, think what to do. Someone touched her arm—a bald, clean-shaven man in jeans and a black T-shirt.

She gasped and pulled away. "Get away from me."

The man laughed and pointed to his eye, then his chest: I. Me.

"Isaac?" she said. The man looked like a pirate.

He nodded and gave her the come-here sign. They walked together to La Marquise, where he borrowed a pen and began to write.

"The police are looking for me—but they want you, I think."

"You were the one at the house."

"I heard you come in, but I couldn't catch you. I was cleaning up after this." He touched the top of his head.

"I don't understand."

"They were looking for a guy in white—with hair and a beard, I presume. What do you think of the new look?"

"How can you be The White Monk without your robes?"

He shrugged. "Monks have shaved heads. Listen, they must know what you look like, too. You need to turn into a brunette or something."

"But . . . what'll the Royces think?"

"The Royces?"

"Oh, Uncle Isaac, I forgot to tell you! I got the job."

"That's wonderful. What's wrong with a dark-haired cook?"

"I can't be a whole different person from the one they met."

"Lovelace, listen. I think this involves my dad. Do you realize how serious that is? He's a murderer."

In the end there was nothing to do but what he said. He gave her money, and she called hair salons until she found one that would take her. When she came out, she was nearly as bald as Isaac, with a quarter-inch or so of crow-black hair, like a gutter-punk.

It did cause comment at the Royces'.

Brenna said, "Jackie? Jacqueline?" as if she weren't sure. "Kind of a new look?"

Lovelace couldn't help laughing at the way she was trying to be tactful. She said, "Awful, isn't it? I could just kick myself. A couple of girlfriends were doing it and they talked me into it."

"I'm glad you didn't look like this the day before yesterday. Charles is waay conservative." She rolled her eyes, then she leaned back and gave Lovelace a long, assessing look, an artist summing up a subject. "But I kind of like it. You have great bones, you know that?"

A boy of about ten came into the kitchen. "What's for lunch?"

"Tim, can't you say hello? This is Jackie."

"Hey, Tim. How about a burger?"

The kid's eyes widened. "You've got to be kidding."

The other kid came in for a burger as well. Paul, his name was. Both of them were blond cherubs, as skinny as their dad was chubby. Bottomless pits. Next time she'd make fries to go with the

171

burgers, and maybe a pie for dessert. She gave the adults some salad and vegetable soup she'd made at home, and then she started making a list for dinner.

Brenna came in again. "We just asked some friends over for tonight. Could you manage four?"

Lovelace shrugged, feeling in control. "It's just as easy as two."

"How about six?"

"Sure, no problem. Want me to make anything special?"

"Whatever you want. And could you stay to serve it? We'll pay overtime, of course. And cab fare home."

"I'll be glad to." Lovelace was liking this a lot. "How about something Asian? Japanese, maybe."

"Perfect."

She grilled salmon with teriyaki sauce, served some rice and spinach on the side and a few other little tidbits—what could be simpler? Not being really up to speed yet, she gave the kids macaroni and cheese. But the Royces acted like they'd discovered gold, and she was it.

She enjoyed the work, but she absolutely basked in the admiration. She was deeply in love.

She liked their friends, too—a psychiatrist and her husband, who was a house painter; a math teacher and his wife, who was a fund-raiser.

What enormously normal people they all were. And fun. After dinner, they went into the living room and put on old R&B albums and danced.

Lovelace couldn't believe people could live like this.

●　　●

It took Daniel a long time to get over being angry. At first he couldn't believe his father could pull something like that—springing a long-gone mother on him—but in the end, he had to admit it was exactly the sort of thing he would do. How could you be mad at a person for being who he was? Besides, as his dad would say, he had bigger fish to fry.

"Why, Daddy?" he had asked. "Why'd you call her? Why'd you make me get on the phone with her?"

172

"Well, I think she might just be an asset to the movement. What do you think?"

"What do I think? I think you must be out of your mind—with all due respect, sir."

He was mad enough to speak like that, but he knew his father was going to hit him. He was braced for it and he didn't care. This mother thing was not an everyday occurrence.

When Errol just laughed, threw back his head and guffawed bigtime, that was when Daniel began to doubt his father's sanity. Something about this woman robbed him of his senses.

"I'm going to go see her, son."

"What do you mean you're going to go see her? Police in fifty states are looking for you."

"The lady lives in Dallas and I'm going there. They got this kind of VIP room in the airport. We're just gonna meet there—I'll fly in, fly out, nothing to it."

"If someone recognizes you, you're dead—and so is the movement."

"Who's gonna recognize me? I'll just be another dude in a baseball cap and shades." He hee-hawed again, and it was enough to make Daniel throw up. The Reverend Errol Jacomine in a baseball cap! Hell seemed to have frozen over.

He got Daniel to make the travel arrangements, booking him under the name Mark Matthews, after two of the Gospels. And as if that weren't enough, he made Daniel go with him under John Luke. "You don't," he said, "expect me to go without a bodyguard, do you, son?"

"Daddy, you know I can't take a gun on that plane."

"You're going have to do the best you can. Be a troubleshooter for me."

"You need to get Pete Joseph to do that. He'd be better—he'd have a clearer head. I'm a little foggy about this one."

"You're going, boy. Don't even think about getting out of it."

The idea was, the woman—that was how Daniel thought of her—would meet Daddy in the airport. Daniel would get him to some VIP lounge kind of shit and say his name, and some flunky would whisk him to some private room where the woman would meet him.

Daniel had never been in one of those VIP kinds of things. It turned out this one wasn't strictly private. He got his daddy in and took him to a bar where there were tables that looked out on the runway. The woman was sitting at one, and he was astonished at how pretty she was.

His daddy said, "Come meet your mama, son."

"No way."

"Come on, goddammit."

"I'll just sit over there and keep an eye on y'all."

He ordered a beer and tried to focus on landings and takeoffs. But they were laughing loudly. They were fucking billing and cooing. For the second time where she was concerned, he thought he was going to throw up.

After about an hour, he went and found a television and watched it. When his dad came over, he had the woman with him. Daniel stuck out his hand and said, "Hello, Mrs. Owens."

She tried to hug him, but he backed away, knowing there were going to be consequences. But his dad was in such a good mood he didn't even get mad. When they were on the next plane back to New Orleans, his dad said to him, "Son, how would you like your mama back?"

"It's a little late for that, isn't it?"

"Now, son, the Lord says to forgive. I have forgiven her and I want you to do it, too. I think she could be a real asset to our movement. She believes in the kinds of things we're doing."

"Daddy, you *told* her? You told her what we're trying to do?"

"Shit, the whole world knows about The Jury. I just told her we're it, that's all."

"She could be working for the fuckin' FBI for all you know."

"Well, she's not. She's with us. Lot of folks are with us. You got to get some confidence, boy."

"How the hell could she help us?"

"She's got money, Daniel. We could use some of that, couldn't we?"

"Daddy, you're living in a dream world, you know that? That woman's nothing to do with us."

"Don't talk that way about your mother."

16

• •

The best Skip could do was get the FBI to tap Rosemarie Owens's phone. She wanted a full-time tail on her, but they wouldn't go for it. "Why not?" she ranted. "Why the hell not?"

Shellmire shrugged. "They don't think it's worth it. They think it's grasping at straws."

"Well, what else are we going to grasp at?"

"Hey, I just work here."

She started calling on all the art galleries in town, asking if anyone knew an artist who wore white and had a beard. There were nearly two hundred listings in the New Orleans phone book, but a surprising number proved to be antique stores. That might have narrowed it down, but plenty of gallery owners knew dealers or reps who worked out of their homes, people who weren't listed in the book, but who knew plenty of local artists whose work had to get sold. Everywhere, she had to say the same thing: No, she didn't know what kind of art he did. He could be a glassblower, he could be into graffiti. All she knew was, he wore white, and maybe he didn't talk much. Everybody said if he wore black and wouldn't shut up, they could probably help her.

Shellmire called the Wednesday after she'd talked to Rosemarie Owens. "Any luck?"

"Not yet. You?"

"Not exactly. But something funny's happened."

She didn't like the tone of his voice. It sounded . . . what? Sheepish. "Oh, no. Something bad, you mean."

"It might have nothing to do with the case."

"Come on, what is it?"

"Rosemarie Owens's husband has turned up dead."

"Dead? What kind of dead?"

"Suicide, maybe. He fell off a balcony."

"Pretty damn suspicious."

"Yeah, well. That's what I said."

"When did it happen?

"Last night. The Dallas police have already talked to Rosemarie."

"And let her go?"

"Hell, she wasn't even in town. She was in Atlanta with some friends."

"Damn convenient."

"Yeah." He sounded a little sulky.

"Anything from the wiretap?"

"Nothing."

"I guess we weren't soon enough."

"Now, Skip, don't get your panties in a bunch about this."

"Don't you dare talk to me that way."

"Just don't get excited. Maybe he was remorseful about the way he treated her. Or maybe he got loaded and fell."

"Turner, will you do me a favor? Get the damn twenty-four-hour tail on her?"

"I think that can be arranged. Sure. We got their attention now."

She could practically see him grinning. She grinned back, though neither could see the other. But as she hung up the phone, she started to think about what this meant.

It's my fault. Goddammit, it's my fault.

She got Steve to take her to a movie that night, and afterward she didn't want to go home. She wanted to go in the Blacksmith Shop and drink awhile.

They talked about the movie and Steve's project and Layne's miraculous cure. They didn't say one word about The Jury, or Jacomine, or Rosemarie Owens. She didn't want to think about it until she had to.

Because it was only a matter of waiting. If she was right, she'd know soon enough.

The next morning Roger Owens's death was splashed all over the paper, with pictures of the tearful Other Woman, the young model who'd succeeded Rosemarie, and a summary of Roger's accomplishments on the planet Earth, which he'd apparently devoted his life to destroying.

Shellmire's call came around noon: "The Dallas police got a letter."

"The Jury?"

He sighed. "They're faxing it over. You'd better come into the office."

In a way, it was like the others, especially so far as the rhetoric went: The Jury wanted justice and couldn't get it through conventional means. Roger Owens was the kind of man who gave philanderers a bad name. Politicians talked about family values to stir up working-class people, while the fat cats who really ran the country, the ones at the top, did anything they damn well felt like, and got their pictures in People magazine. And that was only the tip of the iceberg.

Global Operations Ltd., which Roger had founded and of which he was the CEO, was the biggest polluter in the world today, having strip-mined thousands of acres in seventeen countries and dumped toxic gunk in every river in every one of those countries. Along with exploiting the land, Global had exploited the poor, paying slave wages under life-threatening conditions, and causing more deaths each year than cancer. He was as much a murderer as Hitler or Idi Amin, yet because of his connections, and because of his money, Owens would never be convicted of anything, let alone punished for it.

"Well?" said Shellmire.

"Shit. Just shit."

"What's that supposed to mean?"

Skip didn't answer. Though she'd done nothing wrong, though

she'd call Rosemarie Owens again, if she could turn the clock back, she was too mad at herself to say anything.

"The guys here don't think it's genuine."

She nodded. "It looks like a copycat. It definitely looks like one. It isn't a criminal justice issue. That's what The Jury's supposed to be into, right? Is that how they're reading it?"

"You got it. This one's all over the map—feminism, environmentalism, you name it. I mean, Owens might have been a bad guy—sounds like he was a kissin' cousin to the Prince of Darkness—but it doesn't feel right. The other issues were cut-and-dried, more or less. At the risk of sounding crazy myself, they were easy to identify with. Popular causes."

"Yeah."

"Is that all you've got to say?"

"The letter is genuine, Turner. I swear to God the thing's genuine. Jacomine killed him for his lady love. Avenged her honor, so to speak."

"Bullshit."

"For a price, Turner, for a price. He's going to try to collect it now. And that's where we come in."

"Would you mind telling me what you're talking about?"

"Listen, have you met Rosemarie Owens?"

"No."

"Well, I've talked to her on the phone, and Jacomine may well have met his match. I tipped her unwittingly—she was ready for him when he called. With a tiny little errand for him to run."

"Wait a minute, now. Hold it. You're a good cop—therefore you didn't tell her he's a suspect in the Jury case."

"No, I just got her to thinking. She had to know he was already a murder suspect. And let me tell you, she's the kind of woman who gives hard bitches a bad name. I'm telling you she got him to kill hubby—by the way, they're not divorced yet—I'll bet she still inherits. But I doubt she actually hired him. They probably just had a nice, friendly talk—real gentlemen's agreement kind of thing. Terms probably weren't even slightly spelled out. But I'll bet Jacomine got the idea a lot of Owens's dirty money might just make its way into his hands if he did his old girlfriend a good turn. Who knows?

Maybe she's going to join up with him—maybe they're the new Barrow gang."

• •

Daniel had rarely seen his father so exuberant. "Things are going great, son. Things are going our way."

Daniel usually stood while his father sat. Today he sat, too. His dad was in too good a mood to complain, for one thing. For another, he felt deflated. Depressed about the way things were going; not at all in agreement with his father.

"Daniel, boy, you want your little girl back?"

"Daddy, you know I do. I'd like to work on that now." That was the closest he dared come to saying what he meant: *I haven't had a spare second, goddammit. I couldn't look for her because I've been too busy gratifying your damn teenage crush.*

"I'm very happy with the way things are going. Aren't you?"

No.

But he said, "The Bazemore hit was real important."

His dad only nodded. It was impossible to rile him today. "Yeah. The Owens thing too. We have done a lot of very important work. For a while now, there'll be no more killing."

"I think that's a good idea."

"We're in tune, boy. We're right in tune." His father just kept nodding and smiling. "Now we've got two projects to do here in New Orleans. Then we're gon' move on. First thing is to get our little family back together. We're gonna find Lovelace and get her to come join us. The second thing is, we're gonna pop a six-foot blister on our hiney."

"Say what?"

"Did I ever mention those run-ins I had with a fat, nasty bitch of a cop in this town?"

"Oh, yeah. Once or twice. Also, it was in *Time* and *Newsweek* and everywhere else."

His father laughed. "Sometimes I can't remember just how far our little movement's come. You do me good, Danny. You know that, boy?"

Daniel was nearly bowled over. His father had never even come close to suggesting such a thing. Maybe Rosemarie Owens was good for him. But he caught himself—good for his dad's mood, bad for the movement.

"Okay, here's your assignment. Find your daughter, Lovelace. Devote twenty-four hours a day to that little job, and if I tell you to do anything else, tell me to go to hell. Now, we had to do those other jobs—they were priority one. But if anything else important comes up, we're gon' just let it go for a while. It's time to regroup, and that's exactly what we're gon' do.

"Okay, got your assignment?"

Daniel nodded, happy to be doing something he knew he could do and had no ambivalence about.

"Now before you go, let me ask you a question. Who's the best-looking young Christian African American we got in our flock?"

"Why, Daddy?"

"Just answer the question, goddammit."

"Well, I guess that'd be Dashan Johnson. Jericho, now. He changed his name to Dashan Jericho."

"Excellent choice. Excellent. Dashan's a nice tall boy, isn't he?"

"Yessir."

"Good. Women like 'em tall. Get Dashan on over here. And one other thing—soon's you get a chance, drive out to the country someplace and go to a hardware store. We're gonna need some dynamite and blasting caps."

Daniel knew better than to ask why. He just made time and did it.

17

• •

Lovelace was falling in love with Brenna Royce—not in a sexual way, of course—but she had taken her on as an idol. Brenna was beautiful, she was creative, she was a great mother, she had fabulous taste, she was wonderful to Lovelace . . . in fact, that could be her number-one good quality.

She couldn't say enough good things about Lovelace's cooking, and that was damn good for the ego, but it wasn't only that—she seemed to really like Lovelace. She was always making tea for the two of them and getting Lovelace to sit down and talk to her. Naturally, this had a down side, as Lovelace couldn't tell anyone except Isaac a single true thing about herself.

So she was evasive to untruthful. She said she lived alone, she'd had a couple of years of college at "a small midwestern school," she'd come to New Orleans to pursue a relationship that hadn't worked out, she was from Virginia, her mother was a schoolteacher, and her dad was dead.

In turn, she learned Brenna and Charles were both from Atlanta, had known each other practically forever and were more or less expected to marry each other. However, they hadn't. They'd each married someone else, and in each case it hadn't worked out.

And so they had remet and remarried.

Lovelace was charmed. "How romantic."

"Oh, I wouldn't say that."

Lovelace hardly knew how to answer. She could have said nothing, but it wasn't in her nature to leave it alone. The question of what these two were doing together had occurred to her more than once. She'd thought all along that Brenna was a much more interesting, much better-looking person than Charles. She said, "You didn't marry for love?"

Brenna looked mischievous. "Both our families have a lot of money."

Lovelace was still trying to grasp it. "But if you had money, and he had money, why did you need to get married? If you weren't in love, I mean."

She spread her open palms. "Our families wanted grandchildren, and we wanted to make them happy. That was one reason, anyhow."

Thinking she was getting the hang of it, Lovelace touched Brenna's hand. "I'm so sorry. I wish there were something I could do."

"Do I look unhappy?"

"No, but you deserve something special. You're such a fantastic person, you deserve to be adored."

"Do you really think so?"

"You're so fabulous. You've got your life under control like nobody I've ever seen. You're so creative and so beautiful. . . ."

Brenna leaned over to brush something off Lovelace's shoulder, or so Lovelace imagined, and wondered what it could be.

And then Brenna was kissing her. She absolutely hadn't seen it coming. If someone had shown her a video of it taken in the future, she still wouldn't have believed it.

Lovelace couldn't help noticing that Brenna was soft and smelled good, felt kind of the way a mother should feel, only Lovelace wouldn't know because Jacqueline hadn't really been around that much.

But she knew perfectly well there was nothing maternal about what was happening. She pried herself away, freed herself of Brenna's lips anyway, but not Brenna's hands.

Brenna's hair brushed Lovelace's neck and she felt Brenna's breath close to her ear. "It's okay, baby. It's okay. Just let it happen. Your job is fine. Charles won't know, and he's impotent, anyway. He'd just be happy you were making me happy. Come on, let's go upstairs. Come on, baby."

"No!" Lovelace sounded like a baby, even to herself.

Brenna broke away and looked at her, must have seen the fear and confusion in her face.

She turned hot-pink, obviously deeply embarrassed. But the embarrassment passed with the flush, giving way to a fine fury. "No? What do you mean no? You're the little seducer. Not me. Don't try to make this my doing."

"I . . . what?"

"That hair, for openers. As soon as you had the job, you went back to looking like your normal self. You might as well have broadcast, 'Baby dyke, looking to get laid. Hey, any takers? Here I am.' Charles and I laughed about it."

Lovelace was so astounded she didn't say a word. Later it occurred to her that her mouth may actually have been hanging open.

"And I'm so beautiful and I'm so fabulous. And you were in a 'relationship' with 'a friend.' No gender. Just a friend, to whom you always referred to as 'the other person.' I've been around a long time, baby, and I know a dyke when I see one."

Lovelace didn't answer. Couldn't think of a single thing to say. She looked around wildly for her purse, grabbed it, and made a quick, graceless exit.

She was lying on the sofa, hands crossed over her heart, staring at the ceiling when Isaac came in.

Seeing her, he started shaking his head, grasping instantly that something was badly wrong. He drew a question mark in the air.

She sat up. "You get right to the point."

He nodded and gave her the reverse wave that means "come on."

"Oh, Isaac, I'm such a fuckup. I loved this job."

He kept waving backward ever more frantically.

"Brenna Royce made a pass at me."

He wrinkled his face inquisitively, obviously meaning, *What the hell are you talking about?*

Lovelace thought he'd learned to communicate amazingly well without speaking. "She said I was the one seducing *her*, but I had no idea, I swear. I told her she's beautiful and fabulous because she is, but I had no idea she's a lesbian! She said she thought I am because I cut my hair."

He sat down and gave the backward wave again, making Lovelace tell the story exactly as it had happened, retelling everything Brenna said and everything Lovelace said.

When she had finished, he came to her and hugged her and said, "It's okay, honey. You couldn't have known it was going to happen. She was trying to convince herself, that's all. She got it into her head you were available, and then she interpreted data any way she wanted to. She told you it was your fault because she feels bad— she's embarrassed. But it *wasn't* your fault. She'll cool down and realize that. Do you want to go back? I'll bet you can."

Lovelace hugged back and let him rub her back, in shock, but not wanting to mention it for fear he'd notice he was talking and stop. He was talking *and* he was hugging—the same Isaac who'd so recently recoiled from her.

When he was finished, she stepped back, looked him in the eye, and rather idiotically told him what he'd done. "Isaac, you hugged me! You spoke to me. I don't believe what just happened. You must really care about me."

She wasn't really sure that was the case. But because she needed the human connection, she pulled him close and hugged him again. She could feel the fastidious contraction of his body; the moment was over.

● ●

That second time, The Monk would have given anything to wiggle away. Hugging was bad enough, but it was a lot worse when someone else initiated it. He could feel their need. He didn't want to be responsible for someone else's need.

And that was without even considering the danger of germ transfer. This was the point of his vows—to keep the human race at bay.

No sooner did the thought appear than he smashed it down.

Where the hell had that come from? The point of his vows was spiritual expansion.

This whole exchange was making him edgy. How dare Lovelace tell him how he felt?

Still, he was furious on her account. Better to focus on that so the anger wouldn't get misdirected. It wasn't her fault he hated human contact.

He said, "Don't be silly. You know I care about you. But don't make too big a thing of my speaking. I've rethought the vow, as it happens. I've decided to speak when I'm not confused—and I most certainly was not confused about this one.

"Look, in some ways, it's just one of those things. The woman never married for love in the first place, her husband's impotent, she just moved here, and you're the cutest thing in the world. Fine, but not your problem. If she's a lesbian, why doesn't she go to a lesbian bar? Or at least find someone her own age. It's just tacky, as these Southerners say, to jump the twenty-year-old cook. And if she's not a lesbian, but simply an opportunist, she's a shithead."

Lovelace laughed. "A shithead?"

"Look, you didn't *do* anything. The woman is a shithead, it's that simple. I forbid you to go back to that place."

Lovelace was still laughing.

"Uncle Isaac! You're so cute when you're really worked up." She blushed as soon as she said it. "Omigod, I hope you don't think . . . I only meant you're funny, I didn't mean anything else."

"Now she's got you feeling bad about yourself. *Goddammit!*"

"You're so human. I had no idea you'd be like this."

He didn't like her saying that. Whose business was it whether he was human or not?

He found a pad and wrote. "I am not human. Quit being such a bitch."

She laughed. "I guess you've always been funny. I just didn't notice because—I guess because it's different when you have a verbal exchange with someone."

And not in a good way, he thought. He wrote, "You're not going back there, are you?"

"How can I? My uncle forbade me." The laughter left her face. "No, I'm not. I wish I could rise above it, but it was just too embarrassing. I think it would be horrible for Brenna, too."

He wrote, "The hell with Brenna. But seriously. Back to Plan A."

"I don't think I recall a Plan A."

"I was going to get you a reference from my friend who used to run a juice bar. You could still get a restaurant job."

"I guess so."

But she looked downcast. He wasn't sure whether she no longer wanted a job or just didn't think she could get one.

"I'm going to call Anthony for you."

Her smile came back. "You'd call him? You'd really talk to him for me?"

For some reason that seemed important to her.

18

• •

Dorise loved two things about church. The most important one was the way it made her feel; as if every day were a clean slate, as if you really could start over every morning and all really was forgiven. In her heart of hearts, as she was lying in bed, tears running down her face, thinking of Delavon and how she didn't bother to find out enough about him to know he was dealing, thinking of Troy and that poor little dead dog, thinking of Shavonne and her nightmares, in the dead of night she didn't believe it. The next day after one of those nights, she still didn't believe it. But when Sunday morning came and that good feeling came over her, she believed it.

The second thing she liked was the music. She wished she had a good enough voice to sing in the choir. The choir in this church was a particularly fine one, and she wasn't good enough. But she enjoyed the hymns and put her whole heart and soul into singing with the congregation. This morning they were doing one of her favorites:

> *What a friend we have in Jesus,*
> *oh what needless pain we bear.*

All because we do not carry
Everything to God in prayer.

It's so true, she thought, and from now on I'm living by it. I'm not doing one thing, I'm not shooting my mouth off, I'm not so much as looking at a man until I've prayed about it.

She was feeling pure and clean and very pretty in a nice blue suit with black high heels as she went to get her chicken and rice dish, to warm it up for the buffet after the service. Shavonne was real pretty too, wearing her Easter dress again, a pretty pink one it took Dorise nearly an hour to iron. But she was sulky. "Mama, do we have to stay? I need to get home."

"What you need to get home for?"

"I got homework."

"Oh, yeaaah. Oh, yeaaah, you need to get home and do your homework. Now I ain't *never* heard that one before."

The girl stomped her foot. "I do."

"Don't you go stompin' your foot at me, and don't you go tellin' me somethin' be true that ain't. You know how long it take to do your homework, and you can just do it tonight instead of watching television."

Another little girl ran up, didn't even stop, just spoke on the fly. "Hey, Shavonne, come on. I got somethin' to show you."

And Shavonne went off, her impatience forgotten. Dorise thought, *I wish I was like that. Why can't I be like that? Lot to be said for bein' under twelve.*

She talked to her mother and her sister, and several women she knew, and then it was time for the buffet and the preacher said the blessing, which usually took him about twenty minutes to do.

When he had thanked the Lord for this beautiful spring day and the congregation's loving church fellowship, and everyone's husband and everyone's wife and everyone's children, and their collective health and the beautiful flowers that some of the ladies had brought, and the lovely music provided by the choir, and when he showed no sign at all of getting to the food, Dorise lifted her head and opened her eyes, just for a minute.

She thought she saw someone she'd never seen before, also

peeking, and she was so embarrassed she dropped her head quickly and peeked a little more discreetly. It was a man, a handsome man in a tan suit, with a pair of the broadest shoulders she'd ever seen, and his eyes were wide open. Looking at her.

No, it couldn't be. She closed her eyes again, and tried to concentrate on all the things the preacher was trying to remind her she ought to be thankful for. When the blessing was over, she refused to look at the place she'd thought she'd seen the man, and got herself a plate and went to get some food.

Somebody had brought greens and somebody else had brought squash, and there was ham and fried chicken, and gumbo if you wanted that, and some sweet potatoes, and lots and lots of different pies and cakes. But Dorise wasn't interested in sweets today. She thought she'd lose a little weight, and so she was thinking about vegetables. There were some nice-looking crowder peas, she saw, and she was about to head for them when she heard a man's voice, almost in her ear: "Is he always that long-winded?"

She almost dropped her plate. It was the stranger, and he was smiling at her. He was tall and very light-skinned, lighter even than Troy, and he looked like he could probably build a house by himself if he wanted to, or maybe lead the children of Israel into the promised land. He was the last kind of man she wanted to be any-where around right now, but she was in church—in the church building, anyway. It wouldn't be polite to pretend she hadn't heard.

She smiled and looked him in the eye. "Yeah. I'm 'fraid he is."

"Well, he does preach a nice sermon. I'm kind of lookin' around for a church; my aunt used to go here so I thought I'd try it."

"Are you new in town?"

"Umm-hmm. Just moved here from Monroe." He took a bite and said, "Oh, my heavens, you've got to try this. This has got to be the best thing I ever put in my mouth."

"Well, I made that, to tell you the truth. It's just this little thing I do with, uh, mushroom soup and stuff."

"My Lord, it's good."

He stuffed some more in his mouth, and Dorise finally got a chance to reach for the crowder peas. But when she had them on her plate, he was still there. "I'm Dashan Jericho, by the way."

"Dorise Bourgeois. We're mighty glad to have you here." She didn't ask him any questions about himself, made no attempt to keep the conversation going.

He said, "Have you been going here a long time?"

"Oh, about a year. Something like that."

"And you like it."

"Mmm-hmm. I especially like the choir." Very neutral. Maybe he'd move on soon.

"Well, like I said, I just moved from Monroe. I was with a law firm there, but when I got divorced, I got a good offer to come work for a firm down here, and it seemed like a good time to move."

"I sure hope you're going to be happy here."

"So far everybody's been real friendly. That's your little girl over there, isn't it? I don't think I've met your husband, though."

"Well, here's my mama. Mama, you met Dashan Jericho? He just moved here from Monroe."

"Why Mr. Jericho, you and your family are very welcome here."

"I'm afraid it's only me right now. I've got one little girl, about your granddaughter's age, but she's with her mother up in Monroe."

Dorise was so unnerved she went and cut herself a slice of coconut cake. She could slip away easily now—wander off in another direction—but leaving Dashan Jericho with her mother was like leaving a helpless rabbit with a great big friendly-looking hound. He wasn't going to know what hit him pretty soon, and neither was Dorise. He'd know everything about Dorise, down to how Delavon had died, and how well she could make a pecan pie, if she left the two of them alone for long. So she went back to rescue him.

He looked broken-hearted. "Oh, Ms. Bourgeois! I'm so very, very sorry I made that remark about your husband. Your mother told me you're a widow, and I feel the biggest fool. You must find me the rudest lout you ever met."

"Lout?" Dorise said, and she laughed in spite of herself. "Is that the kind of word they teach you in law school?"

Seeing his confusion, she stopped herself. "I mean, I guess I don't know that word. I bet there's lots of things I could learn from you." *Oh, God.* She stopped. "I didn't mean to say that." Her cheeks felt hot enough to blister.

He smiled kindly, as if nothing had happened. "May I get you some coffee?" She nodded, feeling numb, and for a few minutes he was gone, giving her time to collect herself. But instead, her heart seemed to pick up speed, flapping like a heron in the middle of her chest. She felt her palms get sweaty.

When Dashan Jericho returned with the coffee, which he handed her only after taking away her empty plate and setting it down for her, he said, "I surely have enjoyed this fellowship here today. It's been a real delight to meet you and your charming mother—I don't know when I've felt so welcome."

"It's been real nice to talk to you, too."

She watched him go around saying his good-byes, looking like a racehorse—lean, long of flank, aristocratic.

Too bad I'm not in the market for a man, she thought. That one'd probably do just fine.

Her mother started in on the way home. "Well, now. I think we got us a buddin' romance."

"Oh, Mama, come on now."

"You know what I'm talkin' about. You saw the way he kep' looking at you, how he kep' comin' back to talk to you."

"He was just bein' friendly."

"No, ma'am, he was not just bein' friendly. I know when a man's interested, and that one is."

"Well, I'm not."

"You ought to be, girl. You ought to be. Trouble with you is, you're always pickin' the wrong man."

"Once, Mama. Just once." She couldn't possibly know about Troy.

"Mmmph. I know all about you and Troy Chauvin."

"My sister ought to keep her damn mouth shut."

"You ought to give that young man a chance."

"Jesus and I've got a deal, Mama. I'm gon' devote myself to Him, and He's gon' keep me out of trouble."

Still, she was disappointed it took two whole days for Dashan Jericho to call. Every time he entered her mind, she banished the thought. No more men for her. Not for any reason. No way; no how.

When she picked up the phone, he said, "This is your Secret Admirer."

She hung up.

He waited half an hour to call back and when he did, he said, "I'm so sorry. That was disrespectful. I'm so embarrassed I almost didn't call back."

She said, "Michael Jordan, if you don't quit callin' me, I'm gon' get my Secret Admirer to go over there and tan your hide."

She hadn't meant to say that. Somehow it just slipped out.

● ●

The wiretap on Rosemarie Owens's phone bore fruit almost immediately after the death of her husband. Skip heard it through Shellmire: "The call came."

"Jacomine? He called Rosemarie?"

"Daniel did. At least we think it was Daniel Jacomine."

"What'd he say?"

"He said, 'Hi, Mom. It's Daniel.' We highly trained G-men call that a clue."

"Then what? What'd she say?"

"She hung up."

"That's *all?*"

"Every crumb."

"Damn. How's the tail working out?"

"Two of 'em. They're depressed as hell. Spend most of their time trying to guess the cost of the clothes on all the fabulously dressed Texans at those parties she goes to. One tank top—three years' salary. That sort of thing. They're thinking of leaping off the same balcony Roger Owens thought so highly of."

"Damn again."

"Yeah."

"Listen, I don't know if a tail's good enough. I think she needs a guard on her."

"Why? I thought she was Jacomine's girlfriend."

"She just hung up on his son. Are we talking possible double cross?"

"Could be. Or maybe the call was some kind of signal. Could be lots of things—maybe she's not double-crossing the Jacomines;

maybe the son's double-crossing the father. Or maybe she just knows her phone's tapped."

"Turner, goddammit, you're like Cassius—you think too much."

He laughed. "Well, nobody could accuse me of looking lean and hungry."

The whole Rosemarie Owens thing had thrown Skip into a renewed panic. She reasoned that if Jacomine would kill someone merely as a favor for a friend, if he could take time out to do that from his self-appointed job as vigilante executioner, he probably had time for her. She knew how his mind worked, and she knew he hadn't forgotten that she had bested him a few months before.

He would probably not go for her. He would go for Steve or Dee-Dee or one of the kids. If she'd been worried before, she was now waking up in the middle of the night in a cold sweat.

Obviously Rosemarie was in touch with Jacomine. Skip only hoped she hadn't mentioned her call—you never knew what a madman would do with a random piece of information.

To make matters worse, Joe Tarantino called Skip and Adam Abasolo into his office. "How's it going, kids?"

Skip said, "Terrible. I'm trying to find the uncle of the kidnapped kid through the art community. Do you know how many artists there are in this town?"

Joe was impatient. "Adam?"

"I'm checking out oddball religious groups."

"Oh, great. Let me reiterate. As I understand it, we're looking for the son of the primary suspect, who may know where the suspect's granddaughter is. We're not even looking for the suspect. And we don't have any other suspects. Have I got it right?"

Skip sighed. She knew it sounded lame as hell. "That's about it, Lieutenant."

"We don't have any reason to imagine he's in town, do we?"

"Only that his granddaughter may be."

"I think we've got to move on."

"But, Joe—"

"Listen, another taxi driver was killed last night. That makes two in a week, you know that?"

Abasolo said, "Little twin heater cases."

"You know, Skip, in a way the captain was right that day. As far as I can see, no one, but no one in this whole department gives a flying fuck who killed that asshole Nolan Bazemore. Most people—policemen included, I'm sorry to say—even seem to sympathize with the guy."

Skip was speechless.

"I know, I know." He patted the air. "I'm giving you a few more days, okay? You, Skip. Adam, I want you full-time on the heater cases. I don't have enough people to waste any more time on this." He was still patting the air, and for some reason, seemed only about half-focused on what he was saying.

Skip exchanged a look with Abasolo. The sergeant spoke first. "What else, Joe?"

"What?" The lieutenant seemed to be coming out of a trance.

"Seems like you've got something else on your mind."

"Yeah. Yeah, I sure do. The superintendent's getting ready to drop a bomb. You know what decentralization is?"

Abasolo said, "That thing they're doing in New York? Busting up the detective bureau?"

"In effect. All detectives are fixin' to be reassigned to district stations. You know what that means, lady and gentleman? It means the Homicide Division as we know it will no longer exist. Everybody'll be working every kind of case within his or her own district."

"Jesus."

"This is what I'm worried about. Look, Skip, I believe in what you're doing, and I couldn't agree less with these short-sighted bastards who think it doesn't matter. For one thing, to help break a huge national case would do a hell of a lot to restore some of the honor to this tarnished old department. For another—call me old-fashioned—but I still think murder's murder. But you're nowhere close and there's not much time. The chief decides to decentralize, you'll be running your butt off covering stick-ups of mom-and-pop groceries. You're not going to have five minutes to check out weird religious groups. If you want to break this thing, you better get some kind of religion yourself."

Abasolo sucked in air.

"You hear what I'm saying? It's now or never, kid."

Just what she needed. More pressure.

If she could have worked twenty-four hours a day, she would have. And so she hit galleries with a vengeance, all the while fretting, trying to think of other avenues to follow.

Lovelace might have credit cards with her—Skip got on the computer and checked for recent purchases. There were none.

There was no record anywhere for an Isaac Jacomine, not even a Social Security number—but that she already knew. She checked the coroner's office for a twenty-year-old white female or a twenty-seven-year-old white male, and again came up with nothing.

Finally, she went home and endured the nightly hurdle of getting through the courtyard without getting bitten by Napoleon. "He's never bitten anyone," Steve said. "What makes you think he'd bite you? He loves you."

"He hates me."

Nevertheless, she went for a walk with the two of them. Truth to tell, Napoleon was the tiniest bit friendlier, meaning his growling had taken on a kind of half-hearted quality. At least, she thought, he makes it harder for anyone to get to us.

But Errol Jacomine was a man who'd killed several times already and who didn't work alone. A German shepherd, however ornery, wasn't really going to stop him.

Steve said, "You know what you need? Comfort food." He made her his special baked potato with sautéed vegetables, and they went over to watch a video with Jimmy Dee and Layne.

"No kids?" said Steve, and she reflected how far he'd come. He hadn't bonded with the kids immediately.

"Kenny's doing his homework and Sheila's at play practice. She'll be back by nine or nine-thirty. I think she's Lady Macbeth."

Layne said, "Beats Ophelia."

"Damn right," said Jimmy Dee. "Good training for her. It's a dog-eat-dog world. Right, Angel?" The black and white pooch wagged her tail, and all was right with the world.

They watched *House of Games*, one of Steve's favorites, and though it met with raves from Dee-Dee and Layne, it was too dark for Skip's mood. She had the willies by the time it was over.

And Sheila wasn't home. "Drink?" said Dee-Dee.

Steve said, "Sure." Skip nodded, distracted, thinking that ten was too late to be out on a school night.

By ten-thirty, there was still no Sheila, and inwardly, Skip was wild. Dee-Dee said, "What is it, kid? You're checking your watch every two minutes."

"I was just wondering where Sheila is."

"Sheila? She's a big girl. And fortunately, doesn't drive yet. Wherever she is, she's with someone's parents."

Skip sipped her wine sparingly, thinking to be alert in case she needed to be. When she saw Dee-Dee begin to check his own watch, and then excuse himself, her heart started to pound.

Layne and Steve were talking about the movie, but she couldn't really follow it. Dee-Dee came back with his forehead creased. "I just made a couple of phone calls. Carol Gauthier's been home for an hour. She said Sheila told her she had another ride."

Skip's breath started getting ragged. "Has she—uh—done this before?" But she knew it was a stupid question even before everyone laughed.

"All the time," said Dee-Dee. "Still . . ." He stared at his watch. "This is a little much."

Skip was sweating. Her heart was beating so fast it felt like a hammer. Her breath was coming in shorter and shorter gasps.

"Hey, hey, you're okay. Let's get you a paper bag to breathe into. Come on, now. You're okay." She heard the words only dimly. She was afraid of passing out and in a way hoped she would—a piece of her wanted escape.

And then a tiny chime sounded through the house, the noise the alarm made when the door opened.

Jimmy Dee yelled, "Sheila! Sheila, is that you?"

Someone brought a paper bag and Skip breathed into it. Around her, she heard parent-child sounds.

"Yeah, I'm going to bed."

"Come in a minute."

"I said I was going to bed."

Dee-Dee left, striding angrily. Though he was making a half-hearted attempt to save her embarrassment, the whole exchange carried easily through the house.

"You're an hour and a half late. Omigod, look at you. Do you always wear your lipstick on your chin?"

"I am not late. We've been out front the whole time. Talking."

Parked on a public street. Not talking at all, if the lipstick was any indication. Totally oblivious to her surroundings.

Vulnerable as a bunny rabbit.

"Sweetheart, you okay?" said Steve when they were alone. "I think they call that a panic attack."

He never called her pet names.

"I can't crack, Steve. I can't. I've got to get this asshole before he—"

"Before he gets Sheila or Kenny? Don't you think you're being a little paranoid? He's not exactly the big bad wolf, you know—he's just one guy. And, as he keeps reminding the world at large, he has bigger fish to fry. I think you're taking this kind of personally. What do you think about going back to Boo?"

The therapist she had seen a few months ago that time when she fell apart at work. Shortly after shooting Delavon.

It was a thought. It was certainly a thought. But she didn't have time. She still had fifty galleries to visit—that was her guess, anyway. She was nearing the end of the alphabet.

As she stood in the shower, an act that often produced clarity, she suddenly thought, *Galleries, schmalleries. I'm just spinning my wheels. And for what?*

She was crying when she came out, and Steve made her tell him why.

"I don't understand," he said. "Isn't that what detective work is? Slogging? Listen, let me help. Let's divide up the list."

They were lying in bed. She laughed through her tears, nestling her head in his armpit. "You never give up, do you?" From the moment they met, he'd been offering to help her do her work.

He was right. All she could do was slog. But she needed a payoff in the worst kind of way. Sometimes it paid off, sometimes it didn't.

● ●

She began the morning at Rhino, moved on to the elegant Arthur Roger Gallery, then had coffee on the run and blew into Rough

Trade, which, its name notwithstanding, was located in a fashionable part of the French Quarter.

Judging from the work she could see, Rough Trade specialized in the work of untrained artists, the sort that were once called "primitive." She asked to see the manager and as she was waiting, amused herself looking at the pictures. Most of them, to her mind, looked as if they had been drawn by seven-year-olds, but there were many things she liked, including a collection of angel faces that looked oddly familiar. Alongside the grouping hung a picture of the artist and a short bio. The man in the picture wore a white robe and a beard. Skip jumped as if someone had leapt at her, hollering, "Boo."

Belatedly she saw why the angels were familiar—though the hair had been darkened to auburn, they had the round face and almond-shaped eyes of the girl in the picture the feds had given her—the one of Lovelace Jacomine.

She devoured the bio like a woman starved for words. The artist, it seemed, was a native South Carolinian who had spent most of his teenage years in and out of juvenile facilities, and his early adulthood in the federal penitentiary in Atlanta, where he had learned to paint. He had also learned to meditate in the joint and now divided his time between his art and his spiritual studies. He was known as The White Monk.

Bullshit, she thought. *It's Isaac.*

"Ah. You like The White Monk?" The voice had a trace of an accent, but nothing recognizable—it could well have been an affectation. "I am Dahveed."

David? Skip thought, but she wasn't about to ask. Dahveed was a slinky, smooth young man of indeterminate ethnic origin and skin that glowed gold. He wore black pants with a narrow belt and a white shirt that might have been silk but probably wasn't; Dahveed simply had a silky way about him.

"Does he live in New Orleans?" Skip asked.

"Oh, yes. In fact, he often paints in our courtyard. The angels are marvelous, aren't they?"

"Wonderful. I own a pair of them, actually. I find them so haunting. I came in to ask about the artist, to tell you the truth—" Her mind raced. Did she want him to donate a painting for a fund-raiser? Talk to a class? Was she simply a fan?

Maybe she was. That might fly fine, New Orleans being the kind of town that celebrates celebrities, however modest.

Her instinct was right. She didn't even have to bring it up. "You would like to meet him, perhaps?"

"Is he here?"

"Of course. One second."

Dahveed disappeared and in a moment was back, looking distressed. "His friend said he had to leave suddenly."

"I need to talk to the friend." Skip produced her badge.

"Damn you. You lied to me."

She shrugged. "Only about my angels—and I'd like to own them."

The shop opened onto a narrow courtyard where a black man hummed as he painted. He said, "How you?" and narrowed his eyes in a way that said her most secret thoughts were known.

She showed him her badge. "Detective Skip Langdon." The man nodded. "Thought you were heat." Now this one *had* been to prison—cons always knew.

"Where's the Monk?"

"Gone."

"He thought I was heat, too?"

The man shrugged. "Guess so."

"Where he'd go?"

"Home, I guess, but nobody know where that is. I'm his best friend and I don't even know."

"Dahveed? You know?"

"He's very secretive. He never would tell us."

"How about a phone number?"

"He wouldn't give us one."

She raised an eyebrow at the other man, the old con.

"Wouldn't tell me either."

"Look. I'm trying to help him. He's not in any trouble, I only want to help. Not only him, but his niece." She saw the surprise in the black man's eyes.

Skip said, "The girl in the picture."

Dahveed was clearly eager to end the interview. "There is only one thing we can really do—when he comes back, we will give him your card."

She was so frustrated she was quite sure that if he'd been alone, she'd have slammed him up against the wall and yelled at him. She was convinced Dahveed knew how to reach The Monk, and equally sure he was going to call and warn him about her as soon as she left.

He'd have regurgitated the information she wanted in about thirty seconds, but there was something about the other one that kept her from going for it. Not only was he street-smart—he'd never tell something he didn't want to—but he had a funny feel about him, an air of repressed violence. If he thought he was helping out a friend, he might get a little too rough.

She crossed the street and went into the antique store opposite the gallery—it was a perfect place for a stakeout, but she didn't dare broach the subject. Shop owners in the French Quarter were a regular retail mafia; the owner and Dahveed probably took each other's UPS deliveries.

But it was a good place to regroup. She pretended to look at silver candlesticks and antique tables, while she turned options over in her mind.

She could contact the federal pen in Atlanta—and would—but she already knew there was little point. She had run Isaac through NCIC and he had no prison record. Evidently The White Monk was a self-invented entity.

As she saw it, aside from beating answers out of Dahveed, there were only three solutions, one of which was also out of the question—burglarizing the gallery for The Monk's phone number. That left two—she either had to stake the place out or send a surrogate in to make an appointment with The Monk—someone posing as a potential buyer. The last, of course, was the simplest solution, but whom could she send?

In the end there was only one choice. Abasolo.

19

• •

Isaac made good on his promise. He called his friend Anthony, the erstwhile owner of Juicy's Juice, and spoke as if he did it every day. "Anthony, how you doin', baby?" Just like that—slang and everything. Lovelace couldn't feature Isaac talking like that.

"Listen, man, I need a favor. Bet you didn't know I had a grown-up niece. No, I'm not kidding, she really is a niece. My brother's an old man—real old man, rocking-chair age. That explains it, right, man? What she needs is a reference. She's a real good cook, and she's trying to get a job cooking. The only trouble is, the last place she worked closed and she can't find the owner.

"No, it didn't close because of her cooking. You be nice now. You know how good I was when I worked for you—remember that? Well, if you could write me a reference and just, you know, put her name on it—"

Here there was a long pause, during which Lovelace's palms sweated and her heart thumped. It wasn't going to work.

"Hey, congratulations, brother! Hey, that's great news. Sure she can cook. I wouldn't bullshit you. Okay, sure. Sure, I'll send her over."

He hung up the phone and reached for his notepad. Damn! He'd started talking; she didn't see why he couldn't just continue.

He scribbled forever. When she thought she couldn't stand it one more second, he gave her the note. "He's opened a new juice stand," it said. "Same menu as last time. His helper's okay but unreliable—he'd like you to come in for an interview. It would mean taking orders, cleaning up, all that stuff, but you'd get to cook, too—in a modest kind of way. He said cooking's about a third of the job. Would you be interested?"

"Sure. At least it would be a jumping-off place."

He wrote, "That's what he said. It's on Maple Street. Go in the morning."

Shit, she thought. *Damn this stupid hair. What if he expects some Betty Coed?*

She got up the next morning and put on lots of makeup, to make it seem she had done the hair trick to show off her fine, bold features. But the bigger she drew her lips, the more she looked like some kid playing with her mom's lipstick.

She put on her only earrings, the ones she was wearing when she was kidnapped, and a short black skirt and a white crop top. That was what waitresses wore, and caterers—maybe it would send a subliminal message.

Anthony hadn't given Isaac a specific appointment time, but she figured ten-thirty was about right. It would show interest, but not excessive eagerness.

Despite the erratic quality of public transportation, she was there by ten-fifteen, and was pleasantly surprised.

Maple Street was way, way uptown, at what was called Riverbend, where the Mississippi took so major a meander, it defined the shape of the city, cradled it into the upriver horn of the crescent that gave it its nickname. To Lovelace's delight, it was the kind of hip shopping area you get in a university town—bustling with coffeehouses, small galleries, an utterly charming bookstore, and, now, it seemed, a juice bar and vegetarian restaurant.

In truth, Anthony's new place—Judy's Juice—was little more than a hole in the wall, but a clean, inviting one, with about three spotless formica tables, a floor you could see your face in, and a bulletin board where you could find anything from a roommate to a ride to Albuquerque.

If I lived here I'd be here all the time, she thought. *I'd go get a book from that bookstore, and I'd come in here and have some carrot juice and a bagel.*

It was the sort of place she'd love to work.

She patted her head where hair used to be, preparing to enter. The minute she saw Anthony she knew she needn't have worried about tress-weirdness—he himself sported handsome dreads. That was the first thing she noticed. The second was that her cheeks were getting hot.

Anthony was a light-skinned black man, or, as they say in New Orleans, a Creole, which used to mean a mixture of French and something else, but nowadays, more often than not, simply meant black and something else. Lovelace had seen plenty of light-skinned blacks in her life, but she'd noticed that in New Orleans, they often had an aristocratic look, an exotic, almost haughty bearing that reminded her of Ethiopians—people who looked as if they'd all been kings or queens in the old days.

Anthony was one of these. He had a nose that could have been modeled by Phidias. He had green eyes as well, and he wore an olive shirt that matched them. His skin was the color of slightly tarnished brass—pure gold, but too refined to shine. His dreads were exceptionally neat and quite long, about shoulder length. He was five-feet-ten, she thought—about her height, though Lovelace wouldn't have cared if he'd been a midget. And he was thin, with good shoulders; he was probably a vegetarian.

So magnificent a man might have caused her to lose the power of speech, but she didn't feel in the least shy. Probably, she thought later, because some piece of her had noticed his wedding ring. Or possibly because he looked friendly. He said, "What can I do for you today?" and gave her a smile that might well have been sincere.

"Are you Anthony?"

"Sure am."

"Well, you could give me a job." She stepped forward and extended her hand. "I'm Lovelace Jacomine."

"Lovelace! My Lady Lovelace. Isaac didn't tell me you had such a pretty name."

"Uncle Isaac's a little vague sometimes."

"He really your uncle?"

"Honest to God. I've always worshiped him."

"Woo! You'd be the only one."

"He's a sweetie, don't you think?"

"Oh, yeah. Pretty worthless cook because he counts to twenty or something before every ingredient he puts in the dish—and that includes sandwiches. But a sweetie for sure."

"Have you ever been to his house? It's all white. He cleans it for an hour every day—hey, I'm nothing like that. I guess he did that part of the job pretty well."

"Well? He did it superhumanly. I couldn't begin to pay him for all the hours he spent scrubbing things. That's why I had to go out of business the first time—went broke trying to pay the help."

"Well, I work cheap. I'm not nearly as good a cleaner, but I make a mean tostada."

"Hey, good. Let's put it on the menu."

"You mean I'm hired?" She smiled when she said it, and realized she was completely confident, a feeling she'd almost forgotten about. She and Anthony were generating enough heat to cook with.

"I guess you are. My helper didn't come in this morning. Third time this month he didn't call, didn't show. All you got to do is turn up, Lady Lovelace, and you can work here as long as you like. Two-fifty an hour suit you?"

At her dumbfounded look, he said, "See? Now if I pay you mini-mum wage, you'll think you're getting a deal."

She went to work immediately, heedless of the cute outfit she'd put on for the interview.

About an hour into it, she thought, *I can do this. This could really be fun.*

By that time, she had the hang of things—the basic routine, at least, and a sense of the rhythm of the place.

Business was good, and it took all her focus to keep up with the job, making sandwiches and serving them, pulverizing carrots and celery. Her mind raced along with her body. *I could come in early,* she thought, *and try out an extra dish or two a day. Isaac's vegetable lasagna, maybe, and some vegetarian chili. Pasta salad, maybe, or potato.*

She ran it by Anthony. "Sure, baby," he said, "just give me a shopping list."

By the end of the day she was spent, and it was not till she was on the bus going home that she had time to let her mind wander. As she passed the neighborhood where the Royces lived, the unbidden image of the two kids' faces, upturned and waiting for their formerly forbidden burgers, suddenly brought hot tears to her eyes.

Other images came: Brenna and Charles dancing to Ernie K-Doe; Brenna in her studio covered with clay, forehead wrinkling in concentration; Brenna reaching for her, kissing her.

The embarrassment that enveloped her when she thought of that rivaled the full-body humiliation of grade school when she got the answer wrong.

The sadness wouldn't leave her. She had bought into the family as if they were hers.

Isaac was gone when she got home, so she was deprived of that distraction. *I'll never get anything right,* she thought. *How is it even possible to screw up that badly?*

She needed desperately to talk to someone, and there was only one person she could call. Michelle. She was in mid-dial when she thought, *Better not. Just better not. Maybe I should go somewhere else. A bar or something.*

It was starting to get dark when she found one, and it looked like an oasis.

Light streamed from the open windows along with the scent of good barbecue. The inside was surprisingly light, for a bar, illuminated by a single naked bulb. The walls were painted an uncharacteristic white, and five or six tables had been set up, with mismatched chairs. Evidently it was a place like Judy's, that served sandwiches along with the juice. Though every single customer was black and male, they showed no interest in her presence. The place had an easy, Caribbean feel.

She bellied up, ordered a beer, and spoke to the bartender. "Do you have a public phone?"

"Sho' darlin'." He gestured with his head. "You need some change?"

He was an older man, sixty perhaps, and Lovelace could swear she saw concern in his face. She wondered what she had done to provoke it—her hair was far too short to be disheveled. Her anxiety must show on her features.

She walked down a long dark corridor, thankful the phone was far enough away to afford privacy.

Michelle answered on the first ring.

"Hi. I need a shoulder to cry on."

"Lovelace, for Christ's sake. Are you all right?"

"Physically, but—"

"This phone's probably tapped, so don't say anything. Just be quiet and let me talk. A lot's happened. The FBI picked me up."

"The FBI?"

"They were looking for you. I didn't tell them anything but—"

"Good."

"Don't interrupt, okay? This is really important. They flew this cop in from New Orleans—"

"*New Orleans.* They know—"

"Lovelace, be quiet. I'm telling you this line isn't safe. Listen to me—this woman's not what you think. She's a cop, but she's really smart and she's really nice. I mean *really* nice; she's worried about you."

"Oh, sure."

"Try to keep an open mind, okay? The main thing is, she's had a personal experience with your grandfather. He kidnapped a kid close to her and the cop got the kid back—but not before some people died. You hear what I'm saying, Lovie? Your grandfather's a murderer. You really can't forget that."

Lovelace hated the schoolteacherish sound of her friend's voice. She spoke petulantly. "He wouldn't hurt me. I'm his own flesh and blood."

"You don't know what he might do. The cops and the FBI think you're in danger. I'm worried sick, to tell you the truth—this is not something to mess around with. I want you to call Detective Skip Langdon at the New Orleans Police Department."

"That's the cop?"

"Yes. She's in Homicide."

"Homicide!"

"I keep telling you—this thing is serious. Call her. Promise me you'll call her."

Lovelace wished she'd never picked up the phone. "Why did they send a cop from New Orleans?"

"Because the thing with your grandfather—the other kidnapping—happened there."

Lovelace felt tremendously betrayed. If Michelle was asking her to turn herself in, whose side was she on? "Michelle, what did you tell her?"

"Look, I had to make a decision. I told her you're with Isaac."

"Dammit, Michelle!"

"Shut up. There's really a lot to say. I didn't know his address, so all I could do is describe him. I'm sorry, Lovelace, but I'm just so damn worried about you—you've got to call this cop, I'm not kidding—this is far, far the best move you could make right now. You need as much protection as you can get from Errol Jacomine."

"Goddammit, you're supposed to be my friend!"

"I am your friend, and I have another message for you. A bigger bombshell than the FBI—are you ready?"

No, I am not ready. Don't you dare say another word. But she managed not to hang up.

"Your grandmother called."

"But my grandmother—"

"Right. Dumped your seven-year-old father at your grandfather's, and hasn't been heard from since. This woman told me the story. That's right, isn't it?"

"Anybody could know that."

"Is your dad's middle name Theophilus?"

"Holy shit."

"Guess who your grandmother is?"

"What do you mean, guess who she is?"

"I mean she's a famous person. Rosemarie Owens."

It took a moment for the penny to drop. "Rosemarie Owens. The one whose husband was just killed. After he dumped her for some supermodel."

"Good thing you read *People* magazine."

"Rosemarie Owens called me? What the hell does she want?"

"Now, that I couldn't tell you—but she said it's urgent. Do you want her number?"

"God, yes." She'd rather call her than a cop.

Michelle gave her the number. "And here's Skip Langdon's," she said. "Just take it down, okay? What can it hurt?"

Things were moving way too fast. Her best friend had betrayed her, her grandmother was not only alive, but some kind of pop culture celeb, and the FBI was looking for her.

This is a joke, she thought, it can't be real, and dialed the number Michelle had given her.

A machine answered, a woman's cigarette-voice. "We may be home and we may not. It depends how intriguing your message is. Start talking when you hear the tone, and you better make it fascinating."

Despite the aggressive tone of the message, the voice was somehow playful, in a Mae West kind of way. She took a deep breath. "This is Lovelace Jacomine calling Rosemarie Owens."

There was a click as someone picked up the receiver. "Lovelace, baby, I've been worried sick about you."

Could this really be her grandmother? This stranger who called her "baby"?

"I got a message to call you."

"I'm so glad you did. I didn't even know you existed until a few days ago, and now you're the most important thing in the world to me."

What in hell did the woman want? Lovelace was speechless.

"Are you there, darling?"

"Is this Rosemarie Owens?"

"Mee-maw to you, sweetness." Was the voice slightly slurred? Had she said "shweetness"? "I'm just so very, very glad you called."

"Michelle said it was urgent."

"That it is, darling. We don't have much time. I want us to meet so much. But now that may never be possible, and I thought that, just in case, I'd better tell you what I know."

"Why wouldn't it be possible?"

"Do you actually know your grandfather?"

"Well, we haven't seen each other in years."

"He's a very dangerous man, sweetness. An extremely dangerous man. If I die soon, I just wanted you to know." Lovelace heard her pause. "I need to take a deep breath. I'm so sorry to tell you, but someone has to. I'm afraid your grandfather's The Jury."

"My grandfather's what?" Her mind searched its files like a computer.

"The people who killed Billy Ray Hutchison, and then Nolan Bazemore, the guy that shot that nice police chief—that honest one—down in New Orleans."

She remembered. The Jury. She'd been self-involved lately, but everyone knew about The Jury. There was no way to avoid it.

"Why are you telling me this?"

"I may be in danger, for one thing, and I wanted you to know."

"Why not go to the cops?"

"I'm so sorry, darling, I just can't do that. There are times when blood's still thicker than water."

"Are you saying you're keeping quiet on my account?"

"I'm just so sorry. I don't know how to say this." She took another breath. "All right, here goes. I'm afraid your father's in it with him. I can't rat out my baby. I owe him that much."

The street slang sounded silly, coming from her.

"Do you understand what I'm getting at? You need to stay away from your daddy right now."

Lovelace was silent, absorbing it.

"Can I ask you a question, darling? Why aren't you in school?"

Okay, that was it. The woman was crazy. She was mad as a hatter. Lovelace got off the phone as quick as she could.

The bartender evidently didn't like the look of her. "Saved your beer for you. You sit down and drink it now."

Lovelace complied, hands shaking.

"You get some bad news?"

"I'll be okay. Do you have any more change?"

"You drink your beer now. I'll give you change in a minute."

What does he know? she thought. *Does he know the FBI's looking for me? Is he holding me here till they can pick me up?*

Her scalp was as prickly as if a large hairy spider had just dropped on her head.

Just be calm, she thought. *He can't know. How could he?* But her mind

209

kept racing. *Rosemarie's phone's probably tapped, too. They did a tracer, and they called him to have him hold me. That must be it.*

She took a long pull of the beer. *Well, so be it. I haven't done anything. Let them pick me up and do their worst. If they're after me because my father's a criminal, that means they're not trying to find me to give me back to him. So that's cool, right? What the hell.*

Once she had gotten past the paranoia, she thought about being the granddaughter of a multiple murderer. *That one's not in the genes, she thought. No way, I don't even know the man. I can just go back to school and lead a normal life. Maybe sell my story to the National Inquirer and retire at twenty.*

She giggled. The bartender said, "That's better. See? Nothin's that bad."

But by the time she'd finished the beer the FBI hadn't arrived. *Damn, she thought, maybe my fate's in my own hands.* She had another beer.

She sat awhile and sipped, turning over the possibilities in her mind. *There's no reason not to go to the cops if they're on my side. And if my dad's a murderer, that would explain a lot of things, actually. Like why he's so damn mean. He's so damn mean because he's not a nice person, as history has proved. They're not going to put me in his custody if he's a murderer.*

Shit. Could my dad really be a murderer?

Okay. Cons of going to the cops: It could be a setup. Maybe that wasn't my grandmother, or even Rosemarie Owens. Michelle might think I've flipped and this is her way of getting me to 'get help,' as she'd probably say.

If it's not a setup, I'll be hounded by the media.

I won't be able to lead a normal life.

Okay. So much for the cons. Pros: Call this a normal life? I might be able to lead a really normal life. Change my name and transfer to Cornell, enroll in the hotel school, and learn to run a restaurant. After the National Inquirer of course—with the proceeds.

Also, I might be safe.

Michelle had said the cop was nice. And not only that, smart. How could calling her hurt?

Lovelace said to the bartender, "How about that change?"

But of course, the cop wasn't working at that hour. What was she supposed to do—leave her name and number?

Well, why not? she thought. They can beep her. If any of this is true, she'll probably call back in two minutes.

But something was wrong with that. They'd look up the number in the reverse directory and come get her.

Well? she thought. *Wouldn't that be okay?*

She was just sober enough to decide it wasn't. She'd talk to the cop first, decide for herself what was going to happen. Besides, she had to let Isaac in on it.

In the end, she ended up saying she'd call back in half an hour; if Langdon was there, she'd talk to her.

She went back to the bar and waited, sucking down another Abita. But when she went to make the call, she didn't feel buzzed at all. She was scared shitless.

Langdon picked up on the first ring.

"This is Lovelace Jacomine. I hear you're looking for me."

"You hear right. We need to talk."

"About my grandfather?"

"Yes."

"I don't know where he is. Or my father either."

"We think they're looking for you—to kidnap you again."

"I wouldn't be surprised."

"Listen, I'm really sorry about what happened to you. Tell me about it."

Lovelace thought: *I don't feel like it, standing up here in this damn dank corridor.* Her scalp prickled again. *It's too long a story for the phone.* She said, "Wait a minute. Michelle said you were simpatico. But you're trying to trace the call, aren't you?"

"Lovelace, you're in danger—I'm trying to help you."

"Well, forget this method. Meet me at seven tomorrow morning. . . ." Her mind searched for a place. "The Camellia Grill."

It was near the juice bar.

But maybe it wasn't a good idea. Maybe the cop would follow her to her job—did she want to be followed? How did they plan to protect her anyway? House arrest of some kind?

Isaac was home when she got there. He indicated a note he'd already written. "What gives? I called Anthony and he said you left hours ago."

She didn't answer. Instead, she wrote him a note: "Are you my uncle or my mom?" and went into the kitchen.

Pasta, she thought. *Some nice, comforting noodles.* She was just pulling things out of the refrigerator when her uncle came in and joined her. He wanted to talk, if you could call it that.

• •

She had forgotten and said the name. If he could just keep his ears from hearing the name, or his eyes from reading it, or his mind from thinking it, he could get through most days okay. But this was the big one, he didn't know why.

Things had to equal out. Lovelace had said it, and so she had to offset it. She had said "Errol Jacomine" and now she had to say "Jesus Christ." The Monk couldn't; that was clear. It had to be Lovelace.

He could ask her to say it, but was that really fair? Would it work? He wasn't sure. It might be good enough, it might not.

And what a hell of a thing to come now, when she was talking about calling the police. It was too much. What was this about her grandmother being some floozy who'd lost her husband to some younger floozy? And she had a harebrained story about his father being a vigilante killer, not that The Monk wouldn't believe it.

Jesus preserve us, he thought, so as to offset the thought of his father. Now he needed to get Lovelace to say it. Did he have to provoke it, or would it be good enough if she simply said it on her own?

He wrote, "I can't do this, Lovelace. I've been running from this all my life. I can't have it in my life, don't you understand?"

She said, "Jesus, Isaac, did I ask for this?"

Oh, thank the gods, she said it. But it probably wasn't enough. She had said "Errol Jacomine"; that meant she now had to say both names, "Jesus" and "Christ." He couldn't leave her until she had. And he had to leave. He absolutely had to get out of here, because if he didn't, there'd be cops all over, and they'd be saying the name and bringing in contamination, and it would be a contamination of the spirit as well as of his house and his body.

He wrote, "I thought I left all that behind."

She touched him, and then withdrew her hand, knowing that he couldn't be touched, which made him so ashamed he wanted to go in the bedroom and lie there till he died.

Oh, no! He couldn't think about death. *That* one was back. "Life. Life," he said to himself, so deliberately he moved his lips.

She said, "What? Did you say something?"

He shook his head.

"Isaac, I'm so sorry. But you don't have to worry. I won't say where you are, or anything about you. I'm meeting her at the Camellia Grill. She'll never even know you exist."

He wrote: "Are you kidding? They have dossiers on everybody. They'll have them on me. They'll know I exist. They'll come here and get me."

"What for?"

"For questioning, I guess. Who knows what for? Can you imagine what would happen to me if I had to go to the police station for questioning?"

"I think it's pretty funny. I bet they've never questioned a man who's taken a vow of silence."

She meant to make him laugh, but he just couldn't. He was thinking of how to get her to say what he needed her to say. He couldn't stand it.

He wrote, "Lovelace, quick. Who's the son of Mary and Joseph?"

"Jesus Christ?"

She had said it, but with a question mark. Was that good enough?

"Say it again."

"Jesus Christ."

"Thanks. Do me a favor. *Please* don't say my father's name anymore." And then he wrote "Jesus Christ," to offset having written "my father."

Lovelace frowned, evidently puzzled, but seemed willing to humor him.

It wasn't good enough. He had used the possessive. He wrote, "In Jesus Christ's name," but he couldn't leave it at that—it made him look too crazy, so he kept on writing. "In Jesus Christ's name, please don't do this."

"Well, what the hell's the alternative? They'll just find us and spray us with automatic gunfire."

He wrote, "I have to get out of here."

"No. I'll go. It isn't fair to put you in jeopardy this way."

But they would find him. They were going to find him. And that was big trouble. Because he couldn't be absolutely sure he wouldn't kill someone.

Oh shit, oh shit, oh shit. That's back.

That was a thought that had been gone for a while. Now, with this mention of the police, he knew the possibility existed. He might kill someone. There was simply no way in hell to be sure he wouldn't. He might have done it already.

He wrote: "I can't talk about this anymore. I have to meditate."

"Okay." She went back in the kitchen, and pretty soon he smelled garlic and onions and squash. She was probably making a vegetable pasta.

He sat there and thought: *I have to get out. I might hurt someone. Even now, I can't be sure I haven't killed anyone; I just can't. There's no way to be sure, is there? Absolutely no way. If there were, I'd know what it is.*

And I can't be sure I won't do it again.

I can't go to prison. I can't control the contamination. There aren't enough showers in the whole prison system of the whole country to control the contamination.

I have to leave.

20

• •

Steve was pulling a roast chicken out of the oven when Skip got back.

"Hi. You hungry?"

"Starved. That looks great, but we've had a development—I've got to call Shellmire. Oops. My beeper just went off." She recognized the number instantly—Shellmire's. Eagerly, she dialed. "I was just about to call you. Guess what?"

"I give up."

"The kid's coming in out of the cold. We're meeting tomorrow— at the Camellia Grill, of all places."

"How do you know it isn't a setup?"

"I don't. We're talking mega-backup. You want to be there?"

"It's no setup. And yeah, I'd love to. Can't though. Bigger fish to fry, as your pal says."

"What could be bigger than this? And how do you know so much about it, anyway? Evidently she talked to Michelle. Do you have her line tapped?"

"Sure we do, we're Big Brother. Our guys heard the conversation, but she called from a bar—we didn't get her phone number. But here's the big news—Michelle's not the only one she talked to. Take a wild guess at who her other phone friend is."

"Her dad."

"You're never gonna guess. I better tell you—her grandmother."

It took a moment to figure out who he meant. "Rosemarie?"

"We've got a majorly interesting tape of those two ladies. Rosemarie told her her grandpa and her dad are The Jury."

"No!"

"Sure did. Why, I'm not exactly sure. I don't think she had in mind Lovelace calling you, but she could have."

"Never mind why she did it—how does she know?"

"Okay, okay, don't rub it in. Guess you were right. There's probably a reason the hubby turned up dead. We got her in custody in Dallas—I was calling to ask if you want to fly over and get in on the interrogation."

"Good God, yes. But I've got bigger fish to fry."

"At the Camellia Grill, along with the burgers."

"Turner, do you realize what this means? I've got to call Cappello. And Joe."

She hung up.

"Steve! The FBI's got evidence pointing to Jacomine."

"Hey, congratulations—hometown girl makes good."

"It's not over till it's over. But, man, this is hot. Maybe they'll finally give me some help. We're this close—" she held her thumb and forefinger an inch apart. "We're gonna get the bastard."

●　　●

The Camellia Grill, which never closes, did at five A.M. the next day, while staff and customers were replaced with policemen.

By six, the transition was complete. By six forty-five, Skip was sitting at the counter, sipping coffee. At seven, she began to feel restless. She kept fighting the urge to look over her shoulder, or even at the door. She was well covered. She stared at her coffee.

A man came in and sat next to her, a man in coat and tie, looking as if he were on his way to work. "Morning," she said.

He grunted and ordered coffee. The place was starting to hum. A woman in a miniskirted power suit flipped in and got something to go—a woman too old to be Lovelace.

Two other customers took counter stools. One—apparently a regular—asked where the usual staff was. The wait-cop shrugged. "Out, I guess."

Skip thought, *That should cover it*. She looked at her watch.

Seven-ten. Still in the ballgame.

Her coffee cup was empty.

She got a fill-up and tried to focus on breathing. In, out, in, out—people were staring. She smiled at the man in the suit, the grunting nonspeaker. "Yoga breathing."

He frowned back.

She thought, *Maybe Lovelace doesn't know what this place is like at this hour. Maybe she thought it'd be deserted.*

There were plainclothes cops outside who'd seen Lovelace's picture. If anyone came near who looked anything like her, they'd follow; and they'd say what they were doing on their radios.

Maybe she's not coming.

She didn't let the thought solidify until seven-twenty. By seven-thirty, Abasolo's imitation of a fry cook was wearing thin. The real customers were getting testy. The place smelled as if there'd been a forest fire. Skip was sweating.

At seven-forty, the owner got pissed and insisted on replacing Abasolo, which, at that point, was fine—the place was full of civilians, anyway.

At seven-fifty, Skip's clothes were soaking wet with flop-sweat. The policemen outside were on their radios more often than not, making progress reports—who they were ought to be obvious to anyone on the block. But Skip had a feeling it didn't matter. Lovelace wasn't coming.

They made it official at eight.

Skip killed an hour or two at Headquarters, doing paperwork and returning phone calls, waiting for the business day to start at Rough Trade. Any idea of sending Abasolo to try a kid-gloves approach now seemed absurd—it could take days, and she was overloaded on adrenaline now.

She got in her car, drove to the French Quarter, and found a parking place. Jittery with coffee nerves and fury, she blew into the gallery like a hurricane.

The door slammed behind her. "Dahveed! Dahveed, come out here! Skip Langdon, NOPD—get your cute butt here in two seconds."

He seemed shaken when he arrived, about half a second ahead of her deadline. "Uh—what is it? Can I help you?" He looked undecided, and she knew he was trying to get up the nerve to ask her to lower her voice.

"I want you to let me walk through your gallery."

"Walk through my . . . what is this?" He actually burst into tears. It was quite a spectacle—she'd never seen a grown man do that. A drop or two on the cheeks maybe, but not a full-fledged tantrum straight from Queen Central.

Dahveed pleaded as if beset by Mongol hordes. "You can't do this. Please don't do this. I promise you I don't have any phone numbers. I swear to you. Please, please, please, please, don't rip apart my place of business. I'm begging you—please. If you have any human feeling."

"Hey, take it easy." She knew she'd come on a little strong, but she must have yelled louder than she thought—or maybe she was just giving off a very nasty vibe.

Revelas came in from the courtyard. "What you doin' to Dahveed? He don't know nothin'."

"Look, I don't want to hurt Dahveed. But I need to find The Monk. Is he here? Is that what's going on?"

"Naw. He ain't here. But I just remembered somethin' I know about The Monk. Maybe it could help you."

She could have screamed. *Just remembered! Goddammit, where were you yesterday?*

She spoke as politely as she could. "What's that, Revelas?"

"Before he started helpin' out aroun' here, The Monk had a gig. Little somethin' to help him get through, you know? Support his paintin' habit."

"Uh-huh."

"Well, look, it wadn't like this." He swept an arm to indicate the

218

gallery. "Dahveed's like a artist hissef. No records, no nothin'. You a artist, you get ya money, that the end of the story. This was a regular bi'ness, you know? Like with records and stuff. Maybe that dude have his address."

It couldn't have been that regular, she thought. The Monk doesn't even have a Social Security number.

She said, "What kind of business?"

"Juice bar. You know—one them carrot-mashin' places; make your yogurt shakes, shit like that."

"Uh-huh. You know which one?"

"Well, I been thinkin' 'bout that. See, mostly I talk to The Monk. He don't talk to me—he don't talk at all, you know about that?"

"Revelas, you know something or not?"

He was suddenly belligerent. "Yeah. I know somethin'. You want it or you jus' want to tear Dahveed place apart? Dahveed jus' a innocent bystander—other brother might have what you want."

Skip suddenly got a tight feeling in her stomach, as if she were standing on the edge of a precipice. If she took a wrong step, she might go flying. Unless she'd misunderstood, he'd already told her something—that meant this was more than smoke.

"Did you say 'brother'? He worked for a black man?"

"Yeah. He work for a brother."

"You remember his name?"

"Don't know his name. He told me, went in one ear, out he other. What I do remember, I remember the name of the sto'."

Skip waited. But the man was obviously pissed off and in a mood to make her work. Finally she said, "Well, what was it, Revelas?"

"Well, now, you ask me nice."

"Oh, forget it. I've got work to do."

But Dahveed shouted, "For God's sake, tell her if you know!"

"All right, bro'. Okay, awrite. I'll tell her for you."

Again she waited.

Revelas pulled out a cigarette and lit it. Finally he said, "It was Juicy's."

"Juicy's?"

"Juicy's Juice. How you gon' forget a name like that? Mother-fucker say he name it after his girlfriend. Bet she love that. Juicy! Huh."

"Now, how would you know a thing like that when The Monk didn't talk?"

"Oh. *Now* you be interested in that."

"That's right. *Now* I be interested."

"Well, we was gettin' to be friends, see. And he tol' me all his friends was brothers."

"I thought he didn't talk."

"Sometimes, if he thought somethin' was real important, he write it down. We pass notes like—you know?"

Skip nodded.

"I said somethin' like, 'You the whitest man I ever seen. Not enough to have white skin, you even dress white.' And that kind of hurt his feelin's. So he wrote me about workin' for this brother who own Juicy's Juice. I laughed, man, I laughed—that just tickle my funny bone. Juicy's Juice. Who in hell would name a bi'ness some-thin' like that? And whose girlfriend would let 'em?"

"But he didn't give you the name of the owner?"

"I tol' you already. He tell me, I jus' don't remember—Juicy's Juice the funny part."

"What city was it in?"

"What you mean what city? Racheer. Racheer in New Orleans."

"Not Metairie or Kenner? Or Algiers? New Orleans—you sure about that?"

"Sho' I'm sho'."

She doubted he was, but it was something, anyway. "You know what location?"

He shook his head. "He never did tell me that."

It was all she could do not to dash for the phone book. She already knew there was no Juicy's Juice in the Yellow Pages—she'd been to every juice bar that was there—but it might be in the white ones.

It didn't matter anyway. There was a way to look it up. She could find out who'd been issued the business license.

She wondered if she should stay and watch the shop for a

while. Dahveed had seemed unduly upset about her being there. On the other hand, she was eager to look up the business license for Juicy's.

She stuck around about fifteen minutes. Nobody came in or went out.

• •

Lovelace felt someone kick at the old tarp that covered her. "Come out, dammit."

"Okay, okay. That was a cop, wasn't it?"

"Oh yes, indeed, that was a cop. What exactly is going on with you and your newly bald uncle, who are about to put me out of business between the two of you?"

"Listen, thanks for not ratting me out."

"I should have, you know that? I truly should have. But because your uncle is such a fine artist—"

"Do you really think so?"

"Oh, yes, I most certainly do. And because you are his model, and because I like The Monk, even though he's completely crazy, I protect you."

"*And* my uncle?"

"No, no, no! How many times must I tell you? How many times must I tell the damn cop? I have no fucking idea in the world where your uncle is. Why in hell do you think I would know?"

"Because I don't know where else he goes, or what else he does. This is his life, so far as I know."

"Yes, well, he usually is here this time of day. What's happened, Miss . . . ?"

"Lovelace. My name is Lovelace."

"Miss Lovelace—I am quite sure you are not, Miss Not-So-Loveless, my funny valentine. What's happened to you, Miss Not-so? What's going on? May I give you some tea?"

"No thank you."

"Ah—a coffee drinker."

"No, I just . . ."

"Well, then, tell me what's the matter while both of us stand up in this hot courtyard with Revelas smirking in the background. He

221

saved the day, you know. Revelas, have you met Miss Not-So-Loveless, niece of The White Monk?"

Lovelace whirled toward the black man, "Revelas! You're The Monk's best friend."

"I'm his best friend, the man sho' is hard up."

"That might be," said Dahveed. "That might well be."

"He a very odd duck—more or less the Platonic ideal of a odd duck."

"Revelas," said Dahveed. "I've said it before and I'll say it again—you talk funny."

Lovelace came close to doing a double take. How could he have such bad grammar and a classical background?

"Prison school, Miss Lovelace." He spoke as if he had read her mind. "Good prison library, too. I never did learn to talk too good, but I got a hell of a vocabulary."

"You aren't my uncle's best friend?"

The man looked as if his nose had been pushed in, and it probably had, in one fight or another.

"Oh, I reckon I am—I'm a little hard up myself."

"Can you help me? Do you know where he is?"

"Well, you ain't really stated the problem, but sounds to me like your uncle must be missin'—ain't at home, ain't here. Must be missin'."

"We talked for a while last night. Then I went into the kitchen; when I came out he was gone."

"Y'all fight?"

"I'd rather not say."

"Course, y'all fought. Somethin' to do with that cop, that be my guess."

"Excuse me," said Dahveed. "I really have no time for this."

He went back into the store.

"Revelas, please. Do you know where he is?"

"Now, Miss Lovelace, you know I'd help you if I could."

"You know where he *might* be?"

"Now that do be a mystery. 'Cause you right, darlin', he go between the sto' and the house. That's about all he can handle, be my guess. Somethin' eatin' that man. Dahveed full o' shit, but he

222

right about that one, almost right anyway. The Monk pretty crazy, all right. First he wear white, then he go bald—just for openers. And we not even gon' talk about kind of stuff he paint. 'Cept you, I mean. Those angel pictures real pretty. But, hey—we outsiders here. That what they call this shit—you know about that? Outsider art."

She shook her head, impatient. "You don't have any ideas?"

" 'Fraid not, darlin'. But I know The Monk be mighty pleased to know you so worried about him."

"Well, thanks anyway, Revelas." *What a nice man,* she thought, though remembering full well what The Monk had told her about him.

She found Dahveed again, doing the crossword puzzle in the *Times-Picayune.* Something seemed peculiar to her.

"Dahveed, let me ask you something. Why didn't you give the cop our address?"

"Why, Miss Not-so, what could be simpler? Because I do not have your address, or the addresses of ninety percent of the itinerant geniuses who pass through these portals. That oversized official of enforcement can get a truckload of search warrants and she will turn up neither address nor phone number. These people want cash and I pay them in cash—I doubt half of them even have bank accounts. For all I know, some don't know how to sign their names.

"Not that The Monk is like that, of course. He reads; he definitely writes. Otherwise, how could he communicate? However, I have a motto: Tell me no answers and I'll ask you no lies."

Lovelace almost laughed. *If I could, I would,* she thought. *I'll bet I could like Dahveed. In a superficial kind of way.*

There was really nothing to do but go to work. She had phoned Anthony that she'd be late, and he'd said, sure, be as late as you want, just let me know and I'll give you a two-cent raise.

She couldn't believe it last night when she came out to announce dinner. The Monk just wasn't there. He wasn't in the bathroom taking one of his endless showers, and he wasn't on the porch sulking.

He was gone.

She had heard him leave a hundred times, so this time he had been careful to be quiet.

He'll be back, she thought. *He's just walking.*

He hadn't come back. She had driven him away. He had been so afraid of his father, and of her father, that he had left his own home, and all because of her.

She could have kicked herself in the seat of the pants. She would have done anything to take back the whole conversation, everything she'd said about the cop. She didn't *have* to see any cop—she could have gone back to Northwestern, or to Mexico to find her mom— she certainly didn't have to see any cop.

Maybe she could have just gone on living with her uncle, hoping her grandfather and her dad and the FBI wouldn't find her. Isaac would have been fine then, his life wouldn't have been disturbed.

But in her heart, she knew it wasn't true, especially after the thing that had happened that morning. She couldn't simply have waited for the blow to fall, the moment when she walked through a doorway and someone grabbed her—grabbed her or her uncle. Isaac would truly have been no safer than she, perhaps less so; he was simply wrong if he thought otherwise.

Still, she couldn't bring herself to meet the cop this morning, couldn't shake the feeling that it wasn't her decision, that it was Isaac's as well. She needed to give him time, needed to talk about it with him, to let him figure out an escape route for himself.

But perhaps he'd found one. It made her feel immeasurably sad that he hadn't discussed it with her, had just up and left.

He hated her, probably. And she deserved it, for coming into his life and endangering him like this. He wasn't a well person, she knew that. But he was more sane than otherwise, she was pretty sure of that. She wondered if his apparent craziness was meant to conceal something else, was simply an act, like Hamlet's antic disposition.

She got off the bus and walked toward Judy's Juice. *Am I crazy, too?* She thought, *Maybe I should just go find the cop now. It's not like I only had one chance.*

But she had promised Anthony she'd be there.

● ●

Dorise thought about it, and realized that not only had she never been out with a lawyer, she'd probably never even been out with a man who had graduated college. A lawyer had an advanced degree, if she wasn't mistaken.

She'd certainly never been out with a man who wore suits to work—a white-collar dude. The phrase was so odd when applied to her life, it was like a foreign language. A movie star would have been more believable—at least she'd actually spent time fantasizing about that. It had a certain familiarity.

A lawyer was the kind of person who lived in the houses she worked in.

The wisdom of what her sister had said came down on her—she didn't hang with lawyers, except when she was the help. She had no idea what she was going to talk to Dashan Jericho about.

Still, he was taking her to Commander's Palace. She'd never in a million years thought she'd get to go to Commander's Palace, and she wasn't sure what to wear, except that maybe it should be the sort of thing you wore to church. And he'd already seen her one good suit.

She got a loan from her sister and went out to Dillard's to buy herself a nice dress.

What would make him proud of me? she thought. *Something red? No, that's for later, to be sexy. For a first date, something black.*

She found it, too; the perfect black dress, made out of some taffeta kind of stuff that caught the light a real nice way and had a little jacket that buttoned at the waist to show off her best asset—her proportions. She went way in at the waist and way out at the hips, and she found a lot of guys thought that was more or less the perfect shape.

She never wore red lipstick, but she got some of that, too, and some perfume that the manufacturers swore had been made in some way that didn't hurt animals. Shavonne had learned in school that they did something awful to a certain kind of African cat to make perfume, and had made her promise never to wear it again. She couldn't see how any Christian could condone such a thing and had instantly agreed. She hoped Dashan would know that there were perfumes that didn't hurt animals.

She would have sent Shavonne to her sister's for the evening, but her sister had said, "Uh-uh, no way. I'm gon' get a look at this dude the whole family's talking about."

So she was baby-sitting on the premises, wearing a pair of sloppy old jeans, a T-shirt, and a slightly sulky look—not exactly an asset. But *I'm only responsible for myself,* Dorise told herself. *The preacher's always sayin' that, when people talk about their husbands drinking and their wives fighting with their in-laws. You can't change anybody but yourself.*

And then she thought: *Maybe this night will change everything.*

She was so nervous, she was still getting ready when Dashan arrived, still putting on makeup; didn't even have the dress on yet. She got a run in her pantyhose putting them on.

Damn! That always happens. Good thing I bought another pair. Hope my sister and Shavonne don't run him off by the time I get there.

When she finally walked into the living room on three-inch heels, in a cloud of animal-friendly perfume, dress rustling, lips glowing, she felt like a movie star—and Dashan's face told her it wasn't just her imagination. He stood up, breaking into a wide grin, and offering what he had in his hand—a single red rose, with some tiny white flowers around it, and a fern frond or something. The whole thing was wrapped in cellophane.

He said, "Look at you! You put this little flower to shame." He was wearing a dark suit, white shirt, and striped tie, like the men at the parties where she worked. She wasn't at all sure she'd ever seen a black man her age whom she actually knew wearing a suit, except to go to church or a funeral or a wedding. She'd been to clubs where other men wore suits, but no man she'd been with did, and not even any man in the group she was with. Delavon had money, but he dressed hip—anyway, he called it that; and Troy sure wasn't into suits.

I been missin' somethin', she thought. *I sure been missin' somethin'. Maybe I should have got saved, started going to church a lot sooner.*

"Mama, can I see the flower?"

"Sure, honey, you go put it in water now."

Shavonne ran into the kitchen, as if there were no time to waste. Dashan and Dorise smiled at each other the way adults do when children do something cute. The whole scene had an oddly domestic feel.

"She sure is a nice child."

Dorise's sister said, "Mmmph," as if to contradict, but neither of the others paid her any mind at all.

Dorise said, "Did y'all have a nice visit?"

"Well, we did. I've just been getting acquainted with your sister here. We had a lot to talk about—my family's in the laundry business. And then Shavonne and I talked about kitty-cats. She likes the striped ones best."

Dorise had to laugh. "Which kind's your favorite?"

Her sister said, "Mmmph" again, jealous as hell—Dorise and Dashan were still looking at each other.

Dashan said, "You know those nice black and white ones? More white than black, though, like with ink spots, and black feet."

"You've been doing some thinking about this."

"Well, everybody has a favorite kitty-cat, don't they?" And he gave her a smile that made her feel like the queen of England.

The restaurant was in this big old beautiful house—more like a mansion, really—and they showed Dashan and her to a table all set with white linen and a candle and flowers—real nice—and then Dashan said, "How about some champagne?"

For starters, they ordered three things so they could taste everything, and then they ate some fish that made her feel like she'd died and gone to heaven, but that was nothing compared to the chocolate cake they brought out after that. Dorise had never tasted cake like that, all full of raspberry and something that tasted as if it would make you drunk.

And all through the meal they drank champagne and other fine wine, none of which was like anything Dorise had ever had in her life.

Jesus, she thought, *you have sent me a prince among men. You must not have meant me to make that promise I made if you sent me a man like this. You must be saying it be time to get serious, find me the right kind of man, once and for all. Good father for Shavonne, good husband for me. I b'lieve I'm ready at last.*

It was like a homecoming. For one thing, so different from being with Troy. Dashan asked her about her work, and about her clients, but he wanted to know about her—how she felt about it and them, not what they had that he could steal. He asked at least a hundred questions about Shavonne—and all of them nice ones, like what were her hobbies? Did she like her teacher? What school did she go to? Not did Dorise ever get tired of taking care of her, how often could she get a baby-sitter.

This was a man who not only wouldn't dream of breaking the law, he wouldn't have to. This was a man doing well—a good Christian man she'd met in church just the way it was supposed to be.

She was so busy congratulating herself, so busy being over-whelmed by her good fortune, she almost forgot to ask him about himself.

He liked his new job a lot, he said, and he liked New Orleans. "Even better now," he said. "If I didn't have a reason to stick around before, I got one now. Let me ask you something—maybe it's something you never thought of, I just want to know."

"Sure, Dashan." She loved that serious look he got, as if what she thought was the most important thing in the world.

"Do you think you're through having children, or would you consider having more?"

She couldn't believe what he'd just said. A man didn't ask a question like that unless he had a reason. She wanted to say, "I'd do anything for you. Just tell me and I'll do it." But she had her wits about her enough to say she hadn't really thought about it. She loved Shavonne a lot, she told him, but she didn't think she'd rule out the possibility of having more kids.

He nodded, as if the answer satisfied him; he was so serious.

So nice.

When he took her home he didn't even try to kiss her, just pecked her on the cheek and said he didn't know when he'd had more fun, she sure was good for him.

Her sister said, "Somethin' funny about that man. He just a little bit too good to be true."

But that's just the way she was.

21

• •

The Monk had been amazed when his niece didn't keep her appointment with the cop. He had left without even his crook, or his emergency money. At first he hadn't had the least idea what to do.

He could have stayed with Revelas, but he didn't know where his own best friend lived, which made him wonder about his life and the way he was living it. Yet how else could he live it, considering the way things were?

He had enough money for a few meals, but a hotel was out of the question. Of course, he had no credit cards—he didn't believe in leaving footprints within the system. He didn't even have a driver's license. One of Dahveed's gay friends had traded him the scooter for an angel mural on his ceiling.

No friends, no money, no plastic—and for the moment, no home. He wondered what it would be like to spend the night in Washington Square. On the whole, he decided, he'd rather be in Philadelphia. There was a nice vacant lot on Frenchmen, though, quite near the square. That might be okay.

He started walking. It would be fine to sleep outside, he thought, because the outside was already dirty—therefore, no need to try to clean it. And no need to take a shower either. It might even be fun.

As it turned out, it was such a relief he started wondering if he was going to end up a street person. He settled in, but found he couldn't go to sleep until he was sure Lovelace had. So he went back to his own house, where he watched till the lights went out.

I'm my angel's guardian angel, he thought, and the thought filled him with such pride, such love that he could have stood watch all night. He liked this a lot—this love from a distance.

Perhaps, he thought, *I can stop being The White Monk and be The White Knight.*

This was a good plan, an excellent plan. As long as he stayed on the street, the police couldn't find him. And as long as he had no house, he didn't have to wash.

He'd still have the thoughts, of course, and some of them might be worse than usual, since he couldn't make them stop by painting. But this was his job for right now—watching over his angel. He was oddly pleased at that.

He was up with the sun the next morning, watching his house— her house now. But she didn't come out. Her meeting was at seven, he couldn't be wrong about that. The Camellia Grill was at the opposite end of town, about as far uptown as you could get and not fall in the river. It could take an hour or more to get there on public transportation. His plan was to follow her until she got on a bus, then get on his motor scooter and be there before her—just to see that everything went okay.

But six came and six-thirty, and then seven, and still she didn't come out. He peeked in the window, and there she was lying on her new futon, peaceful as a real angel. He was touched—she could have slept in the bedroom, but she had kept it clear for him.

All of a sudden she sat straight up, as if she'd sensed him there, and he had to duck. He couldn't really hide in his own neighborhood— what to do?

Finally, he went to Pamela's, and wrote her a note asking if he could come inside. She said, "Sure, Monkie, whatever your white little heart desires." Pamela was such a nice woman; she never asked questions. She'd never even mentioned his shaved head.

He simply walked in, sat on the sofa, and turned toward his own house so he could see out the window. Pamela said, "You want anything?" but he pretended he hadn't heard. There were two great things about not talking—people thought maybe you were deaf and maybe you were crazy, and if you acted as if you were one or both, they left you alone.

Lovelace finally left at about nine. He got up and followed, without even a word to Pamela, knowing she wouldn't care.

When I start talking, he thought, *I'm going to have to do something nice for that woman.* He was aware that that was the first time he'd actually thought about talking again.

Lovelace set out walking through familiar territory, straight to Rough Trade.

What the hell, he thought, and pretty soon a big woman went in, six feet or more, with wild, crazy hair.

I'd like to paint her, he thought. *She's terrific-looking.*

When the woman came out, she just kind of stood in the street for a long time, and it came to him that she was doing what he was doing—watching the gallery.

She must be the cop, he thought. Lovelace must have decided to meet her here. *Maybe she tried to turn me in. Maybe she thinks I'm going to kill somebody.*

But eventually she left, and Lovelace came out and walked to the streetcar. The Monk took a taxi home and got his scooter. She must have gone to work, he reasoned. Where else would she go? He parked near Judy's Juice, and found a place to hide. Sure enough, there was his angel behind the counter. He stayed with her.

The whole thing was familiar and not familiar. *I wonder if I'm doing this because I have to,* he thought. *It sort of feels like it and sort of doesn't. But I think it's like wearing white or keeping silence. I think I have free will on this one.*

He found it gave him an odd sense of peace and purpose, almost fulfillment, like painting. *That must mean I want to,* he thought. *Other people live like this all the time. Other people do things just because they want to.*

He caught his reflection in a window and saw that he still had twigs on his clothes from sleeping outside. He didn't bother to remove them.

• •

Skip went straight to City Hall and looked up the business license issued to Juicy's Juice. It had been given to an Anthony Earls in 1992. It had probably gone out of business. Going backward, she looked up Earls. Six months ago, he'd gotten another license—for Judy's Juice on Maple Street.

Now that sounded more promising. She headed straight over.

She realized what had happened—Judy's opened after the phone book came out; therefore it wasn't listed.

She had parked and was more or less ambling, not really thinking about anything much except that this was probably another dead end, when she heard a man's voice, loud and alarmed. "You get on out of here. You leave her alone now!"

She stepped up her pace, and when she could see in the window of Judy's, she ducked out of sight, grabbed her radio, and called for backup.

It looked like a holdup in progress. One man, evidently a look-out, faced the door. Another faced the counter, pointing a gun at two people behind it. One of them was a black man with dreads, the other a nearly bald woman.

The man facing the door was white, wearing a blue shirt, khakis, a Saints cap pulled low, and a pair of shades. The other one, also wearing a cap—a blue one of some sort—was speaking in a voice too low for Skip to hear. She heard part of the woman's answer: "You're crazy," and her heart sank. Resisting a holdup was as likely as not to be fatal.

She crossed the street, planning to pose as a passerby and get a better look in the window. By the time she had a view, the man in the blue cap was behind the counter, fighting with the black man, who was evidently Anthony Earls. The other joined him, laying Earls out with one blow. Blue-cap grabbed the woman, but she pulled back.

She heard one of the men say, "Lovelace, for Christ's sake," and she made a hard, dangerous decision not to wait for backup. This had to be Daniel: Surely the man wouldn't shoot his own daughter; and there was no time.

Dodging cars, she ran across the street, hearing as she ran the blessed sound of a siren. She pulled her gun. "Police! Drop it."

The man shot at her and she returned fire. He fell. The other one slipped into what looked like a kitchen. The bald woman shouted, "Daddy!"

Behind the counter, there was blood everywhere. Blue-cap was lying slumped against the wall. Skip's head whirled, a side effect, she knew, of that other shooting, the one the year before. She heard the woman say, "Don't shoot him. Don't shoot my daddy!" and she turned toward the woman, her mind's eye full of a little girl in pink shorts, crawling toward her mother.

She couldn't have looked away more than a split second, but by the time she turned back, officers with drawn guns were pouring through the door. She said, "He's in there," and gave her attention to the girl, mouthing the obligatory lies. "Lovelace. It's okay. It's okay now." She bent over the fallen man, and saw that the wound was in his head. She felt bile in her throat, so strong she thought there was a good chance of disgracing herself. She swallowed, but more saliva flowed. She turned away. "Give me a cloth, quick."

The girl handed her something, possibly an apron or a dishcloth, and she pressed it to the wound, though there was barely any blood. With action, her nausea was starting to pass.

She heard a quick movement behind, and fearing Lovelace meant to run, she whirled, but another officer had caught the girl, and was holding her tight, murmuring that it was all right: the all-purpose lie in emergencies.

• •

The Monk cursed himself for failing at first to recognize his own brother. He saw the two men go into the juice bar, and saw the one with the blue cap pull a gun, the other one turn to face the outside. *Daniel?* he thought, and saw that it was. He ran for the phone on the corner. He never stopped to consider whether or not to talk. He was giving his location to the 911 operator when he saw the woman, the big cop, threading her way through traffic. He hung up and went back to watch, from the safe side of the street. As he ran, he heard a siren, getting louder.

He was nearly there, nearly directly across from the juice bar, when the street exploded. He took cover in the nearest shop. Pedestrians screamed and scattered. Three more ran into The Monk's shop. By then, the shooting had stopped.

People were screaming, shouting, one woman was crying. But from across the street came a huge bubble of silence, a void of noise so oppressive it felt like a thunderstorm. A police car hurtled into view and stopped with a squeal of brakes. A uniformed officer leapt out, and another car hurtled, braked, and squealed. Another officer, gun drawn.

Silence.

Silence.

Oh, Christ, is she alive or dead? I have to get over there.

People were clustered at the door of the shop. He tried to break through the cluster, not even stopping to consider whether or not to speak. "Excuse me," he said, as if he did it every day.

No one moved. A woman said, "You can't go out there."

He could have explained. He could have said, "My niece is over there," and the crowd would probably have parted, but he didn't want to give out information. The last thing he wanted to do was draw attention to himself, have the police take him into custody, make him sit for hours, God knew what.

He simply said, "Excuse me" again, and continued to elbow. No one wanted to physically restrain him, and more police cars were pulling up, all squealing their brakes. There were no other cars: they must have sealed off the street. Police were all over the place now, swarming like hornets, and just as dangerous.

He kept elbowing, and gained the door in time to see two policemen handing Lovelace into a marked car.

Thank the gods.

He waved to the nearest policeman. "Officer, I need to talk to that woman. She's my niece."

The cop shouted, "What?" And the car drove off.

He started to cross the street, "Where are they taking her?"

"Let's try to keep the street clear, sir."

"She's my niece. I need to be sure she's all right."

"Sir, I'm really going to have to ask you to get back on the sidewalk. We're letting people walk on that side now."

The Monk wasn't at all sure the cop had heard him. He took off walking on the side he was permitted and retrieved his scooter. They'd probably take her to Headquarters, he thought, on Broad Street. He'd go there and try to find her.

He putt-putted along in severe traffic, and had gone only about a block in ten minutes when he finally saw a clear path, if he passed on the right. This was the good thing about a scooter—it could do that. He zipped out and just as he did, noticed a dude about half a block up the street stepping off the curb, and walking around a white pickup.

Uh-oh, it looked like he was going to open the door and get in. Cursing, The Monk slowed to accommodate the setback. The man got in and closed the door, just as The Monk came up on him. Perfect timing, he thought, and glanced to the right as he passed, to make sure the man was in and the door properly closed. The man looked like Daniel.

He tried to look again, but he was already past. He had forgotten about Daniel. This man wore shorts and no hat—it hadn't occurred to him it was Daniel. He realized he'd assumed, in the back of his mind, that his brother had been arrested.

He worked his way back into the line of traffic, watched in his mirror as the truck pulled out, and did the same. Once again, The Monk pulled over to the right, between the traffic and the cars parked on the curb, and drove to the end of the block, where he turned around and came back. Traffic was still creeping, but the truck had passed his corner. He came up on it slowly, not even slightly worried that his brother would recognize him with his head shaved. When he was parallel, he glanced over again.

Daniel.

He pulled ahead, circled the block, and found himself again behind the truck. He memorized its license plate, and then he followed it.

It parked on Magazine Street, and The Monk pulled over into a driveway, as if he lived there. He watched as Daniel entered a house, whose address he noted. He pulled out of the driveway, parked the scooter, sat down as if he were a street person, and watched the house for a while. No one came or went.

What now? The Monk thought. *Do I keep watching? What happened to the other man? What happened to the big cop? Is one of them dead? It's my fault if they are. They could both be dead and it's my fault. I could have moved faster; I could have tried to stop them myself rather than tried to call the police. They could both be dead and I'm responsible. I've got to get out of here. I've got to go home.*

But he knew if he went home, he would have to clean the house and shower for a long time and someone could come while he was in the shower. The police could come. On the other hand if he didn't go home, he might kill someone else. Should he go home or not?

He walked down the block and got a sidewalk table at a coffee-house, where he drank espresso and kept up his watch. After a while he switched to water, but kept his table. It grew dark and still he watched, trying to decide what to do next.

At the house on Magazine, all was quiet.

Finally, he decided to check into a hotel. At least he'd be inside, where he couldn't hurt anyone. The problem was, his money stash was back at his house, and by now Lovelace might have told the cops where he lived. They might already be watching his house.

He couldn't move. But when they came out to get the tables for the night, he had no choice.

He drove back slowly, stopping at the end of the block to see if there were any strange cars on the street.

Things looked normal. Everything was quiet.

22

• •

Lovelace had recognized the cop as soon as she came in shooting—Skip Langdon, the one Michelle said was so nice. To her surprise, the others were nice, too—the ones who took her to Headquarters and got her coffee and asked if she was hungry while she waited for Langdon. She had requested Langdon, and they said, yes, Lovelace was going to get to talk to her, but it was going to be a while. Another female cop came in, Sergeant Cappello, a nice-looking, calm-seeming woman dressed in a black pantsuit. She asked if Lovelace needed anything, and Lovelace asked her if Anthony was okay, and if she could talk to him.

"Not now," she said. "They took him to Charity."

Charity Hospital. Lovelace happened to know his wife was out of town. She jumped up. "I'd better go stay with him—he's probably by himself."

But the sergeant explained to her she didn't think that was a good idea; Lovelace had better just wait for Langdon. She started feeling trapped, and wondered if she was. She thought about asking for a lawyer. She wasn't a criminal, she was a victim—could they hold her against her will?

On the other hand, what lawyer was she going to call, and how was she going to pay him? Maybe she should call Michelle—her parents could get her a lawyer.

She was about to ask to make a call when Langdon appeared and stuck out her hand. "Hi, I'm Skip Langdon."

Not Detective Langdon. Skip. Lovelace liked that. Langdon wasn't playing games with her. And she liked the way Langdon looked as well. She was even taller than Lovelace. The shape of her face and her nose were what she thought of as Irish, though she didn't know why. The eyes were slightly almond-shaped, and they were a vivid green. Maybe that was it. Then she had this curly, tumbling hair, which was pinned up, but barely, and smooth, pretty skin, brownish-gold, like a baguette.

There was something about her that was very down to earth, casual even. Maybe, if you got right down to it, even a little sloppy. She was slightly overweight, for one thing, and her butt jiggled inside a pair of linen pants that tied with a drawstring and that were almost floods—but when you were as tall as Langdon, Lovelace had no idea how you ever got pants that were long enough. She had enough trouble herself. The cop's tucked-in cotton tank top was a bit on the tired side, and sort of a khaki green that almost went with the beige pants, but not quite.

She moved awkwardly, too, like a girl who'd never had ballet lessons. She didn't seem even slightly intimidating.

Lovelace said, "I'm Lovelace Jacomine. But you know that."

"Sit down," said the detective, and they both did. "You have no idea how worried about you I've been."

"I heard you were looking for me."

"Night and day, young lady. Night and day."

She asked again, "How's Anthony?"

"He's okay. They sent him home."

"How about the other man—the one with my dad?"

"Not good." A shadow crossed the cop's face.

"Dead?"

The cop nodded, and Lovelace thought she looked as sad as if a relative had died instead of a man who'd tried to kill her. Skip said, "The other man is your dad?"

"Uh-huh. Did you find him?"

"He's a pretty slick operator, you know that?"

The cop was starting to play games. Lovelace hated it when someone answered a question with a question. She spoke sharply. "Is he okay? Tell me."

"Take it easy. I'd tell you if I knew. He got away. Tell me something, will you? Why does your own dad want to kidnap you?"

"To take me to my grandfather."

"And how do you know that?"

"My grandmother told me. At least, a woman who said she's my grandmother, but those two haven't seen each other in a million years as far as I know. I can't figure out why she thinks that."

"How about if you start from the beginning."

And so Lovelace did, beginning with her dad's kidnapping her on the Northwestern campus and ending with the shoot-out at Judy's Juice.

When she had finished, Langdon had only one question, having apparently heard most of the story from Michelle. "Where," she asked, "did you say your uncle Isaac lives?"

"I didn't say."

"I thought you said the Bywater."

Had she? "My uncle is a very strange, very wonderful man. He's been terrific to me, and I'm not about to violate his privacy."

"Lovelace, a man got killed today, but he fired at me first. Do you realize what that means? He'd just as easily have fired at you."

"He would not. My dad wouldn't let him."

"Do you think your dad would shoot your uncle—to try to get to you, maybe? How close are they?"

Lovelace felt her heart leap to her throat, closing it. She tried to take in air, and couldn't for a moment. She truly hadn't thought of that. But she knew as well as she knew how to make carrot juice that the best thing she could do for her uncle was keep quiet.

She said, "I really can't tell you where he lives."

"If your grandfather finds out, he might kill him just for revenge—for harboring you."

"Kill his own son? Listen, my family's nuts, but we don't kill each other." *Not yet*, she thought. *At least not yet.*

Langdon said it. "Not yet, you mean. I'm telling you, Lovelace, we need to get your uncle some protection."

"If you can't find him, how's my grandfather going to?"

"They found you, didn't they?"

For no reason, Lovelace felt her eyes fill. "They're not going to find him!" She couldn't believe the sound of her own voice, which seemed suddenly about eleven years old.

Langdon glanced at her watch. "I've got to go for a few minutes. Will you be okay?"

Lovelace nodded, thinking, *She's leaving me to stew. How dumb does she think I am?*

It seemed hours before the cop came back, though it was probably only about forty-five minutes. In that time, Lovelace had gone back and forth a hundred times—should she tell her or not? In the end, she felt she had to respect Isaac's wishes.

Whatever way the cops had found her was probably the way her dad had—and if the cops couldn't find Isaac, then neither could her grandfather.

When Langdon came back, she had a list with her—of all the crimes her grandfather was wanted for. She also told the story of a body she had found; when she got to the part about the cigarette burns, Lovelace put her hands over her ears and screamed Isaac's address.

• •

By the time Daniel got back to Magazine Street, he had begun to hate the Langdon cop almost as much as his father did.

He had gone through the kitchen of the juice bar, barged through the back door, and found himself in a small courtyard. There was a brick fence which he managed to scale, with the help of a garbage can for a boost, and again he found himself in a courtyard, a pleasant one with a green wrought-iron table, on which someone had left a newspaper and a mug of coffee or tea.

There was a side entrance to the courtyard, at the end of which there might be a locked gate—or it might be unlocked. This fence could be scaled as well, or he might simply be able to walk out the gate—but then again he might not, and cops would be coming over the brick wall in a minute.

There was also the back door of a house.

He grabbed the paper and the mug, tried the door, and to his relief found it open. He went in, closed it, turned the key, which had been conveniently left in the lock, and listened. Behind him, he heard men scrambling into the courtyard. Inside the house, he heard a kind of dull roar, as if plumbing was in use.

Reasoning that the cops would do as he had, assess the situation and pick the easiest exit, he listened. Someone tried the door and then he heard running.

He crept upstairs, where there were two bedrooms facing each other, saw that both were empty, and noticed a third door, which was closed. The sound of running water came from behind it— apparently a bathroom. Silently, he opened the door, and saw a closed shower curtain. Whoever was behind it was going to scream when they realized they weren't alone. Man or woman, they'd remember *Psycho* and wail their lungs out. If there was a window on the other side of the curtain, Daniel was dead.

He thought of jerking the curtain back and commanding silence, but the person would almost certainly scream anyway. He had to prolong the silence as long as he could. This door, too, had a key in it. He closed and locked it.

Then he took off his cap, shades, and shirt, exposing a black T-shirt. He was unzipping the legs of his old safari pants, the kind that could be turned into shorts in thirty seconds, when the person in the shower startled him by bursting into song. It was a sadly off-key version of "Amazing Grace," delivered in a female voice.

You wouldn't start a song, he reasoned, if you were about to turn the shower off. Also, since it was a woman in there, she might put on her makeup or dry her hair before she came out of the bathroom. And he was ready to go.

So he shoved the bundle under one of the beds, very gently unlocked the bathroom door, slipped quietly downstairs, and walked out the front door. Seeing a cop across the street, he made as if to lock the door and walked down the porch steps, bold as a banker. When he was far enough away from the house not to alarm the showering woman, he shouted, "What's going on?" to further estab-lish his bona fides. The officer only shook his head and continued his search. Summoning all his willpower, Daniel began to whistle "Amazing Grace."

Walking briskly, as if he had to be someplace, but not so fast as to seem alarmed, he made his way to his truck, where he noticed for the first time that he was shaking so hard he could hardly find his keys. All he could think about was how angry his father was going to be.

But to his utter surprise, the elder Jacomine, fiddling at his desk, broke into a smile when his son entered the house. "Look what the cat dragged in."

"Dad, we fucked up." Might as well get it over with.

"Oh, yeah, I know. Been listening to the radio. Thought you were the one down, boy. I've been worried."

"You have? About me?" Daniel was unaccountably touched.

"You're my son, aren't you? Why wouldn't I be worried?" His dad did not get up to hug him, but then he never did that. This was as good a reaction as could be expected.

"We didn't get her, Daddy."

"I know that, boy. I know that. Just tell me what happened. How'd you get away?"

So he got to tell that part first, which was a blessing, as his father would say. When he told about unlocking the bathroom door, his father actually shivered. "Boy, you got balls of steel."

Daniel shrugged. "I spent years learning how to survive."

"Well, I'm proud of you. Real proud." And without warning, he leaned back in his chair and laughed until he had to reach for a tissue to wipe his eyes. "So that woman might not figure out what happened for days."

"Could be years if she doesn't clean under her bed very often—and from the look of it, she doesn't."

"Still, there's the locked back door. And you brought the paper and mug in—damn clever to think of that, by the way."

Daniel basked in his father's too-rare praise. "She'll just think she did it herself. You know how people are—she'll say to herself, 'I must be crazy; I did that and forgot about it.' "

"You didn't tell me how my granddaughter is. How'd she look?"

"Great. Except for being bald." He raised an eyebrow. "I don't understand kids anymore—she dyed her hair black and cut it so short she almost looks bald."

His father actually laughed. "She probably thinks that's some sort of disguise. So tell me something else, boy." The laughter was gone now. His father leaned forward on his desk, eyes narrowing. His dangerous look. "How'd a smart boy like you let Devil-Woman follow him to that juice bar?"

Well, fuck.

He wasn't going to take this. He'd done so well even his father admitted it; he wasn't about to get blamed for something he didn't do. "Daddy, I swear on my darling mother's head—" that ought to get him "—I didn't get followed. I didn't spend all those years in Idaho learning survivalist techniques so I could do a damn-fool thing like that."

"Well, how do you account for the fact she got there at the same time you did?"

"If she'd followed us, we'd never have gotten as far as we did. The woman's a detective—she did what we did; looked up Isaac's last employer."

His father stood up. "Detective, my fucking foot. Son of a mother-fucking bitching bastard. That woman's the spawn of the demon Lilith and the clove-footed beast from below." He was spitting. " 'Therefore says the Lord God . . . behold, I am against you; and I will execute judgments against you in the sight of the nations. And because of all your abominations I will do with you what I have never yet done and the like of which I will never do again. . . . You shall be a reproach and a taunt, a warning and a horror, when I execute judgments on you in anger and fury, and with furious chastisements—I, the Lord God, have spoken.' "

His voice dropped, and it was low and terrible. "God will be the instrument of her destruction and he will work through me and he will work *now*! Not soon. Not when all my petty plans are laid. He will work immediately! The female beast from the darkest corner of hell must be destroyed before we can proceed with our master plan—before justice can be done for the people of these great United States. She stands in our way and she must be removed."

Even to Daniel, he sounded nuts. All he could think was, *Thank God he's mad at her instead of me.*

It could so easily have gone the other way.

"We've got to escalate this Shavonne thing. Forget that fucking Dorise; forget all that finesse and careful planning. God doesn't have time for that. God wants to act now.

"Go get Shavonne. Go get her right now. Don't even change your clothes. Just go get her."

"Uh . . . Daddy . . . I don't actually think I know a Shavonne."

His father seized the heaviest thing at hand—the stapler on his desk—and threw it at him. It caught Daniel square in the forehead, in the spot damn-fool kids like his daughter called "the third eye." The kind of pain it caused was something like a cut and something like a heavy blow and, oddly, something like a tickle, yet the way a tickle would be if it were the worst pain in the world.

Daniel staggered backward, automatically throwing a hand up to his forehead. It came away wet and red. Blood filled his eyes. He hit a table leg and staggered. His father gave no sign that he noticed. Instead, he picked up his phone and said, "Get Dashan Jericho over here," in a voice so thick with menace, Daniel feared for Dashan.

His father looked at him again and for the first time seemed to notice the blood. He said, "Son, let me get you something for that." He walked out of the room and came back with a towel. It was the first time in memory Daniel had known him to get something for himself, much less for someone else. "We've got to get you better," he said. With one hand he handed the towel to Daniel, with the other he guided him into a chair. Daniel sat there applying pressure to his wound, feeling befogged and slightly nauseous, until Dashan arrived.

Dashan began his greeting, which would have been, "Hey, Daddy," Daniel thought, but he got no farther than the first "D."

"Dashan, where's that little girl go to school?"

"Shavonne?"

"Of course, Shavonne. Look alive, son. Who've you been working on? You have been working, haven't you, Dashan?"

"Of course, Daddy. Dorise and I are thick as thieves."

"Well, I don't give a shit about Dorise. Your assignment was to get as close as you could to Shavonne. Now, where's she go to school?"

"McDonogh Number Forty-three, Daddy. Her teacher is Mrs. Pearl Rivers, and the principal is Felix Pitre."

"Fine. Now you two boys go over there and hold it up at gunpoint. Get that kid and bring her here. You get followed and the Lord will take his vengeance."

"Daddy, there's no need for that. I've been doing my work. Shavonne'll leave with me. She loves me."

Daniel's dad screamed. "Did you hear me, you jackass? Did I say use guns or didn't I? What did I tell you?"

"Yessir. You said use guns, Daddy. And that's what we're going to do."

"And I mean use guns. See that at least one shot is fired, you hear me? And nobody gets hurt and nobody gets followed."

"Yessir."

Daddy nodded. "Good. The Lord lift up his countenance upon you and give you peace."

This last was so incongruous Daniel almost wondered if his dad were drunk.

"Let's go, Dashan."

"What happened, brother?" Meaning his wound.

Daniel winced, knowing it would set Daddy off again. His father was around his desk before either of the others saw him move. "I'm going to kick your butts." He raised his foot and kicked Dashan into the wall. "Get up, boy," he said to Daniel. "Now turn around."

In the car, on the way over to the school, Dashan said, "Man, you must have done something *really* bad. He's so mad at you it's getting on me."

"Well, my man, usually he is. But this time it's not me he's mad at. It's somebody else."

"He sure is mad."

"Yeah. So we better not fuck up—what you know about burglary?"

Dashan said, "Are you kidding? I'm a computer nerd."

"Okay. Let me think about this."

They drove around until they had a plan, though in the end it was all Daniel's plan. Daniel had spent his life studying survival; Dashan had spent his bent over books. He could drive, Daniel thought.

The first thing—to buy some time—was to cut the phone lines. That should be easy, as most public buildings have phone boxes outside. They went to buy supplies: wire cutters, coveralls, a couple of new caps. They already had plenty of guns.

Daniel left Dashan in the car, sweat running down his cheeks. *He's not going to last,* Daniel thought. *I just hope he gets through this one.*

In his coveralls, cap, and shades—this time the reflecting kind— Daniel found the phone box and cut the wires. Then, toolbox in hand, he went to the principal's office and asked for Shavonne Bourgeois's room number.

The secretary was a black woman of about thirty, with straightened hair and about sixty extra pounds. She had a round, pretty face and wore no makeup. She was chewing gum.

She said, "If you need to leave something for her, I'll see that it gets there."

Daniel might have argued with her, might even have tried to sweet-talk her, but there was no time for that. He said, "Take me to her, darlin'."

The woman looked puzzled, as if she couldn't believe someone would talk to her like that.

He said, "Her dad's been in an accident. He's not expected to live."

"Omigod. Stay here and I'll get her."

"I'm going with you."

The woman stood up and walked around the counter. She was nearly at the door when she seemed to remember her job.

She turned to him. "Sir, I really need authorization from the child's parents. I'm sorry, but I—"

"Her mother's at the hospital." He looked over her shoulder at three curious faces, two black, one white, all female. "Look, could we talk in the hall?"

The woman shrugged shoulders that looked massive—though not unattractive—under dark green fabric. She crossed the threshold and almost the second she did, Daniel put the gun to her head.

"Let's go."

Fortunately, it wasn't far. The woman wet her pants almost instantly and hyperventilated the entire way. He didn't know how long he had before she passed out.

He shoved her into the room. "Get the teacher out here."

But the teacher didn't have to be asked. She took one look at the secretary and without even a word to the kids, click-clicked to the door of the room. "What is it?" she hissed.

Daniel showed her his gun. "Shavonne Bourgeois. Now."

"I'm sorry, but I really can't—"

He shoved the gun in the secretary's temple so hard she jumped. "You can, or I'll kill her."

Without flinching, the teacher turned around; an extremely cool customer, also black, a lot older than the secretary. "Shavonne, can I see you a minute?"

As soon as the girl was close enough, Daniel grabbed her. The teacher made a noise like someone who's been hit, and literally grabbed for Shavonne. Took her around the waist and pulled. Daniel had her arm. Shavonne, suddenly the object of a tug of war that might result in mayhem, screamed, "Mama. Mama, Mama!"

Daniel hit the teacher with the gun, its butt to her temple. The sound was ugly, even to him.

The secretary, seizing the distraction, started running down the hall, screaming, "Help! Help! Kidnapping! Help!"

Daniel fired a shot, and she fell down. He didn't think he'd hit her—hadn't even aimed for her—but she lay still.

Room doors were cracked and timid heads peeked out. However, one man, a large black dude Daniel thought might have been a coach, flung open his door and lunged.

Daniel didn't have so much as a split second to make a decision. He simply fired, more or less a reflex.

The bell rang, signifying school was out for the day.

Only later did Daniel remember that Daddy said no one gets hurt. It occurred to him to throw himself from the speeding car.

23

• •

Cappello got the call while Skip was questioning Lovelace. The girl was still screaming when the sergeant came in. Skip knew from Cappello's face the worst had happened. *What can be worse?* she thought. *I killed a man today.*

Another man.

Cappello took care of the girl first. "Calm down, Lovelace. Take a deep breath."

Skip said, "What is it?"

Cappello said, "Let's get her squared away." She turned to Lovelace. "You okay, darlin'?"

Lovelace shut up quickly. Nodded, looking terrified. "Is it my uncle?"

"No, baby, it's not your uncle. Langdon, you through here?"

"Yes."

"Lovelace, we're going to have to put you in protective custody for a while. Stay here a minute more. I'll send someone for you as soon as I can."

She didn't wait for an answer, just left the interrogation room, Skip following.

"What is it?"

"Someone's kidnapped a little girl at school, just as the kids were getting out for the day. The FBI's over there—they want you right away."

"Why?"

"I'm afraid it's a kid you know. Shavonne Bourgeois."

"Oh, shit! It's Jacomine. Oh, shit—Shavonne. I never thought of that—I thought Sheila or Kenny. I never thought Shavonne. Oh, God, the man's evil. I swear to God he's the devil. Always one step ahead, no matter how I think I'm in control."

"Hey, hey. Take it easy."

The tirade had been involuntary. She expected Cappello to tell her how paranoid she was, possibly even to take her off the case. The sergeant said, "You want to sit down?"

"I'm okay, goddammit. I'm just mad." *And scared half out of my mind.*

"We need to talk about this. Let's go in my office." Cappello would probably send her to Cindy Lou this time—a definitive vote of no confidence. It would end up in an administrative reassignment, and she needed to be on the case. She could have bitten her tongue off.

Still, there was nothing to do but follow the sergeant like a puppy-dog.

Cappello made her sit, though Skip was far too antsy to pull it off with any grace. She wanted to stand; she wanted to pace. She wanted to chew nails and pound walls.

Cappello said, "You think Jacomine kidnapped Shavonne to get to you somehow." She sounded like a shrink, humoring the patient.

"I know it sounds crazy, but he *is* crazy. I'm telling you, Sylvia. . . ."

"The FBI agrees with you."

"What?" Skip hoped her mouth wasn't hanging open. She said, "Shellmire."

Cappello nodded. "Shellmire knows all about you and Delavon. He knew exactly who Shavonne was, and apparently the feds huddled and came up with the same theory you have."

"Do they have any evidence?"

"None." But she hesitated.

"What?"

"Well, I guess the whole terrorist thing got to them. And, frankly, maybe the fact that it was a white guy."

"I don't get it."

She shrugged. "Obviously it wasn't the kid's father. He cut the phone lines and marched right in wearing coveralls and those insect glasses—scary as hell. And he shot someone for no reason."

"Dead?"

"Not so far."

Skip sighed. "If there's a Jacomine M.O., that's more or less it—terrorist tactics, senseless violence."

"Listen. How're you holding up?" It was the same question Cappello had asked before, when Danny LaSalle had shot Herbert. It meant, "Are you going to make it, or are you going to fall apart after shooting that man today?"

"I'm fine." It was more or less true. She wasn't fine, but she wasn't falling apart either—at least not yet. She was running on adrenaline. "What about Public Integrity?"

That was the department's name for Internal Affairs, the cops who policed cops. She had been scheduled to report immediately after talking to Lovelace—standard procedure when an officer fired a shot.

"Later. The chief wants you out at the school. You're the only officer familiar with the case—and you may end up at the center of it. The whole goddamn city's exploding, and he doesn't want to look like an idiot."

"Too little too late."

She could have sworn the sergeant suppressed a smile. "Go. Abasolo's waiting for you."

Great. She finally had help.

It was bedlam at the school. The streets were clogged with parents and schoolbuses, trying to get the kids home. Emergency vehicles were everywhere, though there had been only three injuries—the shooting and two slight injuries resulting from a fall and a gun butt to the head.

Feds and policemen swarmed, streaked with sweat and looking disoriented. There was an odd sense of panic in the air.

An army of press was there. As soon as she and Abasolo emerged from their car, a familiar figure started toward them.

"Shit. Jane Storey." A former print reporter who'd been trying to nail Jacomine almost as long as Skip had. They'd pooled information once, and she'd had more than Skip. Skip owed her. And now she worked in television, which made her about ninety times as visible.

Abasolo said, "Let's just duck her."

"Right."

Jane waved. "Hey, Skip."

"Hey, Jane. Sorry. Can't talk now."

"I've got something for you."

That was the last thing she'd expected to hear. It stopped her in her tracks.

Jane said, "What's happening today? Is it the heat or what?"

"Big news day, huh?" This was New Orleans—you didn't get away without small talk.

"Listen, you know that Maple Street thing? That guy you shot? I know him."

He had been tentatively identified as Darnell Roberts, twenty-eight, no known address. That was all they had. Skip said, "You know him?"

"Yeah. From a long time ago—when I did the story on Blood of the Lamb." The name of Jacomine's flock.

"He was a member?"

Jane nodded. "Whew. Fanatic's more like it; he was the press liaison or something. Called me up and more or less made a threat. Course he said later he never said it. So what do you think? Was that juice bar thing connected with Jacomine? Is our favorite bogeyman surfacing again?"

Skip rolled her eyes. "No comment, Janie."

"Well, let me tell you something. You know who the getaway car is registered to?"

"What getaway car?"

"This one. The one in the McDonogh forty-three kidnapping."

"No comment, Janie." She didn't even know someone had gotten the plate.

"Well, I do. Darnell Roberts. You think these two things are connected?"

Abasolo said, "Holy shit."

251

"I'll take that for a yes. What do you think the asshole's up to?"

"What do you think?"

The reporter rolled her own eyes, "No comment, Skippy."

Skip and Abasolo went to find Shellmire, who had just talked to the principal. He was sporting two kinds of forehead cleavage, horizontal and vertical. "Skip, this is nasty."

"Tell me about it."

"It's about you. You know that, don't you?"

"Oh, yes."

"But what he wants, I don't know."

"I do. He wants me dead, but he wants to torture me first."

"You know what? In any other situation, I'd call for a shrink. But I have a bad feeling you're right."

Skip was so used to the idea that hearing it put so baldly didn't even give her goose bumps. She said, "Has anyone talked to Dorise?"

"The mother? Let's do it now." He gave her a hard stare. "You know what, Langdon? I like your sangfroid."

"It's an act. I'm shaking on the inside. Have been for weeks."

"That's a good thing. Otherwise I'd worry." And for a second, he rested a hand on her shoulder. "Listen, maybe I should go alone. You shot this woman's husband, didn't you? She might not see you."

"You know damn well I did. But I'd like to try. Let me tell Abasolo."

She caught up with the sergeant. "AA, I want to go with Shellmire to talk to the mother. How about if you stay here and pick up what you can?"

"You got it. I'm sure she doesn't want to see both of us." He'd been with her when she shot Delavon.

As Shellmire maneuvered out of his parking place, Skip said, "She lives in Gentilly. Moved away from the East. Too many memories, I guess."

He said, "I know that—I got her address from the school. But how do you know that?"

"I've kept up with the family. But—you know—I've been pretty private about it." She stared out the window, thinking.

"Meaning, how did Jacomine know kidnapping this kid was going to get to you?"

252

"Yeah. He's got to have sources within the department."

"Have you actually been to visit?"

"Not exactly."

He turned to her and raised an eyebrow.

"Watch your driving, will you? I . . . uh . . . leave little trinkets sometimes. For Shavonne."

"Uh-huh. Well, maybe The Jury's been watching you."

That one did give her goose bumps. She was silent for the rest of the trip.

They found Dorise with a district officer, a school official, her mother, and her sister. She'd apparently gotten over having hysterics and was now sitting pitifully on an old gold-covered sofa, tearing tissues into shreds.

Shellmire displayed his shield. "Agent Turner Shellmire, FBI. This is Detective Langdon."

Dorise nodded, turning to Skip. "I know Detective Langdon. You my secret admirer."

"Pardon me?"

"That jus' a little joke I tell myself. You leave little presents for Sh—" Apparently, she couldn't say the name. "For my daughter."

"I do, yes."

"Well, that's real nice of you. I know you feel bad about what you done, but I don't hold it against you. It was God's will. I know that."

Skip felt tears and lifted her chin, knowing that wouldn't hide them.

Shellmire said, "Is there someplace we can talk?"

As if he'd given a signal, the mother and the sister got up. The older woman said, "We go in the kitchen."

The school official said, "I better be going now," and the district officer rose as well. He spoke to Dorise. "You be sure to tell the detective everything you told me. Will you do that for me?" He gave Skip a meaningful look, and Skip in turn glanced at Dorise. The large woman who was Shavonne's mother slumped in her chair, obviously as miserable as if her daughter were already dead.

In a moment, she straightened, turning her attention to Skip and Shellmire. "Won't y'all sit down?"

"Thanks."

"I don't know what it is with me. I jus' cain't seem to find me a good man—seems like every man I meet got the devil in him." She plucked a tissue from a box someone had placed close at hand, and started crying anew.

Skip and Shellmire glanced at each other, alarmed, not having the least idea what to make of this.

She was nodding now, over and over again, and rocking her body as well. Cindy Lou had once told Skip that this movement was one people used to induce a mini-trance as a kind of comfort mechanism. "I know who got Shavonne. I know 'zactly who. Only problem, I don't know his address. Everything my sister said true as the word of the Lord."

"You know who kidnapped Shavonne." Skip thought she sounded like some particularly lame psychologist, repeating what the patient said.

"Oh, yes'm, I know. I sho' do know. He call himself Dashan Jericho and he say he a lawyer come from Monroe, but I bet a year's salary that ain't his name and ain't where he from, and he ain't no lawyer. Oh, why, oh, why didn't I listen to my sister?"

A voice from the kitchen said, "I hear that," and Skip thought her sister must be a small-minded bitch. She said, "Tell us about him, Dorise."

"Oh, he handsome, he slick as shit. He ax me out, and took me for a big ol' ride. Yes ma'am, my sister said he seem too good to be true, and she sho' be right about that."

"What makes you think he kidnapped your daughter?"

" 'Cause he entirely too interested in my little girl. No man I ever met in my life be that interested in my child. I shoulda known. I just shoulda known."

Skip and Shellmire were silent.

"He ax me what school she go to. What her teacher name. What her hobbies.

"Y'all see what I'm talkin' about? I didn't see nothin' comin'. Nothin'. I just thought he love chirren. He told me he had a little girl of his own. You know what I really thought? I thought he auditionin' to be Shavonne daddy. He axed me if I be willin' to have more chirren—now what you gon' make out of that?"

254

Skip could see exactly what was bothering her—she probably thought he had a mile-long record of child abuse, and maybe he did. Maybe she and the FBI were wrong about this one. She felt the tension in her shoulders let up a little.

Maybe, she thought, *this isn't my fault.* And knew, even as she thought it, she was as crazy as Dorise. If the man was a pedophile, it wasn't her mother's fault, and if he were Jacomine's flunky, it wasn't hers. But she wondered how healthy a person would have to be not to feel responsible.

And she also remembered what Jane Storey had said about the car—that it was registered to Jacomine's late follower. The kidnap had Jacomine written all over it.

Shellmire said, "How do you know this Dashan Jericho?"

"I met him at church. Where in God's name you *s'posed* to meet somebody? He walked into that church like he own the place, pick me right out, and ax me for my phone number."

"Did he meet Shavonne that day?"

"Oh, yeah. Oh, yeah, he sho' did meet Shavonne. Then later on, he talk to her while I be gettin' ready to go out. They talk about what color kitty-cats they like—you ever hear of a grown man doin' that?"

Skip said, "Fathers do—and uncles. People interested in kids, sure." She was nodding, not wanting Dorise to feel any worse than she had to. "Did he ever do anything inappropriate?"

"What you mean by that?"

"Did he touch her in an inappropriate way?"

"Not when I be aroun' he didn't. Lemme ax my sister." She raised her voice. "Sister! Sister, lemme ax you somethin'."

The sister came back to the living room, a shorts-clad, slightly messier version of Dorise, heavy though still in her twenties. "You ever see Dashan touch Shavonne?"

"No. He be real careful 'bout that. Never got nowhere near her. He sho' did watch her though. Mmm-mmm. He sho' did watch her."

Shellmire said, "Mrs. Bourgeois, did he ever say where he lived?"

"Well, I don't know why—I never did ax. I thought he just be a gentleman, not tryin' nothin', you know—tryin' to get me over there."

"Do you have a phone number?"

"No. He always call me—I thought he be so nice. Always call me."

"Do you have anything—anything at all—he might have touched?"

"What you mean?"

"A glass or something. For fingerprints."

"He didn't touch nothin' far as I can remember."

"Okay. What about a description?"

"Tall, light-skinned brother. Powerful man; good-lookin'! Yeah, he sho' is good-lookin'."

"He's a black man?"

Dorise looked at her as if she were crazy. "Course, he black. You think some white man's gon' want a great big ass like mine?"

"Ms. Bourgeois, the kidnapper was white." She felt slightly guilty about withholding this salient fact even as long as she had. But she had wanted Dorise as upset as possible to keep her talking.

"He white? The kidnapper white? Oh, thank you, Jesus! I didn't kill my little girl. Oh, Lord, I didn't do it!"

Skip thought, *Don't be too sure.*

She and Shellmire got a more detailed description and the name of the church where Dorise had met Jericho.

It came as no surprise that the pastor didn't know him, and didn't know who did. Jericho had attended church only the once, had cut a wide swath of admiration through the female congregation, and had never been seen again.

He wasn't listed in the New Orleans phone book or in the Monroe book, he had no criminal record and no Social Security number—in short, he appeared to have sprung from nowhere for the sole purpose of helping Jacomine snatch a little girl away from her mother.

Skip felt her shoulders tighten again.

She and Shellmire were working out of FBI headquarters. Abasolo joined them to report on the scene at the school. He had only one piece of pertinent information. "There was a driver, and the witness thinks it was a male. But she couldn't say for sure if he was black or white. Or even, for that matter, that he was definitely male. Too busy getting the plate."

Skip said, "Bless her for that. The address on the registration didn't check out, I presume?"

"You presume correctly."

She turned to Shellmire. "Do you guys have someone watching Isaac's house?"

Shellmire shrugged. "Shore, honey. We're the FBI. Doesn't mean we got diddly, though."

24

• •

Taking the precaution of leaving his scooter around the corner, The Monk hesitated, not able to make a decision to return to his house.

He thought of walking by and checking out all the parked cars, but what if the cops knew what he looked like now? Maybe they'd talked to the neighbors—maybe Pamela had told them.

Actually, he was pretty sure Pamela wouldn't tell them anything.

But then again she might if they told her he was in danger. Or if she suspected he'd killed someone.

Did she suspect? Did other people suspect? Did he look as if he'd killed someone, or was it all internal?

The Monk felt even more undecided and unable to think, and vulnerable to odd ideas, than usual. *I know*, he thought. *Actually, I really know. I know I didn't kill anybody, but how can I be sure? Maybe I did.*

But the thought disappeared almost as soon as it surfaced—at the moment he had more immediate pressures, and he'd noticed that when he needed to focus on something, the crazy thoughts went away and he was better able to think with his real mind. He thought of it that way—he had a real mind and a crazy one. It was just that the crazy one took over so often.

He suddenly had a thought: *I could just call Pamela. I know her last name. Why not give her a call? She might know something.*

He got his scooter, went to the Cafe Marigny, looked Pamela up, and dialed before he had time to think about it.

"Pamela? Hey. This is Isaac next door."

"Isaac?" She sounded utterly mystified.

"The White Monk."

"You're not The Monk. The Monk don't talk." Now she was mad.

"Pamela, it's me, honest—please don't hang up. I talk if I have to. It's been kind of a weird day—I need to ask you something."

"Where you callin' from?"

"Cafe Marigny. Why?"

"Walkin' or what?"

"I've got my scooter."

At the word "scooter," there was a change in her voice. "Well, maybe you are The Monk. I'm gon' take a little ride. Meet me by Hubig's Pies."

The Monk didn't like this at all—Pamela almost never left her house. She hated to drive almost as much as he hated to speak. What in hell was she doing?

It would take her longer to get to the meeting place than it would him. He decided to go right away and do what he'd been doing for days, it seemed like—hide and watch.

But sure enough, along she came in her ancient Ford Fiesta, alone as advertised, making the car look like a toy. No wonder she hated to drive; it must be hideously uncomfortable, given the miniature car and the oversized body.

He tapped on the window and slipped in beside her. "Darlin', when I get rich, I'm gon' buy you a Cadillac."

"Monkie! Baby, it really is you!" She leaned over and gave him a big hug, entirely forgetting to be solicitous of his touching problems.

He realized suddenly what it had cost her to come here—if she didn't think it was The Monk, who was she expecting? Whoever it was, she'd come out alone on a dark night to a block some people wouldn't go to in broad daylight—and all for a man who'd never spoken to her, who'd been the beneficiary of her good will and never given a thing back.

259

His eyes flooded. *I really do need to buy her a Cadillac.*

"Hey, if you could talk, why didn't you say so?"

"It's pretty hard to say anything when you're not talking. I never mentioned my vow of silence?"

"Monkie, you never mentioned a *damn* thing."

"Well, I always said I'd talk again if I weren't confused about what to say. And right now only one thing comes to mind."

"What?"

"Help me, Obi-Wan Kenobi, you're my only hope. Help me, Obi-Wan Kenobi, you're my only hope. Help me, Obi—"

She was laughing. "I never knew you were funny."

"Never more serious. Pamela, I've got some problems."

"You're not kidding, Monkie. The police are watching your house. Hey! Does this have anything to do with that pretty girl? I was so happy you finally got a girlfriend."

"I hate to tell you, that's my niece."

She wouldn't let it go. "You're not in trouble with the law, are you?"

He felt himself closing down. "How do you know it's the cops out there?"

"Well, I didn't till a few minutes ago. A woman turned up and talked to them, and then—uh—she went in."

"How'd she get in?"

"You don't want to know, baby. I asked her what she thought she was doing, and she showed me her badge. That's how I know it's the cops."

"Big woman—crazy-looking hair?"

"Yeah. How'd you know?"

"You don't want to know."

"So what can I do to help you?"

"I guess you did it. I wanted to know whether it was safe to go home."

"I'd say come home with me, but that might be a little close for comfort."

He nodded.

"You got a place to stay?"

"Sure. I'll figure something out."

"You need money?" She reached into her blouse and pulled out a ten-dollar bill. "It's all I got but you're welcome to it."

"No, no, I'll be fine. Really."

"Come on. Take it."

"No, I can't. But, listen, don't forget."

"Don't forget what?"

"That Cadillac I owe you." He managed to slip out without taking the money. But the memory of Pamela reaching into her bra for him almost broke his heart. Tears nearly blinded him as he chugged down Dauphine, having no idea where to go.

In the end he went to a bar.

Not being a drinker (but on the other hand, not being opposed to drink), he ordered a beer, then a Coke, then another beer, and on like that so that no one would throw him out.

Since he still wasn't talking except when he had to, he amused himself by watching television rather than talking to his fellow drinkers. It wasn't something he often did, but you couldn't really meditate in a bar, with half a six-pack inside you. And tonight he had a reason—he wanted news of the debacle on Maple Street.

When the teasers started, he began to think he was going to get a lot more than he bargained for: "Exclusive tonight! Religious group terrorizes city!"

He stopped drinking beer.

It was the lead story. "Police believe a religious group headed by the Reverend Errol Jacomine, a former candidate for mayor of New Orleans, is responsible for kidnapping a student at a Gentilly school and attempting a second kidnapping that resulted in a man's death. Jane Storey has that report."

The Monk felt panic rise in his throat. His heart began to pound like a piston.

His first thought was that he liked Jane Storey's looks. She was a youngish blonde, softer than most reporters, looking more as if she came from Kansas than Central Casting. He wondered how she got away with showing her real face instead of a makeup mask.

She was standing in front of a blowup of a city map. "Police have confirmed that a shoot-out at a juice bar on Maple Street today was actually a botched kidnapping. Detectives are withholding the identity of a man killed in that attempt, but we have confirmed that the getaway car in a kidnapping two hours later at McDonogh Forty-three in Gentilly—" here she pointed on her map "—was registered to the same man, who was a follower of the Reverend Errol Jacomine during his ministry in New Orleans. The victim is an eight-year-old girl, Shavonne Bourgeois. The identity of the intended victim in the juice bar shoot-out is being withheld, but sources close to the investigation say that it is a twenty-year-old woman with close ties to Jacomine."

What followed was a detailed report of the school kidnapping, followed by one of the "juice bar kidnapping," followed in turn by a lengthy history of Errol Jacomine's checkered history and suspected crimes.

The Monk was shaking when it was over. The things that shocked him were these: A second man had been shot in the school kidnap, though he was in "stable" condition, whatever that was. His father, for reasons he couldn't begin to fathom, had kidnapped a child—not Lovelace, but a child. And his brother had been the instrument of it.

The station even had a police artist's drawing of the gunman at the school. It didn't look exactly like Daniel, but there was no doubt in The Monk's mind.

He went back to his vacant lot, but couldn't even begin to sleep. He tried meditating, though his blood was full of alcohol, and that was no better. In his half-drunk state, it should have put him to sleep, but his mind was like a cricket.

Hey! he thought suddenly. *Hey. The name.* He had listened to it seven or eight times and hadn't felt a thing. That was the way his other mind was—his crazy one. You didn't have the least idea what it was going to do when. One thing he'd noticed, though—focus made a difference. If he absolutely had to do something—or, as in this case, simply get through something—his real mind, his sane mind, seemed to get the upper hand.

If he ever needed it, he needed it now. He had to think. He laced his hands behind his head and stared up at the sky until it began to lighten, and then he called the police from a pay phone. He had to wait until Langdon called him back.

262

• •

There were witnesses at the school, witnesses at the scene, and an army of anonymous tipsters. There were also some hate calls from people who thought the police should leave a man of God alone.

Yet there was nothing—not one shred of information—that could shed light on where the hell Jacomine actually was.

Skip thought that she would like to kill Jane Storey—and possibly everyone else in the media.

The FBI called in a psychologist, and Skip asked for Cindy Lou as well. But it was a waste of taxpayers' dollars. Both said they thought Jacomine had fixated on Skip and believed he could get to her through Shavonne. By "get to her," they seemed to mean mess with her mind. But what he might do next they couldn't say, and Skip had nightmarish visions of cut-off ears and fingers.

Shellmire wanted to know if Jacomine was "decompensating, as you fellas say." The FBI guy said he didn't know. Cindy Lou said, "Law, man, I would have said he was decompensating last time he pulled something like this. But he got away with it and he did it again. What if he is decompensating? It doesn't seem to make him any easier to catch."

Skip wasn't about to argue with Cindy Lou when she decided to go all practical and nonshrinky—which she often did in police work. But Shellmire said, "Look, there was the getaway car. That was really careless if he doesn't want us to figure out who's behind this."

"But maybe he does want us to figure it out. One thing we know about this man—he's mean as the devil himself. If he didn't want that, you can bet those two guys who pulled the job are getting the worst punishment of their lives right now. He used to do that kind of thing with the Blood of the Lamb folks—and for tiny little things. Real big, nasty stuff, for hardly anything. Public humiliation, beatings, you name it."

Skip said, "Maybe that'll take his attention off Shavonne for a while."

And she saw a terrible compassion come into her friend's face—not for Shavonne, but for her. She knew Cindy Lou. She probably had to bite her tongue not to blurt out, "I wouldn't count on it."

Next to the parent who got the plate number, the secretary from the school had probably been the most helpful. She'd sat with the police artist until they were all reasonably pleased with the sketch they released to the media.

Lovelace had been taken to a hotel, where she'd immediately fallen into a deep sleep. When she woke up, they showed her the sketch, but she couldn't say whether or not it was her dad.

Asked if she'd be willing to help with her own sketch of Daniel, her shoulders started to shake and she looked down to hide her eyes. Which left Skip, who had really only seen him in a cap and shades.

She tried valiantly, but when her sketch was compared with the one the secretary had worked on, it was impossible to tell if they were the same man.

So they couldn't be sure Daniel was the gunman in the school kidnap. But what, Skip thought, did it matter? They had Darnell Roberts's plate number, and that was almost as good for linking Jacomine to both crimes. The car, however, was probably hidden by now—no officer had seen it, and everyone in the state was looking.

Two FBI agents were ensconced with Dorise, and her phone, with her permission, was tapped. Two others had been dispatched to St. Philip Street, to Skip's house, at Shellmire's insistence. "Look," he said, "These people are into kidnapping, and they're trying to get at you. We can't take a chance on them trying for Sheila or Kenny."

She didn't protest. There was nothing to do but go home.

It was midnight, but Steve was up, drinking a beer and reading. He stood and came to her. She thought how kind his eyes were. "Tough day."

"The worst. I need wine."

He went to the kitchen to get it, while she took a shower. She put on a cotton caftan and joined him in the cantaloupe-colored living room, grateful to have someone to come home to.

He said, "I feel so helpless. I just wish there were something I could do."

"You feel helpless. This is the worst damn thing I've ever worked on."

"Oh, I don't know. . . ."

"It is. I swear to God. It's so personal. Like some kind of crazy duel between Jacomine and me. And I can't just not participate. Did you know you have two bodyguards?"

"I feel like a rock star." He was keeping it light. "How's Lovelace?"

"Poor kid. Nobody knows what to do with her. Her mother's off somewhere in Mexico, and she can't be sent back to school with these crazies on the loose. She's more or less in jail, although it's a hotel. At taxpayers' expense." But she found she didn't want to talk about the case anymore. Couldn't. Couldn't even finish her wine. After she'd sat silent for ten minutes, holding her glass and staring at the wall, Steve plucked it from her hands. "You want to talk about it?"

She knew he meant the man she killed. "Television, huh?"

"Uh-huh." He gave her a good hard look. "You're doing okay. I didn't know if I was going to get a whole woman tonight or a bag of Skip McNuggets. So far I'm impressed. You're fine, kiddo. You're okay."

"I'm in denial." She smiled, but he didn't let her get away with it. He gave her another hard stare.

"Are you?"

"Well, I might be. I'm so exhausted I can't honestly say one way or another. I think you're right, though—I might be all right. And that kind of scares me."

"You mean it gets easier after the first one?"

She clenched up her shoulders and closed her eyes. "God, I hope it's not that. I just think I've made my peace with it."

"Let's go to bed."

They held each other as if it were their last night together.

When her beeper went off, she was dreaming she was walking on a roof, trying to rescue a cat. The sound registered as a burglar alarm. In the dream she panicked, started to slide down the pitched roof. The cat yowled, and Steve shook her awake. "Skip. You were dreaming."

"My beeper." Half-asleep, she dialed her office.

"Langdon, you want to talk to someone named The White Monk?"

"Jesus." She came fully awake. "What's the number?"

A man answered; a simple "hello."

"This is Skip Langdon. Did you call me?"

"You're in Homicide, aren't you? I think I might have killed somebody."

"Who is this?"

"You know me. I'm The White Monk."

"Do you have another name?"

"Isaac Jacomine. How's Lovelace? I need to see her."

"Where are you, Isaac?"

"I'll come to you."

"Is somebody hurt? Why do you think you killed somebody?"

"If I didn't already, I might. You need to lock me up. I need to be locked up."

"Tell me where you are and I'll be there right away."

"I'll come to you. Tell me where you are."

She said again, "Is someone hurt? Tell me if someone's hurt."

"I don't *know* if anyone's hurt." His voice was genuinely bewildered, utterly frustrated, the voice of a child who doesn't understand what the grown-ups want.

"Tell me where they are and we'll send somebody over."

"Look, I'll meet you at police headquarters." He hung up.

Steve said, "Well?"

"I sure as hell don't know what that was. But I think I'm up."

"Damn. You need a good night's sleep."

He's always thinking of me, she thought. *I wonder if I could ever be like that?*

She called Shellmire, who said, "Do you think it's really The Monk?"

"Got no idea. This killing thing doesn't make sense."

Shellmire was impatient, eager to get things moving. "Listen, we'll send a car for you. The guys watching the house'll stay there. I don't want your family left alone and I don't want you driving by yourself. Now, do this: Tell everyone in your household to stay there till further notice. Hear me? Nobody goes to school or work. Nobody goes anywhere. Nobody comes over. I'll meet you as soon as I can—I live on the North Shore. It'll take a while."

"They're going to love that."

In fact, Steve said, "Oh, peachy. '*General Hospital*,' here I come. Oprah, you're my girlfriend. You're calling Dee-Dee, right? I can't face him this time of day."

Dee-Dee said, "Darling, what's up? I've still got my sleep goggles on."

"House arrest, Dee-Dee."

"Oooo, baby. You must know what I did last night."

"I think it's only a crime in Georgia, but here's the deal." She explained.

"Good thing Layne spent the night. He can play games with the kids." Layne, a puzzle maker by profession, knew every board game, card game, and parlor game ever invented in any country.

"Layne spent the night?" That was something new, given his allergy and Dee-Dee's discretion.

"Separate bedrooms, of course."

The FBI car was there in less than fifteen minutes. When Skip walked into Homicide, a smallish man with a shaved head was waiting for her, wearing black, not white. Bits of grass and weeds clung to his T-shirt, as if he'd slept outside. He had five o'clock shadow all over his skull.

She said, "I thought you wore white."

"My disguise." To her surprise, he smiled. "You can't say it didn't work."

As she shook hands, she noticed he smelled as if he hadn't showered lately.

"Sit down, won't you? Would you like some coffee?"

He looked pathetically grateful, and Skip realized that she liked him. There was something infinitely sweet about this man, something uncomplicated and basic. She hoped he wasn't a murderer.

She got him his coffee. "Shall we go someplace private?" The only choice was an interrogation room, but she sensed he'd do better there than in the detective bureau, with its noisy comings and goings, and the random prisoner sitting shackled, waiting to be transferred.

He seemed to relax a little once he'd had some coffee. She tried to put him at his ease a little further; she didn't think bullying would work on this man. "Isaac, we've been worried about you."

"I know." He seemed slightly ashamed.

She turned on the tape recorder she'd brought into the room. Isaac said, "What's that for?"

She smiled. "Just something we do."

"Am I under arrest?"

"Of course not. We're not going to arrest you unless you committed a crime." She paused. "What's this about killing somebody?"

"I'm all right here. I can't hurt anyone while I'm in here."

He didn't seem as if he'd hurt a fly.

"You're a monk, aren't you? A religious man. I'm sure you wouldn't hurt anyone without a good reason."

"I might've. I'm trying to think—I might've."

"Do you have a problem with your memory?"

"No. It's not that. I just can't be sure. Listen, I might know where Daniel is."

"Daniel? Is it Daniel you might have killed?"

"I don't know. I need to see Lovelace."

"I can't let you see Lovelace if you're dangerous."

"I'm not dangerous to Lovelace. The last thing I would ever do is let any harm come to her."

"Tell me where the person is you think you might have killed. He could be lying there hurt—we might be able to get to him in time."

"You don't understand. I think I *might* have killed someone; I just can't be sure I didn't."

"Tell me about it."

"There's nothing to tell. I just might have killed someone, that's all."

Her frustration was mounting. She was quiet, sipping her own coffee. *Count to ten, Skip. Don't blow this.*

She said, "Can I ask you something? If you don't want to tell me what happened, why did you call?"

"To tell you where I saw Daniel."

"And where was that?"

"A house on Magazine Street." He gave her the address.

"How did you happen to see him?"

"I followed him there. I was watching Lovelace to make sure she didn't get into trouble. I saw those two guys go in the juice bar, and I went to call 911 and then you were there. I hung up and took shelter, and then when I saw Lovelace get in a police car, I left to try to meet her here. But on the way I found Daniel."

"You found him." He sounded perfectly sane when he was expaining himself, precise even—until he got to the punch line.

"I just saw him on the street—in a pickup. I followed it, of course."

"You just happened to be at the place where there was a shooting, and then you just happened to see a man the police were searching for, whom nobody else could find. . . ." She heard her voice rising.

Isaac shrank down in his chair. "You don't have to believe me."

"All right. You followed the pickup. Then what?"

He spread his arms, palms open. "Then Daniel went in."

"And after that?"

"Then I watched the house for a while, but no one came out or went in. I couldn't decide what to do, but I knew I couldn't go home because you were watching my house."

"Yes?"

"So I found a place to go and I saw that thing on television. That Jane Storey thing."

"Umm-hmm."

"I didn't know they had that little girl. I had to do something."

"Did you see the artist's sketch?"

"Yes."

"Did you recognize it?"

"I think it was Daniel. It didn't really look like him, but if my dad's behind this thing, it's him."

"Why didn't you call us immediately?"

"I didn't know what to do." He jumped at a noise behind Skip; Shellmire came in.

Skip said, "Hey, Turner. This is The White Monk."

"Well, hey, Mr. Monk. We been mighty worried about you." He was giving Isaac his good ol' boy routine; he must sense the same thing she had about Isaac. That he wasn't a man to push.

"This is Agent Shellmire, Isaac. Why don't you tell him what you told me?"

Patiently, Isaac told him, Shellmire saying, "Uh-huh, uh-huh," every time he paused. When he had finished, Shellmire said, "Tell us about the person you think you killed."

"I don't really think I killed anybody. I just think I might have."

Skip found herself grinding her teeth. She excused herself, and sat at her desk rubbing her temples, trying to think what to do. In a moment, Shellmire followed. She said, "What do you think?"

"Let's get somebody on that house." He used her phone to order surveillance, and she was grateful. She could have gotten someone herself, but the department was so hugely understaffed, any help was welcome—even from the feds.

Especially from the feds; they had money.

"Okay. Let's divide the labor."

Skip looked at her watch. "Why don't you work on The Monk some more? I've had him for half an hour. I guess I better wake up the assessor."

"I was hopin' you'd say that. I hate gettin' cussed out this early in the day. The Monk's more my speed; too holy for cussin'."

"Hey, I just remembered something—Lovelace told her room-mate he didn't talk much. Maybe this is what she meant."

Shellmire shook his head. "He's a case for that good-lookin' police shrink."

Skip snapped her fingers. "Great idea. Let's sic her on him."

She called Cindy Lou. "Lou-Lou? Get up."

"Girlfriend. It's not even seven yet—and you kept me up late." But it was a feeble protest; Cindy Lou couldn't stand to miss anything.

"We got The Monk. He says he might have killed somebody, but he won't give us any details."

"So? Interrogation's your department. Whatever happened to the rack and the iron maiden?"

"I've got a feeling something's off here, but I can't be sure. He seems sane; he just talks crazy."

"Sounds like half my exes."

She called the assessor next, asked who owned the house on

270

Magazine Street, and after that, it was hurry up and wait till he could get to City Hall to look up the address. She rejoined Shellmire and The Monk.

For a grueling fifteen minutes she listened to the same phrases over and over: "I might have. I don't know. How can I be sure?"

Finally, she and Shellmire decided to vary the routine. They asked The Monk about his father, his brother, his art, his relationship with Lovelace, everything they could think of that might shed some light. When he wasn't confessing to murder, he seemed normal—if you didn't count the shaved head, the vow of silence (which he told them about), and the all-white house (which Skip had seen for herself).

At seven-thirty, the assessor called with the name of the property owner—a Mrs. Julia Diefenbach, who was evidently an absentee landlord, as her tax bills were sent to Los Angeles.

Oh, boy, Skip thought, *five-thirty on the West Coast. She's going to nominate me for a medal.*

A woman answered on about the fifteenth ring—the merest trickle of sound. "Hello?"

"Mrs. Diefenbach? Sorry to bother you so early. This is Detective Langdon, calling from New Orleans."

The voice said, "Oh, my Lord. Oh, my Lord. Has something happened to Jamie?" Skip thought she must be about ninety-three, and not too well.

"No, no. Everyone's fine. I'm just calling to find out who lives in your house on Magazine Street."

There was a long pause; a pause so long Skip feared she'd gone back to sleep. But apparently she'd merely been paging through her too-crowded RAM space. Finally she said, "I don't b'lieve I own anything on Magazine Street anymore. I used to, but I don't b'lieve I do now."

"Do you know a Daniel Jacomine?"

"No, I don't b'lieve I do. Jamie handles all that; my grandson."

"Does he live in New Orleans?"

"Why, yes, he does. Let me see now, does he live on Magazine Street? No, I b'lieve it's Prytania."

"Jamie Diefenbach? The same name as yours?"

271

"Well, it's James really, but we just always called him Jamie."

James Diefenbach was awake, alert, and a pain in the butt; he was a lawyer and a hardnose, who absolutely declined to give information until Skip told him what the call was about.

She went and got Shellmire, who was still talking in circles with The Monk. "Mind getting tough with someone? People quake in their boots when they hear those three little letters."

"Ah. Famous But Incompetent. Isn't that what you people call us? And then you come around begging when the chips are down."

Nonetheless, he performed the extraction like a dentist—a referral to a rental agent named Jay Fingerer.

Skip looked at her watch again. Nearly eight. Bad and good—bad, because chances of a confrontation before the streets got crowded were pretty much gone. Good, because everyone was probably up now, and not so grumpy.

Or so she thought. The rental agent was plenty grumpy, and an hour away from his office, what with taking kids to school, and another appointment. "Mr. Fingerer," she said, "this is a matter of life and death. Could you possibly send someone else to look up the record?"

"Life and death? It doesn't have anything to do with those kidnappings, does it?"

Damn. All I need. "I'm afraid I can't say what it's about. All I can tell you is we badly need your help, and there's really no time to spare."

"Hey, I hope they don't have a time bomb in there."

Me, too. She also hoped Fingerer's immediate circle didn't include members of the media.

Apparently, she impressed him with the urgency of the problem. He called back in fifteen minutes. "I think I've got something hot for you. The guy gave his name as Melvin Gibson. Like Mel, you know? Like it was the first name that came into his head. Know what else? He paid us in cash. I remember him now."

For a moment she considered asking if Gibson looked like the police sketch of the McDonogh kidnapper, but she decided against it. If it was Daniel, his own brother couldn't identify him from that.

Fingerer was still talking. "He rented 'em both."

"I beg your pardon?"

"That's a duplex. He rented both sides of it—paid first and last month's, plus a security deposit."

"When?"

"About two weeks ago."

25

• •

They moved to FBI headquarters—Shellmire; Skip; Cappello because she was Skip's sergeant; the FBI psychologist and Cindy Lou; Abasolo; Joe Tarantino, the lieutenant in charge of Homicide; and Captain Marshall King, one of the superintendent's stooges. King wouldn't make a move without calling the chief, but Skip preferred him to the superintendent—he had a reputation for half a brain at least. She finally had the department's attention.

But now it was the FBI's case—technically. Department lore had it that the FBI assumed command only when they thought they could get some good fast ink. If they were optimistic, there was going to be skirmishing.

King left the room and stayed gone a long time. When he came back, he was accompanied by Harold Goerner, the Special Agent in Charge, and he was tight-lipped.

The fighting over command was over—at least for the moment—with predictable results. The feds could always unload it if they thought the case was turning to dog poop.

Goerner was a short, thick man, not pear-shaped like Shellmire, not soft-looking, just ursine. He was alert and straight-backed, like a recent Marine recruit. He had dark hair, a dark mustache, and a slightly irritated manner, as if he'd snap at you if you offered him a cup of coffee. Skip disliked him almost on sight.

She and Shellmire exchanged glances. They had ridden over together, speculating on who would "assume on" the case and what the consequences would be in each scenario. Skip said the feds would dump it. "Want to bet?" Shellmire said. "You don't know about our secret weapon."

"What?" she said, "What? Tell me, dammit."

"Uh-uh. But you're gonna like it. I wish I could say the same for Goerner."

"What's he like?"

"He's like some dude whose father was in the military and woke him up every day at five A.M. and threw him in a cold shower. And then later he couldn't decide whether to rebel or conform."

"I don't get it."

"It's like he's pissed off all the time, because he thinks he's supposed to be a real hardnose and he doesn't want to, but he's got to or he'll disappoint his daddy. So he's not only a hardnose, but a pissed-off hardnose."

"Charming."

"Tell me about your guys."

"They're all solid except for King—I don't really know him."

"So he's a wild card."

"And possibly a loose cannon."

Shellmire shook his head. "You're the loose cannon, Langdon. Are you going to behave?"

She was only half-insulted. She wanted to do this her own way, though what that was she couldn't have said. She just knew that she did, and that it must show. And then there was her past record.

When they were assembled in what resembled a war room— maps on the walls, pointers, coffee, and telephones—they put together a plan. A simple plan, but a woefully incomplete one, due to variables they couldn't control.

By ten o'clock, they had the two phone numbers assigned to the duplex in Mel Gibson's name, lists from the assessor's office, names and numbers of all the neighbors—in short, a complete dossier of the block where The Jury was holed up.

Officers had been dispatched to get everyone to leave their houses on this block and the three surrounding streets.

As soon as that was done, police would simply close off the block and surround it. When they were in position, along with all the TAC units they could muster—NOPD's and the FBI's for starters—a hostage negotiator would phone the house. And then what happened was anybody's guess.

Goerner turned to the psychologists. "Doctors Taylor and Wootten?"

The FBI shrink shook his head and drummed his pencil. He looked pale, but that was probably his natural state. "I've got two words for you," he said. "Remember Waco."

Cindy Lou nodded. "We've got to consider these people a cult. When you've got somebody as crazy as Jacomine, you've got a lot of blind followers and a guy who thinks he's God and probably has a headful of chemicals. They don't mind dying because they think they're saving the world. You're on a mission from God, the FBI's pretty small potatoes."

"Dr. Taylor?"

He was smiling, his body turned toward Cindy Lou. "Dr. Wootten has a way of cutting through bullshit."

"So what you're advising is—"

Taylor whirled to face him, turned off his smile, and finished Goerner's sentence: "Don't fuck up."

The room was starting to smell sour from sweat.

"And read their minds," said Cindy Lou.

Goerner stared at her, looking uncertain, evidently pretty sure she wasn't making a joke, but unable to explain her words any other way.

"I hear they make listening devices powerful enough to pick up a conversation in a house across the street. Surely the FBI has some of those babies."

"Thanks for your input, Dr. Wootten. I assure you, all legal methods of intelligence gathering will be employed." Goerner fixed his mouth in a prim line, which Skip took to mean a device was already being installed, probably in a house next door.

•   •

Daniel turned over in bed, his body sore, his brain muzzy, his mood somewhere between desperate and hopeless. He recognized in himself the depression that had dogged him at various times throughout his life. Lovelace had it, too; it was genetic, the shrinks said. When it hit, he didn't even want to get out of bed. That idea he'd had yesterday, the one about throwing himself from a car, still seemed a viable plan—except that he could no longer get access to a car.

He half wished he'd done it.

He couldn't see any good coming from this thing. Somehow it had gotten seriously out of hand. What was kidnapping children about? Lovelace, he could see—she was his own daughter. But why this little black girl? Why endanger her?

She wasn't in danger, Daddy said, not for a second, she was gonna be just fine. But Daniel had shot a man trying to get her. He might be just fine eventually—according to the TV news, he probably would, but he'd already had to go through a lot of pain, and there was going to be more. And Darnell Roberts was dead. What was the point of it all?

He was even starting to wonder if there'd been any point in killing Nolan Bazemore. He had been so proud of that.

But his father seemed to have gone crazy. Or perhaps had always been crazy. Now he was the first lieutenant of a crazy man, living with a cadre of people who worshiped a crazy man and who thought he could do no wrong.

Daniel thought, *Who am I to doubt?*

But he did. He had spent his life alone, or nearly alone, except for that brief period with Jacqueline, and groups were not his talent.

He had turned Shavonne over to the sisters, who tried to feed her and take care of her, but all she would do was scream and cry and wet herself. So they taped her mouth and locked her in a room.

And Daddy called a prayer meeting. Everybody came, all the people from the other side of the house, and all the ones from this side, and the ones who lived outside as well, the entire inner core of

The Jury, once an appropriate twelve people; now eleven. They were crammed into Daddy's living room that he used for an office, sitting around on Home Depot nine-dollar plastic chairs and pillows on the floor.

First they prayed on general principles, which lasted thirty minutes if it lasted one. And then Daddy said, "We lost a brother today. We were twelve good men and true and our number has shrunk." Then with no planning at all, they held an impromptu funeral service, which included eulogies to Darnell, with Bible readings, hymns, everything you might have in church—Daddy was a preacher and he treated this like a church service.

Daniel had to admire him—his skill and his energy—though, after Jacqueline left him, he had stopped believing in God. He was here because he thought his dad wasn't doing the God thing anymore. He thought this thing was about justice.

When Darnell had been properly remembered, and Daniel, for one, was near starving, Daddy started in again. "We are in for a siege, seekers of justice. Are y'all up to it?"

Everyone cheered.

"We have come to a time in our movement when a blight must be removed before we can go on. Little Shavonne Bourgeois, an angel in our midst, will be the instrument of that delivery, which will be done before the sun sets tomorrow. I can promise you that. Before the sun sets tomorrow. Do you believe me?"

A great cheering went up that left Daniel cold. Yet, not wanting to call attention to himself, he went along with it. "Some of us may not live. Are you ready for that?"

Cheering again.

Daniel felt his hands go cold. What was happening here?

"But most of us will live. We will leave this place with a police escort. Yes! And we will have with us our daughter, Lovelace Jacomine, from whom we have been so long separated, and we will also have vanquished that instrument of Satan himself, Detective Skip Langdon!"

He waited for silence. "Sometimes, in fact, I'm not sure Langdon is not Satan. But then I remember she is only a woman. And I know that we will destroy her. Like the children of Israel, we will go into

278

the wilderness. We will take shelter in another safe house that our brothers and sisters have prepared for us in a faraway city—" this was news to Daniel "—and we will accomplish this because the Lord is with us."

Daniel couldn't stand it. "But, Daddy, how are we going to get there?"

"Do you doubt that we will, boy?"

"No, I just—"

"There is always one among us. A doubter. Possibly a traitor. Let me tell you about my son. My son is a brilliant strategist. He led both of our commando raids today. The first was not successful and re-sulted in the death of our brother Darnell. Yet this was not the fault of our brother—my son Daniel. He acquitted himself well in that raid."

This time, Daniel realized, the cheering was for him.

"He was prevented from his mission by the female demon, Skip Langdon, well known to all of us. We quickly recouped and made plans for the removal, once and for all, of Detective Langdon. And my son was sent on a second mission, a benign mission in which our little sister Shavonne was to be assisted in coming to us. A mission to be accomplished with no bloodshed. And yet there *was* bloodshed! *Specifically* against my orders.

"Anyone, even my own dearest son, can make a mistake. And my son did. My son shot a man, inflicted pain for no reason. Now, Errol Jacomine does not play favorites. Errol Jacomine is willing to admit that when his own dearest, most cherished son has made a mistake, even that son must be punished. Is there anyone here who agrees with me?"

Daniel had not realized how ominous cheering could sound.

His father said, "Daniel, it isn't my decision."

Daniel stood up, furious. "The hell with this. I've about had it, anyway. This is it. I'm leaving the movement."

"You're what, son?"

Daniel didn't answer. He strode toward the door, and had his hand on the knob when someone grabbed him from behind.

"Dashan! Come on, this is me, Daniel. You got to be kidding."

They tied him to a chair and questioned him.

"First things first, boy. What did you mean you're leaving the movement?"

For the first time, Daniel felt fear; understood that his father hadn't been kidding when he said he didn't play favorites. Low profile was best. "I didn't mean anything. I was upset."

"If you were leaving, you must have had someplace to go. Where were you going, boy?"

"Nowhere. Back to Idaho."

"You were going to Langdon, weren't you? You are the betrayer." His father's voice rose, full of hellfire. And then he lowered it, almost to a whisper. "Weren't you even going to kiss me first, boy? Like Judas?"

Daniel didn't reply.

"Daniel, Daniel, what are we going to do with you?"

Leave me alone. You're right—there's nothing for me out there.

But he held his peace.

"Son, we've got a tradition in the Following. And that's who we are—we might be The Jury, but we're still God's children. Still the Blood of the Lamb Evangelical Following. You haven't been with us for most of our history, so you don't really know our traditions. Sister Kathleen, tell him our tradition."

Kathleen was a woman of fifty who looked ten years older. She was a white woman who seemed beaten down by life, tired before her time with childbirth and work. She said, "We choose our own punishments."

His father said, "Do we still have our paddles, Matthew?"

"Yes, Daddy. Or we could use belts."

"Need those to keep our pants up." His father laughed, as if this were light conversation. The other Jurors laughed as well, and the sound was as sinister as their cheering.

"See, what we do," his father said, "is we let each person have a turn either with paddles or belts. As many strokes as he or she deems necessary. Keeps it fair, that way. Everyone knows what could happen if he or she decides to betray us, knows how hard he or she has worked for what we have. So he is both punishing and reminding himself how important it is not to make a pact with the devil."

I can do this, Daniel thought. *I can just breathe deep and get through it.*

280

"That's one option. The other's even more fair. It depends on the mercy of the good God. We can untie you, son, and you can pick your challenger. The Romans of old set Christians to the challenge." He paused, ever the showman. "Course, they loaded the dice a little more than we do. We don't have any lions here. We do not require you to fight to the death. But you may choose a gladiator's contest, if you like. If you are innocent, know that God will give you the strength to overcome your opponent. And if that happens, know that we will cheer your victory."

Daniel thought of a medieval witches' punishment he'd heard about: You threw the suspect in the water, and if she didn't drown, it proved she was guilty.

He thought crazily, *What's the punishment for winning?* and somehow knew that it wasn't such a dumb question.

Nonetheless, the contest was the only choice he could stomach. He was a good fighter and in good shape. Dashan was the biggest of the bunch—he would almost certainly be able to take Daniel, but at least it would be a fight rather than passive submission.

"What do you choose, boy?"

"I choose the contest."

"Very well. Let the games begin."

Daniel remained tied up as he watched the others clear the dining room for the match. Since it had hardly any furniture in it, that didn't take long, but Daniel used the time wisely. He took deep breaths, psyching himself up. He was almost looking forward to it when everyone suddenly left.

Every single person.

He had his eyes closed, didn't even notice them disappearing. He simply noticed that it seemed unusually quiet and when he opened his eyes he was alone. Sitting there in the pitch-dark. They had turned the lights off so quietly he hadn't even heard a click.

He thought, *Maybe I can get out of this,* and began to work on his bonds, which were only a couple of extension cords, anyway.

Dashan was good, though. They held. Daniel had succeeded only in making his wrists bleed when he was seized with panic. Where the hell had they gone?

They came back in improvised robes, in most cases bathrobes, in some, women's caftans or muumuus lent to the men. They were holding candles and singing "Onward Christian Soldiers."

It would have been laughable, the song itself and the way they were dragging it, except that it had the quality of a dirge. The entire procession was way too serious, too incongruous, to be anything but grotesque. He felt an underlying menace that he couldn't put his finger on, but that had nothing to do, he thought, with his personal danger. It was a wild electricity in the room, an energy, almost a presence, and it was like a dog with rabies, something feral and carnivorous driven by a force it couldn't understand.

They stood around him in a semicircle.

His father addressed him. "Daniel Jacomine, you have chosen a gladiatorial contest. The women among us are ineligible for the challenge and I am likewise ineligible. Of the remaining men, you may choose your challenger."

For a fraction of a second, Daniel felt something like hope. *There has to be a catch*, he thought. *There just has to be.*

"Choose wisely," said his father, "and the good God will protect you."

Wisely. What would be wise? There was bound to be a double cross, but he was too frazzled to try to figure it out, too wired by the wait and the ritual.

He looked at the men. Surely Dashan, being the biggest and most powerful, was the poorest choice. He could probably take any of the others. But who could say? Maybe they all had black belts. One, named Ellis, was about five feet tall and young, but he couldn't choose that one—it wasn't even sporting.

So not Dashan and not Ellis. That left two. There wasn't much difference, but the one named Pete was slightly bigger than Al; he was the older of the two, but he looked like a pretty good opponent.

I'll choose fairly, Daniel thought. *I'll just try to be fair.*

He said, "I choose Pete." The slightly bigger one.

"You choose Pete," his father said. "Is Pete your choice, son?"

Daniel began to think he'd made a mistake. But what was the alternative?

He said, "Pete is my choice," unconsciously entering into his father's ritualistic cadences.

282

"Pete is your choice. Is that a fair choice, Daniel?"

"I think so."

"What do you think, people?"

Daniel winced before he heard the chorus of "No's," knowing already that no other response was possible.

"They don't think it's fair, Daniel. Pete's a good ten years older than you. You could probably lick him with one hand tied behind your back. So I tell you what we're gonna do. We're gonna tie one hand behind your back."

The Jurors shouted, "Amen."

Daniel thought grimly: *They seem to have done this before.*

"I warned you to choose wisely," said his father. "What do you think would have happened if you'd picked Dashan?"

Too late, Daniel saw it coming. "We'd have had to tie a hand behind *his* back."

Daniel was right-handed, so they tied that one back.

Just when the fight was about to begin, Daniel's father stopped it. "Pete, you've had the flu, haven't you?"

"Yes, Daddy."

"You feeling okay?"

"Little under the weather. That's all."

"We'd better give Daniel another handicap. Wouldn't want y'all to think I play favorites."

They blindfolded him.

When it was over, his father said. "How you feel, boy? Did we knock some sense into you?"

In fact, he didn't feel anything except sore.

And this morning he felt almost more depressed than sore. But when he got up, the balance quickly shifted; sharp, shooting pains made the walk to the bathroom a Himalayan trek. When he finally made it, he pissed enough blood for a transfusion.

He didn't flush the toilet, left it instead for someone to find.

He was awakened by a scream. After that, he was vaguely aware of rustlings around him; comings and goings, and someone praying. His father, maybe.

● ●

"God won't take your baby, Dorise. He couldn't do that, 'cause He already took your husband, and He a merciful God."

So far, Dorise thought, *I haven't noticed.*

But her mother was doing the best she could to keep her spirits up, and she bit her tongue. *One thing I got,* she thought, *I got a good mama.*

Her mother had moved away when she got married for the second time, but she had always missed New Orleans. She had moved back when her husband died three months ago, and Dorise had seen the way her faith had gotten her through. It was her mother who'd gotten her to go back to church.

"Mama, I got something to tell you. I promised Jesus I wasn't gon' look at any man again, and I did, and now look what's happened!"

"Jesus wouldn't want you to do that, honey. It's not your fault what happened to Shavonne."

When her mother said it, she could almost believe it. But she didn't really believe the other thing—that God wouldn't take her daughter. He would if he felt like it, and then the preacher would just say it was God's will, and she'd still be supposed to swallow that "merciful" bullshit. She knew families that had lost three or four members in shootings. She couldn't even answer her mother. All she could do was cry, and wait for the phone to ring.

She couldn't understand why these FBI guys thought the kidnapper would call her. She couldn't offer any ransom—she didn't have anything to give. It seemed much more likely he was a pedophile who'd torture and kill her daughter—except that she didn't put it quite that way to herself. It was just a vague crimson cloud in her head.

It was around two in the morning when her mother finally got her to pray. She couldn't honestly say it was comforting, but, since she was on her knees, she did find it made her want to sleep. And once she went to bed, she didn't want to get up.

Her mother tried to rouse her at eight, then again at nine, and at ten, finally brought her some orange juice and made her sit up. "Honey, you can't stay in bed the rest of your life. You got God's work to do."

Dorise wasn't honestly sure she even believed in God anymore, but she wasn't going to say that to her sweet mama. She was a grown woman, but she put her head on her mother's bosom and her arm around her neck. Dorise was wearing the T-shirt and shorts she'd gone to bed in, her mother a fleecy, rose-colored robe. They were sitting like that, her mother stroking her hair, when the phone rang.

"Should I answer it?" asked her mother. It was probably bad news. The po-lice calling to tell her the worst.

"No!" She put her hands over her ears.

"You crazy, girl?" Her mother picked up the receiver.

She said, "Yes?" like some lady on television, somebody who lived in a mansion. In a minute, she hollered, "Praise the Lord!" and the phone tumbled out of her hands.

"What is it, Mama?"

"Shavonne. Shavonne calling." She was rooting around on the floor, trying to find the phone. There was only a dial tone when she finally did.

The two FBI agents pounded into the bedroom. "Was that her voice?"

Dorise was crying.

"Hang up. Hang up the phone." One of the men did it for her. Dorise stared as if it were a dead thing that might come alive. It rang again.

She answered slowly, so as not to break the spell, if that's what it was. "Honey?"

"Mama?"

"Shavonne, honey, is that you?" The two agents were scrambling back to their equipment.

"Mama. Mama, I'm all right. They treatin' me good and they need love . . ." Her voice sounded the way it did when she read aloud, unsure of each word, figuring each one out as she went along.

"Where are you, honey?"

"Love less. They will trade me for love." Each word separate, slow. "Love less."

"What you say, honey? Tell me again."

A man spoke into the phone. "Tell the police we want Lovelace. We'll call again."

Dorise felt as if her whole body were being torn by exploding sobs she couldn't control, that seemed not even a part of her, something far away and destructive.

285

26

• •

"They called Dorise," Shellmire said. "An agent's on his way with the tape."

Everyone shouted questions, Skip fairly shrieking hers: "Did she talk to Shavonne?"

He ignored them all, shouting over them. "I'll run it down, if everyone'll just be patient." He looked wilted. Skip thought he must have already sweated a gallon, and the day had hardly started.

The man's going to be dehydrated by noon.

But so much could happen between then and noon; there was so very much to lose.

"They put Shavonne on and apparently had her read a prepared statement. She said she's okay and they'll exchange her for Lovelace. At least that's what it sounds like. Then a man came on and said they'd call again later."

"Lovelace for Shavonne. Why on earth do they want her?" Skip was thinking aloud. She didn't like it. There had to be more.

King said, "Are the hostage negotiators on the scene?"

Shellmire shook his head. "Penny Ferguson's going to be

handling the negotiation." He looked at his watch. "She should be here in about ten minutes."

They drank coffee and waited for her, Taylor drumming his pencil nervously the whole time. Skip thought, *Wouldn't you know he'd be a psychologist.*

Ferguson arrived with another agent, carrying a briefcase that might have held a change of clothing. She was a petite woman with a neat pageboy. Her hair was sun-streaked brown, the kind of hair that looks natural and costs plenty. Her well-tailored pantsuit was a deep olive, almost black but not as severe. Her silk blouse was a lighter olive that brought out the green in dark hazel eyes. The whole effect was pleasing to the point of soothing. It occurred to Skip that this was no accident.

Ferguson introduced herself in a voice that washed over the group like mother's milk—warm and nourishing, just sweet enough to make you want more. Skip felt instantly comfortable; she noticed even King was smiling. "Agent Ferguson," he said, and his own voice seemed to have lost some of its edge.

"Sorry I'm late. I just got in from Washington."

Shellmire said, "Agent Ferguson's the best we got—I call her our secret weapon. We flew her in 'cause she's got a voice could make you kill your grandma if she wanted you to. Fortunately, she usually just wants you to give up your life of crime."

Ferguson smiled, and she had the teeth of a movie star, an all-American, girl-next-door kind of grin that made you glad she'd gone into law enforcement instead of white-collar crime. "I'm what they call a VNL—till they know me, of course."

Cindy Lou said, "Abasolo, you can close your mouth. She's wearing a wedding ring." Because she was a consultant, and not a police officer, Lou-Lou could say anything she pleased and always did, which made her Skip's hands-down hero. *Yes*, she decided, *those two have definitely been flirting.*

The sergeant gave the psychologist one of his devastating grins. "Don't be jealous, Lou-Lou. I like my women mean."

King asked the question everyone else was holding back: "What the hell's a VNL?"

"A Very Nice Lady, Captain. But that's only what I look and sound like."

Shellmire said, "Whew. We got guys in prisons all over the country still don't know what hit 'em."

Ferguson sat down, apparently feeling she'd established her credentials. "Morris briefed me," she told Shellmire. "And I'm quite familiar with the Jacomine case, as well as The Jury."

"Okay. The only new development we got is they want to exchange the victim for Jacomine's granddaughter."

"What kind of weapons do they have?"

"We don't know."

"How many people are in there?"

"Don't know that either."

"Are we set up at the scene?" She was firing questions like darts, the VNL momentarily banished.

"We have a command post next door and the block's surrounded."

"Do they know we're there?"

"So far we haven't heard a peep out of 'em. Not so much as a curtain flutter. The street's blocked off, but we've got people walking up and down now and then, to make it look normal. So far as we know, they don't have the least idea we know where they are—or who they are."

The two psychologists, along with Tarantino and Cappello, were released. That left Shellmire, Skip, Abasolo, King, and Ferguson, who entered the command post in two groups, like people arriving for a business meeting. Goerner was already there.

The furniture had been stripped from the living room and piled in the dining room, replaced by folding tables and chairs, and a baffling maze of phones and electronic equipment.

"How'd you get this stuff in here?" asked Skip.

A man she didn't know pointed to a side window. "Brought it in from the other side of the house." He pointed next to a front window. "See those roofs? TAC unit's already in place."

Ferguson took off her coat. "Shall I make the call?"

"You better listen to this first. The Rev's been on the phone." The speaker couldn't have been more than twenty-two; he wore khaki shorts and a polo shirt. His head was almost as smooth as The Monk's, and he had on glasses. "I'm Will Kohler, by the way."

Shellmire made the introductions. Kohler said, "Shall I play the tape?"

The instant Goerner nodded, Jacomine's voice filled the room. "Rosie, honey, how the hell are you?"

"Darling, I just stepped out of the shower. Could you give me twenty minutes?"

"Are you wearing a towel? With maybe a pair of high-heeled what-do-you-call-'ems?"

"Mules, sweetcakes. 'Bye now."

The woman hung up and Jacomine swore. Then he hung up himself and dialed again. Rosemarie Owens's machine answered.

Kohler clicked the tape off. "We timed him. He called again in exactly twenty minutes. Listen to this."

"Rosie, honey."

"Darling, I'm so glad to hear from you. I could just hug your evil little neck. But I've got to be somewhere in ten minutes. Call me there, will you?"

She gave him a number and hung up. Kohler fast-forwarded. "She's a fast thinker, but of course she didn't know about this little setup."

Jacomine's voice again: "Rosie, what's going on?"

"My home number isn't safe, baby. How've you been? I've been so worried about you."

"That wasn't nice what you did to me, baby. Disappearing off the face of the Earth. 'Specially after I did that little favor for you."

"I had to be out of touch for a while. The FBI came calling."

"I was getting the dumb idea you just didn't want to talk to ol' Uncle Earl."

"Earl, this is serious. We really can't talk for a while."

"Well, we have to, sweetness. I've got me a situation here. I need you to send a plane for me and a few of my friends. You know that island you own off the coast of Florida—the one with the airstrip? We need you to take us over there."

"You think I've got planes at my disposal?"

"Charter one, Rosie—and make sure it can't be traced to you. Or your heirs are gonna die before you do."

"What the hell are you talking about?"

"That cute little Lovelace is quite a kid. I know you want to meet her sometime."

"Earl Jackson, you're just as crazy as you ever were. You've got to promise to leave me alone, now—do you hear me? You really can't call on my phone."

"I don't have to, honeybunch. I sent somebody to help you. He's watching you this minute, and he'll introduce himself real soon. I know you still love me, honey. You do, don't you? You have to because of what we did together. That thing last week—you remember?"

He rang off, and this time Rosemarie did the cursing.

Kohler turned off the tape. "Neat, huh?"

Goerner's face twisted like so much dough. "Shit! What about Owens?"

"We don't know yet. We monitored the call from here and then got in touch with the office in Dallas. But she was gone by the time they got there. We haven't heard from them since." He checked the time. "That was forty-five minutes ago."

"Oh, Lord, what else?"

"Well, sir, there is something. Several somethings."

Goerner glared as if Kohler were the perp.

"We have laser surveillance equipment that'll go through their wall, as long as we've got our window open. Theoretically, we can hear all over the house, but some things come in better than others. So far we've got seven discrete voices. We don't know how many more there are. We've got a few conversations about cooking and household chores, and one that seems pretty interesting. Shall I play it for you?"

"Certainly. For Christ's sake."

"This one's kind of fuzzy at first."

It began with a blur of voices, one of them female, one male. And then one that was clearly Jacomine's. "What do you mean he can't walk?"

The female voice answered. "Tara says we might have hurt him last night. I think you should come up and see him."

Instead, his voice bloomed into a shout. "Daniel! You get your tail down here."

Silence.

"Daniel, goddammit!" Again a shout. Then a lot of rustlings and scrapings.

Kohler said, "He must have been sitting down. We think he got out of his chair and left the room."

"And how long ago was that? Before or after the Rosemarie incident?"

"After. About ten minutes ago. That room—" Kohler tapped the wall "—the one closest to us—is the one he's apparently using for an office. When he's in there, we do pretty well. When he's not, we don't."

Ferguson said, "What do you think? Do we call?"

Goerner put both hands over his face, and drew them down to his chest, his fingertips ending up on his mouth—a man frustrated and nervous. *Headed for a heart attack*, Skip thought.

"Yeah, sure. Make the call."

Ferguson sat at a folding table and dialed, showing not so much as a wrinkle in her green silk. "Hello. This is Agent Penny Ferguson of the FBI. I wonder if I could speak to the Reverend Jacomine?"

The phone went dead.

Kohler said, "This is cool. All calls from their number to any FBI office get put through to here automatically. So when he calls back—" He was interrupted by a ringing phone.

Giving Goerner a smug look, he answered it himself. "Federal Bureau of Investigation." There was a pause. "Agent Ferguson? One moment." He punched buttons and looked up at his audience, canary feathers dotting his chin.

The nerds, thought Skip, *shall inherit the Earth*.

Ferguson answered with her last name. The caller rang off.

After that, they waited.

If Jacomine and his followers were holding a council of war, they weren't doing it in the office.

Finally, they heard someone reenter the room, and a few minutes later a phone rang. Ferguson jumped, ready to go. Kohler held up a hand. "It's ringing at the Bourgeois house. We're set up so we

291

can hear the whole thing." He adjusted something—the volume, Skip thought.

They heard Jacomine say, "You shouldn't have called the FBI. I said, tell the *police*."

"What you mean, don' call the FBI? Let me talk to my baby." Dorise sounded indiscreetly furious.

"We're disappointed in you, Mrs. Bourgeois."

"What you talkin' disappointed? You kidnap my chile from a public school, you think my house ain't crawling with FBI? What you think I'm gon' do to get 'em out of here? They here right now, and they got my phone tapped. They say they don't, but I know they do. What you think I can do about that?"

All right, Dorise! Skip had no idea whether she'd been coached, but she liked it. It had the sound of "I-can't-beat-'em-and-neither-can-you."

"Good. Then I'll talk to them. Have Agent Ferguson call us, please, gentlemen."

In the command post, a collective sigh went up when he rang off.

Ferguson checked her watch. "We'll give it ten minutes. To fray their nerves a little."

"Why not?" said Goerner. "Mine are shot. They might as well catch up." His hand was torturing his hair, as if he might tear out a hunk of it. Skip would have felt sorry for him if his voice didn't sound as if it could cut concrete.

When the allotted time had elapsed, Ferguson dialed again. "Agent Ferguson calling. I had a message from you."

"Ah, yes. Agent Ferguson. Apparently, you know where we are."

"Yes. And we have the block roped off and surrounded. But you expected that, didn't you?" She waited a moment. "How are you doing in there? Is Shavonne okay?"

"She's doing great, Agent Ferguson. We're not gonna hurt that child."

"Why don't you call me Penny, Reverend?"

"Looks like you know my name, too."

"Oh, yes."

"All part of the plan, Penny. All part of the plan. Now here's what I need. You just give me my granddaughter in exchange for Shavonne, and then give me and my friends an escort to the airport. Now, what could be simpler?"

"How many people are in there with you?"

"You'll be told when the time comes." He spoke sharply. "You just get me my granddaughter."

"Does she *want* to join you?"

"Of course. Sure she does, Penny—we're doing more for justice in this country than you and every damn police force in every state combined."

Goerner balled up his hands in victory-fists—it was an admission of guilt.

Ferguson stayed cool. "Well, Reverend, is there anything you need in there? Have you got enough food and supplies?"

"That's not really your concern, is it?"

"I'm a little worried about Daniel."

He hesitated before speaking. "Now, why in the hell are you worried about Daniel?"

"Is he okay?"

"You tend to your own knitting, Miss Agent Penny Ferguson." The phone went dead.

Goerner's mouth worked like he was chewing. "Fuck."

There's got to be more, Skip thought. *There just has to be.*

She had butterflies that felt more like bees, partly from fear and tension, but partly from excitement. As the negotiator talked with Jacomine, an idea started forming in the back of her mind. It was so outlandish there wasn't a chance of talking anyone into it—and yet she couldn't get it out of her head. She was reasonably sure this particular situation—therefore this specific opportunity—had never come up before.

It was going to meet resistance, though. Maybe this wasn't the time to bring it up.

Kohler, wearing headphones, was making keep-it-down signs. When he had their attention, he turned a dial, and they heard a woman, apparently in Jacomine's office. "He needs a doctor, Daddy. This is not something to mess with."

"It's God's call, Tara. We've done the contest a thousand times and nobody's gotten hurt before."

"Daddy, he's getting worse. He can't even get up to go to the bathroom." Her voice was panicky.

"Now, don't you worry about it, you hear me? Go on out of here now. I got a phone call to make."

They sat tensely while he dialed a number and got no answer.

27

• •

Skip's mind raced. Finally, she could stand it no longer. "Agent Goerner, I've got a thought."

He looked at her from under beetle brows, his expression saying this better be good. "What?" Rude. Barely acknowledging her.

"Look, *we* know we'd never exchange one hostage for another, but evidently they don't know that or they wouldn't be asking for it."

"What are you getting at, Langdon?"

"Lovelace is nearly as tall as I am. Nobody'd notice the difference without having us side by side."

"So?"

"Well, I bet anything her grandfather hasn't seen her in years— the only one who'd recognize her is Daniel, and sounds like he's out of commission."

"You want to change places with her, is that what you're saying? You want me to send you in there to get killed?"

"I'd have a gun with me. We could work that out."

"Absolutely not. You crazy, Langdon?"

"Besides," Shellmire said, "Jacomine might not know his own granddaughter, but he most assuredly knows you."

"Not with my head shaved, he doesn't."

Ferguson said, "Gentlemen, take this woman seriously. Do you hear what she just offered?"

Abasolo was staring straight at Skip, as if sizing her up, deciding whether she was up to it. They'd been through a lot together—his opinion meant a lot. "The gun thing's not so hard," he said. "You could pad something so they don't feel it when they pat you down."

"Forget it," said King. "She's not doing it."

Goerner glared at him.

Abasolo was still looking at her. "There's this guy who does theatrical makeup—we've worked with him a few times."

"Are you guys in kindergarten or what?" Goerner snapped.

Skip said, "Listen, please. We can't let Jacomine take control."

"Excuse me, Officer Langdon. The Federal Bureau of Investigation has had some experience in these matters."

Stung, she crossed her arms and glowered.

● ●

Jacomine called back. "Penny, I want to meet you."

"Well, let's talk about that."

"I have something for you."

"What is it?"

"It's a Polaroid picture of Shavonne. We just took it."

"I'd like that, Reverend. How about if you let me speak to Shavonne a minute?"

"You don't trust me? Is that what you're saying?"

"I'd just like to be able to reassure her mother, that's all."

"Penny, you must really underestimate me. You really think I'd call you up and not let you talk to Shavonne? Sure, I'm gonna let you talk to Shavonne. Shavonne, honey, come on over here and talk to Miss Penny. Okay. Say hello."

A childish "Hello" galvanized the room.

"Shavonne? Hi, honey. How're you doing?"

"Fine."

"Your mama says to tell you she loves you." Ferguson was improvising here. "You want me to tell her anything for you?"

For a moment there was no answer, and then some sibilants, like whispering. Finally the child said, "Tell her I want to come home real bad."

Jacomine spoke again. "Okay, Penny, how long will it take you to get down here?"

"Not long—a few minutes, maybe."

"I'm gonna send a pregnant lady out with the picture. She'll be unarmed and so will you."

"I thought I was going to get to meet you, Reverend."

"Well, I'd love that, Penny, I really would. But I'll be watching you from inside. It'll be just like we met."

"I'm coming myself; I want you to come, too."

"Don't be ridiculous, honey. Be there in ten minutes if you want the picture." He hung up.

"Dammit!" The Ferguson underneath the VNL was starting to show. "It's pretty fucking hard to negotiate with someone who isn't there."

Once again, Jacomine called back. "Oh, yeah. One other thing. Bring my granddaughter."

"Are you ready to give up Shavonne?"

"We're not at that stage yet, Penny. Here's what's happening now—I'm giving you a picture of Shavonne; you're giving me a look at Lovelace."

"Well, now, Reverend, what if Lovelace doesn't want to see you?"

He yelled through the phone. "Well, goddammit, ask her! You goddamn, incompetent, motherfuckin' bureaucrat! This is how the taxpayers' money gets spent? You be there in ten minutes. With my granddaughter."

Goerner said, "Fine. Let's give him a picture of her. We get one of Shavonne, he gets one of Lovelace."

"Wait a minute, I've got a great idea." Skip spoke like a cheerleader—anything to get them to listen. "I accept the fact that you won't send me in there. But why not let me impersonate her out on the street? Why don't I get made up and come with Penny and talk to him—tell him I don't want to join his stupid movement."

Ferguson said, "We might get some mileage out of that."

Goerner drummed his fingers—now that Taylor was gone, it seemed someone had to do it. "We might. We might."

King looked wary.

"I'm worried about the voice problem," Shellmire said. "You sound like you and she sounds like a young girl."

"Maybe I don't have to speak. At least at first. If Lovelace is willing, maybe we could completely switch identities." She was making this up as she went along. "Abasolo gave me an idea when he mentioned hiding a weapon under padding. I'm heavier than Lovelace, but we could pad her clothes—because nobody knows what she really looks like. The only constants are height and eye color—and I'll bet you a million dollars her grandfather's never noticed her eye color. Get her a curly wig, police uniform, and Bob's your uncle. Meanwhile, I shave my head, dye the stubble black, and wear kids' clothes—jeans or something. They see us across the street, more or less together, they get used to the idea that the curly one's me— voices might not matter so much."

A tiny muscle under Goerner's left eye was twitching, forcing him to close it slightly, so that he looked more like a thug than an officer of the law. "Okay, I'll go for it. It might buy us something. What, I don't know—but I don't see the down side."

Abasolo said, "Let's go talk to Lovelace."

They found her watching television and pacing. "That mess on Magazine Street—my dad's in there, isn't he?"

"I'm afraid so," Skip said, and told her everything except that her father's life might depend on ending the standoff as quickly as possible.

Lovelace considered the switch. "Sure," she said finally. "I don't see any harm in that—I just don't want to be a party to anyone's getting hurt."

Skip was hard put not to roll her eyes. Someone was definitely going to get hurt.

Lovelace said, "There's only one thing—I need to talk to my uncle first."

"Fair enough," said Abasolo, as if it were a huge concession. "And we have a little coaching to do. Skip has to get shaved and dyed, so I'll take over if it's okay with you."

That should cement the deal, Skip thought. Women found Abasolo hard to resist.

He took Lovelace away to see Isaac and to make a tape of her voice, while Skip twitched under the hands of a hairdresser, enduring the removal of the silky curls she regarded as her best feature. Though she was turned away from the mirror, a great sadness came over her as they fell on the floor. She'd had them all her life. *Get over it,* she thought. *This isn't your identity. It's only hair.*

But she thought there was a good chance she'd cry about it later.

Dye wasn't necessary. The hairdresser sprayed the inch-long locks with something that was probably meant for Halloween parties, and then sheared them off to a quarter of an inch.

"Ready?" he said, finally.

"I guess so."

The hairdresser whirled her around. "Omigod. I kind of like it." He nodded. "You got the face for it. Cheekbones."

The only problem was, it in no way resembled Lovelace's face. Though Lovelace was thinner, what baby fat she had was in her face. Makeup rounded Skip's a bit.

Abasolo was waiting for her. "Ready to meet your double?"

"No comment about the new me?"

"Langdon, you're a cool customer. You know that?"

It was something like what Shellmire had said. *If they only knew,* she thought. All during the shearing, she had sung to herself to avoid thinking about Steve, or the kids, or what would happen if she died today: "Let the Good Times Roll."

Lovelace had been fitted with a new, rounder figure, a police uniform, and a toy gun that looked exactly like a real one—the sort more than one kid has been shot by a cop for brandishing.

On the way back to Magazine Street, Abasolo filled her in on the thing they'd withheld. "We have some bad news for you. We think your father may be ill—what's wrong, we don't know, but we need to try to get him out of there. How are you going to be with that?"

She gave him as level a gaze as a woman ten years older. "What do you mean by that?"

"Are you going to fall apart? Can you stay in character?"

"You mean if I find out he's dead or something?"

Skip thought, *She gets right to the point. That's probably good.*

Abasolo said, "Yes. That. And if his condition changes."

299

"If he dies while we're doing it."

"Yes."

She nodded, having apparently asked herself the question and found the answer. "I'll be okay."

Skip gave her a pat. "Good girl."

Lovelace smiled. "The hairdo looks better on you."

"Thanks." She smiled back. "Here's what's going to happen first. We're pretty sure how it's going to go. If it doesn't, don't say anything. I'll ad-lib." She outlined the scenario, with a few possible variations, all worked out on the phone with Ferguson. There'd be no time for Ferguson and Lovelace to talk before the show started.

As they neared the taped-off area, they had to fight their way through media vans and cameramen. Shellmire and Ferguson were standing in the middle of Magazine Street, Shellmire holding a megaphone. Abasolo said, "What's the situation?"

"Ferguson's been holding them off. We came over in ten minutes like they asked, but they wouldn't give us the picture till they saw Lovelace."

Skip said, "Well, here I am."

"I like it. It's good." He turned to Lovelace. "Don't shake hands—pretend you already know me. Agent Shellmire, FBI."

"Officer Jacomine, NOPD."

The name made Skip shiver, even when a young girl said it.

Skip said, "I don't really get the point of the picture. We've already talked to her."

"Let's don't worry about that now. Penny, you ready?" Ferguson whipped out a cell phone and called.

"Reverend, look out the window. Your granddaughter's here."

Though they could see no sign of activity at any of the windows, Skip waved.

Ferguson said, "Listen, I really need *you* to give us the picture." She paused. "Well, if I'm coming over, you at least need to come out and show yourself."

She listened. "Well, look, okay, I'll deal with Bettina. But I've got some other things to tell you. Lovelace wants to know how her father is."

Ferguson waited a minute, then put her hand over the phone and

300

spoke to the others, all part of the act for whoever was looking out the window. "He says, why don't you ask him yourself, but I'm afraid we can't . . ."

Skip made a show of grabbing for the phone, but Ferguson snatched it back and kept talking, knowing she could be heard at the other end of the line. "I'm sorry. It's not an appropriate time for you to talk to him. You'll have to wait until we have the picture."

Skip moved her mouth, but Lovelace spoke, her lips hidden by her cap, and by Shellmire's shoulder. "Tell him I want to speak to my dad."

Ferguson did, and waited while he answered. "I know it's not part of the deal," she said, "but you're not letting us see you. Look, if she can't talk to Daniel, why don't you at least let her see him?" She paused.

"Okay, okay—you're counting to ten. You want to give me the photograph now. Hold it, Reverend. Can you hold it just a minute? Okay, we can do it now, but just do me one favor, to show good faith. Give me the picture you took an hour ago, and a new one, too. Deal? Okay, I'm coming."

She held the phone toward them so they could hear Jacomine counting, and began to walk across the street. As she did, several members of the TAC unit stepped into view behind her, on the sidewalk opposite the house, rifles raised.

The door opened and a pregnant woman stepped out.

Ferguson mounted the porch. Both women started at a noise behind them—something being pushed through the mail slot. The pregnant woman stooped, picked it up, and gave it to Ferguson.

Ferguson looked at it, nodded, and said, "Is everyone all right in there?"

The woman said, "I'm going back in now."

When Ferguson returned, she had two Polaroid pictures, one of a small black girl in a blue T-shirt, the other still developing. As it came into focus, they saw that it was the same little girl, still wearing the T-shirt. The only difference was that the first one was a head shot, and the second was full-length. The little girl was wearing jeans.

Skip gave a slight nod to confirm it was Shavonne.

Ferguson spoke into the phone. "Okay, we're satisfied." She listened. "Sure. You can talk to her now."

She handed the phone to Skip, who had a tape in her pocket, prerecorded by Lovelace after her visit with Isaac. Skip flicked it on and lip-synched, "Grandpa, how's my dad?" She turned it off, ready for the next sound bite when she needed it.

"He's fine, honey. You look good—or you will when that hair grows out."

"Why can't I talk to him?"

"Come over and join us; then we'll all be together."

They hadn't known what he'd say, had simply recorded a generic bit to get the point across. "Please, please give yourselves up. I'm so afraid for you."

"Are you kidding? We're Jacomines. Nothing's going to happen to us. We need you, Lovelace."

Skip put her hand over her face, as if overcome with emotion, unable to go on, and gave the phone back to Ferguson, shaking her head, simply unable to say another word.

Ferguson said, "She's a mess, Reverend. Don't put her through any more of this." She listened a minute and folded her phone. "He said he'll call us back in an hour."

28

• •

Kohler had a tape for them, a call to Jacomine just before they talked to him. But before he played it, he took Goerner aside and when Goerner came back, he took Lovelace aside. Skip couldn't hear any of what they said, until Lovelace raised her voice. "I have a right to hear it. I'm not a child and I won't be treated like one."

Goerner murmured some more.

Lovelace answered, "That's my dad over there. I swear to God I won't continue with this unless you let me hear it."

Goerner's lips were tight thin lines, wild things that wanted to get loose and say what was on the agent's mind: *Fuckin' civilians! Goddammit, how the fuck did I get talked into this crap?*

At least that was what Skip imagined he was thinking. A similar, faintly guilty thought had crossed her own mind: *When you're running an operation you need obedient soldiers, not volunteer labor.*

Still, she wasn't running it, and she thought a little irritation a small price to pay for Lovelace's cooperation.

Ferguson joined the duo and spoke to Goerner. "It's okay. She needs to know what's going on as much as the rest of us."

She was playing the good cop, but also, Skip thought, she was

303

reminding Goerner that negotiation was her business, that she could handle Lovelace if she needed to be handled.

He shrugged and held up his hands like Ferguson walking to The Jury's safe house. "Okay, okay. Let's just play the goddamn tape."

Kohler looked so smug, Skip wanted to slug him. He flicked the switch for the tape.

A man's voice spoke, a voice Skip didn't recognize. "Daddy, Ms. Owens wants to talk to you."

"Put her on."

There was a rustling, then silence.

Jacomine said, "Baby, you there?"

"Your fucking thug kidnapped me."

"How're we doing with that plane?"

"Goddammit, Earl, are you still Mr. FedEx in the sack? Faster than the competition ever thought about being?"

"What's that supposed to mean?"

"You are the most impatient man in the history of the world."

"Rosemarie, did it ever occur to you we might have a reason for it? Lives are at stake here."

"Did it ever occur to you they wouldn't be if you weren't playing your little game?"

"Our son's life is at stake."

Silence.

Finally Jacomine spoke again. "I didn't want to tell you, honey, but Daniel's had an accident. He needs medical attention. Bad."

"What's wrong with him?"

"Well, we don't know, exactly, but he's pissing blood. He's moaning, and in and out of consciousness."

They could hear her draw in her breath. "Earl, that's not something you can mess with. Leave Daniel there. I swear to God if you don't, I won't lift a single finger to help you. I don't care if you kill me if you endanger that boy's life."

The phone went dead, and they heard Jacomine say, "Goddammit, Rosemarie, you can't hang up on me."

There was silence for a while, then another man said, "You okay, Daddy?"

Jacomine said, "You know what, Dashan? This is a good thing. The Lord just provided. I was going to use Bettina—but you know how much she would have hated to leave us. This is better. What you think, Dashan?"

"You're right, Daddy. You sure are right."

Skip thought: *I wonder if he understood that any better than I did?*, and then Jacomine said, "Sarah Jane, for Christ's sake, when's lunch?"

Kohler flicked it off.

"That's all?" asked King.

"That's it."

Shellmire said, "Anything during the negotiation?"

"Yeah, but nothing worth playing. I guess they're going to call us after lunch."

"I hope they all get E. coli."

Sandwiches were brought into the command post as well, along with soft drinks and another round of coffee. Abasolo, King, and Kohler ate. Lovelace nibbled.

Everyone else fidgeted.

When the call came, Goerner said, "Let it ring a few times."

Finally he said, "Pick it up" and Kohler answered, again going through the charade of transferring the call to Ferguson.

"Hello, Reverend."

Jacomine said, "Here's the deal. We got a real problem. We got a sick man in here. We're gonna trade you my son Daniel for my granddaughter."

"Daniel's sick?"

"Daniel's real sick. We need y'all to get him to a hospital."

"Can he walk?"

"Afraid not. We'll just have to put him out on the porch and y'all can pick him up. That okay with you?"

"What about Shavonne?"

"Well, now, she wants to get back to her mama. Real bad. But we can't give you two for one . . ."

"Now, Reverend, you know we can't trade you anybody. Lovelace doesn't want to join you. We can't make her."

"I've got a feeling she'd change her mind if she knew how sick ·

305

her daddy is. But it wouldn't be fair to give you Daniel and Shavonne. So we'll take that big clumsy cop off your hands in exchange for one sweet, innocent little girl."

"What cop is that?"

Skip whispered, "Me," and Jacomine's voice boomed out, "That Langdon bitch. Daniel and Shavonne for Lovelace and Langdon. Take it or leave it."

"Reverend, listen . . ."

"You listen, Penny. I'm just about out of patience with you. You got my number—call me when you're ready to deal." Once again, the phone went dead.

Skip said, "It had to be. I knew they wanted me."

Goerner looked puzzled. "What for?"

"The Rev and I have a lot of history. Bottom line, he wants to kill me. But use me for a hostage first to get wherever they're going. After that, arrange some particularly nasty form of torture—the Rev's famous for torture—and then, I don't know. Burn me at the stake, probably."

Goerner pulled at a hunk of thick hair. "Out of the question."

"Well, I don't like the idea much myself."

In a small voice, Lovelace said, "What about my dad?"

Skip spoke before anyone else could. "There's only one chance. We say Lovelace changed her mind when she heard about her dad. She'll be happy to join them. We say okay, the deal's fine—"

"For Christ's sake, Langdon. No law enforcement agency in the world makes deals with terrorists."

"Oh, please. Don't treat me like a child. No one *honors* deals with terrorists. You guys'll turn an exchange into a snatch any time you get a chance."

"You want to go in there yourself." Goerner was still trying to grasp it.

"As Lovelace, yes. But the whole point of never making deals is to send a message to the next guys. Negotiators make deals all the time—'Promise I go free if I give up my little son and daughter?' 'Sure, we'll take real good care of you.' Then, bam, he's in the slammer. Deals, yes. Followed by double crosses. All I'm suggesting is a different kind of double cross—think of it as a Trojan horse."

"Then who do we send in exchange for Shavonne? Abasolo in drag? And what's the point, anyway? They'll just kill both of you."

"We arrange for one at a time—first Daniel, then Shavonne. If I go as Lovelace, they won't be expecting a cop, and they won't be expecting a weapon. They'll pat me down, but I'll have the gun hidden well enough that they won't find it. Then I'll just have to make a move before the second exchange—which won't occur in any case."

"Uh-uh. You're not trained for that kind of work. Anyway, how do we know there aren't twenty of them over there, all armed with assault rifles? What are you going to do, pick them all off? Or maybe just one of them's armed—and that one shoots Shavonne."

That had been worrying Skip as well. But she said, "I just don't see what else we can do—this is something we *can* do without being completely at their mercy." She shrugged. "Okay. I'm happy to listen to alternate plans. Penny, you're the negotiator—what do you suggest?"

For the first time, Ferguson looked rattled. Not falling-apart-rattled, like Goerner—but profoundly unhappy.

"I don't know. I just don't know. This isn't like some psycho who's mad at his wife and threatening to kill his kids. That kind of person at least half wants to be talked out of it. Religious fanatics at least half want to become martyrs."

The phone rang again. Goerner waved at Kohler, giving the okay to answer it. Jacomine didn't even bother to ask for Ferguson. "What's your fax number, FBI? We just took another picture of Shavonne and we want to send it right over to you."

Kohler gave it. They gathered round the fax machine, the air clogged with tension.

As the picture slid out, the point of the first photo became clear. A collective gasp went up. Even the smug Kohler for once lost his cool. "My God!" he blurted.

The photo showed Shavonne standing up in the same jeans and T-shirt as before. She was also wearing a down jacket with two sticks of dynamite jammed and taped into it, an alarm clock attached somehow or other. It was a primitive time-bomb. As graphic a warning as a finger in the mail.

Another fax came through, a handwritten note: "It's set for three P.M. sharp. We're prepared to die with her." There was a P.S.: "By the way, it can be detonated earlier. Use gas or fire one shot—and that's it."

Goerner's face was grayish. "Fuckers. Goddamn motherfuckin' FUCKERS!"

It was two-fifteen.

The phone rang. "Did y'all get my fax?"

Ferguson said, "Reverend, you've got to remember she's just a little girl. She didn't volunteer for this. I know you're a Christian. Listen, I'm Irish Catholic, myself, and I know God is a merciful god. Doesn't he expect us to be merciful as well?"

"Penny, shut up, will you? Let me talk to Lovelace."

"We had to send her away for a few minutes. I'm sure you didn't want her to see that picture, did you?"

"I most assuredly did. I want my granddaughter to know her grandpa means business. That saving her father is completely within her power. We don't get her, we don't get Langdon, that bomb goes off, Shavonne dies, I die, Daniel dies, everybody in the house dies."

Even as his words filled the room, agents and engineers in headsets were working, calling the bomb squad, making plans to move the command post—first the people, then the machines.

When the call was over, Goerner said, "Okay, we can't stay here. Everybody out the window—there's a van around the corner. Not you, Langdon. Let me talk to you. Turner, you too."

Skip huddled with him, not sure what to expect.

"Look, there's no point in calling the psychologists. They already gave us their opinion—but just the same, I'm gonna get people on the phone to 'em right away. If they say what I think they're gonna, which is that this guy's crazy enough to do it, I've either got to let him do it and kill that little girl, or gas the place and rush it, thereby getting maybe twenty people killed, or send you on what could very well be a suicide mission. Turner here says you think on your feet, and you can probably pull this thing off if anyone can. I want to know something—are you as crazy as that asshole?"

Skip's feet and hands were blocks of ice. *No*, she thought. *I take it all back. No way in hell am I going in there.*

She said, "Give me five minutes. Let me think about it while we move." She was aware that her voice sounded sluggish and without enthusiasm.

Kohler said, "Something's coming in." He turned up the volume. "He's talking to the mother."

Jacomine was saying, "Ms. Bourgeois, you got a fax machine?"

"We have one over at the church."

He was going to fax Dorise the picture. He was probably going to fax it to the *New York Times* after that. Tomorrow Shavonne would be dead, and Dorise and the whole world would know that the FBI and the New Orleans Police Department had done nothing to stop it.

The world was one thing—Dorise was another.

Skip knew Shellmire was thinking what she was and that, despite that, he'd actually be relieved if she said no.

Goerner probably wanted her to do it. The feds would look like jerks if they relinquished control at this point; he had to do something to save his ass.

Goddammit, she thought. *I wish I were a Christian. Or something. Maybe I'd be braver.*

She caught Shellmire's eye. "I think I've got to take a shot at it."

"No, you do not have to. You had to kill a man who was trying to kill you. You don't owe that kid a damn thing just because he was her father."

His words had the opposite effect they were meant to have. She thought of the people she knew that Jacomine had killed, and she thought of pregnant Bettina, and she thought of the man she had killed the day before, to save Lovelace from her own grandfather.

She said, "I want to do it, Turner."

They took her to the tactical command post, where the leaders of the TAC units were busy sweating bullets. Goerner outlined the plan, and as he talked, Skip watched the men's faces screw up in dismay and worry.

Their names were Vinterella and Platt. Vinterella, the one from NOPD, was someone she knew slightly. She liked him and thought he liked her, but he was already shaking his head.

"Skip, we've never worked together. How we gonna do this if we're not on the same page?"

"You and Agent Platt have never worked together. Have you?"

He kept shaking his head. "Shit. Shit, shit, shit."

"Listen, I know the risk. I've just spent the last ten minutes psyching myself up for this. You and Platt can plan your nice maneuvers all day and all night, but, realistically, these people are crazy as bats. You know and I know I'm the only chance that kid's got."

"We have to think about the risk to our guys, too."

"This way there's less risk to them. If you try to storm that place you're probably going to lose somebody. If you don't, the kid'll probably die, so you're probably going to. If I'm already in there—say with a hidden transmitter—you've got an edge."

Platt spoke for the first time. "The question is, will you have a chance?"

"Give me one, guys. Come on. Tell me what I've got to do and I'll do it, okay?"

Vinterella let his face relax. He was talked into it. "All right. Let's do it."

Platt gave the after-you sign. "You're the explosives expert."

They sat down at a small table, and Vinterella began to draw. "Here's the alarm clock here. See this screw in it?" He showed her the faxed photo and put a loupe on top of it. She could barely see a speck where the screw must be. She turned back to the drawing.

Vinterella had added a wire and a blob representing a battery. "See there's a wire on the screw, which is attached to a battery on the kid someplace. Maybe on the back of the jacket. There could even be more than one battery. Know what's attached to the batteries?"

She shrugged. "Blasting caps, I guess."

"Right. So here's how it works—if the clock hand touches the screw, the bomb detonates."

"So I have to cut the wire."

"Yeah, if you've got the guts. Most cops won't touch a device. You know that, don't you?"

"I don't think I'm gonna have time to wait for a bomb expert."

When the meeting was over, they put Lovelace on the phone. "Grandpa, I'm really worried about my daddy."

"He's holding his own, Sugar-pie. But I'm not gonna lie to my granddaughter—he really does need a doctor."

"Can I talk to him?"

"I'm sorry, honey, but the only phone we got's downstairs, and he's upstairs. He can't really walk down, the condition he's in."

"What would I have to do if I traded myself for him?"

"Oh, you'd be part of us. You'd be part of the most important justice-seeking organization in the history of the world."

"You know, I—" she spoke slowly "—think I'd kind of like that." They all held their breath. Ferguson had felt it would be better for her to ask more questions about the movement, but they were aware of the time constraints—at this point, the goal was get in, get out—just get it happening.

Ferguson took the phone. "Hi, Rev, it's Penny. Listen, we've tried real hard to talk your granddaughter out of this thing, but we haven't succeeded. We have only one condition. You give us Shavonne first."

"Penny, honey, call me back when you're ready to talk." He rang off as usual, and this time Ferguson smiled. "I think I'm getting a feel for him. You have to turn his hang-ups against him—like in aikido, or something."

Skip barely listened. She was sitting on the floor, meditating. It wasn't something she was good at, generally finding it hard to sit still, but somehow she had to get her nerves to quit dancing like electric currents in a science fiction movie.

Ferguson called Jacomine and told him he'd won: They'd transfer Lovelace and Daniel first. Again, the room held its collective breath—if Jacomine said the transfers had to be simultaneous, it was over. Skip half hoped he would.

"Very good," he said. "We're ready."

"The only requirement," Ferguson said, "is that Lovelace wants to see her dad first." If he said yes to this, they'd wiggle out of it, saying she'd changed her mind for some reason. Since he was the only one who could identify Lovelace, they couldn't take a chance on his seeing Skip, but they had to make it Jacomine's idea to keep them apart.

"Impossible," he said. "I'm sorry to tell you Daniel's been unconscious for an hour."

"Are you sure he's still alive?"

311

"Of course, he's still alive. Are you crazy? But he's not going to be if you assholes don't get a move on. We're taking him down the steps now."

"Okay, we'll send two paramedics to get him. Then we'll send Lovelace."

"No deal." Again, the hang-up; again, the redial.

"Here's how it'll work," he said. "Two people will bring Daniel outside. Your two paramedics will carry the stretcher, so we can see their hands at all times. They will be covered from inside the house. Lovelace will walk with them. Our two people will hand Daniel over and receive Lovelace."

Ferguson handed the phone to Lovelace. She said what she'd been coached to say. "Grandpa, I need to walk in by myself. There's media out here. I want the world to see me walk in."

"Well, of course, honey. You can have anything your little heart desires."

Skip fought nausea. She was way past "Let the Good Times Roll." She thought of the peaceful feeling the witches always gave her. *What would they do?* she thought. She tried deep breathing, chanting as she breathed. *I breathe in courage and strength and the spirit of all the warrior women who have gone before me. I breathe out cowardice and ineptness and failure.*

She was making this up as she went along, and it wasn't working.

She dropped the last part and tried to think in specifics. Were there any warrior women? There was Kali, the Hindu goddess of destruction, or anyway, that was close enough; there was Boudicca, the British queen whose army slaughtered seventy thousand Roman invaders; there was Athena, chief strategist for Zeus; there was Deborah, the Hebrew warrior.

And of course, there was Joan of Arc, but Skip wasn't going to mess with that one.

She tried their names. *I am Kali, goddess of destruction, I am Boudicca, leader of the Celts, I am Deborah . . .*

The one that worked was Kali. She imagined herself with a necklace of severed heads, a demeanor so savage her face alone could probably destroy mere mortals.

Or anyway, make them fuck up. That's all I ask—just make them fuck up.

And stay with me in there. Don't leave me alone with those assholes.

How odd this was did not occur to her; all she knew was that she'd never been more scared in her life, and she certainly wasn't going to pray to the Christian god. For one thing, she never had; for another, Jacomine claimed to have Him sewed up.

•   •

Abasolo had seen to it that when the makeup expert fattened Lovelace up, he padded a pair of jeans for Skip, making them pillowy at the top, as if a blouse had been tucked in, and sewed in a holster. She had tried them on briefly at Headquarters, but, because this mission wasn't yet authorized, a cursory fit was all there was time for.

The clock read two thirty-five as she changed into them. Expertly, Abasolo patted her down. "No good," he said, "I can feel it." There was no time to send for the tailor.

"I wonder," said Ferguson. She turned her back and took off her bra. "Padded."

They improvised, and when they were done, several experts could feel nothing when they patted Skip down. It was two forty-five. They gave her a second gun—a tiny North American .22—in a bra they had padded with tissues and handkerchiefs. Neither was going to be easy to get to, but it was the best they could do in the allotted time.

In the second bra cup, they fitted a small wireless transmitter and a tiny pair of wire cutters.

Goerner was pale, but strangely calm, as if he'd finally worked off all his nervous energy. All he said was, "Get a move on, y'all," in a quiet, almost serene voice.

King sat in a corner biting the side of his index finger. They'd practically had to tie him up to get the operation going, and bitter words had been exchanged before he finally called the acting chief, who agreed instantly; in fact, so quickly Kohler joked that he must have already spent a few hours dodging reporters. Skip suspected that wasn't the whole story.

She'd noticed Abasolo talking very quietly on his cell phone—he'd probably called Joe Tarantino, who had briefed the chief before

King called. Throughout the whole day, Abasolo had moved like some dark, knowing shadow, anticipating what had to be done, smoothing the way for it.

The two of them—he and Skip—had always been a great team, but this was something new. *I'm going to owe him big-time,* thought Skip. *That is, if I'm around.*

She tried to clear her brain, banish thoughts of mortality. *Breathe in, breathe out. The hell with chanting.*

Ferguson said, "Okay, everyone?" and dialed.

The psychologists had been called and had agreed this was the only alternative.

The TAC unit was at the ready, with strict instructions to stand by until Skip came out, or asked her bra bug for help, or it became clear from the bug that she was out of commission.

The bomb squad was ready to dismantle the bomb if Skip couldn't.

An ambulance was parked a block away, ready to make a show of arriving for Daniel. More emergency vehicles were seconds away.

Ferguson held up a finger; Jacomine had answered.

"Hey, Reverend, how you doing?"

"All our people are at peace with God. We are ready to die in twelve minutes." He sounded ominously calm.

"The paramedics are here, Reverend." A siren could just now be heard. "I'm bringing them both over now—Lovelace and Langdon. After we have Daniel safe, an unarmed member of the bomb squad will bring Langdon up the steps. You will send one person out with Shavonne."

"Send Langdon up alone."

"Reverend, there won't be time—"

"Whose fucking fault is that?" He hung up.

The first part of the operation went exactly as both parties had agreed. As soon as Daniel lay on the porch, and Jacomine's two goons stood beside him, hands in the air, Skip—in her Lovelace role—walked onto the porch with the paramedics.

The first thing she noticed was that they hadn't lied about Daniel. His eyes were closed and he was moaning, apparently unconscious.

One of the goons was black, one white. The black one was a large, handsome man, who nicely matched Dorise's description of Dashan. *I hope,* she thought, *I don't have to tangle with that one.*

The white one was older and smaller, but he had a spare, mean look that Skip didn't like, and thick ropy wrists. A fight with him wouldn't be a picnic either.

She didn't smile at either one of them, tried instead to look small and scared. On one account, at any rate, she wasn't acting.

They made a sandwich of her, Dashan first entering the house, then Skip, then the white man.

She cased the place quickly. The front room of the house was meant to be lived in sideways—that is, the fireplace, instead of being dead ahead, was on the right wall.

This room opened into another, with pocket doors that were wide open, so that the two were really one. It was full of furniture, and there was practically none in the front room, the one in which Skip stood. It had probably been emptied into the second, except for one chair, which was full, and a heavy table that was apparently used as a desk. The one window was also to the right of the door. A man holding an assault weapon stood looking out, but probably couldn't see much.

All that was expected.

What was not were two smiling women, waiting for Skip with arms outstretched. She heard the words, "Welcome, sister," though from which one she didn't know, and felt soft arms enfold her. Her face snuggled into someone's shoulder. Somewhere in the distance she was aware of Dashan and the other man clumping up the stairs.

Upstairs, she thought. *Jacomine's running this from the second floor.*

In the room's one chair sat another woman, holding Shavonne, bomb in place.

Skip had half expected the faithful to be gathered round the girl, praying and kissing their asses good-bye. The fact that they weren't was a good sign, she thought, a sign undermining Jacomine's statement that they were all ready to die. He evidently expected to be obeyed by the forces of the law.

That could work in her favor.

The second the hugging woman let her go, Skip's hand went to her waist, drew her gun, and jammed it into the hugger's abdomen. "Now I've got a hostage."

The man with the gun whirled, but remained in place.

Feet sounded on the stairs, men coming down, probably Dashan and his buddy.

The second woman started for the stairs.

The woman holding Shavonne started praying, tears running down her face, terror in her eyes. "Merciful God, deliver us . . . help us, oh God of Israel."

She wasn't going to be a problem, but Shavonne clung to her. Skip pushed her hostage, hard, toward the man with the gun, and while they were both still unbalanced, she jerked at the girl. When Shavonne turned toward Skip, the face of the clock loomed as large as Big Ben. It said three o'clock, straight up.

But the second hand was still sweeping. It was four seconds from the screw.

It could take that long just to get the wire cutters out of her bra.

Skip thought, *I should pray, too.* She was aware of noise in the room, the other two coming toward her.

Her hands shook and sweat ran into her eyes as she ripped the jacket open and off the child. The popping snaps sounded like firecrackers.

So hot, she thought. *It's so damn hot in here.*

Without even taking aim, she threw the vest into the second room, and dived under the table, Shavonne's body under hers. The building exploded.

29

• •

She swallowed dust and rubble, and she was hit by flying objects, but for the most part the table protected her. She said into her bug, "We're all right, I think."

Shavonne whimpered, and Skip tried to move a little, so as not to crush the child, but she found herself absolutely unable to speak words of comfort, only to lie there, very still, until they pulled her out.

Someone said, "Can you walk?" and she had absolutely no idea what the answer was. But her muscles moved, and she did walk, through a bombed-out shell. Seeing what she saw, she couldn't believe she'd survived. She later learned someone else had carried Shavonne out, but she had no recollection of being parted from the child.

She had thrown the bomb diagonally, and most of the damage to the house was on the other side, the left, and toward the back. Still, the house was totalled.

She was so deeply in shock that she didn't protest when they put her in an ambulance and took her to Charity Hospital. Abasolo rode with her.

"You're okay, Skip, you're okay." The usual lies.

He held her hand tightly, but she couldn't stop the shaking. Her body was reliving the explosion over and over again, like aftershocks of a quake.

"Close," she said. She meant it was a close call, but she couldn't say it. She couldn't say anything for a long time, not until she had been examined and pronounced well, and Cindy Lou, who had shown up almost immediately, had fought her way in and said, "Valium, okay? Have pity on the woman."

They made her swallow something, and gradually the shaking subsided.

Cindy Lou said, "Steve's on his way."

Involuntarily, Skip's hand went to her head. "Oh, shit. My hair."

Lou-Lou laughed and Skip was aware that this was a normal sound, a real-world sound. "You might be getting better, girl-friend."

She was well enough to go home, but that was about it. Steve got her upstairs and into bed, wrestling off her clothes, removing the .22 and the bug without so much as a comment. He woke her briefly to ask if she wanted to see the news, but she shook her head, noticing it felt slightly strange—lighter and smoother, she wasn't sure why—and she went back to sleep.

She awoke the next morning feeling surprisingly normal, except for a choking mass of something in the back of her throat. She rolled over onto Steve and wouldn't let go until he pushed her gently. "My leg's asleep."

When she spoke, she realized she was hoarse. "Shavonne?"

He stroked her bald head. "She's fine."

To her vast surprise, she started crying, and when she was done, the mass in her throat had dissolved. "That wasn't fun."

"What, crying? I know. It really hurts your eyes."

She rolled over, flinging an arm over her head. "Oh, shit. I'm not cut out to be a commando."

"Actually, intelligence agencies the world over have been faxing fabulous offers. A few came in from Hollywood, too. My favorite's the one from some dude named Broccoli—is he a man or a vege-table? Says you're the new Jane Bond."

She couldn't even laugh. "He's wrong. Also he's dead."

"I like your new haircut."

She turned away from him.

"Seriously."

"I don't *ever* want to do that again."

"If you do, don't tell me, okay? Only good thing about it, I didn't know till afterward. That, and my girlfriend's currently the most famous woman on the planet."

She sat up. "You better give me the stats. What happened in there?"

"Three dead, four injured, three unscathed. All law enforcement personnel in one piece."

"Which group is Jacomine in?"

His face was suddenly serious, even a little panicked, as if he were afraid of disappointing her. His voice sounded puzzled. "There's something funny there."

She gave him a kill-the-messenger glare. "What?"

"He wasn't there."

"What do you mean he wasn't there?"

"He wasn't in the rubble."

"Are you trying to tell me he got away?"

"Not necessarily. Maybe you blew him into such minute smithereens he disappeared."

She was shaking her head, refusing to buy it. "This is a joke, right?"

Before he even answered, she flung the covers aside, got out of bed, and started rummaging for clothes. Steve said, "Shellmire called. They're questioning the survivors at the federal building."

She arrived as angry as she was scared the day before. Shellmire came out to greet her. "Nice job, Skip. Incredible job."

"How'd he get away, Turner?"

"Oh, shit. It's too embarrassing to talk about."

"Tell me."

"Did you ever hear about the case where the perps were passing something along, and all the surveillance team ever saw them do was dump trash in a Dumpster? Turned out it had a hole in it and it was up against a wall with a hole in it, and there was another Dumpster on the other side. Or that was more or less it. Famous case in FBI annals."

"Shit. How'd Jacomine work it?"

"A uniquely New Orleans twist. Armoires."

She saw it instantly. "Two bedrooms back to back—the armoires in exactly the same place, only you'd never notice."

"Yeah, well, we might have noticed those bedrooms also had closets." He sounded chagrined. "But in the heat of the moment—and I do mean heat . . ." He shrugged.

"How'd he get out of the house?"

Turner shrugged again. "Made himself invisible, I guess. Or more likely waited till no one was looking—till after dark, probably."

"We've got seven survivors, right? And no one blew the whistle?"

"Oh, yeah, someone did. The pregnant woman—but not till after the baby was born."

"A baby? You mean a baby came out of all this?"

He grinned. "Bouncing girl, doing fine. Bettina got injured somehow or other—flying wall, probably—and they had to do a C-section. It was a while before we could question her."

"Who's the father?"

"She won't say."

"Oh, God. Spawn of the devil, as Aunt Alice would say."

"Could be. Speaking of which, Daniel's doing okay, too."

"What about Rosemarie?"

"Sorry to say she hasn't turned up. She did charter a plane, but needless to say, Jacomine chose an alternate mode of transportation."

"Shit, shit, shit."

"Didn't your mother ever tell you that's a very unoriginal and undescriptive word?"

"Wrong. It exactly describes what I feel like and what we've got."

She was so angry about Jacomine she threw herself into questioning the survivors, unwilling to brood, just wanting to work her mood off, until Cindy Lou called to ask her to lunch.

Skip looked at her watch. "Lunch? It's two o'clock."

"You haven't eaten, have you? Come on—I've got a new boyfriend."

"With your record, it's probably Dashan." Lou-Lou's boyfriends always had a fatal flaw.

"It's a thought," she said. "He's not only homicidal, he's got a real bad head injury. If he comes out of this sick enough, I might consider him."

They went to Mona's, a Mideastern restaurant said to be fashioned from an old gas station, and famous for unique alfresco dining—it may once have had windows, but it no longer did. Until she actually had a falafel in hand, Skip didn't realize she was ravenous.

"You're really tearing into that poor sandwich."

"You know what? I haven't eaten in twenty-four hours—more, maybe. Listen, you want to be my shrink? I swear to God that was the worst thing I've ever done—how come in the movies everybody's all beaming and happy after a disaster?"

"You've had close calls before. Why was this so much worse?"

"I don't know. I had more time to think about it, I guess. Lou-Lou, I really didn't think I was going to pull it off. I've never felt that way before. Do you know how lucky I got? We didn't know if there were ten people in there or fifty, and we had no idea where they were. I could have walked right into the lions' den."

"You did, actually. It's just that the lions were a little preoccupied."

Skip nodded, and swallowed the last bite of her sandwich. She considered ordering another. "There weren't that many when you realize how big the house was—they were all spread out, trying to cover every entrance."

"Would you do it again?"

"Not for a million dollars and a castle in Spain. Not if I got to be queen of England. No way and uh-uh." She wondered if Lou-Lou would ask how she felt about the people who had died in the blast and the man she had killed the day before, but she didn't and that was good, because Skip didn't want to talk about it.

She felt oddly separate from their deaths—"in denial," Lou-Lou might say, but if denial would work that was fine with her. She had shot Delavon in the middle of a family reunion; these other deaths were not so real, and she wanted to keep it that way.

"Do you know who's the cutest thing in the world?" Lou-Lou was saying. "Hey, Skip—you with me?"

321

"Oh, yeah. The new boyfriend."

"Not really. That was just a joke, but honestly, he's adorable."

"Who?"

"The White Monk."

"Oh, God, he's perfect for you. He's a sweetie pie, which would be a welcome change, and has delusions you could work on the rest of your life."

"What delusions?"

"About killing somebody. Either that or he's a liar, but I kind of think he really thinks it."

"That's no delusion. That's just his OCD."

"His what?"

"Obsessive-compulsive syndrome. He doesn't think he killed somebody, he just thinks he *might* have."

"Oh, right. That's what *he* says. What's the difference?"

"OCD is a very interesting thing—people who suffer from it are like philosophers, in a way. They want to know how you can really know something. Because they can't. They're pretty sure they didn't kill somebody, but they just can't be absolutely sure. They're pretty sure their hands are clean, but they still might have to wash them twenty-seven times a day. They can remember checking the door thirty times to see if it's locked, but they still can't be sure it is."

"Oh, my God."

Cindy Lou nodded. "It's not a fun thing to have. And Isaac's kind of a case—you usually get washers or checkers or doubters. He doesn't seem to be into checking so much, but he's got all the other stuff in spades. And he's got a shitload of 'shoulds' on the conscious level. Poor guy."

"What about not talking?"

"That seems to be voluntary—the washing and stuff isn't. See, the other philosophical question OCD brings up is free will. They *have* to do certain stuff."

"Why do they have to?"

"Something just tells them they do."

"What causes it? Having a dad who's the closest thing to the devil?"

"No, it seems to be chemical. Drugs help. Isaac didn't know

what he had till I told him. He's hugely embarrassed, of course, to be found out—but I'm going to send him to a shrink and get him some vitamin P or something. He could get a lot better."

•   •

The Monk could hardly bear the thought of her leaving, though it was going to be a lot easier being on his own again. Human relations were difficult for him, and they were about to be harder now that he'd decided to give up his silence. But the time had come for that, and for other changes. It had never occurred to him that he didn't have to clean and shower and count—he'd simply thought he did. He'd never questioned it. So he would try Prozac or whatever it was they wanted to give him, and then he'd have more time to paint.

The time had come to paint differently, too. He would finish the pregnant Pandora, the one Dahveed hated, and he would go on to paint other things.

Other women.

First the beautiful psychologist, then the magnificent bald detective. When the detective's hair grew back, he'd paint her that way, too.

And he'd paint his mother if she'd let him. He was going to call her soon.

Lovelace was getting her things together now. He had bought her a backpack and a duffel to go back to school. He thought she was sniffling a bit, crying perhaps, because she'd miss him. Or maybe she was getting a cold.

He said, "You'll come back this summer, won't you? Anthony says you're the best assistant he ever had."

"I'd like to, but I've missed a lot of school—I might have to make it up this summer." She turned toward him, and he saw that her nose was red. "I'll come next year for sure. For JazzFest, maybe."

He must have shown his distress. She said, "Oh, no, that's way too long. Let's do a family Thanksgiving. Just you and me—and anybody else you want except Mom and Dad. And your dad, of course." She shuddered a little at the mention of her grandfather.

He moved toward her. "You've been good for me, you know that?" He recognized as he said it how uncharacteristic it was. It probably scared her to death.

Sure enough, she stepped away. "In what way?"

You put me back in touch with women. After your mother, I sort of flipped out, I guess.

He couldn't tell her that. He couldn't tell her that it was her mother he painted, not her—that he hadn't known she'd grow up to look like Jacqueline, but that was why the angels looked like her.

No one knew better than The Monk that Jacqueline in no way resembled an angel. But he was an artist, he could make her what he wanted.

Jacqueline had seduced him when Daniel left her. He hadn't at first realized what an enormous thing it was to sleep with his brother's wife, not until his father caught them and explained it—in fact, made them an example in front of the entire congregation.

He had tried with another woman, the one he met when he first came to New Orleans, but when he thought about it, his heart wasn't in it. It was a lot easier to take vows of chastity and silence than to try it again.

He thought that soon, when his hair grew back, he'd start dating again.

● ●

Skip had to go by the office before she went home, to pick up her messages and do some paperwork. It was something she dreaded, since the place would be crawling with media.

What are you supposed to do, she thought, say *"I can't talk—I'm having a no-hair day"?*

They grabbed at her, ran at her, stuck metal phalluses in her face. They asked her how it felt to be a hero and what she thought about Jacomine's disappearance and other nonquestions guaranteed not to lead to a Pulitzer.

She kept her eyes fixed on a spot about ten feet in front of her so that if the camera caught her, she would look neither blank nor unfriendly, but busy. A person with bigger fish to fry.

She was so busy with this technique that she missed the people waiting for her in the reception area outside Homicide, and had to be sent back out. They were Dorise and Shavonne, dressed as if for a wedding, Dorise in a royal blue suit with black heels, Shavonne with her hair in braids fixed with pink barrettes, a pink dress and white Mary Janes; her Easter outfit, probably.

Not long ago it was Easter, Skip thought, though it seemed a century.

Shavonne carried a plant with a spike of purple blossoms on it.

"Hi." She looked Skip in the eye, not down at her shoes the way kids her age tended to do, and her smile seemed a little unruly, something with a mind of its own, inclined to materialize when its owner was supposed to be serious.

Skip said, "Hi," and shook hands with Dorise.

Shavonne held out the plant. "This is for you. It's an orchid. Have you ever seen one?"

"Not one that pretty."

The girl looked back at her mother. "Mama, see, I tol' you. I knew she was gonna think that." She turned back to Skip. "Can African American girls be detectives?"

"Sure. Plenty are—would you like me to introduce you?"

Dorise said, "You don't have to do that, darlin'." She seemed diffident, perhaps a little intimidated at being at police headquarters. "We came down because we just wanted you to know how much we appreciated what you did."

"It was my job." *And I owed you big-time.*

"Darlin', I hope you don't ever, ever feel bad about that other thing." Her eyes got filmy. "You gave me back my child. I thought I'd lost her."

Shavonne looked as if she hadn't the patience for any of this. She put the plant on the nearest chair, and put her arms up to be hugged. Skip had no time to bend down, and so it was an unbalanced hug— Skip's waist and Shavonne's sweet thin shoulders. She wondered if Shavonne knew who she was—that she was the white po-lice who had killed her father—and something in Dorise's face told her she did, and that she was hugging her anyway.

Skip went back to her paperwork.

Later, on the way out, she managed to dodge the reporters, but that night she found herself at Jimmy Dee's for dinner, where she had to tell her story under much more severe—if more intelligent— questioning.

"Weren't you scared?" asked Kenny. "I would have been terrified."

Sheila rolled her eyes. If she were scared, she'd never admit it.

"I *was* scared. I was petrified."

"Would you do it again? I mean, if you had to?"

Sheila said, "Of course she would, stupid. It's her job."

"Shut up. I asked Auntie."

Skip's fingers gently rubbed the stem of her wineglass; her knee grazed Steve's. She was full of pasta and good feeling. "Sure," she said. "If I had to."

She barely remembered what she'd told Cindy Lou at lunch. That was centuries ago.

ABOUT THE AUTHOR

JULIE SMITH, a former reporter for the *New Orleans Times-Picayune* and the *San Francisco Chronicle*, has written seven novels featuring Skip Langdon. The first book in the series, *New Orleans Mourning*, won the Edgar Award for Best Novel. Smith recently married and moved back to New Orleans, where she lives in an 1830s Creole town house with its very own ghost and serial murder story.